Hol

this book. Pl

DIVIDED HOUSE

DARK YORKSHIRE - BOOK 1

J M DALGLIESH

First published by Hamilton Press in 2018
This edition published 2020

Copyright © J M Dalgliesh, 2018

ISBN (Trade paperback) 978-1-80080-241-4
ISBN (Large Print) 978-1-80080-001-4
ISBN (Hardback) 978-1-80080-786-0

Look out for the link at the end of this book or visit my website at **www.jmdalgliesh.com** to sign up to my no-spam VIP Club and receive a FREE Hidden Norfolk novella plus news and previews of forthcoming works.

Never miss a new release.

No spam, ever, guaranteed. You can unsubscribe at any time.

For H, M and RT

DIVIDED HOUSE

"He who is unable to live in society, or who has no need because he is sufficient for himself, must be either a beast or a god."

Aristotle

CHAPTER ONE

THE GENTLE CLICK-CLICKING sounds carried through the darkness. She didn't know from where they originated but the noise appeared distant and the repetition was somehow hypnotic. With precious little else to occupy her thoughts, she spent many an hour trying to figure out the source. Initially, she considered that they might come from a nearby industrial unit or workshop. However, those thoughts had gone now. The sounds were constant and almost never altered in pattern, no matter what the time of day or night. Not that she knew when one passed into the next.

Standing on her bed, little more than a stinking mattress on the floor, she reached up to the vent. A slight breeze brushed over her fingertips. On tiptoes, she opened her mouth in a vain attempt to inhale the clean air. It was useless. There was so little to be had.

Hearing what she thought was a movement beyond the door, she looked in that direction. Dropping back down, she sat herself on her bed and hugged her knees, willing the door to remain closed. The sliver of artificial light creeping under the threshold created something of a paradox for her. The feeling of comfort that is usually drawn from light was absent. In here the opposite was true. The darkness, as wholly encompassing as it was, brought the only respite from her torment.

A memory from childhood, one long forgotten, came to mind. The warmth of the light, illuminating the landing beyond the bedroom door, signified that protection was near. A bad dream or a sense of loneliness could be relieved within moments of a frightened call to her attentive parents. Not so in this place. Her parents were long dead now. She chastised herself for the fleeting notion that she would be better off with them. Not doubting that that was true, she forced her family to the forefront of her mind. They had to be her focus as well as her motivation for the things that she had done, and would still have to do, in the coming days.

Reminding herself of the core principles instilled in her over the recent weeks, *compliance, obedience and willingness*, she knew that those words would be their salvation. The key to getting out of this damp, stale, environment, lay in practising those virtues. The teachings at mass had not been too dissimilar. On occasion, there were sermons focusing on the torment of the world, the family unit and the conflicts within your soul. Challenges would lie in your path. Some were set for you to rise above, others to battle and all to overcome, lest they devour your spirit. For now, she was living through such times. There was still hope and her faith remained strong.

The door stayed closed and she stared at it for a few minutes. The sound was only a trick of the mind. She was grateful. The moment that it opened her nightmare would intensify. Another draught from above brought much needed fresh air into the room. The ventilation system had to run somewhere. She considered, not for the first time, whether the vents served other buildings as well. If so, there was always a chance that someone would hear her pleas. The urge to scream at the top of her voice through the grate was almost overwhelming. Remembering, however, that unnecessary noise brought about punishment, she kept quiet. Memories of previous experiences flashed back through her mind. They were a stark reminder. She didn't want to go back in the pit.

She never wanted to go back there. Besides, no-one had ever come to her aid before when she had called out. Why would this time be any different? No, she had to follow the rules.

Thoughts turned to the man who currently occupied the pit. Thankfully, for the moment at least, he lay still and resolutely quiet. Was he courageous and resilient or incredibly stupid and obstinate? You cannot always control what happens to you but you can control your reaction to it. That had been another lesson learnt throughout the duration of her time here. It was sound instruction. This life had become manageable, more or less. Much to her anger, it appeared that others were either unable to understand that message or unwilling to give in. Such behaviour was selfish and impacted on everyone else. The one in the pit could be placed in that category, for he refused to be nullified under any circumstances.

He was a fool. Why couldn't he understand the way of things, it wasn't complicated? Follow the rules and life becomes bearable, or at least more so. Several others had come and gone which meant that there was a route out of this place.

A sound emanated from the next room. This time she was certain. He was coming. His boots broke the shaft of light that crept under the door. It was time. Withheld breath and an unbroken gaze in that direction, she waited to hear the key turn in the lock. Feeling her heartbeat quickening, she willed this to be the last time. Her spirit dissipated as the telltale sound came to her ear. She whispered what was expected of her.

"Compliance, obedience and willingness."

CHAPTER TWO

THE PUB WAS QUIET, not unsurprising on a cold Monday evening in November. Lendal Cellars, Caslin's favoured haunt, was set well below ground in the vaulted brick ceilings of the former Lord Mayor's wine cellar. The lack of natural light, irrelevant at this time of year, and recessed lighting gave him shadows in which to seek comfort.

Taking out his phone he checked the time. He would be late again. A raised voice caught his attention. Seated in a booth, at the far end, were a couple deep in conversation. Returning focus to the pint before him, he swirled the remainder and drained it in one fluid motion. Caslin fancied another. He stood up and pulled on his coat before glancing around and heading for the men's room. Passing out of the main bar, he caught sight of a man's hand roughly clasping the face of his partner. Stopping briefly in the doorway, the woman met his eye. The moment passed as she was released from the grip with a sharp push, her eyes brimming at the reprimand for some apparent indiscretion, the details of which were lost on him.

The door swung closed. The corridor was narrow and despite a succession of wall mounted lights, still felt oppressive. Caslin made his way up a flight of stairs, casting a fleeting glance towards the discreet security camera, mounted in the ceiling. Entering the men's room, he first checked that the cubicles were empty before reaching into his coat pocket and retrieving a plastic vial, secreted within. Gazing at the white powder that it contained, he took a deep breath before catching his reflection in the mirror. An involuntary expression of melancholy stared back at him. The door opened as another entered and he closed his palm, concealing the vial and replacing it in his coat. Instead of what he'd planned, he stepped forward and turned on the tap. Leaning over and cupping his hands under the stream, he lightly doused his face.

The newcomer passed by, coming to stand before the urinal alongside him. Caslin glanced over. A look that didn't pass unnoticed.

"Problem?" he asked, nonchalantly.

Caslin eyed the man warily, contemplating how pleased his partner must currently be to be rid of him, if only for a trip to the gent's. He was of middle age and well dressed, with once dark hair, now shot through with grey. His face was heavily lined, amplifying the effect of too much sun on tanned, leathery skin.

"No. Not me," Caslin replied. *Should he say something?* It wasn't really any of his business, certainly not personally and without a complaint, not professionally either. *Morally?* Well, that was altogether different. He drew himself upright and took a deep breath, adjusting the position of the waistband of his trousers and clearing his throat. Without looking back, he left the men's room and returned downstairs. Entering the bar, he glanced at the woman, a young lady would've been more apt for she was far younger than the man she was with. He offered her a slight smile as he passed. She returned it, nervously. Almost as an afterthought, he turned back to her. She was staring at the wine-glass in her hand.

"You don't have to put up with that, you know?" he said bluntly.

Her eyes flicked up at him and away. Shaking her head, she replied, "You don't know him."

"I don't need to," Caslin replied. "Whatever it is you think he has, it isn't worth it." She met his eye with a brief expression of hope but that dissipated as the door to the bar creaked open. Her partner stepped through and immediately drew a conclusion about the subject of their conversation. He glanced down at her and she fell silent, head bowed. Squaring up to Caslin, he shoved him backwards with two flat hands against his chest and then raised a finger pointedly.

"Who the hell do you think you are?" he asked aggressively.

"Now, calm down—"

"Piss off," the man stated, advancing. Reaching out to grasp the lapels of his coat, Caslin deflected the move with his forearm. The movement drew an angry response and Caslin barely managed to avoid the blow as the man lashed out, with a closed fist. Stepping to the side, he used his assailant's body weight to pull him across, putting him off balance. Pressing home the advantage, Caslin pivoted, sending his opponent to the floor, upending a table on the way down. He was showered in alcohol and glasses as he hit the ground. With a howl of frustration, he rolled and tried to rise, his face contorted with uncontrolled rage, but Caslin was upon him in an instant. Driving home a right cross, he sent the man sprawling to the floorboards once again.

"Please!" a woman shouted, barging in between Caslin and the fallen man, pushing him away. "Please, stop," she implored him. Caslin stepped back, stunned at the interruption as he watched her kneel by her partner's side. Blood was pouring from his nose and he appeared dazed, the rage replaced with shock and fear. She glanced up at Caslin, a flash of anger in her eyes.

"You've got to stop doing this kind of thing, Nate," a voice said from behind. Caslin glanced over his shoulder at the barman, standing some twenty feet away, eyeing proceedings. Other patrons were now watching with a mixture of trepidation and bemusement. "You'll get yourself barred if this keeps happening."

Caslin turned on his heel and stalked away. Waving away the barman's protestations, he headed for the exit. Pulling his coat about him and climbing the steps, he left the Cellars. Picking his way through the light throng of people, out and about amongst the narrow streets of the old city, he hurried on. The students were entrenched again, in mid-semester, and tourists still milled about in York, even at this time of year.

Passing a couple of buskers at the entrance to Dean's Park, he cut through, circumventing the Minster. He took the next left onto Chapter House Street. The car was parked nearby, he was almost certain. With a bit of luck, he'd only be a half hour late. Skipping over the cobbles, he reached the corner and swore. The plastic wallet glued to his windscreen angered him more than he could have believed possible.

"And the hits just keep on coming," he said aloud.

Tearing off the offending article, Caslin unlocked the car door, the fob having stopped working months ago, and got in. He threw the ticket into the passenger footwell, alongside the last one. The key was in the ignition as his phone rang. Gently rolling back his head, he closed his eyes and took a deep breath. Taking the phone from his inside pocket and pressing the answer tab, without looking at the screen, he knew who it would be.

"Caslin?"

"Yes."

"Are you coming in today?"

"On my way, as we speak," he said, turning the key. Most of the dashboard lit up although fewer icons than earlier in the day. "I've had some car trouble."

"Okay. I was just getting a bit worried because you-"

Caslin ended the call. It was 10:24 p.m., Harman had waited five minutes more than the day before. *Progress*, he thought, as the car stuttered into life. The old Volvo squeaked as it ticked over. Caslin dabbed the accelerator a couple of times and observed the plume of blue smoke illuminated in the glow of the brake lights. Having wiped clear, the mist from the windscreen with the end of his sleeve, he swung out into the light city centre traffic and headed for Goodramgate and the ring road. Ten minutes later, he pulled into the car park at Fulford Road. Reaching over to the glovebox, he retrieved a can of deodorant. Giving himself a healthy blast to mask the smell of Lendal's, he followed it up with a couple of breath mints and made his way to the entrance. Most of the four-storey building was in darkness. Only the occasional rectangle of light punctuated the façade as cleaners, and those on late-turn, worked through.

Despite the cold he was sweating as he entered reception. The room was well lit but the counter was closed, with only a sign indicating a buzzer to push for assistance. Caslin reached the secure entrance to the left and punched in his code. The lock clicked and he passed through. Making a beeline for the vending machines, he selected a white coffee, before resuming his course to the third floor. Looking at the contents of the cup in his hand he observed the film that had formed on the surface, fleetingly wondering what on earth caused it.

He made it up the stairs having burnt his fingers only twice and pushed open the door with his free hand. One person was present as he walked in, apologising as he did so.

"No matter," Harman replied. "I don't have anything on tonight anyway."

You have to say that, Caslin thought. Personally, he would have been livid if the situation had been reversed, and for the second night in a row.

"That's okay, then," was what he actually said.

Would it really have killed him to get to work on time? Maxim Harman was far too nice a lad to be doing this job and too placid when people took advantage of him. Perhaps in time, he would learn to sharpen his elbows a bit but Caslin was unsure that he had it in him. Judging by how Harman was regarded by the rest of the team, it would be fair to assume that they thought likewise.

Harman was the youngest member of the group, only two years in the job and already in CID. Sponsorship through university brought a certain level of expectation which was further enhanced by having the Chief Constable of Northumbria Police for a father. Many thought that was a combination to unlock the door to a fantastic career, but it certainly led those around him to form opinions as to how he got there.

"Anything for me?" Caslin asked.

"No, it's been pretty quiet. There was a break-in at a pharmacy over in Bishopthorpe Road, this evening."

"What was taken?"

"I don't know yet but the secure cabinets are unbroken," Detective Constable Harman shrugged. "The keyholder's going to do an inventory. Although, I've asked him to hold off until scenes of crime get there to check for prints. They smashed a window at the back to force entry."

"I hope you told him that'll probably be tomorrow. They won't be paying out overtime for a junkie on a smash and grab."

Caslin sensed Harman hadn't considered that.

"No," he said, "I didn't think. Should I give him a call?"

"Either that or expect him to be a little shirty the next time you speak."

Harman promised that he would. There was little else to report. It was a Monday. Caslin sat down in his chair and casually glanced at the paperwork on his desk. Cold case files that had been exhaustively investigated the first time around but not yet signed off for removal to the archives. Caslin knew. Just like everybody in the office knew. He was being kept "busy".

Late turns and night shifts, along with a caseload that was either unsolvable, or plainly not worth the effort and resources required to get a result. He was up to his eyes in counterfeit goods, petty mail-fraud and ringed cars. Nothing that set the imagination alight and most would barely scrape past the desk of a trading standards officer, let alone a Detective Inspector. He was sure that the cases in the folders before him were as cold as ice. The perpetrators were no doubt well on their way through their next enterprise. The chances of success were slight but Caslin knew that wasn't the point.

The office had a DI already in Michael Atwood and he was deemed sufficient for the detective chief inspector. It wasn't paranoia. Atwood had his own office and got the lead on anything that came through whereas Caslin had the caffeine shift and a desk in the corner of the squad room. He sighed as Harman bid him goodnight. Leafing through the collection of menus he kept in his top drawer, Caslin considered how things had changed for him. He tried not to think about it too much, it depressed him. There was a Chinese that delivered within five miles, for nothing. The smell in the office in the morning would cause much consternation though. *Chinese it is then.*

Monday the 6th November was going to be a quiet night.

———

HAVING DEVOURED a starter of prawn toast, mini-spring rolls and seaweed, Caslin was setting about his Kung Pao Chicken when a head ducked around the door to the squad room, accompanied by a rapping of knuckles on the frame.

"Got a sec?"

Caslin nodded, wiping some sauce from his chin with the back of his hand. The uniformed officer entered. He was traffic. Caslin had seen him around but didn't know him directly.

"What can I do for you…?" Caslin enquired.

"Thompson, Sir," the newcomer proffered.

"Of course, Thompson," Caslin said. "What can I do for you?"

"We've got a guy downstairs in custody, Daniel Horsvedt. The Sarge thinks you should take a look at him. We thought he was under the influence after we were called to a collision with a motorcyclist."

"Where is that name from, The Netherlands?"

"I thought Germany."

"No matter. The accident, was it his fault?"

"Not really, Sir. But that's not what might interest you. No priors or anything outstanding against the identification, and the pickup itself was clean."

Caslin was instantly suspicious. A glance towards the clock saw that it was a little after a quarter to midnight. Was this uniform trying to offload a basic collar onto CID so they could go home on time?

"And why would this interest me?"

"He has some gear in the car that doesn't quite add up."

House-breaking kit, Caslin thought. "Go on."

"He had a bag behind the driver's seat containing some cable ties and a hammer. A can of pepper spray was also wedged in the crease of the driver's seat."

"Hardly the Great Train Robbery though is it, anything else?"

Thompson nodded, "The name he gave doesn't ring true. It ties with the vehicle but describes a thirty-year-old male, 5'9 and heavy set, with dark hair. It's not even close. He's much older, 6'2, skinny as a rake and bald as a badger's arse."

Caslin raised an eyebrow at the last.

"Sir, sorry, Sir. He just isn't right, particularly as he speaks with a Scottish accent. He apparently moved here from abroad in 2010 when his background in the UK begins but he's got a hell of a strong accent. What with that and the registered name, it doesn't scan."

"Still possible. If you learn English from scratch, you can take on the accent of those around you. Maybe he had a Scottish teacher at night-school or something."

Caslin was thoughtful for a moment as he processed the information. He could pass this one on to the day shift, Harman or DC Holt could endeavour to get to the bottom of it. On the other hand, he could show some interest, his meal could wait until later.

"Come on then, let's take a look at what you've netted."

CASLIN FOLLOWED PC Thompson down the corridor. He frowned and rubbed at his chest. The spring rolls were already repeating on him, he had eaten too fast as usual. They dropped down two flights of stairs and hung a left towards the custody suite. Caslin jumped. A high-pitched alarm sounded throughout the station, instantly setting his heart racing. Reacting first, he barged past Thompson and took off down the corridor. Another body stepped out of a doorway, only just managing to step aside as Caslin bellowed a warning. Crashing through the double doors to the custody suite, he arrived alongside two others entering from the yard. Confusion reigned as the custody sergeant was nowhere to be seen, the cell block was deserted. Shouts were going up from all over. Caslin headed for the interview rooms with the others close behind. An officer stood in a doorway and Caslin eased past him to get a look.

A man in a polo shirt and blue jeans lay outstretched on the floor with Sergeant Allen kneeling alongside. A chair was upturned to the right. A shocked officer stood on the far side of the room watching events unfold. He looked over and met Caslin's unasked question with an expression of bewilderment, spreading his hands wide and shaking his head.

"He just... I didn't..."

The man on the floor appeared to be fitting, his arms and legs in spasm. Sgt Allen recoiled as the semi-conscious figure violently convulsed, eyes tightly shut, straining every muscle. He coughed involuntarily, yellow bile and vomit spewing from his mouth.

"Jesus Christ!" Allen exclaimed, backing off.

"Get an ambulance, fast," Caslin shouted, at no-one in particular.

Someone standing behind him made the call. Moments later the alarm was silenced, by whom Caslin didn't know but he was thankful. It got your attention but also made it impossible to concentrate. Seconds passed that seemed like hours. Caslin felt a hand on his arm move him forcefully aside as another entered the room. It was the FME, the local doctor on call for the police that evening. Allen made way and the doctor knelt down. Pulling on a pair of latex gloves, he started by opening the man's eyelids and passing a light over them. The convulsions had stopped, as had the fitting and from his viewpoint at the door, Caslin could see that the patient was unresponsive to the intense light of the torch. He wasn't sure if he was still breathing.

"How long has he been like this?" The doctor glanced up at all present, in turn. Caslin shrugged but another spoke up.

"A minute, maybe two?"

"What happened?"

"I… I don't know," the constable stammered. "He was sitting there, and then he just… threw himself forward and collapsed over the table."

"He's not breathing. Where's that ambulance?" the doctor asked without looking up. He opened the unconscious man's mouth and peered inside, running a gloved finger within.

"On its way," a voice announced, from behind. "Five minutes, tops."

The doctor began heart massage and requested Sergeant Allen to continue the compressions as he put a resuscitation kit over the unconscious man's face. He hesitated for a moment before proceeding to blow air into his lungs. Caslin backed out of the room and into the corridor. The area was not wide and felt even more cramped by the number of people in attendance. Everyone in the station, barring the cleaning contractors, appeared to have answered the call.

"Someone get out in the yard and direct the paramedics when they arrive."

A constable eased his way past everyone and ran outside. Caslin pushed his way through the throng. Gently gripping PC Thompson's forearm as he passed, Caslin guided him away. They continued on until they were back in the custody suite and out of earshot. Another officer walked by and Caslin kept his voice low to ensure that they would not be overheard.

"Concentrate."

"Sir?"

"Is there anything you missed out?"

"What do you mean?"

"The arrest. Come to think of it, from when you initially arrived on the scene to the moment that you left custody to speak to me. Anything at all?"

"No," Thompson replied, looking a little concerned. "You can't think that we had—"

"No," Caslin was firm. "No, I've no reason to think anything at all. Just answer the question, are you sure?"

"Yes. I think so."

"You need to do better than I think so," Caslin snapped. "You need to be damn sure."

The constable looked back towards the interview rooms as a paramedic rushed past, escorted by a colleague, disappearing from view.

"Is this the right time to discuss this?" he said, his voice wavering.

"Look, there's a distinct possibility that this guy isn't going to make it."

"How do you know that?"

Caslin glanced over his shoulder, checking that they were still comfortably out of earshot of anyone else.

"I don't, not for sure but it's not looking good, is it? This is probably the only time you're going to have to get your story straight in your head. I want to know everything, every detail, however small and insignificant you might think it is. I'll give you five minutes to think."

Without waiting for a response, Caslin turned and walked back towards the interview room. The crowd was dispersing. He ran a hand through his hair and realised that he was sweating heavily. Sergeant Allen came out as he approached, the doctor slightly behind him. The ashen look on his face, and that of resignation on the doctor's, confirmed what Caslin had already suspected. Neither of the men spoke. Drawing the doctor aside,

Caslin ushered him away whilst Allen began directing proceedings.

"I'm keen to hear your thoughts on cause of death, Brian."

Brian Frampton was an experienced local GP, working with the police for many years. In Caslin's mind, that gave his opinion some weight. The doctor appeared reticent.

"I'm not a pathologist. It would be pure speculation—"

"And yet, you have an idea?"

Frampton shrugged, his mouth opening as if to speak but merely shook his head.

"I saw you hesitate before resuscitating him. I would understand without a resus kit but with one? What went through your mind?"

"I really think that you should wait for—"

"Look, I'm hardly going to quote you on it, am I?" Caslin reassured him. Frampton appeared to relax. "You have my word." The last struck home and the doctor nodded his agreement. Before saying anything further, he took a last look beyond Caslin to ensure that no-one else was able to hear what he was about to say.

Arriving at a side door to the yard, basically a fire exit from the main building, Caslin passed through and out into the night. He shivered against the cold and drew his coat tightly about him. It was well below freezing and a hard frost already lay on the cars. Looking around, he easily picked out the burgundy Toyota pickup on the far side, sparkling in the moonlight. Making his way over, he saw that it was actually a glaring red. A cursory check saw him survey the damage along the offside panels where the motorbike had delivered its glancing blow, the rider was exceptionally lucky by all accounts.

The remainder of the bodywork threw up the usual dents and scratches that a vehicle would carry after two decades on the road. The tyres were in good shape with deep enough tread for the conditions. There was a great deal of mud, mixed with salt, ingrained on the tyre walls and all along the length of the vehicle. Caslin took a quick glance over his shoulder, as he pulled on a pair of latex gloves. Opening the passenger door and looking inside, he saw that the cabin was pretty Spartan. There was a small collection of assorted food containers on the passenger seat and in the footwell. The side pocket of the passenger door was stuffed with assorted rubbish, none of which was noteworthy.

A second check that no-one else was in the yard and Caslin opened the glove box. He rooted around and found a couple of Ordnance Survey maps, one for the North East and another for the West Midlands. They were both a bit dog-eared around the edges. He found an old mobile phone that didn't power up when he switched it on. Returning to the glove box, there was a small packet of replacement bulbs and a grey plastic box containing the socket piece, for the locking wheel nuts. There was also a black wallet that Caslin assumed held the service record. He opened it and a cluster of sheets of paper slipped out, one landing inside the car and the others dropping to the tarmac.

Caslin scooped them up. The first was a printed receipt for an exhaust and wheel check from a garage in York. The next was a leaflet for a ramblers' association and lastly, an electricity bill in the name of a "C McNeil". It was dated for the March of that year. Caslin didn't recognise the address but he could tell from the postcode that it was local to York City. He thought about it for a moment, then took out his notebook and a pen, jotting down the name and address before carefully putting the papers back in the wallet and replacing them in the glove box.

There was little else to draw his attention to, so he closed the door to the pickup. Walking around to the front, he took down the registration number. Finally, he opened the driver's door for a closer look at the contents of the side pocket, amongst the broken glass from the window above. There were bits of cellophane, scrunched up crisp packets and confectionery wrappers, along with some used tissues and what looked like fuel receipts. From the date range of the latter, it was clear that this vehicle covered some miles. Satisfied that there was nothing else to see of any value, he shut the door and returned to the office, thankful to be out of the cold. All of a sudden, he felt like he was crashing. Leaning his back against the wall of the deserted squad room, he took a moment to gather himself. He should have called in sick tonight.

Once seated behind his desk, Caslin picked up the phone and put in a call to the control room. He requested the details of the registered keeper for the pickup and noted them down. As soon as he replaced the receiver, he had the thought to run a check on the name and address from the utility bill as well. He would follow that up later. In the meantime, he was going to check out Horsvedt's home address.

The address was out in the sticks, a name and a postcode. He went online and brought up a map showing the location. The pin on the map put it somewhere off the B6265 between Pately Bridge and Grassington. Caslin remembered the former from his childhood. His father had once taken them to a farm nearby on a shoot. Tearing a page from a note pad, Caslin jotted down a few words before neatly folding the paper and placing it on Maxim Harman's desk for the DC to find when he started his shift.

It was 5:56 a.m. on Tuesday 7th November.

CHAPTER THREE

CASLIN PICKED up the pace as he made his way down to the rear yard, deciding to leave from there, rather than run the gauntlet of bumping into any senior officers, roused early due to the events of the night. The rear gate opened as a Transit pulled into the yard and he slipped out. The sun had risen and it was looking like a beautiful day. There was barely a cloud in the sky and the gentle easterly breeze was cold but not stinging as it had been recently.

Caslin buttoned up his coat anyway and headed for his Volvo. He pressed the fob in the hope that it might come back to life but it didn't. Putting the key in the lock he wrestled with the frozen mechanism before the click brought a smile to his face. Dropping into the seat, he turned the key in the ignition and after a few attempts. The engine fired up. He flipped on the rear-view demister, set the heater and blowers to maximum and got out of the car, leaving the door ajar. He set about raking the ice from the windscreen with a credit card when a recognisable voice called to him. His heart sank.

"Good morning, Detective Inspector."

"No comment, Mr Sullivan," Caslin replied, without looking over.

"Oh, come on, that's just mean on such a fine day as this. You must have something to say, especially knowing that your colleagues from the IPCC will be due in at some point today. It'll be something of a reunion for you, won't it?"

"You're up early, Jimmy. Did the wife turf you out again?"

"She left a long time ago, living down in London with the kids. How's yours, by the way?"

Caslin stopped scraping and took a measure of the man alongside him. Sullivan was in his forties. His clothes appeared to have been thrown on in something of a rush and his hair was unkempt. The journalist cut a feeble first impression. For a fleeting moment, Caslin remembered looking at himself in the mirror and thought the unthinkable.

"She's keeping well, thank you for asking. Please excuse me, I have to be somewhere."

Caslin thought that he could see through the windscreen well enough, at least to get out of the car park and away from the unwanted attention. He got back into the driver's seat and pulled the door shut. Sullivan tapped gently on the window. Begrudgingly, Caslin pushed the button and after sticking for a moment, the window cracked open.

"You and I have a lot more in common than you think, Inspector," Sullivan offered up a business card through the two-inch gap, Caslin took it. "We could be of mutual use to each other you know."

"There are laws about that sort of thing, Jimmy."

Sullivan spread his hands wide, "Not suggesting anything untoward, Inspector. Just keep it in mind."

Caslin put the car in gear and reversed out from his space. He turned on his wipers to clear the residue of the melting ice and made his way across the car park towards the exit. The question came to mind, and was instantly dismissed, of how the journalist was so quickly in the know. Sullivan was a shark with contacts everywhere; apparently also within the walls of Fulford Road. He was about to pull out onto the main road just as his phone rang. Fishing around inside his jacket, he drew out his mobile and was surprised to find that it wasn't anyone from Fulford. Tapping the screen, he answered the call.

"Oh," said a familiar voice. "I figured you wouldn't be up and I'd get your voicemail."

"Hi Karen. No, I was already up. New number?"

"Yes."

"How're you?"

"Really well, very well."

"That's nice," Caslin lied.

"I hadn't heard from you about the weekend."

"The weekend?"

"Yes, please don't tell me you've forgotten? I've left you several messages."

"Ahh…"

"The kids. Coming to you on Saturday…"

"Oh, yes, yes."

"You had forgotten, hadn't you?" Karen said, her tone accusatory. "For crying out loud, Nate, when are you going to start taking an interest in anything apart from yourself? It's not good—"

"Maybe you should've got your solicitor to tell mine. That's how I usually hear from you. It would make the most of them. We're paying enough, after all."

"Well, maybe you should return calls and then it wouldn't have to go through the solicitors, would it?"

"Seriously, have you seen the running total? Mine's astronomical. My guy drives a Porsche. It's no bloody wonder, really."

"Grow up, Nate."

Caslin took a deep breath. He didn't need this. There was a pause at the other end too. For a moment, all that each of them could hear was the other's breathing.

"Does it have to be like this?"

Another pause before Karen replied, "No, it shouldn't."

"What train are they going to be on?"

"It gets in to York at 11:10. You will be there won't you?"

Caslin bit his lip, *as if I would leave them standing on the platform,* he thought. "Yes, of course."

There followed more silence, "Anything else, Karen?"

"When are you going to call your father?" her tone softened a little.

"Has he been badgering you again?"

"Yes, and I'm running out of things to say."

"Can't you just tell him?"

"He's your bloody father, Nate!"

"I'll get around to it."

"When?"

"Soon. Look, I'm in the middle of something. I'll have to speak to you later."

"Nate…"

Caslin hung up. Eyeing a break in the early morning traffic, he thrust the car into gear and accelerated. His intention was to circumvent the city centre to the south. He was aiming to pick up the westbound A59. The route finder had indicated a journey of nearly an hour and a half. The words of Sullivan rang in his ears as he negotiated the pre-rush-hour traffic of York. Remembering the journalist's appearance and marital status, Caslin knew Jimmy was certainly correct in part of what he had said, for they did have a lot in common.

The traffic flowed steadily, with the majority of commuters heading into York and not out of it. Caslin found his stomach groaning. With the benefit of hindsight, it may well have suited him to wait for the refectory to open before heading out. However, staying at Fulford Road for another hour or so increased the likelihood of being collared by DCI Stephens and having to stay put. Besides, he wanted the opportunity to follow up on Horsvedt's address. Caslin got along with his boss, up to a point. Frank Stephens was looking to see out his time, comfortably at that, and the last thing he wanted was controversy but then again, who did?

As he sped past, he caught a glimpse of an advertising board for a roadside café four hundred yards ahead. The urge to pull over and grab something to eat tugged at him but he knew that pressing on was more important. He could eat later. The address he was heading to was somewhere within the Dales National Park. Passing through Pately Bridge a little after 8 a.m., he kept his eyes peeled for any sign of Radford Farm, the registered address of Daniel Horsvedt's pickup. Once he hit Grassington, he knew he'd gone too far and made a U-turn. He was guessing that the building must be set back from the road as all those that he had seen were clearly marked. After driving for five minutes, he almost missed it for a second time. An unmade track left the highway, roughly three quarters of the way between the two towns, heading north. A large tree on one side and some sprawling undergrowth on the other shielded the turning, making it almost invisible from the main road.

The track had been laid with some form of hardcore to help maintain a continuity of the surface but nonetheless, was pitted and uneven. Caslin felt his car bottom-out in places. He wound his way along the side of a fallow field, with a thick hedge delineating the boundary. The other fields immediately adjacent or surrounding it had winter vegetable crops, which would soon need harvesting. Caslin figured that the house sat approximately a quarter of a mile off the main road, sited in a hollow and surrounded by a large copse of trees, thickest to the north and east. The house itself was no surprise, a traditional farmhouse of stone construction, two-up, two-down, with a clay pantile roof. At first glance it was clearly in need of some maintenance.

Caslin pulled the Volvo to a stop a short distance from the building so that he could take a better look, keeping the engine ticking over. The exterior pointing was crumbling around the stonework and the sash window frames were rotten. One upstairs pane was broken, with a triangular piece of glass missing from the corner. The roof tiles were heavily laden with vegetation, some were slipped or missing, and the guttering was coming away at various points. There were no vehicles in front of the house or in the car port to the side. Under the corrugated roof of which, there stood a well-stocked log store. Caslin parked up and walked to the front door, set within a makeshift porch that was a later bolt on. Little more than a single skin lean-to, it would provide scant protection from the harshness of a Yorkshire winter.

Rapping his knuckles on the door, he waited. A thick curtain draped across the inside made it difficult to see within but there was no movement as far as he could tell. He knocked again, this time more forcefully. Still there was no response. He tried the door handle but it was locked. Kneeling down, he propped open the letter box. There was no mail piled up on the floor and nor did any sound come to his ear. It appeared as if Horsvedt either lived alone or his cohabitants were out. Either way, Caslin wasn't getting inside, not legitimately anyway.

Making his way around the side of the house, he noted that within the log store there was no mould or damp visible to the wood. It was clear that much of it had been cut recently by the pale hue of the inner edges and piles of sawdust lying at his feet. There were no tools left out to battle the elements. A toddler's ride along car sat out in the open, off to his left.

The layout to the rear of the property was standard, with three windows at ground floor level. One of which was into the kitchen, with a door off to the left. Another was the same size, most likely the second reception room and the third was far smaller, set to the left of the door and opaque, perhaps a pantry or cloakroom. Caslin peered through each in turn but could ascertain nothing of note. The two windows to the upstairs were shrouded in net curtains and in a similar condition to those at the front. He tried the rear door but found it was also locked. Caslin's phone trilled once again and he hoped it wasn't Karen calling back for round two. It wasn't, it was Fulford.

"Caslin," he answered abruptly.

"Where are you?"

"Michael, good morning," Caslin replied.

"Morning. Where are you? The Guv wants to know," DI Atwood said, with open hostility in his tone.

"Just checking out the lay of the land. I'll be back in the office later."

"Later is not good enough, Nathaniel. He wants you here pronto and asked me to remind you that a report on last night's incident is expected upstairs."

Caslin winced.

"I'm on my way."

He hung up. The events surrounding the death in custody didn't seem quite right to him and the visit to this address was doing little to alter that feeling of unease. Perhaps this man lived alone but if so, choosing an isolated location such as this, struck him as an odd decision at his time of life. Caslin had learned to trust his instincts over the years. Doing so hadn't always panned out but he couldn't ignore the feeling. He walked casually back to his car. The sun was above the tree line and the copse gave him shelter from the wind. The little warmth offered felt pleasant on his skin. Giving one more thoughtful look in the direction of the house, he opened the car door and got in to begin the drive back to the station.

Without knowing why, his father suddenly came to mind. Caslin knew that he would have to call him. There was a limit to the number of excuses Karen could, and would, give before his father would get wind that something was up. She was right, it was his responsibility and his father only lived in Selby. There was no valid excuse. He decided to call him later that day and arrange to drop in for a chat. The parking permit came to mind and he thought he should probably make that call today as well.

CHAPTER FOUR

IT WAS PUSHING 11 a.m. by the time Caslin walked back into CID at Fulford Road. DS Hunter glared at him as he threw his coat across the back of a chair, pretending not to notice her scowl, thereby not asking the question she had intended to draw. She answered anyway.

"The DCI's on the warpath. The Super's been chewing his backside about your report."

"That's unusual."

"How so?"

Caslin smiled, "Usually they get annoyed *after* they read my reports."

Hunter allowed herself a slight smile. Caslin looked around the office. DC Holt was nowhere to be seen. A quick glance at the coat stand told him that DCs Harman and Underwood were in the building. Both had easily identifiable fashion traits. Underwood dressed to impress with her professional attire, plucked from the most fashionable outlets on the high street. Her slender figure and chiselled features were well framed by fastidiously styled-hair and make-up. All of which certainly ensured that everyone saw her coming, which was most likely the intention. She certainly got his. He would check her out when he thought he could get away with it, almost a daily occurrence. DC Maxim Harman wore nothing but the best, tailored suits and Egyptian cotton. How either managed it on a constable's salary, Caslin could only guess. As if reading his mind, Harman appeared at the doorway, making a beeline for him, notebook in hand, an eager expression on his face.

"What did you find out?"

Harman whipped a little elastic band off of the notebook and flicked through to the relevant page.

"Daniel Horsvedt. A thirty-three-year-old Czech national, relocated to England in 2009, as far as we can tell, anyway. The Border Force has him coming in and out of the country on a fairly regular basis from then on. His rig was registered around the same time, whereas the Toyota pickup came to him in early 2011," Harman glanced down at his notebook. "March 15th, to be precise."

"His rig?" Caslin enquired.

"Yes. It looks like he's an independent haulier."

"Strange."

"What is?"

"I didn't see a rig at the house. Might explain why the access track is so torn up, mind you. To be fair, I wasn't looking for a truck but it'd be pretty hard to miss."

"You would think," DS Hunter chimed in. Turning to Harman, she frowned. "Is this what you've been doing all morning?"

Harman nodded as he went over to his desk and released his computer from hibernation. Soon they were both looking at the Companies House web portal.

"He registered himself as DH Haulage in the May of 2010, filed mandatory accounts when required, including this past April."

"Anyone else listed on the file?"

"Yes," Harman clicked a link to bring up the company details. "Here it is. An 'Angela Horsvedt' is down as Company Secretary. I figured it was his wife, so I checked out the electoral role and they share the same address. I could check to see if I can find when and where they were married. Not sure if it would be in the UK or not though."

Caslin patted him on the shoulder.

"Yes, do it. Good work. It leaves me with more questions though."

"Such as?"

"Well if we have Mr Horsvedt, then where is his rig and while we're at it, where is Angela?"

"Driving the rig?" Hunter chipped in again.

Caslin shrugged, taking her comment more seriously than she had intended.

"Doubtful, but I guess we can't rule anything out, just yet."

"What do you want me to do?" Harman asked.

Caslin suggested that Harman look into Angela and see what else he could find. If she was married then where was she from, what was her maiden name? Daniel was a common European name but was Angela an anglicised variant of a continental name, or not? She may be more local. Caslin had no idea where this investigation was heading, but he was damn sure that it was worth his while to keep digging. Something was going on and he intended to find out what.

Caslin excused himself from the office and went to the men's room. No-one else was present when he entered and pausing in front of a mirror, he reluctantly examined the reflection. His eyes were sunken and dark rimmed. What with that and the stubble growth, he had the appearance of a man who had been out on a bender for the last twenty-four hours. Running the cold tap, he threw some water over his face, giving it a fierce rub with his hands in a vain attempt at bringing back some colour. He found his thoughts drifting first to his father, and then to his wife. Deciding that he was inclined to think of neither, he pushed them from his mind.

Returning to the office, he quickly typed up a report of the events as he saw them on the previous night. Having printed it out, signed and dated it, he hurried upstairs to hand it in. Returning to CID, he bumped into Harman on the stairs.

"The DCI is looking for you."

Caslin smiled, "Of course he is." He had been on his way back down with the intention of seeking out Frank Stephens himself, but changed his mind. "I'm popping out again and I want you to come with me."

"Alright," Harman replied, with a note of caution in his tone. "Where are we going?"

"I got pulled away from the Horsvedt's house earlier before I was done. I don't want to sit around waiting to see if anyone contacts us. I've got the urge to force the issue a little and a second pair of eyes wouldn't go amiss. You up for it?"

"I feel like I know them already," Harman smiled, falling into step.

The two of them made their way outside. Caslin felt the cold once more. The wind was up again and it tore through him. The thought occurred that it was going to be a long winter.

"My car or yours?" Harman asked, pointing to a little blue and white hatchback. Caslin considered it for a moment and elected to drive.

IT WAS the afternoon before they made the turn on to the winding track, leading up to Radford Farm. The sky had clouded over and the promise of the early morning sunshine had been replaced by a thickening mass of grey. Somehow the day seemed colder and far more threatening than it had at sunrise. Very little had changed since Caslin's morning visit. There were still no vehicles parked in front or to the side of the house and the nets continued to shroud the interior. The old house stood stoically in a foreboding, winter landscape. Caslin parked up and both officers got out, walking to the front door. Harman pointed towards a patch of hard standing out front, which Caslin hadn't noticed on his previous visit. It was perfect for parking a rig on.

The breeze had stiffened and the bitter snap looked like it was settling in for a while. Maybe the early snow that they were talking about would come after all. Once again, the knocking produced no response from within.

"How old do you think this place is?" Caslin asked casually. He looked closely at the pane of the door, almost willing himself to see beyond the curtain.

Harman appeared thoughtful, "Turn of the last century, maybe earlier."

Caslin didn't reply but headed around the back as he had done that morning. The younger man followed, their footfalls crunching on the gravel beneath their feet. Once he was at the kitchen door, Caslin tried it again. As expected, it was still locked and his focus turned to the door frame, his gaze a picture of concentration. Harman was about to ask when Caslin began feeling along the top edge of the surround.

"There might just be…" Caslin said quietly, almost to himself. He withdrew his fingers and clapped his hands together to shake loose the debris.

"What are you looking for?"

Caslin ignored the question, his eyes scanning the immediate area around them. A small two-person bench was off to their left, in a poor state of repair. Either side of that stood two medium sized flower pots. Both had plants within that had not been cared for in some time. The same could be said for three hanging baskets with detritus hanging limply over the sides, indicating the contents were far from their best. It was hardly the season for outside cultivation but still they were there, swaying slightly in the cold easterly. Caslin's eyes fell on the flower pots at their feet. There were lighter rings of dried mud ingrained in the concrete slabs laid beneath them. Surely it couldn't be that simple? Kneeling down, he tilted the first pot and rolled it to the side. Sure enough, underneath lay a key.

Caslin picked it up and examined it, turning it in the palm of his hand. It was a standard Yale design and, despite a few rust spots, it slid into the lock of the kitchen door with ease.

"You're not going to..." Harman exclaimed in a hushed tone, as if frightened that he would be overheard.

Caslin smiled, "Well we didn't come all the way out here just to drive home again. Been there, done that."

"But we can't break in. We don't have grounds or authorisation—"

"Ssshh," Caslin raised a forefinger to his lips and lowered his own voice, in a mock conspiratorial manner. "I won't tell if you don't. Besides, who's breaking in? We have a key."

Caslin unlocked the door, his eyes widening as the reassuring click of the barrel turning came to ear. A smile, reminiscent of a naughty child breaking a parental rule, lit up his face as he eased open the door.

"Damn it," Harman whispered.

"Tell you what. I'll have a quick looksey inside, while you check that the rig isn't parked around here someplace. Just in case I missed it earlier. That way, this is all on me."

"Like that would cut it with the DCI."

Caslin ignored the protestations and quietly walked into the kitchen. He was pretty certain that the place was empty but nevertheless, entered with caution. Harman stood at the doorway, shifting nervously and putting his weight first to the left, then the right. Caslin figured the lad would learn. A detective had to walk the line carefully but on occasion, when the need arose, he also had to know when to cross it.

The kitchen was a reasonable size and would be described as "rustic". Not only the walls but also the ceiling, was clad in pine strips, varnished to a high sheen many years previously. Despite the gloss finish, the wood sapped the light from the room. Low level cabinets stood against two walls, arranged in an L-shape around a standalone table and three chairs. There were a handful of wall mounted cabinets. Several had doors whose hinges had dropped slightly, giving them a crooked appearance.

Caslin opened the first and found some packets of rice and assorted dried pasta. The second had a few tins of vegetables and a can that had lost its label. He picked it up and noted the use by date stamped on the bottom. It read 11.02.09. Caslin opened the door to the fridge and recoiled at the smell. There was a flaky scum across one shelf. Caslin turned his attention elsewhere. The Belfast sink had scale residue beneath the dripping taps, offering up streaks of blue and green. He guessed that it had been installed long before the style came back into fashion in the utility rooms of the middle classes. A freestanding range was set at the end of the room, a flue rising from it, leading off at an angle. On the far wall there was a door leading to a reception room. To the left of that was another, Caslin assumed it was the pantry. A quick check and that was confirmed although it proved to be largely empty.

Caslin made to leave the kitchen, progressing further into the house. Glancing over his shoulder as he went, he spoke to Harman.

"Are you coming?"

Without another word he moved on. Behind him, Harman shook his head and with a last glance over his own shoulder, tentatively followed. They found themselves in a sitting room that must have been decorated in the fifties. The flock wallpaper was an assault on the eyes. The colours had long since faded and been replaced by a yellow tan, lending the room a dreary, dated atmosphere. It felt oppressive and the small forward-facing window, shrouded in nets, did little to ease that. The room smelt musty and was sparsely furnished with a two-seater settee and armchair combination. The pattern on the stained fabric was of vertical stripes, faded blue and cream in colour, far from their glory days. The carpet was a motley concoction of dark colours, woven together in a repeating, hexagonal pattern. Taken as a whole, the person who had put this decorative ensemble together did not have an eye for complementary furnishings.

There were a few pictures hanging on the walls. Nondescript landscapes, copies of originals by artists that Caslin had never heard of, framed in overly ornate surrounds that did little to enhance the work. The open fire was the focal point that dominated the room. The hearth was made up of crazy-paving stonework with a matching surround. The chimney breast itself was clad in pine, maintaining a measure of continuity from the kitchen. A clock hung to the left of the window, the ticking of the hands resonating in the silence. Caslin was struck by the irony of marking time in a room where it had been forgotten.

Crossing the room, Caslin looked out of the window to the front of the house. The single-glazed pane had a simple latch at the point where the sashes came together. A draught of cold air could be felt filtering through. There was farmland as far as the eye could see, the main road obscured by distance and foliage. If you hadn't just driven off it, you would never know it was there. The old house gave out the odd creak and groan but despite this, Caslin was struck by the silence. This place was isolated.

A copy of the *Yorkshire Post* lay folded on the floor to one side of the armchair, some unintelligible words scrawled across the page above the lead photograph. He scanned the paper in search of a date. It was from September. Caslin indicated that they should move on. As expected, they found two bedrooms upstairs, one of which was set out with a double bed and a small dressing table. There were two imposing wardrobes containing both male and female clothing. The second was a child's room, with a cot and an assortment of games and toys piled in one corner. All the bedding was made up.

Returning downstairs, they inspected the second reception room, a dining room that doubled as a store room cum office. Boxes were stacked at one end, black marker pen handwritten across them in a language that neither man could read. Underneath the front window was a small desk, a mass of papers scattered upon it. Multiple box files and folders were stacked to the left and right. There was a pedestal with three drawers. Caslin indicated that Harman should take a look while he continued on.

Caslin found that the bathroom was nothing surprising, small and cramped, shoehorned in under the stairs. The usual toiletries that one would expect were present. Despite needing a good clean, the room was insignificant. He returned to where Harman was leafing through some papers in one of the box files.

"Anything interesting?"

"Possibly," Harman replied without looking up. "We've got copies of invoices here. It looks like our man did long haul stuff. You know, trans-European deliveries."

"Anything to suggest where he is now?"

"You mean other than in the morgue, waiting on a pathologist?"

"Yeah, that kind of thing."

"No, sorry. There isn't anything dated recently that I can see. Although we've got a VAT file here for the last financial year. It may show up some recurring jobs. Maybe he has ongoing contracts."

"Maybe. When we get back to Fulford, give your new friends in the Border Force a call and have them keep a watch for his rig. You never know, he may turn up in Dover or Hull. When did you say they last recorded him coming or going?"

Harman frowned, "I'm not sure that I asked, sorry."

"Ask."

"You don't think it's him, do you?"

"Say again?" Caslin looked up.

"The guy we have on a slab. You don't think he's Daniel Horsvedt."

Caslin's eyes were scanning the room.

"We'll know soon enough. What do we have here?"

He moved across the room and stood before three shelves that had been cobbled together out of mismatching off-cuts, largely supporting random items. An old shoe box full of receipts, a snow globe with a miniature Santa sitting in his sleigh, alongside an assortment of fishing publications. Caslin's attention had been drawn to a loose photograph, that had lain flat, but whose corner was sticking out from beneath a couple of magazines. He reached up and took it down. The edges were creased and it had a small tear in the top right-hand corner. A family shot of a man with his arms wrapped around a woman, clutching a baby. The man was heavy set with dark hair and she was blonde, with curls that reached to her shoulders. Both parents were smiling and the sun shone brightly around them. It could have been taken in the garden outside.

Caslin held the photo up for Harman to see.

"Looks like we found our Mr Horsvedt, anyway."

"Matches the description but he's certainly not who we have in the mortuary."

Caslin turned the image over and was disappointed not to find a printed date.

"Pity we don't know when this was taken, though. We still don't know for sure it is him."

Harman reached for the picture, Caslin relinquished it.

"I could help with that."

"Be my guest."

"My guess is this past summer."

Caslin narrowed his gaze, "Explain."

Harman pointed at the photo, "The T-shirt he's wearing was only printed this year."

Caslin squinted as he looked more closely, making out the partial lettering "Spar" and "sea" written in red on the front. He looked quizzically at Harman, who smiled.

"Sparta Prague played Chelsea in the Europa League, this year. It's a T-shirt commemorating the match. Sparta's name is printed first, so they were at home and that leg was played early in the year, after the group stages were over. The weather looks warm and the shirt has faded a bit, probably in the wash. Cheap print."

Caslin had to admit he was impressed.

"I want you to get a list together of local GP surgeries, vaccination clinics, that sort of thing. Then start phoning around. Babies need their boosters. Speak to the local Health Visitor team as well.

You never know that could give us more of an insight. Families with young children don't tend to drop off the face of the earth, not unless they want to or…"

"They get help," Harman finished.

"Exactly. Perhaps, if we're really lucky, someone might give us a lead on the parents."

Caslin took the photo back and slipped it into his inner breast pocket. Harman didn't comment. They returned to the kitchen. Caslin leant on the back of one of the chairs and let out a deep sigh, glancing over to Harman, who frowned.

"What do you think?"

Caslin shook his head slightly, "Well lived in but also, not. If that makes any sense?"

"I think so. Their clothes, toiletries, kid's toys are here but basics like food aren't. And where are the other family pictures? You tend to take more than one, if you have a camera, don't you?"

Caslin thought about his own house back in London but chose not to comment further. He changed tack.

"And what about the day-to-day stuff that we all accumulate? Unless they're just really tidy. Let's go and see if we can find that rig."

They went outside, Caslin locking the door behind them and returning the key to its rightful place beneath the pot. There was no sign of Horsvedt's rig anywhere in sight of the house. There was a dilapidated shed, or workshop, built against a hillock at the edge of the copse of trees to the north but the cab of a lorry would never have fitted in there. Caslin looked at the time. It was 2:15 p.m., the middle of the day, and he was dead on his feet. Tossing his car keys to Harman, he decided to try and get some sleep on their way back to the station.

That didn't happen.

CHAPTER FIVE

DCI STEPHENS ROSE from behind the desk, the low winter sun behind him silhouetting his ample frame. It was standing room only for Caslin and DC Harman.

"Nice of you to put in an appearance, Nathaniel."

"Just working the case, Guv."

"Yes, so I'm told. May I introduce Gerry Trent." Stephens indicated the man before him, seated alongside Atwood. Both men turned their heads to those standing. "Gerry has been assigned to investigate the unfortunate incident last night."

"Unfortunate is a description that is yet to be determined," Trent said softly, rising to greet Caslin with a smile. His brow furrowing as he spoke.

Trent was an officious looking man, well into his fifties with greying hair which had long since departed the crown of his head. He wore half-moon spectacles and the impression they gave, settled on his angular nose, was that of an academic. He lifted himself to his full height as he stepped towards Caslin. The folds of his charcoal suit were well creased and the material didn't settle as he adjusted his jacket. He was certainly not one who spent his salary on his wardrobe.

Stephens cleared his throat, "Well yes, of course. It was a turn of phrase that's all."

"Never mind, Sir," Caslin spoke before anyone else. "Our friends at the Commission are particularly finicky over the detail."

Trent smiled again but it didn't reach his eyes, "We do tend to follow the letter of the law, to its fullest. A virtue in our business, I think all here would agree?" he glanced at Caslin. "Well, almost all."

Caslin returned the smile. It was as if an arctic blast had passed through the room. Stephens still stood, quietly observing, whereas Harman and Atwood flatly refused to make eye contact with anyone. For his part, Caslin seemed more than content to meet the gaze of the newcomer from the Independent Police Complaints Commission.

"And we will provide any assistance that you should need in your investigation," DCI Stephens piped up, breaking the silence that clung to the air.

"I understand that your officers have already been doing so?" Trent indicated Atwood with a flick of his hand, the latter looked away momentarily.

"We've been trying to locate next of kin," Caslin said, mentally noting that his fellow DI was prone to chatter. "Sadly, without any success, thus far."

"Is that so?"

"DC Harman?" Stephens asked.

The constable hesitated for the briefest of moments.

"Yes, Sir. There was no-one at home today. We think that he lives with his wife but no, there was no sign."

"And no-one has filed a MisPer?" Trent enquired.

Stephens shook his head, "Not yet, but it's still early."

It was a reasonable question. They all had experience of loved ones filing missing person reports when the relative in question had merely been on an extended night out, often turning up several days later than expected. By the same token, thousands of people went missing each year in the UK never to be heard from again. It was fair to say the majority vanished by choice rather than coming to any misfortune.

"May I ask a question of you?" Caslin said to Trent, who indicated he could. "What are the boundaries of your investigation?"

"There are no boundaries, you know that. I will determine the cause of death and what led to it. Nothing more, nothing less." He took the measure of Caslin's expression. "You expected a different answer?"

Caslin shook his head, "Not at all. The IPCC have taken some kickings in the press in recent years, so I'm sure you'll be keen to avoid another."

"We want to get this tied off as soon as possible."

"But not too soon. We wouldn't want anyone accusing you of a sloppy investigation."

Trent's demeanour shifted towards hostile, his tone matching it.

"I have never led a shoddy investigation, I expose others'."

Caslin bristled, "This case is not as simple as you may think."

"Is that so? Perhaps you can enlighten us, Inspector."

"Do we have a preliminary result from the pathologist, yet?"

Trent shook his head, "I'm hopeful that we will tomorrow."

"Well in all probability, I expect you'll learn that he took his own life." There was a stunned silence from all in the room.

Stephens appeared the most surprised and more than a little irritated that he was only learning of this now, "Why would he do that?"

"Haven't a clue. Maybe he didn't want to talk to us?"

"And with what evidence do you base that on?" Trent asked flatly. His expression appeared to be one of genuine interest and not the scepticism that Caslin had expected.

Caslin thought for a moment, "Call it... a hunch."

"A hunch?" Trent replied. There was the scepticism.

"Or good old-fashioned police instinct, if you would prefer?" Caslin replied defensively, the beginnings of an angry knot tightening in his chest.

"Well if that is all you have, then I would recommend you get some rest, you look like you need it. May I remind you that a policeman was present throughout unless you're telling me different? This man didn't tie his shirt into a noose whilst alone in his cell. This isn't South Africa in the '80s."

"Perhaps you should wait for the report before dismissing it out of hand," Caslin countered. "That is what policemen do, weigh up evidence and *then* form their conclusions. Of course, if you were a police—"

DCI Stephens asserted himself and took control, "Gentlemen, the IPCC are here at our request having had this case referred to them, and we will offer our assistance in any way possible. Inspector Caslin has submitted his report, a copy of which I have here," he pointed to a folder on his desk, "and should there be anything else, you only have to name it." The last was said to Trent who nodded acceptance with good grace. "Now this investigation will run its course and maybe it would be best if we continued this conversation, should it be necessary, tomorrow. I'm sure we all have our own work to do. You—" Stephens pointed at Harman, "most certainly do. Where are you with 'Ticketing Express'?"

"Err... I'm working on it, Boss."

"Work faster, fewer distractions. Yes?"

Harman nodded and within moments the impromptu meeting broke up and they all filed out, except for Caslin, who was requested to stay behind. As Atwood left, he almost imperceptibly glared at Caslin, closing the door behind him. Stephens offered him one of the vacated chairs but he declined.

"Is he going to cause you a problem?"

"In what way, Sir?"

"Don't piss me about, Nathaniel. You and he have previous. You'd have to be a blind man not to see it."

Caslin sighed, his shoulders dropped a little but inside he could still feel the rage building, "He was the supervising officer that oversaw my last case, down south."

"The reason you ended up here, you mean?"

"That's one way of looking at it."

"Well this time he's not here for you, so make sure you stay well clear. I need his sort in my station like a hole in the head."

"Understood. May I go?"

"Before you do, perhaps you could tell me why this suicide theory of yours is not mentioned in your report?" he tapped the folder on his desk.

"You said it. It's a theory. May I go?"

Stephens nodded. Caslin guessed that the DCI now saw that potentially there was more to this than he had realised. Perhaps even more than Caslin was currently letting on. For now, the senior officer appeared happy to let it go, but sooner or later, it would need to be said. Stephens had always acknowledged that Caslin was a capable detective but had resisted when asked to accept him onto the team. It was no secret that he still didn't want him there.

Caslin knew his card was marked. The DCI was old school and saw people like him as career men who built reputations as swiftly as they destroyed them. At least Frank Stephens was upfront about his views. There was little room for career-minded officers in his team, only methodical, dogged police work. No glamour, no attention. Careers happened if you worked hard and were not processes to be managed. Caslin was sure that he could read his superior's mind, seeing the question repeating over and over: 'What becomes of a career man who has blown his career?'. Caslin sensed the perception of him was as a walking time bomb and no-one wanted to be near him when he went off. One thing was certain; Frank Stephens would be standing well clear.

Caslin reached the door and turned the handle, before the DCI called after him, "And have a wash before you come back tomorrow. You might not care what people think about you around here but I bloody well do!"

Caslin paused for the briefest of moments before leaving. It was a fair comment. He had looked awful that morning and it was doubtful that eight hours on he would appear any better. It was clear to him that Stephens didn't like having the IPCC in his station, bad smells tended to linger. Trent's arrival had been a shock, far from pleasant, and it had left a bitter taste. There was only one answer for that, the only answer Caslin had.

CHAPTER SIX

CASLIN'S MOOD had not improved by the following morning when he made it up to the third floor of the station, shockingly hung over, and entered a packed CID. Taped to the door was a crudely enlarged and photocopied publicity poster for the latest James Bond film. Scrawled across it in capitals were the words 'WANTED DEAD OR ALIVE'. His suicide theory had clearly found its way out of Stephens' office. Caslin held the door open with his left hand and indicated the homemade sign with his right. No-one inside, sitting at their desks, met his eye.

"Very bloody funny," he said flatly to a chorus of laughter from within.

DC Holt was the first to look up, grinning as he spoke, "Well these spooks are hard to find. We thought we'd better make a start."

More laughing.

Caslin walked in and pulled out the chair at his desk, "There isn't an ejector seat fitted to this is there?"

Holt shook his head, the grin widening. Caslin was about to sit down but changed his mind, pulling on the coat that he had just removed and headed for the exit. DS Hunter looked like she was about to ask where he was going before thinking better of it.

Caslin moved with purpose and nearly collided with Maxim Harman as he rounded the corner in the corridor. The latter had a cup of coffee in his hand and almost threw it over him.

"Sorry, Sir," Harman said weakly.

When Caslin reached the stairs, he called after Harman.

"Do you know where Hope Street is?"

Harman nodded, "It's just off Walmgate, on the east side, edge of the old city walls. Why?"

Caslin thought for a moment before ignoring the question.

"Good. Get your coat and I'll meet you downstairs."

Harman hesitated, "The Guv wants me on this ticketing scam. He'll have my backside if—"

"Now!" Caslin said forcefully. "You can make up the ground on that later. Hell, I'll even help you. Come on," he encouraged the DC to get a move on, turning his back and setting off.

Harman let the door swing shut and scampered down the corridor after the rapidly diminishing figure, trying not to spill his drink as he went but failing miserably.

"Where is it we're going again?"

———

CASLIN EYED a sandwich shop on Walmgate. It was a little place, squeezed in between a newsagent and a dry-cleaners. He decided they would stop there on their way out. Hope Street was in an old estate set just within the ancient city walls, a stone's throw from the Barbican that lay beyond them. It was an estate of brick terraces with a diverse community. From memory, Caslin knew that Dick Turpin was buried somewhere nearby, in the graveyard of a church that itself had been long gone for many years. He glanced around as Harman pulled up at the kerbside and put on the handbrake. It struck him that there was something ironic about the highwayman being buried amongst the residents here, for he too had crossed social boundaries. A fleeting thought crossed his mind as to whether there was a criminal gene that permeated certain areas down through the ages? He doubted it.

Number twelve was a maisonette, located between two larger properties. The dark blue paint of the front door was peeling around the edges and the window frames were also in need of a lick of paint, as the top layer of white was flaking off to reveal another of deep brown. There was a collection of plastic bins, grey and green, alongside recycling crates, all arranged haphazardly on the concrete pathway leading up to the buildings. Some had plasticised numbers stuck to them, whilst others were crudely hand painted. Loud music could be heard banging out from one of the upper windows of the terrace and Caslin prayed that it wasn't from number twelve. His headache was clearing but he still felt a little tender.

Harman rang the bell and stepped back to wait. A few of the neighbours passed by in the street and the two men felt very conspicuous as eyes fell upon them. Caslin felt they were easily identifiable as police. After a wait that made him wonder if they were being ignored, a woman opened the door. She was in her late forties, had light brown hair that was tied back at the nape of her neck, with a fringe that hung low across her forehead. She drew her dressing gown closer about her as the chill of the outdoors hit home, viewing them suspiciously. They introduced themselves, showing her their warrant cards and reluctantly, she invited them inside.

The hallway was narrow and cluttered, with stairs off it to the bedrooms above, leading into a larger reception room that could accommodate a three-piece suite. Once, it was white leather but now it showed signs of discolouration and wear. The smell of cannabis prevailed in the room as did the distinctive stale smell of cigarettes. A television was fixed to the wall, far too large for the room and was quickly muted, sparing the visitors a dose of daytime chat. As they each took a seat, Caslin was relieved to see that the dressing gown covered jogging bottoms and a sweater.

"We're looking for a 'C McNeil'. We believe that name is registered at this address?"

"That would be me, Chloe McNeil," she said, taking out a packet of menthol cigarettes from a pocket in her dressing gown, along with a disposable green lighter, and sparking up. "What's this about?" she asked, between drags.

Caslin explained the events that had led them to her door. He left out the grislier details as he was acutely aware she probably had some connection with the deceased as yet to be determined. Surprisingly to Caslin, she failed to react in any notable way to the information. If she was missing someone there was no apparent concern. The pickup was not known to her, nor was the address of Radford Farmhouse, and she had no knowledge of anyone by the name of Horsvedt. Were it not for the utility bill in the vehicle, there would be no link to her at all. Caslin could feel his frustration mounting. As a last resort he described the deceased as best as he could remember. Chloe stubbed out her cigarette vigorously as he spoke, causing ash to spill over onto the coffee table as she disturbed the pile. Just at the last of his description she hesitated momentarily, but it was enough.

"Sound like someone you know?" Caslin asked tentatively.

Chloe McNeil glanced over at him, her mouth open and lips slightly apart. An expression that was hard to read. She finished stubbing out the butt and rose. Crossing the room to the mantel above her coal-effect electric fire, she picked up a photo that had been tucked behind another frame. Pausing with it held in both hands before her, she stared intently at it, before passing it to Caslin.

"Is this him?" she asked softly.

Caslin examined the photo. It was a shot of Chloe with her arms draped around a man, taken on a bright sunny day, evidently some time ago. The edges were tatty, with both figures in the picture appearing several years younger. Chloe's hair was darker, not greying as it was now, and the man she sat with had a nineties flat-top. However, the likeness was unmistakable, they had found their man. Caslin handed the picture to Harman as Chloe McNeil withdrew another cigarette from the box and lit it, her hands shaking almost imperceptibly. He cleared his throat.

"I'd like you to attend an identification. We need to be certain."

"But it's him, isn't it?" she interrupted.

Caslin remained non-committal, "We need to be sure. Who is it, in this picture?"

Chloe took a long draw on her cigarette, exhaling heavily before she spoke, "My husband... my... ex-husband, Garry. Garry McNeil."

Caslin waited a moment, letting the information sink in. He gently elbowed Harman to get his attention.

"Perhaps a cup of tea might be in order?"

Harman took the hint and pointed in the direction of what he assumed was the kitchen. A slightly shell-shocked Chloe nodded and smiled appreciatively.

"I've not seen him in a while," she said after a moment. Caslin only now noticed her voice was gravelly in tone. Gingerly she seated herself on the arm of one of the chairs.

"When did you last see him?"

Chloe thought for a moment, clinging to her cigarette as she did so, "About seven or eight months ago I reckon, got to be... yeah. He came around every now and again, after we split but he keeps his distance now, since the divorce."

Caslin nodded his understanding and couldn't help but wonder if his marriage was heading the same way. The sounds of a kettle boiling came to him from the kitchen.

"Do you know where Garry has been living?"

She shook her head, "No, and to be honest I couldn't have cared less!" Caslin was a little taken aback. Chloe seemed to notice and quickly responded, "We didn't break up on the best of terms, Garry... well, he found it hard when he came back to civvy street."

"He was in the forces?"

"Yeah, the Rifles. He did his twenty and came out," Chloe thought for a moment. "2008. Pretty sure it was in the June."

"You say he found it hard?"

Chloe nodded, "He struggled to hold down work. It was always casual, labouring or security."

"Security?"

"Agency stuff. Night watchman at factories and the like. He had a stint on A and E at the weekends for a while."

"Any idea what he had been doing more recently?"

Chloe shook her head. Caslin passed the photograph back and Chloe's eyes lingered on it for a moment.

"It wasn't always bad though. This was taken at Glastonbury in '91, I think. We had fun back then, old rockers now…"

Harman reappeared with a tray of mismatching mugs and placed it down on the table before them.

"Do you have anyone that we can call for you, Miss McNeil?" Caslin asked.

She shook her head, "There's no need. When do you want me to do the…" she searched for the word.

"Identification?" Harman answered. Chloe nodded.

"As soon as we can arrange it. This afternoon if you feel up to it?" She said that she was although appeared less than enthusiastic. That was fair enough. In all his years on the job, he was yet to come across anyone who looked forward to identifying their loved ones. Even the disgruntled ex-lovers found it distasteful, if not overwhelming. "I'll set the wheels in motion."

Caslin left Harman in the room with her. She was withdrawing into herself but that was natural, she was in shock. Taking out his phone he was about to call Fulford when it buzzed. He answered it and to his surprise it was Frank Stephens.

"You'd better get back here."

"I think we've identified our man, Guv."

"That's the good news, then," Stephens said genuinely. "You can fill me in when you get here. Bad news, depending on how you look at it, is you were right."

"About what?"

"The preliminary is in from the pathologist and it would appear that your man topped himself."

"We're on our way," Caslin said and hung up. He had resisted the urge to say "I know".

CHAPTER SEVEN

"GARRY MCNEIL DIED of cardiac arrest, having first slipped into a coma and suffered a pulmonary oedema, according to the pathologist," DCI Stephens said, sitting back in his chair as if the weight of such news had settled heavily upon him.

Back at Fulford shortly after 3 p.m., Caslin had joined the meeting. Michael Atwood was at the DCI's side and Gerry Trent was notable by his absence. DS Hunter sat alongside both Constables Holt and Harman. Caslin had taken the remaining chair.

"What brought that on?" Caslin asked. Everyone was processing the information being divulged from the document Frank Stephens held before him.

"He had ingested cyanide. Apparently, a capsule had been loosely sewn into the waistband of his jeans. We found the hole for which after Dr Taylor produced the cause of death."

"That's a bit cloak and dagger," Atwood stated.

"Too right it is," Stephens agreed. "Let's have a recap. What do we know about this McNeil character?"

"He was forty-nine years of age, former military, having served for two decades. Recently divorced and has been struggling to adapt to civilian life over the past seven years," Caslin offered.

"Known income sources?"

Caslin shook his head, "Still to be determined. Nothing regular, as far as we are aware."

"What connection do we have with Daniel Horsvedt?"

Harman spoke up, "Preliminary investigation shows no discernible link through work or criminality. Neither man has been on our radar, past or present."

"Any idea as to why McNeil had possession of Horsvedt's vehicle, or indication as to why he tried to pass himself off as the former?"

"Maybe he borrowed it from him and didn't have insurance. It wouldn't be the first time," Atwood suggested.

"We'll have to find a link between them for that to be the case," Caslin added. "That leads us to a bigger question though."

"Which is?" Stephens asked.

"Where is Daniel Horsvedt? I know it's early days but the border police haven't come up with anything to show that he, or his rig for that matter, have left the country recently."

The conversation was interrupted by a ringing desk phone. Stephens answered it and accepted the call, putting it on loudspeaker for everyone to hear.

"Go on, Dr Taylor, we're all listening."

"Thank you, Frank. Good afternoon ladies and gentlemen," there was a murmur of greeting from those present as the pathologist joined proceedings. "Apologies for my absence but I was required to follow up with the detail as soon as possible."

Caslin was struck by the softness of the tone in the doctor's voice. The thought distracted him briefly from the subject matter in hand.

"What have you been able to ascertain, Alison?" DCI Stephens asked.

"The Hydrogen Cyanide dosage was well over 200 milligrams, almost twice what would have been considered strong enough to kill Mr McNeil. 1.5 milligrams per kilo of bodyweight could be fatal, depending on the person. Even if he'd been admitted to a hospital immediately, knowing what he had ingested, it remains highly doubtful that he would've made it."

"Any idea where he got it from? I mean it's not exactly freely available at your local pharmacy," Caslin inquired.

"There is a possibility that there's a chemical marker that may, or may not, help trace the source but…"

"But?" Caslin pressed.

"Well, it's a guess but judging from the method of delivery, I would find such a marker to be unlikely in this instance."

"Do you have anything else for us, Alison?" Stephens asked.

"Not at this point. I'll get the full report to you as soon as I can."

"Thank you for your time," Stephens said as he hung up. Caslin was already missing the sound of her voice. Stephens refocused on his team before him. "So, we have virtually nothing as it stands now? At this moment in time we have no idea as to where McNeil was living, working or getting his money. Nor do we know why he was pretending to be someone else on the night that he died. Let alone, where that person is and no clue as to the motive for suicide. Do I have that, about right?"

The DCI had stress in his voice. Caslin recognised it and momentarily felt a twinge in his chest. The question was rhetorical and no-one responded directly.

"We have a name, that's a start," DI Atwood said. "Once released, we may get more leads coming our way."

Caslin shook his head. How Michael Atwood had made DI was a mystery to him. He was always looking for an angle to either get up the ladder or make it known that that was where he was heading. If there was anything of potential risk to his credibility, a case that looked too messy for him, he would find some way to duck out without appearing to do so. Caslin had a phrase for people like him, referring to them as "Teflons". As far as he could work out, Atwood had no major collars on his record and moved between positions, and constabularies, frequently. No doubt the regularity of his departures ensured that his misjudgements never got a chance to catch up with him. He had only been in York for ten months, following a two-year stint in Child Exploitation and Online Protection within the National Crime Agency, and was rumoured to already be engineering a transfer. God only knew where to, this time.

What he did have going for him though, was the ear of their boss. However, if Caslin's DI had suggested waiting for the public to proffer information in a case like this, rather than taking a proactive approach, he would have hit the roof. Maybe that was one reason why his own career was prematurely on the way back down.

"I'm not going before the press this evening with nothing more than a name and a suicide," Stephens exclaimed. "We've bloody had the guy for two days. If I don't give them more than that, they'll damn well start making it up. This case takes priority. By all means, continue with anything else you've got on but we need movement on this."

It was a fair point. The red tops loved a case like this and had the dead man been an immigrant, or an ethnic minority, they probably would have had a field day with it, by now. As it stood, there was a limited window of peace before the status quo would evolve.

From the outset it was made clear that an investigation into the death in custody was off limits, this was firmly in the control of Trent and the IPCC. As long as all information was freely passed to them, then CID could look at the surrounding matters, until such time as they were deemed relevant. Caslin felt that such a large team wasn't required but had to admit that the case was unusual and no-one knew where it might lead.

Caslin's absence from the station that morning, accompanying Chloe McNeil to the identification of her ex-husband, had kept him blissfully ignorant of the media scrum that had been developing outside. The interest continued to gather pace once it was announced that the dead man remained, for the time being at least, unidentified. Local news crews had been reinforced by advance teams from some of the national papers and, judging by how slow a news week it appeared to be, the national television press was expected to pick it up soon enough.

The DCI shook his head. He indicated Atwood, "Michael, could you look into where McNeil got the cyanide from? Nathaniel is right. It can't be easy to come by, so we may get a break there. Nathaniel—"

Caslin looked up, he had been momentarily lost in thought, "Yes, Guv."

"You've already made a start. Get into this guy's life, shake the tree and see what falls out. Find a link to this Daniel Horsvedt while you're at it. So far it seems like he's a ghost. I want to know that he exists and, if possible, where he is."

Harman glanced at Caslin but said nothing, the latter pretended not to notice.

"Will do, perhaps Maxim could assist?" Caslin asked. "I'll need help with phone records, bank accounts and such like."

DCI Stephens looked over at Harman who remained passive, for his part, "Okay, but I still want something on that online promo site that you've been working on, by the end of the week."

Harman nodded enthusiastically. Caslin felt a little guilty, for it was he who had been dominating the constable's time in the past day or so. They agreed to meet again at 6 p.m. for a catch up, before the press conference. The room emptied as the group left their DCI to contemplate what he was going to say to the waiting media. If he could have wished for anything at that moment, it would have been for an announcement of a Royal wedding or a celebrity death, anything that the press would love, if only to take the pressure off for a day or two.

HARMAN FELL into step alongside Caslin and once sure that they were out of earshot of anyone else, he spoke.

"Why didn't you mention the photo of the Horsvedts that we found this morning?"

Caslin steered the younger man into the gents, as they passed by, with a gentle hand on the shoulder. He quickly checked that the cubicles were as empty as the rest of the room.

"Why didn't you?"

Harman stammered, "Well… I—"

"Because we picked it up on an illegal search."

"Yes."

"So, stupid question, right?" Harman nodded his agreement. Caslin continued, "With the IPCC hanging around we play it by the book, at least that's how it's written down."

"Yes, Sir. I understand."

Caslin read the expression on his colleague's face. It was one that conveyed far more than merely concerns over their procedural misdemeanour.

"What else is playing on your mind, Maxim?"

"Is it that obvious?" Harman asked. Caslin nodded. "It's that picture you found."

"What about it?"

"The baby. Adults are one thing but…"

"I know. I'm thinking the same. I want any information you can dig up on Horsvedt and McNeil's bank accounts. Let's find them, fast."

Harman was happy to oblige.

CHAPTER EIGHT

"ANYTHING?" Caslin asked.

Harman glanced up, a frown etched on his brow that made him appear well beyond his years.

"Depends on what you consider as useful."

"Give me something."

"I've got a couple of bank statements, one for each of them. They don't show any significant balances or transactions, but we may get some financial history from the branches themselves."

"Well, that is something. You won't have to phone around every branch in the high street asking if they were customers. What activity is there?"

Harman slowly scanned the paper in his hand.

"It looks like all the direct debits went out of Daniel's account, TV licence, rent and utilities. Angela's looks like a building society savings account, with sod all in it, I might add."

"That's somewhere to start. Find out who they were paying their rent to, who owns this place? They should be able to put some more detail onto the Horsvedts. Is there enough in the account to cover the bills? I mean, we don't know how long they've been missing. Unless there's a bottomless pit of cash they'll run out, if no-one's earning."

"Are they missing now, then?"

"Well they're not here, so figuratively speaking, yes. But you're right. They may only be missing to us. The balance?"

"A little over £150 and no withdrawals in this statement, it's dated July."

"That won't go far. Did you find any red letters around the place?"

Harman shook his head. Caslin hadn't either, which set him thinking.

"Any newer statements?"

"Not that I've come across but we'll see. Strange though, isn't it? If he is around, then where are the more recent ones? He's quite organised with the accounts of the business. Although that said, there's nothing recent there either."

"And let's not forget that the power's still on. These days, they're keen to kick your door in and fit prepayment meters if you don't cough up regularly."

"Speaking from personal experience, Sir?"

Caslin ignored the question and went out of the room, heading into the kitchen. His frustration was mounting. The longer they spent looking at this the more questions he seemed to be asking, but the answers were not forthcoming. He had been involved with similar cases in the past where every avenue appeared to be a dead end, or each door turned out to be locked. All he needed was a break and it didn't need to be big. He just hoped that they would find it soon. Either that or the Horsvedts would turn up out of the blue, in a car packed with suitcases and a bucket and spade, then perhaps he could forget the whole thing.

Choosing one of the chairs at the kitchen table, Caslin reversed it and, having first tossed his notebook to the table, sat down. He crossed his arms on the rim before him and leaned forward, resting his chin. He was confident that he had covered the basics but even so, the Horsvedts were still a blank which felt wrong to him. The couple had a son. As best as they could figure he was not even of pre-school age yet and had slipped under the radar of the local health visitors. That in itself was an indication that the family were relatively new to the area and perhaps ignorant of UK childcare procedures. Unless they wanted it that way. Caslin had no reason to think so but it was a consideration, nonetheless.

There appeared to be barely a trace of them in Yorkshire, which was adding to his frustration. Caslin had been working this case solidly now for several days and felt that he should be further along than he was. Two adults going missing was a common enough occurrence in his profession, but the idea of a toddler vanishing without a trace was a major concern for him.

DI Atwood had failed thus far to come up with anything productive on the cyanide. It was of significant strength but, as Alison Taylor predicted, had no chemical marker that could lead them back to a supplier. This was a mystery in itself. The poison had been encased in glass, a throwback to the days of the Cold War, which made for interesting trivia but useless in terms of their investigation as it led them nowhere. The specialist forensics lab in Leeds had promised to examine it further but they had implied that no-one should get their hopes up.

A request had gone out to Europol to see if any of the names were under investigation, or even suspicion, but that too had drawn a blank. The vain hope that a lack of information would encourage the press to find another story to lead with had evaporated quickly. It appeared that no news only led them to greater and greater speculation. The latest from the red tops listed McNeil as MI5 with links to counter-terrorist investigations. That one had made Caslin smile. He guessed that they would have him charged with the Kennedy assassination by the end of the week if something juicier didn't turn up.

He glanced around the room, vainly hoping to see something that he had missed. A note pinned to a cupboard that had fallen and been swept under the cabinets, or perhaps a scrape or scuff to the furniture that didn't seem quite right, anything that could spark his imagination. He threw his head back and looked to the ceiling, exhaling a deep sigh as he did so. The clear head that he had been working with was clouding over as the minutes ticked by. Caslin closed his eyes and returned his chin to the comfort of his forearms.

How long he sat there like that he didn't know but Harman clearing his throat, snapped him from his thought process. The DC held an archive box before him and indicated it with a nod of his head.

"This should keep me busy for a while. I've got financials for the business as well as their personal accounts. With a bit of luck, we should be able to track where they've been, if not where they are."

Caslin nodded but something told him that the break they were looking for wouldn't come from the contents of that box. Instinctively, he felt that the financials would be a cold lead and would probably only throw up more questions.

"I'll head back to Fulford with these."

"Good lad," Caslin said, feigning interest but saying nothing more.

Harman shuffled past and as he reached the threshold of the door he paused, propping it open with his shoulder. Glancing back at Caslin, he looked about to say something but changed his mind and left, the door swinging shut behind him. Caslin was once again alone with his thoughts.

He decided to leave, needing to put some distance between himself and the case, having had enough of sitting there asking the same questions over and over. He had thought of little else for days and that had the effect of creating a form of tunnel vision, analysing the same thoughts time and again. For the life of him he could only come up with two plausible explanations, either the family had fled from something in a hurry, leaving their possessions behind, or they had been caught up in something altogether more sinister. The former seemed more likely as they had no evidence for the latter. If that was the case though, some trace of them should have surfaced by now, a cash withdrawal, ferry tickets, a child's prescription, something. They still knew very little about the family and it was bugging him.

Caslin had flicked out the kitchen light and was pulling the door to behind him when his phone began to ring. He answered the call and continued on to where his car was parked at the front. It was DC Holt. The two exchanged pleasantries.

"I've got the info on the registered owner of the farmhouse from the Land Registry."

"Go on."

"They had to search their archives. Apparently, it hasn't changed hands for decades, so had never migrated onto the computer, hence why we couldn't bring it up sooner. Who'd have thought that, eh? Usually it's only those grand houses that stay in families for generations, until the relatives can't afford the inheritance tax and grant the house to the National Trust instead."

Holt was not only the office comedian but also the chatterbox. Caslin grew impatient.

"So, who owns it, Terry?"

Holt didn't notice his irritation.

"Oh yeah, hang on. It's here someplace."

Caslin had reached his car and unlocked it before he got an answer, shaking his head as he heard the shuffling of papers in the background whilst the DC rummaged around on his desk.

"Here it is, a Sylvia Vickers."

"And who is she?"

"Good question. The title deed was transferred to her name back in the summer of 1938, presumably an inheritance. I guess it was from her father, a Gordon Tremell, who died that same year."

Caslin thought for a moment before speaking, "I imagine that would probably make Sylvia quite old."

"Agreed. I did a search and she hasn't come up on file, but there is an S. Vickers on the electoral roll, living in North Yorkshire."

"Give me the address."

*

Caslin rooted around in his pocket with his free hand for his notebook, failing to hide his frustration at not finding it quickly.

"I'll text it to you, Sir," Holt offered and Caslin gratefully accepted. The address was a residential care home in Goldsborough, which was east of Knaresborough. Realising that it was more or less on his way back to York, and he could make it there in about half an hour, Caslin decided he would stop by. "Do you want me to call ahead?" Holt asked.

Caslin declined the offer and hung up, belatedly thanking the DC for his efforts as the phone touched the lining of his coat. Maybe he would get some answers today after all. With renewed optimism, he turned the car around and headed for the main road.

CHAPTER NINE

It was a good twenty miles or so before Caslin took the turning left onto the Ripley Road, heading directly through Knaresborough and on towards his destination. The care home was based in an old Victorian building, possibly the original rectory for the village church located nearby. The car park was gravelled and set within well maintained grounds. Bringing the car to a crunching halt, he parked up next to a sign directing visitors to present themselves at reception upon arrival.

There was a snap in the air and Caslin shivered as he crossed the short distance to the entrance, trying the door to the porch but finding it locked. Both the inner and outer doors were glazed, allowing an un-obscured view to the illuminated hallway within. What he perceived to be the original panelling on the walls stood out with its richly engraved detail, and Caslin considered how such features were sorely lacking in the buildings of the current day, which saddened him. The resounding chime of the doorbell echoed within and was answered shortly after. A rather ascetic and officious looking woman in a charcoal-grey business suit eyed him warily, as she turned the key in the lock and tugged violently at the door. Evidently severely warped, it eventually succumbed and juddered open, its edge scraping harshly on the tiled floor.

"Visiting hours are eleven to three and then six until eight, with very few exceptions," she said haughtily.

"And this is one of those exceptions," Caslin said, producing his warrant card.

THE OFFICE WAS SET out in what had probably been the drawing room of the house. Once again, the panelling caught his eye amongst the period features on display. An imposing marble fireplace competed with the original sash windows to be the eye catching centrepiece. Caslin warmed his hands on the radiator while he waited. These houses were beautiful but they were draughty as hell. He concluded that the place must cost a small fortune to heat during the winter. The walls themselves were adorned with paintings of regal looking men and women, all depicted sitting or standing, perhaps documenting the familial inhabitants or owners of the house. Caslin couldn't be sure as no names were detailed beneath them.

Having been ushered into the office by the manager of the home, but not considering herself senior enough to deal with a police enquiry, she had left him to his own devices before disappearing to find one of the owners. After a wait of nearly half an hour, one of the oversized four-panel doors creaked open and a gentleman strode forward. In his early fifties, slightly built and carrying himself with confidence, he offered a warm hand to Caslin who took it.

"I'm Dr Spencer Oliver, co-owner of Goldsborough Residential and you are?"

"Detective Inspector Caslin, of York," Caslin produced his warrant card again which the doctor examined closely.

"What can I do for you, Inspector?"

"I'm looking for a lady, Sylvia Vickers. I understand she is a resident here."

"May I ask what this is regarding?"

"Her name has come up in the course of an investigation. Any more than that, I should really say to her."

Dr Oliver frowned slightly, "I see. However, I cannot understand how that would be possible, at all."

"Well if I can speak with her, then we may be able to shed some light on it."

"Patients are entitled to their privacy, Inspector. I'm not sure that I am able to give out any information, unless of course you have a warrant?"

Now it was Caslin's turn to frown, and he felt a sense of irritation creeping forward with the man before him.

"I was unaware that this was an institution?"

"It isn't, Inspector, but nonetheless—"

"Nonetheless my arse, Dr Oliver, is she a resident here or not?"

Dr Oliver seemed taken aback but equally resolute in his stance on the matter. Caslin decided that a full-blown slanging match was not in his interest and adopted a gentler approach.

"I can understand you wanting to protect the privacy of your patients. However, we are looking into the whereabouts of a family who have vanished without a trace. Their residence is owned by Mrs Vickers, I just need to ask her some questions about those people. Only to find out more information that's all."

The man before him responded to the tactful line and his previous rigidity appeared to soften if only a little.

"Well in that case, I will take you to her. I'm not entirely sure what you are expecting, though."

Caslin was led from the office, down a corridor to a set of stairs where they ascended to the first floor and turned right. There was little activity and Dr Oliver explained that most of the residents were downstairs having their evening meal. Only the bedridden, or more aggressive, residents ate in their rooms.

They stopped by a corner at the rear of the house, the last door before the second flight of stairs, outside a room that was numbered 17 and was slightly ajar. The doctor held out his hand to indicate Caslin should enter. For some reason that would still escape him, even later that night, Caslin was hesitant as he gently knocked on the door and pushed it open.

"Mrs Vickers?" he enquired, as he walked in.

The room was lit by a single bedside lamp, was of a reasonable size and had two double-aspect sash windows on adjacent exterior walls. The curtains were open and Caslin could see a rising moon in the evening sky. Sylvia Vickers lay in bed with arms to her side, palms down, the sheets tucked firmly in place. Her eyes were open but she seemed lost in thought, staring straight ahead. Her breathing appeared shallow, in her skeletally thin frame, and was aided by an oxygen tube supplied via the bottle cradled next to her bed. On the far side, her left arm was attached to an intravenous drip.

"Mrs Vickers?" Caslin asked again, purely out of courtesy, as he stepped further into the room. The elderly lady not only failed to acknowledge his presence but appeared to be completely unaware of her surroundings.

"Now you will understand why I cannot believe that Sylvia is a part of your investigation, Inspector."

Caslin indicated the still form of the woman and then he spoke in a hushed tone.

"Is she always... I mean, is she aware of us at all?"

Dr Oliver shook his head and came to stand at the foot of the bed, crossing his arms before him and tilting his head slightly to one side.

"Her condition has not deteriorated, though. That at least is the good news. Sadly, she has been like this for some time now. We keep her as comfortable as we can and she has days that are better than others."

"How long?" Caslin asked whilst trying to locate his notebook in his coat pockets, concluding that he had probably left it in the car.

"As long as she has been resident here, more or less. She was brought to us seven or so, years ago and sadly, I don't think that she has ever clicked on as to where she is."

"Who brought her to you, a relative?"

Dr Oliver shrugged, a gesture that could be interpreted as indicative that he couldn't remember, rather than he didn't care.

"I can take a look in her file but as far as I can recall, she has no relatives. She certainly has never had a visitor that I am aware of."

"Not one?"

"Again, I'll check her file, but no."

"So, who pays for her care?" Caslin was determined to leave there with something useful.

"The State. She had some funds when she first arrived but they were drained rather quickly. Shall we go back to my office and I'll see what else I can give you?"

Caslin nodded and they retreated from the room. He was disheartened, but hopeful that there may still be something fruitful in her records. A family member, or at the least another lead to follow, however tenuous, would count in this case. Caslin thought that ignorance of her own predicament may well have been a blessing in disguise. When an elderly person reached this stage and condition of life, it was conceivable that family might choose not to visit for fear of upset or, which was often more likely, being unduly inconvenienced. After all, if the relative was effectively in a coma and totally unaware, then what was the point? Heartless, uncaring and selfish, perhaps but as Caslin frequently found in his line of work, these were common traits in people.

THE SOUND of the rain drumming on the rooftop matched Caslin's mood as he sat in his car. The storm had shattered the clear, frosty landscape that had been forming only an hour previously. The engine was running and soon enough the heater would be blowing warm air, rather than cold, onto the windscreen. Giving in to his impatience he pulled the sleeve of his coat down over his hand and leant forward, wiping the glass before him.

The case file for Sylvia Vickers had proved to be useless. She had been transferred to the home in Goldsborough eight years ago, along with several other residents, from another care home that had been due to close down, its owners having gone under. The chances of finding records from there would be non-existent. The disappointment was intense, for the details that now remained were incredibly limited. The basic information of date and place of birth, along with medical status and prior conditions notwithstanding, Caslin was leaving with almost nothing. No visitors had been recorded coming or going and the bedridden lady inside had outlived her husband by twenty-two years.

Caslin shuddered at the thought of the life that she had and couldn't help but wonder what his future had in store, would his own children make time for him or was he destined to sit alone, staring at somebody else's wall? Fortunately, he was still some way off it. Turning his thoughts to other lines of inquiry he was hopeful that Harman would be able to shake something out of the bank accounts. The Horsvedts were paying rent for the farmhouse and if the money wasn't going to Sylvia Vickers, it was certainly going elsewhere.

In every investigation there would be a moment when he felt lost and at that point he would believe that he wasn't doing his job properly. He wasn't quite there yet but was certainly well on the way. Events always left a trail, no matter how slight. Caslin firmly believed that a crime scene would talk, provided the investigator was prepared to listen. A brief search of his car had failed to turn up his notebook and he wanted to review what he had written down. There was something in there that deserved more credence than he had given it but he hadn't been able to bring it forward. Caslin hated that and it was happening too often.

A moment of clarity came to mind, an image of him tossing his notebook to the kitchen table at Radford Farm. He swore. The last thing he wanted to do was to head back there, but it would be far less inconvenient to do so on his way home than making a new journey the following day.

Caslin sighed and glanced back at the care home, the darkness punctuated by the occasional room lit from within. Turning his thoughts to the forthcoming weekend, he knew he had to address a problem. Belatedly acknowledging that his workload had suddenly increased, alongside a realisation that his one-bedroom apartment was too small for the visit of his two children, he had logistical issues that he could no longer ignore. There was a solution but he found it less than palatable. Taking out his phone he scrolled through his phonebook, located the number and dialled it. The phone rang a couple of times before it was picked up. Caslin smiled as he spoke, lightening his voice as best he could.

"Dad?" he asked casually, "Here's the thing…"

IT WAS after 9 p.m. when Caslin pulled up again at Radford Farm. The rain had ceased but the cloud cover lent the building a deeply foreboding appearance in the darkness, the illumination from his headlights doing little to pierce the eerie façade. Turning off the engine, he spent the next ten minutes rummaging through the boot of the car for a more substantial light source, before giving up and instead using the screen of his phone as a makeshift solution.

Rounding the corner to the rear of the house, he picked his way up the path and momentarily felt the hairs on the back of his neck prickle, stopping him in his tracks. Had he heard something or seen it in the corner of his eye? Was it primeval fear preying on him in the darkness? He listened intently but other than the breeze passing through the nearby copse of trees, there was nothing to focus on. Accidentally glancing at the screen of his phone he cursed, the bright light further ruining his limited visual acuity. As a child he had been afraid of the dark, not unusual in itself and adults could often attest to the same, although most would never admit it. It was nature's way of keeping you alert.

The longer he remained still, the more ridiculous he began to feel. Telling himself that his mind was definitely playing tricks, he resumed his course. Stepping up to the rear door to the kitchen, Caslin knelt by the plant pot and lit up the area as he reached for the hidden key. Standing, he placed the key in the lock and turned it. The key held firm. It took a moment for him to realise why. Slowly moving his free hand from key to handle, he twisted it and the door cracked open. There was a brief moment of confusion as possibilities entered his mind. Had he left the door unlocked earlier?

For the life of him he couldn't remember. He had had his phone in his hand when the call came through just as he was leaving, the call from Terry Holt with the Vickers information. The key had been in his hand when he shut the door. Once more he paused and listened intently, but again he could barely hear anything apart from the wind and the light traffic noise emanating from the distant road. Even that soon died away.

Gently he eased the door open, immediately regretting doing so as the hinges creaked, sounds that he was sure would carry. Peering into the gloom he strained to make out the interior, remembering the various locations of the furniture, and brought his phone to bear. All seemed to be as he had left it and he caught sight of his notebook on the table. There was that feeling again. He took a deep breath and exhaled slowly, tentatively taking a few steps into the kitchen. If there was anyone there, they would most certainly have seen him arrive, the headlights from the car would have given him up in seconds. *The car.* There was no other car in the driveway and equally no lights on in the house as sure as they would've seen him coming the same could be said for them. Any light from within would have been easily visible upon approach.

The sense of relief was palpable. Caslin smiled to himself and, shaking his head, sought out the light switch and in a few seconds, was bathed in neon light as the tube flickered into life. He blinked at the brightness. Smiling as he dismissed his paranoia he moved into the front room, turning the light on in there as well. There was a brief flash, accompanied by a popping sound, as the bulb blew. Instantly the circuit breaker kicked in and the house was plunged back into darkness.

"Bollocks," Caslin said aloud.

His mobile was already back in his pocket. He fumbled around for it and then fumbled yet more as he tried to unlock the handset. The screen sparked into life, bathing the fireplace in indirect light as Caslin angled the device away from his eyes. Then he saw it. A brief glimpse of something before it was gone. Caslin focused his attention on where he had been looking, slightly above and to the left of the mantel but unsure of exactly what had caught his eye. He slowly passed his hand back across in an effort to recreate the movement and on the third pass he saw it again, a pinprick of bluish light, maybe a reflection.

Taking a step towards it, not wishing to lose sight of the point on the wall, he caught his shin on the edge of the coffee table, cursing again as the distraction made him lose his focal point. He was scanning the wall once more when a scrabbling noise from behind drew his attention. Turning to see the cause, everything was plunged into darkness once more. Faint sounds came to his ear, then slowly began to fade away. Caslin thought to search for the phone that was no longer in his grasp but he didn't, the surface of the floor felt cold against his face, firm and yet pleasant.

The darkness was no longer something to induce fear but was somehow, strangely comforting.

CHAPTER TEN

IT WAS RAINING AGAIN. Caslin felt at ease. Outside it was still pitch black. The night was not yet over but other than that it was impossible to tell how long he had lain there. A little time passed before he could figure out what had happened. The surface felt rough and cold against his face. He was on the floor but where? Something was trickling slowly down the side of his neck, it was irritating. Investigating the cause with his left hand he reached up, a process that sent shooting pains through his head. It felt damp and sticky to the touch. Had he fallen? *No, there was someone else here.* A flash of panic came to mind, the fear that he was not alone there in the dark. *The lights went out.*

Gently easing himself up on to all fours, against his body's will, a wave of nausea swept over him and he vomited. His forearms and hands were splashed with something warm. Remaining as he was for a moment, his fear forgotten, he took in deep breaths until it passed. It was so dark that he couldn't see anything before him but he had a vague notion that a wall was off to his right and, gingerly, he crawled towards it. With fingers outstretched he felt the textured surface of the wallpaper and levered himself into a sitting position, his back against the wall. There he sat trying to focus, his breathing ragged and coming in short, rapid gasps. The nausea had passed but his head was banging, far worse than any hangover he could remember. Applying pressure to the base of his neck seemed to help as he sought to make sense of it all.

Listening intently to everything that may be around him, all he could focus on was the sound of the rain. If he wasn't alone earlier, he felt confident that he was now. Had they wanted to further harm him they had ample opportunity while he was out. Perhaps they had left him for dead. Thinking on it for a moment, Caslin dismissed the notion. His head hurt, and how bad the wound was he didn't know, but he was hopeful it would turn out to be superficial. That was a blind hope. More likely he would, at the least, have a concussion if not a fracture.

Caslin was still groggy but he managed to locate his phone without too much drama. Looking up Harman's mobile number, he called him. The phone rang a number of times and just as he feared the voicemail would cut in, he heard a familiar and yet monotone voice.

"Hello."

"Maxim?"

"Sir?" there was a heavy pause. "Do you know what time it is?"

Caslin didn't. He hadn't looked and if the truth were known, he wouldn't have cared if he had.

"Yeah, it's late. Get over to the farm."

There must have been something in Caslin's voice that alerted Harman to the seriousness of the moment for he suddenly seemed wide awake, concern edged into his tone.

"What's happened, are you out there?"

Caslin closed his eyes and took a deep breath before answering.

"I'll explain when you get here. Oh… bring a torch and…" he winced as a stabbing pain tore into his head, "a clean shirt."

"A clean… okay, leave it with me."

Harman didn't question any further. At that time of night, Caslin was sure Harman would be making the journey in half the usual time, despite the foul weather. Caslin glanced at the time, 3:48 a.m., he still couldn't figure out how long he had been unconscious for and was struggling with the basics. *What was he doing?* There had been something that got his attention but he couldn't remember what. He was trying to stand when it came to him.

Using the screen of his phone to illuminate the room, he cast a glance around everything before him with a renewed sense of determination. Stepping towards the fireplace, this time avoiding the coffee table, he reached the far wall. Rather than mess around trying to catch a reflection as before, he began to slowly run the flat of his hand along the wood panelling, gently stroking it as he went. It didn't take long before Caslin found what he was looking for, a small depression in the wood. The cladding was varnished pine, smooth to the touch, allowing any inconsistencies to be clearly identifiable. There was the odd knot or two that he came across that hadn't been filled, but this was different.

Caslin closely examined the find, a small indentation with a rough edge to one side. The light was reflected by something metallic trapped within it. He was so intrigued that he had forgotten about the bang to the head although it still throbbed. The object was recessed by about three millimetres, and there was no chance of removing it with his fingers. Carefully he made his way into the kitchen, deciding to check the pantry for the fuse box. Maybe he could get the lights back on. The brief search proved fruitless and he returned to his original task.

A quick search in the drawers yielded a kitchen knife with a narrow, pointed blade, probably for gutting fish. Taking it, he returned to the living room. As carefully as he could he tried to prise out the object, eventually managing to tease it out. By this point, the wall was lit by the phone held in place between his teeth. Its glow cast a bluish hue over proceedings. Before it could be examined properly he dropped it from the palm of his hand, a gentle clack-clack ensued as it bounced off the slate hearth and disappeared into the darkness. Once more Caslin found himself on his knees, searching in the gloom. Only this time he knew what he was looking for and in any event, he had easily identified it before losing it.

CASLIN CAUGHT sight of the headlights long before hearing Harman's car on the driveway, thereby realising how his assailant had got the drop on him with such ease. A beam of torchlight guided the DC into the rear of the house. It had gone 4:30 a.m. as Harman stepped in, shaking off the rain as he did so, to find Caslin seated at the kitchen table using a wet hand-towel as a makeshift compress on his neck.

"Sir? Are you alright?"

"Find the fuse box and get the lights on, then I'll tell you all about it."

It took Harman a matter of minutes to switch the lights back on. The fuse box was in the main entrance hall and easily accessed if you knew where to look. Caslin appeared far worse than he had realised, once he was able to examine his own reflection. There was a fair amount of blood that had soaked into his shirt and despite Harman's concerns, Caslin insisted on remaining where he was, a doctor could wait. Caslin described everything that he could remember about his attack but it wasn't much, he had heard little and seen even less. There was no sign of an intruder. The integrity of the building was still secure and, apart from a kitchen chair that seemed to have been knocked over in the darkness en route to the back door, there was nothing to indicate anyone else's presence. That is apart from Caslin's bleeding wound. A quick scan of the rooms made it appear that nothing had been removed, as far as it was possible to tell.

Caslin allowed Harman to investigate whilst he remained in the kitchen, nursing his head. They had found some ice cubes in the freezer and had packed them into the towel. Once the bleeding stopped, he could clean up properly and get changed. The young DC had impressed upon arrival. Not once had he complained about being pulled out of bed in the early hours, nor had he questioned why Caslin had been at the farmhouse alone at that hour. In a perverse way, Caslin judged him to be slightly lacking in confidence for not asking. By rights, he should be read the riot act for going off half-cocked alone. That said, there was no indication that his presence there should have led to violence.

Harman finished his sweep with a scout around outside. There were some fresh tyre tracks in an area of mud that wasn't frozen solid by weeks of sub-zero nights, but little else of note. How could Caslin have missed another car parked outside? Returning inside, Harman came to stand before him and asked what he had on the table.

"I found this embedded in the wall."

They both examined it closely. Although greatly compressed by the impact, its origin remained unquestionably obvious.

"What is it, a .22?"

Caslin nodded his agreement. A .22 calibre bullet was recognisable by its size in comparison to others, being far smaller. They were virtually impossible to confuse with larger calibre rounds, even in this condition.

"It would be interesting to figure out its trajectory. Was it a bored tenant just shooting the breeze, pun intended, or...?"

"Or?"

"... something else entirely?" Caslin finished, rolling his tongue across his lower lip as he did so.

"It's certainly not normal to sit in your living room, putting bullets in the wall."

"You would be surprised at how people pass the time," Caslin shrugged. "I know I was for the first ten years in this job. That's not what's troubling me, though."

"What is?"

"Who was here tonight, and why?"

"Clearing up?"

Caslin nodded, "Possibly, but what for? We didn't find

anything incriminating, apart from this anyway," he indicated the mashed bullet on the table.

"Maybe we missed something?"

"I fear that we've missed quite a lot."

"Should we get scenes of crime out here?"

"Yes, first thing… or soon, seeing as first thing was several hours ago. We'll have to go back over everything with a fine-toothed comb. A full fingerprint search, particularly there," he indicated the rear door. "Let's also see if we can get anything from this bullet. If we're lucky, ballistics might get a match against something in the database. It could give us a break."

"Could we get any forensics off it, to see if it was used to wound someone, do you think?"

Caslin shrugged, "Incredibly slim chance at best. A .22 has about as much stopping power as an asthmatic granny and roughly the equivalent in penetration. If this bullet hit anybody, it wouldn't have passed through and certainly not embedded itself so far into that wall."

"Odd choice for a criminal then, as a weapon of choice, I mean."

"But for an amateur, or someone who doesn't move in the right circles, it might be all they could get."

Harman hesitated before he spoke again.

"Are we, potentially, looking at a murder here?"

Caslin reflected for a moment before answering, choosing his words with great care.

"I don't know, if I'm honest. Although there's definitely more going on."

"And your attacker?"

"Maybe it was the Avon Lady, aggrieved because payment was late."

Caslin was irritated. Yet more questions, no more answers and a thumping headache to make it even harder to focus his thoughts. Reluctantly, and under extreme protest, he agreed to allow Harman to take him to the hospital to get his head checked.

If only he had had a pound for every time someone had said that. They could call SOCO on the way and have them sent out to the house to make a start on the preliminaries. Caslin figured he could return to see them and pick up his car later.

HARMAN'S CAR was in stark contrast to Caslin's beaten up old Volvo. It was a nearly new hatchback. Close to top of the range, Caslin figured, by the built-in satellite navigation system, heated seats and numerous other gadgets whose purpose he could only guess at. Harman seemed to notice his DI checking out the interior as they drove through the early morning traffic.

"Nice car for a DC?"

"I beg your pardon?" Caslin asked.

"Is that what you were thinking? Nice car, on a DC's salary."

"Who can't afford a nice car these days?"

Harman took his eyes off the road and glanced across.

"You?"

"Something like that, yes. A present from your father, was it?"

Harman smiled, it was a knowing smile. Caslin was taking the piss.

"That's what everyone thinks isn't it? Daddy's seeing me alright with everything, career, car, extra money to supplement my meagre wage."

Caslin didn't reply. He didn't need to confirm it. That was what the squad room thought, right or wrong.

"It's not true, you know," Harman continued.

"I know."

"You know what?" Harman said, taking a right turn onto the A59 towards York, heading for the hospital on Wiggington Road.

"That it's not true."

"But I never said—"

"Look, I don't think you're here because of your father, okay. Irrespective of what anyone else says."

"They all think it. Maybe they're right but if so, I've had nothing to do with it."

"It certainly won't harm your career, him being your father. It *will* harm your workplace relations, though. There isn't much you can do about that. Just like I can't stop what they say about me."

"Which part?"

Caslin laughed. True enough, *which part do they talk about the most?*

He casually asked, "The demotion, my last case in Old London Town, or my links to the Masons?"

Harman also smiled, "Any of it true?"

Caslin blew out his cheeks, staring at some far-off point in the distance through the passenger window, declining to answer by way of his silence.

"Sorry Guv", I didn't mean—"

"You can't stop people talking. Don't add fuel to the flames and do your job, that'll keep them quiet. If your luck holds, anyway. At least, that's what I hope for. The degree of success it brings… well… if it doesn't, then you'd best get promoted above them."

There was silence for the next few minutes, Harman effortlessly negotiating the early morning traffic. The younger man seemed lost in thought. Caslin didn't mind. His head was banging and the peace gave him a chance to try and think.

"Just do the job. I'm not too sure I'm cut out for it, if I'm totally honest," Harman stated, clearly having spent time mulling over the advice.

"It's a bit early to think that, Maxim. You've only been in the job five minutes."

"Why did you sign up?"

Caslin returned his gaze to the fields that were flashing by at speed, his answer not as quick to come to mind. At different times over the years he had been asked that by an array of people in multiple scenarios, be it his wife, colleagues or an interview panel. At first thought he knew that each time he had given a different answer, they may even have contradicted each other if laid out for scrutiny. To his wife he argued the case for a strong career, to his colleagues, the action and as for the interview boards, they got the stock answers of "to make a difference where it counts" or "to uphold the principles of the justice system". Was there a grain of truth to any of them?

Caslin had, over the years, reconciled his decision to join by presuming that all of his reasoning was relevant, perhaps his motivations were changeable, like the shifting sands of Morecambe Bay. His father had walked them out there as kids, explaining the dangers as the tide came in. Perhaps he hadn't found his understanding of why he had made his choice just yet. Maybe one day it would come to him in an epiphany. He had never been one for acting on impulse but furthermore, he had never had long-term goals that he had focused on from childhood. That was Stefan but not him. His brother had spoken of joining the army aged nine and never once deviated from that course. At sixteen, with the agreement of their parents, he signed up and a week after his eighteenth birthday was deployed in the Balkans. A choice that Stefan never voiced regret about, could Caslin honestly say the same?

"Sometimes I wonder," Caslin said softly in reply.

Harman took that response as an indication of not wanting to discuss it further and answered his own question regarding himself.

"It wasn't expected of me. If anything, my father was a little disappointed when I told him I wanted to follow in his footsteps. Not that I used those words, mind you." Caslin glanced over but said nothing. "I read Computer Science at university and I was darn good at it too."

"Then why?"

Harman shrugged, "I may have been good with computers but I couldn't see myself at it for years. My father has had a great career and we had a good life when I was growing up. It's an important job, a real challenge."

"It certainly is. You should remember though, not everyone makes Chief Constable."

"I know that," Harman smiled. It made his appearance seem even more youthful than he was. "Can I ask you one more thing?"

Caslin glanced across at him and nodded slowly.

"Why do you drive such a crappy car?"

Caslin laughed. It was genuine.

"On a DI's salary?"

"Exactly."

He sighed, "Give it a few years, get married and bang out a couple of kids. Then get yourself a decent divorce solicitor and you'll know why, soon enough."

"Did you have to sell it, your last car?"

"The wife's got the car," Caslin smiled ruefully. "The kids, the house, even the bloody dog and soon enough, what's left of my pension... provided I can stay in the job until I hit my thirty."

Both men were laughing as they pulled up outside Accident and Emergency.

CHAPTER ELEVEN

FOURTEEN GREEN ONES, three in matching blue and, for some inexplicable reason, one solitary brown chair, were all arranged in a square, facing inwardly towards a low level table supporting a stack of assorted magazines. As if the mind-numbing boredom of the wait wasn't excruciating enough, everyone had to endure staring at each other forlornly. They were all participating in an undesired competition, each hoping that they would be seen next. However, there were no numbers here, no queue that served those waiting the longest first. Just a screen on the wall running a looped recording of a rescue services documentary, no doubt an effort to reassure the viewers they were in safe hands. Caslin hoped that the crew of "Heli-med 6" would be available if he was ever rear-ended by a lorry on the M62.

Taking out his phone, he remembered that he had been told to turn it off earlier and thought better of switching it on. Glancing at the clock on the wall he saw that it was 9:32 a.m., almost three hours since his arrival with Harman. On reflection he shouldn't be too annoyed, his initial triage assessment had been within twenty minutes, seeing a doctor within the hour and dispatched to x-ray soon after. That was where the time had begun to drag. How long could it take to produce the images?

A nurse strolled by. It occurred to Caslin that she was in no particular hurry to get where she was going and she proceeded to give him a stern look as he held his mobile before him, reminding him somewhat of his aunt Bethany. With an exaggerated cough and a nod towards a laminated sign prohibiting mobile use, she waited until Caslin returned the phone to his pocket with an accompanying, sarcastic smile. Therein she resumed her course, an indignant expression upon her face.

Turning his attention back to the motley crew seated around him, he sighed. There were four people present and he passed the time attempting to determine their injuries and likely causes. Caslin felt a bit of a fraud as his appeared the most basic. There was a pensioner who must have had a fall. He sat in silence, clutching his left arm with his right, resignation written all over his face. A younger lady had sat with him, presumably his daughter or perhaps a carer, but she had left him there some time ago, possibly heading for the canteen to get some coffee and had not yet returned.

Caslin realised then that he hadn't eaten since lunchtime the previous day, his stomach groaned. He could also have done with a coffee. Over to his left was a man in his twenties, his hair closely cut, slightly built and sporting several days of stubble growth. His coveralls gave him away as working with machinery, stained with oil and well worn. He was seated with his left ankle supported on a plastic stool. Using all of his powers of deduction, Caslin could work out what had brought him there.

The remaining two people had been passengers in a car that collided with a van, on the morning commute. Caslin didn't engage them in conversation but overheard them complaining bitterly about how working-class people didn't know how to drive. They felt that such people should be given a sterner examination before being let loose on the roads. Caslin hoped that their suspected whiplash injuries were severe and painful for some time to come. However, he shared their view on tougher driving tests albeit regardless of background or social status.

The clock on the wall now read 9:36 a.m., he felt the need to check that it was accurate and moved to pull out his phone, before realising that he was obsessing and changed his mind. *How long does it take?*

"I thought you might need this."

A voice from behind snapped him from his reverie. It was Harman and he had coffee. Caslin gratefully took the foam cup and removed the plastic lid, sipping at the contents. It was hot and bitter but still tasted good.

"How did you get on with SOCO?"

Harman had left Caslin as soon as they made their way up to the x-ray department, stepping out to call in the request for the scenes of crime officers to head out to Radford Farm.

"I couldn't get through to anyone. I left a message for them to get back to me."

"That's a little odd," Caslin mused openly, gently blowing on the top of his cup.

Harman nodded his agreement as he first wiped down the seat with the flat of his hand before sitting down next to Caslin, folding up his raincoat and placing it on the next chair along.

"If I've not heard back in half an hour, I'll try them again, maybe they're having a briefing or something. Any word on your x-rays?" Caslin ignored the question, stifling a yawn. The headache was subsiding and the overwhelming feeling now was one of tiredness, perhaps caused by the waiting around but he felt it, nonetheless. "Any more thoughts on who attacked you last night? A burglar?"

Caslin shrugged, "I don't know. It could have been but..."

"The place didn't look like it had been hit by a burglar, did it?"

"Agreed. If we weren't sitting here, me with a bang to the head, I'd never have known anyone was there last night. Maybe I disturbed him. Is that clock, right?"

Harman glanced over and then at the watch on his wrist.

"Pretty much, yes. Are you getting bored?"

Caslin breathed out, "I've had enough of this."

With that his treatment in the hospital was over and they were on the ground floor heading for the main exit within minutes. The daily press of those coming to work, heading to appointments or visiting patients, was in full swing and conversation was nigh on impossible as they manoeuvred against the flow. There was a small kiosk, well stocked with books, magazines and confectionery, opposite a cafeteria near to the entrance and as they approached, Caslin had a thought. He stopped in his tracks, catching Harman by surprise for he had made it to the exit before realising he was alone. Turning around with a quizzical look, he waited.

Caslin stepped into the kiosk and, after queuing for a short time, emerged and rejoined his colleague. Once out in the car park he broke the seal on the cellophane, opened the box and took out a cigarette. Harman said nothing as Caslin struck the roller to the flint and lit his first smoke in six years. Taking a deep draw, it felt like he had never been away.

"Long day," he said, in response to the unanswered question.

He took out his phone and switched it back on. Within moments the phone began to beep with a voicemail notification. Inhaling another draw, he dialled his inbox. Caslin coughed, the aftertaste wasn't quite what he had remembered and he suddenly felt quite ill. It was hard to hear the message above the noise of the traffic. Harman pointed out the direction of the car and both men began to walk. Giving up on the call, Caslin hung up the phone. Almost immediately it began to ring.

"Caslin," he answered abruptly, blowing out smoke and discarding the cigarette long before he had to. A passer-by scowled at him for littering. He scowled back.

"Are you on your way into Fulford Road?"

Caslin was taken aback. It was Frank Stephens. His voice sounded distant and more than a little harassed. It was a bad line and he assumed the DCI was on a mobile.

"I've got Harman with me, we'll be in shortly. We had a development last night—"

"That will have to wait."

Caslin ceased walking and listened patiently as Stephens went on. His ashen expression conveyed the gravity of the conversation as Harman glanced across and he also stopped. The call was over swiftly and Caslin reached for his newly purchased pack of smokes but instead of taking one out, he took aim and tossed them into a nearby litter bin. He felt sick.

"What's going on?"

"Change of plan."

THE JOURNEY TOOK a little over an hour, in high season it would probably have taken much more. They caught sight of the transmitter in the distance, the landmark they had been advised to head for. Then the abandoned Beacon Windmill came into view with the bay off to their right, they were just over a kilometre west of Ravenscar, well into the North York Moors. Turning left onto Scarborough Road, heading in a northerly direction, they reached their destination.

Neither man was familiar with the area. No doubt, like most Yorkshiremen, Caslin had holidayed near Whitby as a child but to his recollection Ravenscar was only ever a name on a road sign. His father had once called it "the town that never was" in reference to the expected expansion that for one reason or another, never happened.

Locating the crime scene proved to be a simple task, it appeared that most of the Constabulary had turned out. Their car was stopped at a cordon a quarter of a mile away. It had been hastily arranged at the bottom of a steep slope, alongside a small caravan park and run of holiday cottages. They showed their warrant cards in order to gain access. Their destination was a car park at the crest of the rise, the eastern-most of two available in close proximity. They were sited yards from the television transmitter that stood out on the high point, visible for miles in all directions.

Harman pulled off the road and parked up on the grass verge, positioning them awkwardly between a van and a patrol car. With Robin Hood's Bay to their right, beyond the stone walling and the rolling moorland to their left, they made the walk uphill. Caslin was breathing heavily as they approached the top and took in the transmitter. It was located next to a small building, within a gravelled compound, encircled by an eight-foot high fence that ran the perimeter. Outside of the secure entrance he saw a charcoal blazer hanging on a concrete fence post, heavily stained with mud and well past its best, it was fraying at the seams of the shoulder. Looking around once more he considered it a strange find in such a remote location, confident that it would be so even under normal circumstances.

DI Atwood was first to see them arrive and having finished directing some uniformed officers, picked his way through the frozen pot holes to greet them. His expression was grim and he dispensed with any pleasantries.

"It's as bad as you probably think," he indicated the scene beyond him.

Caslin looked past his colleague towards the scene, taking in what he could, which wasn't much. Discounting the official police tape, the forensic officers in their disposable coveralls and the other uniforms milling around, there was nothing to indicate what had been described to him. Clearly, this was a major deployment. A police helicopter was circling above them and that added to his feeling of unease. He had never relished visiting crime scenes steeped in violence, particularly in circumstances such as this.

Both car parks, neither able to accommodate more than six cars at best, were shrouded by trees and brush that masked them from the road. They were haphazardly created parking areas, roughly poured concrete that had begun to disintegrate long ago, allowing vegetation to grow through. The approaches were in a poor state of repair. Any driver would need to take great care to avoid damage to their vehicle.

Michael Atwood led them through the massed ranks. There was the level of activity one would expect but a noticeable lack of banter that often accompanied a crime scene. Usually the mood, even at the most extreme, could be lifted by dark humour but not here. The main focus was on a silver Mercedes, an estate, which exact model Caslin couldn't tell from the front but it was modern and in bad shape. As the others began pointing out details to one another, Caslin took a moment alone.

The car was beached on the verge just beyond the entry point, its rear having perched itself on top of the bank within the over-grown brush, amongst the trees. The wheels beneath had driven themselves deep into a pile of gravel whilst trying to break free. The stones seemingly having been there for some time, Caslin guessed they were left over from a resurfacing job. Turning his attention to the car he observed the near side indicators were blinking. The windscreen had three distinct bullet holes sited in close proximity to the driver's side and the remainder of the glass had shattered but had not been displaced.

Caslin caught his breath, a sudden intake of cold air that froze his lungs, it was uncomfortable and somehow fitting for the occasion. Moving around to the offside he found the door open. Its window had also shattered and the glass had fallen in and around the driver who was slumped half out of the car. The body faced inward, almost as if he was seeking something underneath the vehicle, thereby obscuring his features.

Caslin knelt as close as he dared without damaging any forensic evidence to get a better look, estimating that the dead man was well into middle age, most likely mid-to-late fifties. His hair was an oily black colour shot with grey, notably at the temples and in front of his ears. The cause of death would no doubt be linked to the solitary bullet hole in his forehead. The exit path of the round had removed a large part of the rear of the skull. If he wasn't dead before that wound was inflicted, then it would have been more than capable of seeing him off. There were several other injuries to his lower back, potentially exit wounds Caslin guessed, judging by the size, angle and impacts into the seat behind. The shooter had most likely been aiming downwards from a standing position.

Caslin glanced around as if trying to build up a mental picture of the events that had led up to this discovery. The car keys were in the ignition and a partially smoked cigar lay in the gravel a few feet away, amongst fragments of glass.

No-one spoke as they continued their examination. In the rear seats of the car was another body, an elderly lady wearing a Hijab. Caslin's best guess put her in her eighties. There was a great deal of blood within the car, sprayed both onto the passengers as well as around the rear of the inside of the vehicle. This woman appeared to have also suffered gunshot wounds both to the body and to the head.

He moved around to the back of the car, noting bullet holes to the passenger windows as well as the headrests. The view of the front passenger seat brought a tightening of Caslin's chest and he paused for a moment, eyes closed, almost having to instruct his body to breathe as he once again inhaled deeply. In the seat was another body, that of a female, little more than a girl and barely in her teens. Caslin's son was possibly not much older. This girl had several wounds to her chest, presumably caused by gunshots but her clothing made it hard to tell and she appeared to have suffered no head injury. That fact did not give him any peace of mind. Considering her passage towards death, he felt that a relatively painless headshot would have been preferable to the agony of a chest wound. Couldn't the killer stomach shooting a child in the head?

"This is a mess, Gentlemen. What can you tell me?"

The voice came from off to their left and Caslin didn't recognise it. Turning, he saw a small group approaching and recognised DCS Kyle Broadfoot, head of the Basic Command Unit and the most senior CID officer in North Yorkshire.

The wind was up and coming in off the North Sea in ever stronger gusts, giving Broadfoot's usually neatly coiffed comb-over a mind of its own. The collar of his overcoat was turned up and he kept his hands deep within its pockets, bracing against the cold. Caslin had only met the man twice, both in passing at regional seminars, and had little on which to base an assessment of him. He had struck him as a fast-track career officer with designs on the Chief Constable's position but that was okay, ambition was a necessary attribute in Caslin's book.

Caslin quickly figured that the question was not directed at him but open to everyone present. Broadfoot brought DCI Stephens with him, alongside two others whom Caslin didn't know. One would undoubtedly be Broadfoot's assistant, most likely the younger of the two, the man in his twenties sporting a green Barbour jacket and frameless glasses. The other would be another senior rank, probably out of the Scarborough or Whitby offices.

Atwood didn't speak and Harman looked like a rabbit caught in the headlights. Evidently, he had never seen anything like this but Caslin had to concede, who really had? Acknowledging Frank Stephens and taking the offered hand of the DCS, he replied.

"You're right. Messy, very messy."

"Early days I know, but what do you think?"

Caslin held his breath and gave the vehicle another once over from where he stood. The thoughts running through his head came to him in a random fashion and, despite all that he had seen in his career, he felt sick to his stomach.

"At least ten shots that I can count, maybe more."

"Closer to fourteen, by my reckoning, anyway," the voice from behind heralded the arrival of Iain Robertson, the lead investigator amongst all the assembled scenes of crime officers. "Although, that may turn out to be a conservative estimate. There appear to be shots from multiple angles. This will take some figuring out."

"Multiple shooters then?" DI Atwood offered.

Robertson frowned, an expression that if truth be told was difficult to read for he was in his late fifties and known as "Bulldog", as much for his heavily lined features as for his tenacity in piecing together a crime scene.

"It's a little early for a statement such as that," he chided in his strong Glaswegian.

"I just meant it as a possibility."

"No need to be defensive Inspector, you may well be right but I need time."

"Sadly, you may not have as much as you would like," Broadfoot addressed Robertson directly. "We already have most of the nation's media camped outside Fulford Road just itching for more sensationalism. We'll not keep the lid on this for long and, once it gets out, they'll be decamping here faster than you can say *hold the front page.*"

Robertson grimaced but he knew the DCS was right. There would be pressure brought to bear on this one.

"Aye, you're probably right, Sir," Robertson replied.

"What do you make of it, Nathaniel?" Broadfoot asked.

Caslin had stepped back to the front of the vehicle to examine some of the entry points for the bullets and almost didn't hear the question.

"Sorry Sir, I was thinking."

"Please think out loud, Inspector."

Caslin nodded, "Not wishing to pre-empt the doctor's findings," he pointed casually to Robertson who smiled, "but we're looking at a large calibre weapon, most likely a 9mm." Robertson appeared to agree with the assessment but chose neither to add nor contradict anything. "I'm not so sure that there were a number of shooters, though, but I could be wrong."

"Go on."

"The pattern of fire is not as random as the visual scene might suggest. Most of the wounds are from fairly close range. The hits to the abdomen of the occupants are closely grouped, centre mass and," Caslin moved to the driver's side of the car and indicated the rear passenger, "couple that with the head wounds... all hard to achieve with moving targets and the accuracy is—"

"Could still be more than one," Atwood spoke up, almost as if in justification of his earlier comment.

"Yes, there might be but I don't see it."

"I think Mr Caslin is correct," Robertson said. Looking to Caslin he asked, "The positioning of the car, right?" Caslin nodded that he concurred but the logic was lost on the others.

"The car?" Harman asked.

"The car park is small," Robertson explained, "tight turning circle. Easy to negotiate if no-one else is around and you want to do a U-turn without brushing the undergrowth or the banks. But to do so in a hurry, that's a totally different scenario, altogether."

Caslin picked up where Robertson left off.

"I would surmise that the driver was trying to get away from their attacker. Like Iain says, in a bit of a hurry. It's an automatic gearbox and I imagine he put his foot down too hard, maybe in a panic, and who could blame him? The car shot backwards, beaching itself. The stick's back in drive, so he was trying to flee. At some rate of knots too, judging by how deep the wheels are embedded. A rear wheel drive car, he couldn't get away fast enough. Most likely he flicked on the indicators in error, or as he fell part-way out of the vehicle having been shot."

"The first person on the scene found the engine still running," Broadfoot offered.

"Who was that, Sir?" Caslin asked.

Broadfoot gestured towards a couple who were talking to a uniformed officer nearby. They appeared to be hill walkers, judging by their all-weather clothes and the backpacks nestling near to their feet.

"They were walking a well-known route by all accounts, skirting Brow Moor and bringing them here. The engine was running on the car but apart from that, the area was deserted. Arrived too late to be very useful, unfortunately."

The last word seemed to Caslin to be a contrived addition but he pushed it aside. What did it matter if this guy was already viewing the case as a career maker? He should be aware however that it could also be a breaker. A certain level of emotional detachment was to be expected, in fact necessary, but not always achievable. Caslin was still haunted by his past and he figured all sane people would be after reviewing scenes like this. Perhaps those better at reconciling the brutality within their own mind made better officers but he doubted it.

"They must have come on the scene relatively soon after the attack. The victims were still warm when the first units responding to the 999 call, reached the scene," Broadfoot continued. "We're setting up checkpoints on all major routes within a fifteen-mile radius, so we might get a hit."

Caslin doubted it. Robertson indicated several places a few metres away where officers had marked points of evidence to be catalogued.

"There's broken glass over there. I'm guessing it will match up with the windows of the car."

"Shots fired at them as he was reversing?" Caslin inquired. Robertson agreed with him before Caslin continued his perception of events, "Then as he beached the car, the shooter most likely delivered several rounds through the windscreen, possibly incapacitating, if not killing, the driver. Then it was all but over."

"Pretty much my thinking also," Broadfoot said evenly.

"With the driver down, the shooter would have had plenty of time to be as accurate as he liked with the passengers. Did we get lucky with any witnesses?" Caslin asked.

Broadfoot indicated for Frank Stephens to pick up the narrative.

Stephens shook his head.

"We have someone else who was present but she's not got a lot to say, either."

Caslin was puzzled but allowed Stephens to take him aside. At the far end of the car park was a trail that led off parallel with the coastline. On a beautiful summer's day, he guessed it would be a great spot to set out on a walk and even in the bleak winter, it still held a rugged charm. The track led onto Brow Moor and they picked their way along before taking a left hand fork, proceeding for a few hundred metres until they then had to push aside some overgrown gorse blocking the path. Caslin noted a way marker as they passed it before cutting across another track and continuing on.

Further onto the moor they went, the water always to their right, heading steadily downwards. In places the ground was boggy underfoot and Caslin wondered where they were going. His footwear was inappropriate for the terrain and he had to tread carefully to avoid falling. In the distance he could see three figures clad in white, a little way off the track, with the backdrop of the bay behind them. The moorland dropped steeply away towards the sea.

The further they advanced through the heather he could make out a small cairn overlooking the water in the near distance. Caslin tasted the salt in the air as he took in the dark patches of ground around them, marking the controlled-burning phase of autumn. Another post, a carved number denoting it as point five on the "Stoup Brow Trail", was where they were directed off the path towards the cairn. A little over eight metres away, and propped up against the stack of rocks, lay another body. Two scenes of crime officers were erecting a tent to be placed over it, which was no mean feat in the wind, whilst another was setting up her camera.

At first glance, Caslin wondered if a passenger from the car had made a run for it and been chased down but quickly realised that the theory was highly unlikely. She was dressed in hiking clothes, a red full-weather coat, walking trousers and solid leather boots. Had she stopped at this viewpoint and come across the killer in full flight across the moor, or had he chased her from the car park, wishing to leave no witnesses? If it was the latter, it seemed an awfully long way for a pursuit and didn't fit with the pattern of the scene. Perhaps she just happened to be at the wrong place at the wrong time, *not the only one either*, Caslin thought as he looked her over. He was struck by something that seemed odd. There was a familiarity that surprised him and gave him pause for thought. Although he was confident that they had never met, still the feeling wouldn't fade.

"Any identification?" he asked.

Stephens shook his head in the negative.

"I'm betting the keys she has on her fit the hatchback in the second car park, though. No-one else has claimed it. The car is registered to Claire Skellon, a resident of York. The age range is a match but we're trying to verify her particulars at the moment. Uniform are on the way to her address as we speak."

Caslin noted her injuries. These were of a frighteningly similar fashion to the others, apparent gunshot wounds to her chest and a further two to the forehead. Her expression was one of deep shock. A permanent look etched into her features that would sadly go with her to the grave.

The victim was in her forties, with sandy brown hair that was noticeably greying, although she had clearly taken care to colour it to offset the aged look. A cursory examination of her boots and clothes indicated, from the signs of wear, that she was a frequent walker. That supposition was reinforced by her athletic build. She wasn't wearing gloves and Caslin, seeing no wedding ring, found himself wondering if she had anyone at home waiting for her. A journey that now, she would not complete.

Caslin knelt down. Her eyes were staring straight at him, blank and lifeless. Her body position was awkward due to the backpack wedged between her and the rocks. Her feet were crossed and her arms lay wide to either side of her. The wounds to her forehead carried traces of powder burns at the edge of one entry point, the killer had been close. The gun must have been pressed against the skin or close enough to it, to allow the propellant to mark. That concerned him. Usually killers opted for guns to give themselves distance from their victim, enabling them a degree of detachment from the violence. Those that preferred closer experiences often chose knives or strangulation.

"What did you see?" he asked her softly.

Confident that he had nothing else to assess, Caslin stepped away, allowing his colleagues to cover the area with the tent. He walked to the other side of the cairn and stood for a moment. Gently buffeted by the wind, he admired the view encompassing Robin Hood's Bay from its northernmost tip and sweeping down as far as Ravenscar, a little over a mile away. The clouds out at sea were ominously dark and he could just make out several cargo ships on the horizon.

There was a lot here to make sense of. At this time any thoughts on a motive were utterly meaningless. *What cause or reason could justify such savagery?* Caslin found cases that involved children were the worst. No matter how bad a crime scene, he could always maintain an emotional detachment but he found that far more difficult when children were present. There had been times in the past when he had got home of an evening and hugged his own tighter than usual. Karen would meet his eye and she never asked, but she always knew. He didn't have to like what he saw in the job, he only had to be successful in his role. He might not be able to prevent such acts but he could avoid their repetition and try to ensure the punishment of the guilty.

He made a mental note to pass that thought back to Harman if and when the subject arose once more.

Caslin would be interested in Robertson's conclusions. He trusted him. The man was thorough and if there was anything insightful that they could use in the investigation, then he would find it. However, he knew in his own mind that he was right. This was the work of one shooter. The rounds dispatched were done so with great accuracy, far too much to have been delivered by automatic rifle or multiple gunmen. No, this was carried out with a meticulous eye for detail, if also with a tendency for overkill. Why the young girl didn't receive the headshots was still bothering him. Was it a simple oversight or was the killer interrupted?

Questions that needed answers. All that Caslin seemed to be dealing with at the moment were questions. He took out his phone and checked the time. His headache was back. DCI Stephens approached him and came alongside.

"It's a bloody horror show."

"That it is. If no-one saw anything, did anyone *hear* the shots? They would have been going for a while." Stephens looked him up and down, as if contemplating the reasoning. Caslin decided to help. "If there was only the one shooter, then he either had more than one weapon or, which I think is possible and somewhat chilling, he took time to reload. I know it only takes a second if you know how but—"

"A second, if you're calm."

"This guy was as calm as you like."

"How can you be so sure?"

"Shell casings."

"What about them?"

"There aren't any, at least not that I saw. The car park should be littered with them. The wounds on the victims are large calibre and I've never seen such in my career associated with a revolver. I know they're around but outside of the movies, revolvers, at least in the UK, tend to be smaller, .22 or 38s. My guess is the shooter's armed with a semi-automatic and if he took the time to clean up, then we either have a professional, someone fastidious about not leaving evidence or at the very least, familiar with our procedures. Whichever way you want to look at it, his actions took time and that means we are dealing with someone the likes of whom I've never come across before. Broadfoot can throw up as many checkpoints as he likes but they'll come to nothing."

"We'll have to see about that. We've got people going house to house but there aren't many inhabitants nearby. Ravenscar itself has only a few hundred residents. There's the B&B at the entrance to the cordon less than a quarter of a mile away, if we catch a break, they might have seen or heard something. The wind is rattling in off the sea though. The sound would have carried inland and away from them."

Caslin indicated the moorland sloping away from them towards the sea.

"What's further down the approach road, beneath us here?"

"It drops away, giving access only to Stoup Brow Farm, a few holiday lets and a disused quarry. Pretty much a dead end, apart from a route onto the farmland. The DCS is setting up a Major Incident Unit and he wants us on it. That's why we're here. The local boys aren't equipped to go at it alone. He's the Senior Investigating Officer and he's giving me control of operations based out of Fulford Road."

"Right," Caslin said, as he looked over and raised an eyebrow in an unspoken query.

"Yes, he knows your background, but he wants your experience."

"Even though he *knows my background.*"

"Don't start with me, Nate. I've got a giant broom up my arse and we've all got to make do. You're on the team and you'd better not show me up."

"Understood," Caslin replied, unsure if the retreating form of the DCI had heard him or not but confident that he wouldn't care either way. "I need to speak with you about the Horsvedt case," he called after him.

The reply was almost lost as it carried on the wind.

"That's Trent's business now, so let him get on with it. Maxim can follow up anything that you've turned over and Terry Holt can back him up, if he needs it."

Caslin cursed. This case should take priority, he knew that and it was a reasonable call, but he hated loose ends. Once again, he turned to take in the view of the bay sweeping out before him. Despite the biting wind, the cold and the scene he had just viewed, he still thought that he was standing in a beautiful spot. Casting a glance sideways at the canvas tent billowing in the wind, he wondered whether Claire Skellon had been able to appreciate it as well.

It was 12:18 p.m. on Friday 10th November.

CHAPTER TWELVE

THE ENTRANCE to the train station was bedlam. The combination of queuing for limited parking spaces, shifting taxis at the ranks and buses negotiating the narrow lanes, was causing consternation. Caslin cursed, which drew a stern look from his father beside him. Having spent three quarters of an hour together, Caslin's impatience was reaching new heights.

Fortunately, they had made it with time to spare. The station clock read 10:55 a.m. but still they needed the driver of an estate car to vacate his space faster. A bus sounded its horn behind them, Caslin was blocking the road, but he ignored the gesticulating driver. His father also had a habit of speaking when keeping silent would be less of a distraction and ultimately, far more useful.

"Have you spoken to Stefan recently?"

"Err... no, not recently. Maybe six months ago. Why? Is he alright?"

"Do you care?"

Caslin bit his tongue, "That's a bit harsh, Dad."

His father shrugged, "He said you hadn't spoken in over a year."

"Maybe he's right," Caslin gripped the steering wheel. The estate was finally clear. Why didn't people know the dimensions of their own car? "In my defence, I have been a little preoccupied."

"With your own life, yes. You could spare some time for others as well though. If it's not too much trouble."

Caslin frowned as he parked up. Suddenly the cost of eliciting a favour from his father appeared too high.

"I'll call him, okay. Is that good enough?" Caslin said. His father shrugged once more. "What's he up to now then? Is he still working at that mail-order warehouse?"

Caslin was irritated as his father started to laugh, "He's not been there for over a year! He was working for a local drop-in centre, doing odd jobs and things, but I think that's also fallen by the wayside."

"What happened this time?"

"How would I know? I don't like to pry," Caslin bit his tongue again. "He's getting out a bit more these days, even has some friends, I think."

"Well that's positive. Where from?" Caslin asked, attempting to sound interested.

"Some group or another. Shared background, I think. It gives them something to talk about."

"Hmm," Caslin looked at his phone as his father continued talking. He wasn't interested and was already thinking about the case. The team were up and running at Fulford Road and Caslin wanted to be in the thick of it.

"Are you listening?" his father snapped.

"Yes, of course I am. What did you say?"

"I said Stefan hasn't got over the army. He still finds it hard."

Caslin nodded. There was no doubt that his brother had had a tough time. What he had experienced in the Balkans and the Gulf could only be guessed at but adapting to civilian life had been one wrench too far. Stefan had been unable to hold down any form of work since leaving the forces. Caslin often feared a professional courtesy call, or worse still, getting a late-night phone call from a colleague requesting he attend an identification.

"Hopefully he can pull it together," Caslin said casually.

"Well, at least his friends' help."

"Say that again," his father's words caught somewhere in Caslin's mind, as if they were somehow significant.

His father looked puzzled, "Stefan's friends must help him. That's all I said."

Caslin glanced across. For a second, he was confused as to why he had asked. Moments later he shook it from his mind and suggested that they head inside. The children would be arriving soon and he intended to be on the platform to greet them.

The impressive statement of Victorian engineering with its cast-iron canopy, spanning multiple platforms, was packed with weekend travellers, both residents and tourists alike. The central bridge that arched over to platforms five and beyond was filled to capacity but the crowd moved steadily, without incident. Conversation was limited as they negotiated the throng and attempted to filter the background noise of public notifications and diesel-electric trains.

Checking the station clock once more he saw that they still had time. Caslin bought them both a coffee from one of the many concessions available, adding a fruit pastry to his order. Returning to the platform, and his father, he handed over the coffee and took the pastry from his mouth.

"Sorry, they didn't have a tea pot."

"Typical, but not surprising. This country was built on tea, you know."

Caslin rolled his eyes heavenward as the lecture began but he endeavoured to tune it out. He glanced along the platform, an anxious man pacing, a gaggle of teenage girls waiting to surprise a returning friend, all with far too little on in this weather, he thought. A mother was attempting to control her three children as they ran to and fro. No doubt their father was coming home. His own father was oblivious to the distractions and continued on. As Caslin understood it the Empire had been built on sugar, primarily off the sweat of plantation slaves, backed by an efficient military and civil service. He had no intention, however, of arguing the point. Quietly he knew that his father had come to the rescue today and he was grateful. Finding a way of conveying that and sounding genuine when he did so, would be essential.

The events of the previous day had determined the change of plan. There was now no chance of him taking the weekend off for the visit of the children as intended, not that he wanted to. The crime scene had dominated Friday and there were still forensic reports to come back to. Robertson had given a briefing late the previous night and confirmed much of what Caslin had suspected. The strict caveat was applied that no definitive conclusions could yet be drawn. In Caslin's mind, that meant this killer was clever enough to cover his tracks.

The checkpoints had thrown up nothing unusual and no further witnesses had come forward to shed light on events, but they remained hopeful. The victims had been positively identified. Those in the car were three generations of the same family. The driver of the Mercedes was a widower, Hakim Al-Asadi, along with his step-mother, Rana. The other was his thirteen-year-old daughter, Aasara. The lone victim found near to the cairn was confirmed as Claire Skellon, an unmarried charity worker. A colleague carried out the necessary visit to the mortuary on Friday afternoon. Her death had barely been a footnote in the morning papers, which instead lavished pages on the tragedy of the Al-Asadi family. They had resided in York, apparently moving there within the previous year and, other than polite conversations, had made little impression on the neighbours. As of Saturday morning, their next of kin had yet to be contacted.

Without a motive directly evident, the team had adopted a late-night brainstorming session and came up with theories ranging from a crazed local gunman to honour killings. Any of which were plausible and could not be discounted at that moment in time. It was a sad statistic that nine out of ten victims knew their killer personally, crimes referred to as "self-solvers", so the team were leaning towards an associate link. Caslin preferred the approach of following the evidence trail wherever it led them but that required forensics or strong witnesses, and he wasn't hopeful of either in this case. Hakim had a son who studied abroad and a younger brother, who lived in Surrey, but he too was out of the country and they had a watch on the airports for his return.

As expected the crime scene was awash with journalists. The story took precedence in the national, and even the international, news. The race angle led the tabloid coverage and the pressure was already ramping up. Caslin had only a brief window to collect his children and take them to their grandfather's house before he was to be back in the office. He wasn't pleased at the prospect of not spending time with them but it just wasn't possible. They were good kids and he hoped they would understand. Karen on the other hand was a very different matter.

The Major Crime Incident Unit had taken over the squad room of Fulford Road for the foreseeable future, so, at least, he could remain local. Caslin's phone pulsed in his pocket. He took it out, much to the frustration of his father who was still harking back to the Empire, and answered it.

"Caslin."

"Sir, it's DS Hunter. The DCI is holding a meeting at midday and we're all expected."

"Subject?"

"We've got a potential lead on a motive, plus some more background has come in. One of the papers is speculating that there's a family feud going on."

"I remember a newspaper running a story about a London bus found on the moon but that didn't make it so."

"I know but the paper hasn't printed it yet, they came to us first."

"In return for what, an exclusive?"

"Perhaps, but it's credible, so we need to look into it."

"How did they find that out before we've even been briefed?" Caslin had been around enough to know how journalists worked.

He dismissed the thought, "Scrub that. What do you have on the background?"

"Hakim left Libya shortly after Gaddafi's regime collapsed in 2012. He brought his family with him. Since then he's been working out of an office in York and occasionally one in Kent, they're registered to a company called GOS."

Caslin looked at the station clock and then the arrivals board. The train was on time.

"What do they do?"

"That's the interesting bit. We haven't got a clue. I did an internet search but turned up nothing apart from some smart offices, a postal address and a VAT number."

Caslin waited for a moment, letting the information sink in. The train was pulling alongside the platform, the noise making it harder for him to have his conversation. He scanned the carriages as the doors began to open and passengers spewed out in an effort to escape the rush, or to make their connections. Caslin's father mouthed that he would find the children.

Moving the phone aside from his mouth, Caslin called after him, "You don't know what they look like."

His father cast him a dark look, "Of course I do! You always send me their school photographs in my birthday card." An inability to conceal the look of surprise at that statement gave the game away. His father added, "Or maybe Karen does. She probably signed your name as well, didn't she, you little shit?"

Caslin shook his head and turned away, returning to his call.

"You're right, that is interesting. Find out more."

"Already on it. Will you be here?"

"I'll be there," he hung up and turned back see his father holding Lizzy's hand. Sean was a step behind and engrossed in something on his phone, rucksack hanging from one shoulder. Lizzie hurled herself into his arms and they embraced fiercely. His son smiled at him from beneath a floppy fringe and promptly returned his focus to the screen before him. Caslin indicated that they should get a move on. His father gave him a disapproving look. There was no need to say the words.

Caslin nodded as he spoke, "I know, Dad. I know."

"Should you let Karen know they arrived safely?"

Caslin was about to answer but his daughter beat him to it.

"I've already told her."

"You have?" Caslin sounded surprised.

"Yes, I texted her. And I told her that Granddad was here, too."

Caslin raised his eyes skyward. Sean glanced up and laughed at his father.

"You're *so busted.*"

"And don't I know it," Caslin replied. They all laughed then. Moments later his phone began to ring. Caslin looked at the display and rejected the call. There were three enquiring faces looking at him. He responded, "I'm driving."

CASLIN MADE his apologies as he entered the squad room. Chairs were in scarce supply and people were making use of desk tops or happily standing, in any free space available. Comfortable leaning against a filing cabinet, Caslin took off his coat and caught his breath. He was sweating from having taken the stairs two at a time. He hadn't realised how out of shape he was.

It took well over an hour and a half to make the round trip from the station to his father's house in Selby and back to Fulford Road. The children seemed quite happy with the prospect of spending time with their grandfather. Lizzie had even professed an interest in the railway. Sean, on the other hand, had his social media and had been lost in cyberspace from the moment of arrival. This was a paradox for Caslin. The technology that allowed everyone to remain connected, managed at the same time to detach the user from the personal relationships that were all around them. Whereas when he was a teenager they would hang out in groups on street corners, today they existed almost exclusively in a virtual world. Was it a leap forward, or was society heading for a rude awakening, with human contact a thing of the past? How would such a country be policed? No doubt he'd be long gone and it would therefore, be someone else's problem.

The briefing was underway as soon as Frank Stephens entered the room. He had met with the journalist in private, along with Kyle Broadfoot, and the information appeared to be solid. Hakim's father passed away the previous year and his inheritance was to be split between his children. The rumours that were uncovered by the journalist were of a dispute over inherited land and property, both in England and in Libya, along with a bank account held in Switzerland. The source for this was a family friend and had been ratified by a business associate of Hakim's.

"What business would that be, Guv?" Caslin interrupted.

"Hakim Al-Asadi worked for a company called GOS, registered in South London and primarily concerned with work in satellite observation."

"What exactly do they observe?"

Stephens glanced across at DS Hunter, indicating for her to take it up.

"*Global Observation Solutions.* I spoke to their Executive Officer this morning. They use software to analyse imagery obtained via satellites."

"Analysis of what and for whom?" DI Atwood asked.

"That was where she became a little vague. Mostly they carry out work for the airline industry but have delivered projects for marine studies, archaeologists, and the oil and gas sector. Apparently, the latter had been a significant growth area for them up until very recently."

"What did Al-Asadi do for them?"

"Low level analysis on geology, rock formations and stuff like that."

"People do that for a living? Who would want to kill this guy?" Atwood asked nobody in particular.

"It's unlikely to be related to his work if that's the case but even so, Sarah, check if he had any issues with colleagues, past or present. You never know," DCI Stephens paused, scanning the information board that was beginning to piece the events of the day together, alongside the victims' backgrounds and associations. "Michael," he addressed DI Atwood, "I want you to see what you can find out about this inheritance. Search their house and get hold of the family solicitor. In the meantime, I want all ports and airports to have an eye out for Hakim's brother. He'll be back sharpish now the story is all over the press and we need to speak to him. He'd have to be under a rock to miss what happened. Even without releasing their names he should put it together. Any word on the son?"

"Yes, Sir," DC Holt replied. "He's on a flight back from New York at the moment, should land at Heathrow around three. Uniform will be waiting for him there to bring him up."

"Good. Nathaniel, can you chase up Iain Robertson for an update on forensics and then have a look at Claire Skellon." the DCI pointed at her picture on the board. "Let's make sure she really doesn't have a relative out there before we release her details to the press and get egg on our face."

Caslin nodded, "Yes, Guv."

He couldn't help but think that his was a task that could be done by anyone on the team. He wanted to be heading to the family home and Atwood, looking decidedly smug, had the most promising line of enquiry on this one.

"Everyone else, I want you to keep digging on your current assignments." Stephens stopped talking as Kyle Broadfoot entered the squad room, with another in tow. The newcomer was young, smartly dressed, and carried himself in a confident manner. The DCI addressed everyone, "Last point of business. The Chief Super has an announcement."

"Thank you, Frank. This is DI Simon Baxter. He's come up from Scotland Yard on an officer exchange initiative and will be assessing our procedures, with a view to recommending improvements. We may be able to learn something about how we do things around here. Don't let it be a distraction. I'm sure you'll bring him up to speed and help him settle in."

Broadfoot left the room and there was a general murmur of welcome to Baxter who smiled politely, taking the hand of anyone nearby who offered it. Caslin acknowledged him with a handshake as the room began to empty. Those with telephone assignments started dialling and conversations began around the room. The noise level intensified so much that Caslin almost missed his phone ringing. It was Harman.

"Sir, I think I have something for you out at the farmhouse."

Caslin knew that he should point out that he had his own work to do and was no longer supposed to be involved at Radford Farm, but Claire Skellon was going nowhere. Who cared if the press had to wait? He stepped out into the corridor where it was quiet.

"I'm all ears."

A FEW MINUTES LATER, Caslin headed out to his car, acknowledging a couple of people in passing as he left the station. Once outside, he scrolled through his phonebook, selected a number and dialled it. The call was answered almost immediately.

"Well, well. It's been a while, Nate."

"It certainly has Sara. For that, I undoubtedly owe you an apology," he paused and for a brief moment there was silence. "Listen, I know we haven't spoken for a few months—"

"Try nearly eighteen."

Caslin winced, "I know but it's been difficult, what with—"

"Karen, the kids, your job, I realise that and I understand," Sara said flatly. "Don't beat yourself up over it, Nate. We're both adults and know how these things work."

Despite believing that she bore him no ill will, Caslin still felt a brief wave of relief pass over him as he formulated the best way to phrase the forthcoming question.

"You'll probably think that this is a bit of a cheek but, bearing in mind your particular expertise, I need to ask a favour. Someone's just turned up in the office and I was—"

"What's the name?"

CHAPTER THIRTEEN

His phone rang and Caslin pulled off the main road into a bus stop before answering. It was Iain Robertson.

"Nathaniel, I thought you would want to know as soon as I did."

"Thanks, Iain. What do you have for me?"

"It's as we thought. One shooter with a 9mm."

Caslin paused, pondering on whether to ask the obvious. He did.

"Any chance of matching the bullets to a weapon?"

Robertson made no effort to conceal a laugh, one of little genuine humour.

"Not a chance in hell, I'm afraid."

"Thought not."

"We haven't found a single casing and believe me we've looked. Each round, which was either lodged in vehicle or victim, has been accounted for and none are in good shape. They all made contact with bone, or should I say bones, before the pathologist or my team got to them. It'll be damned hard to match the rifling, even if we had the gun which we don't."

"Not yet, but if we did?" Caslin asked, hopefully.

Robertson waited as he mulled over his choice of words, always one to be exact.

"I have plenty of rounds to choose from. If you find me a weapon, I'll do what I can."

"Good enough. Any idea of the type of gun used?"

"Do you want me to do all your work for you?"

Caslin laughed, "That would be nice. I know, a 9mm but other than that, you can't say."

"You see, I don't need to be everywhere. If I turn up anything else, then I'll let you know."

"Thanks, Iain," Caslin said. He was about to hang up but Robertson stopped him.

"Have you had a word with Alison?"

"Alison?"

"Yes, Dr Taylor, the pathologist. She turned up some interesting thoughts on the victims. I left you a message."

"Sorry, I didn't get it. Such as?"

"You should speak with her directly, really. I know she's in her office today. You could catch her if you're quick."

Caslin thanked him and ended the call. Glancing at the clock on his dashboard he sighed. Harman would have to wait. Restarting the engine, he swung out into traffic and headed back to York.

MORTUARIES GAVE HIM THE CREEPS. Ever since he had paid his respects to his grandfather as a child he had dreaded entering them. Now largely desensitised to seeing dead people due to his professional capacity, he still preferred to read the report rather than view the body. Dr Taylor had insisted on this occasion. Reluctantly he had agreed.

"As you can see," the pathologist said, pulling back the sheet covering the second body they were now looking at, "the wounds are still a close grouping, centre mass. But over here on this one..." she led Caslin to the other side of the room and drew back the sheet that hid Claire Skellon from view, pointing to the wounds to her head.

Caslin looked but still couldn't see what she was getting at.

"I'm sorry, Doctor, could you treat me like an idiot?"

"Not necessary," she smiled warmly and he found it attractive, wholly inappropriate under the circumstances. "This woman, two shots to the head and two to the sternum."

"Like all the others," he said, before adding, "apart from the girl. Are you suggesting that this was a professional hit? That is certainly what we're—"

"I would say without doubt that the shooter has firearms training, you don't need me to tell you that. Whether it's a professional hit, or not, is beyond my sphere but that's not what I'm getting at here. Take a look at her forehead." Caslin leaned in, although at the same time trying to keep his distance. "The two to the body were from several yards away, as was the first to the head," she indicated a wound slightly lower than another, "but the second was point blank."

"The powder burns?"

"Exactly. I would think that the barrel, if not in direct contact, was almost touching her skin judging by the halo effect of the powder burns."

"Well, I figured that from the crime scene. And this is significant in your eyes because?"

"One direct hit to the head and two in the chest. Similar to the Tsunami effect adopted by police marksmen," Dr Taylor said, referring to their method of targeting. "The shock waves generated would kill the host if the bullets hadn't already done so but why did the shooter feel the need for the second, close-up head shot?"

Caslin had to admit it, she had a point. Claire Skellon would have been dead before she hit the ground. Once the killer made up the distance on her, he would have seen that. The shooter had matched the professional standard for a kill already. The last shot, delivered at point blank range, seemed unnecessary.

"We're considering that she may have run and he chased her down. Perhaps he was angry?"

"Well, I'll leave the speculation to you, Inspector. I just found it odd. None of the others exhibited wounds of a similar nature."

"They were in a car, she was on foot."

Dr Taylor shrugged, "True enough."

Caslin thanked her, requested her written report as soon as it was available and made to head out to the car. Dr Taylor called after him.

"Aren't you the lead in the Garry McNeil case?"

Caslin stopped and looked back.

"Not exactly and anyway, that's largely been turned over to another body. Why do you ask?"

"Oh, well, I finished up the post mortem report today, following the preliminary briefing that I attended over—"

"The phone," Caslin finished. "I was there."

"That's right. I mentioned it to Iain earlier, in passing, and he said that you would be interested in anything that I uncovered." She turned away and began packing her notes into a leather holdall. "I must have been confused, I'm sorry."

Caslin found his curiosity piqued and came back to stand alongside her.

"What is it? I'm not technically on the case anymore but…"

"You would like to know anyway?" Caslin nodded. Dr Taylor smiled again. He still liked it and he noticed that she was not wearing a wedding ring. "It's not actually pertinent to the cause of death, and barely gets a mention in the report, but Mr McNeil had quite an extensive brain injury."

"Extensive? I hadn't noticed."

"Well it was above the hairline and received some years ago."

"How extensive an injury and when did it occur?"

"He had severe damage to the frontal cortex. It would've required major reconstructive surgery. Probably well over a decade ago, maybe even longer. I'm basing that on the healing of the scar tissue."

"What could have caused that?"

Dr Taylor shook her head.

"Impossible to say but it was a heavy trauma. A fall from height or a traffic accident, perhaps. His chances of recovery would have been slight at the time."

"Would he have been impaired?"

"I wouldn't have thought so, not in the longer term. At least not physically."

"Mentally, then?"

"Well, that area of the brain deals with judgement, mental analysis and those sorts of processes."

"Morality?"

Dr Taylor nodded, "I guess so, yes. I would need to review his medical history, to make a determination as to what extent that may have impaired him, but..." she paused in reflection, "it is certainly possible."

Caslin thanked her again and, as he left, was considering how he could engineer another meeting with the pathologist at a later date. The chill in the air had messed with the estimated time of death in Ravenscar and had now been set at between seven and ten, in the morning. The sun rose late however, and Caslin found it hard to believe the hiker was walking in the dark with no head torch, so he favoured a later time. He was unsure whether this information aided them in the least. Usually times of death offered up leads to potential witnesses or lines of inquiry but this case was different, the isolated scene giving up little.

He turned on his phone and it beeped twice in rapid succession. The first text was from Lizzie to say that she was helping set up a new track for an A4. Caslin guessed it was a locomotive and smiled, she was enjoying it more than he ever did. The second was to remind him of a briefing to be held in Fulford at 2 p.m., he made a quick calculation in his head. There was no way he could get out to meet Harman and back in time.

He called Harman to give him the bad news. The rain had ceased but it was still cold. The winter was going to be a long one, he thought, as the phone buzzed in his ear. Eventually it went to voicemail and Caslin hung up without leaving a message. He got into the car and set off back to Fulford.

———

THE ATMOSPHERE in the squad room was intense. Everyone was busy researching their assignments but evidently no-one felt that they had struck the right chord. DS Hunter argued strongly that she was on to something with the angle of an honour killing. Friends of the dead schoolgirl intimated that she was due to spend the following summer abroad and furthermore that she had voiced concerns as to whether she would return next term. Hunter saw that as an arranged, or forced, marriage situation that required closer scrutiny. DCI Stephens agreed.

DI Atwood notified them that he was on his way to speak to the brother of Hakim Al-Asadi, who had been detained voluntarily at Gatwick Airport upon his return to the UK. The team eagerly anticipated his response to the suggestion of a family feud. This was certainly the DCI's preferred lead in the absence of anything concrete, although for Caslin, it still left too many unanswered questions. If the brother planned to inherit, then he hadn't factored in the son, studying abroad, who remained as a block to that end. Moreover, there was little evidence, other than hearsay, to indicate that there was any feud at all.

"Nathaniel, what have you turned up on the hiker?" Stephens asked.

Caslin was snapped from his thoughts.

"Little, Guv. She spent a great portion of her time in a charitable profession, setting up and managing refuges for battered women. She was unmarried and a committed member of a local Baptist Church, by all accounts. Currently unattached, according to her colleagues, and she was devoted to her work. She didn't have time for much else."

"Have you contacted the next of kin?"

Caslin failed to hide his irritation at the suggestion. Such contact was seldom done by anyone of his rank. The thought occurred that family members could shed light on her activities, or even be complicit in her death. That angle needed to be looked at but Caslin felt it was a nigh on certainty that there was nothing in it. The woman was as boring as a wet Sunday afternoon.

"We've not found any as of yet. Her associates were a bit sketchy on her background but are asking around for us."

Stephens was unimpressed, "Since when does *Joe Public* carry out our investigations? I want to brief the papers as soon as possible. The more I give them the less they hassle us. When I say *us*, I really mean, *me*. I want the family informed today."

Caslin accepted that. He knew he should be taking the task more seriously although he remained nonplussed.

CHAPTER FOURTEEN

THE SUN HAD SET by the time Caslin pulled up. After the briefing he made a swift exit from Fulford Road, heading west towards Grassington. He tried Harman again and once more got his voicemail. His sense of guilt ensured that he made the trip that late in the day although Claire Skellon was predominantly on his mind. He cursed himself for the belated thought that he should eat dinner with his children. They wouldn't be with him much longer and he had seen precious little of them in the past few days if not months. The illuminated clock on his dashboard read 17:28 just before he switched the ignition key to off and the lights went out. With a bit of luck this wouldn't take long and he could still salvage something of the evening.

Stepping from the car, he was momentarily struck by how dark it was inside the house. So preoccupied was he upon his approach that only now did he notice that no lights were visible, the area lit only by the moon that hung in a cloudless sky. Were it not for Harman's car, Caslin would be forgiven for thinking he'd wasted his time. He retrieved the torch from the boot that he had recently acquired from stores. The metal casing felt cold to the touch as he tested the battery. The light reflected from the rapidly forming frost. He wanted to be prepared just in case the lights had tripped, or been tripped, once again. Could his attacker have returned? Caslin hoped not. Suddenly faced with that prospect, he quickened his pace to the rear of the house. Using the torch, he scanned the inside through the windows as he went but there was no discernable movement within.

Reaching the back door, he found it locked. Tilting the flower pot with his left foot he saw the key was in situ. Withdrawing his phone from his pocket he dialled Harman again. As the phone rang, he shone the beam along the nearby tree line but saw nothing out of the ordinary. Again, the call passed to voicemail. Caslin swore. Taking the key, he unlocked the door and went inside, for a moment debating whether or not to put the lights on before flicking the switch. The fluorescent tube stuttered into life, the buzzing of which was the only sound that came to his ear. Confident that he was alone he progressed through the house. Initially he glanced through each room but, having found nothing untoward, then retraced his steps, only this time with a more methodical approach.

Disappointingly he came to the same conclusion, there was nothing new. Not prone to overreaction, he could feel a gnawing sensation building in the pit of his stomach. Making his way back through the house he thought he heard something, freezing at the entrance to the kitchen, he listened. Had he imagined it? The briefest flicker of movement outside was followed by footfalls on the gravel path. Caslin had a moment to choose his course of action. He took off through the kitchen and out of the back door like a man possessed. A figure glanced over its shoulder as it rounded the corner, giving up on a subtle retreat and taking flight. Caslin discarded the torch, making up the ground easily, almost too easily. Doubts set in just when they collided. The men came roughly to the ground together. The fleeing man letting out something of a whimper as the wind was knocked from his lungs.

Caslin swiftly found himself on top, one hand to the throat of his quarry and the other reaching for his handcuffs. The moon was partially obscured as they struggled in the darkness. Caslin secured one wrist, eliciting a howl of pain from his captive.

"Inspector, please!"

Caslin stopped. He recognised that voice. Torchlight illuminated the two men on the ground. Caslin, by now, up on his knees and breathing heavily. The struggle was over. The glare from the torch momentarily blinded him before it was cast onto the man at his feet.

"Sullivan, what the bloody hell are you doing here?"

The dishevelled journalist looked up, his breathing ragged, speech coming in short bursts as he sought to gather himself.

"Inspector Caslin... I have a nose for a story... you know that."

Caslin shook his head and rubbed a weary hand across his face. Looking up beyond the torchlight, he thought better of asking Harman a similar question. That would have to wait. Fishing out the key to his handcuffs, he released Sullivan's wrist. Both men stood and set about brushing themselves down.

"I could have you for trespassing on a crime scene."

Sullivan cleared his throat, whilst rubbing an invisible mark on his freed wrist.

"What crime would that be?" he glanced around. "So, this place is linked to the Ravenscar killings."

Caslin shook his head and smiled.

"You could not be wider of the mark, if you tried."

"Oh, come on, Caslin. This could be the biggest case to hit Yorkshire since the Ripper. You can't tell me you're not working it."

"I'm not bloody telling you anything at all, am I?"

"What are you doing out here at this time on a Saturday, if you're not? Come on, you've got to give me something!"

Caslin turned and made to head off back to the house.

"Goodnight, Jimmy."

"I'll only keep digging," Sullivan called after him. "I'll make it up if I have to!"

Caslin spun on his heel and strode forward. The journalist took a step backwards and visibly shrank before the oncoming officer.

"I'll tell you something. You've had a lucky break tonight. You could've been finding yourself spending a night in the cells but I don't fancy the paperwork. So, I'll put this in the nicest way possible, in a way that I think you'll understand… fuck off!"

Caslin stalked away, Harman falling into step just behind.

"Can I quote you on that, Inspector?"

"JESUS CHRIST, Maxim. Where the hell have you been?"

Harman was taken aback, "I've been here, Sir."

"Then why didn't you answer your bloody phone?"

"No signal," Harman replied apologetically. "Come with me and you'll see why, but I'll bet my pension that you're not going to believe it."

Harman led them back outside and, having first made sure that the journalist had left as instructed, followed their torchlight down the side of the house and around to the double doors of the workshop. They were of tongue-and-groove construction, painted blue, matching the shell of the building but in an equally poor state of repair. One of the two appeared to be locked in place and unmoved in years but the other swung open effortlessly. The hinges were well oiled. Caslin peered into the gloom. There was little light penetrating within. Glancing at Harman before putting the beam of his torch inside, Caslin stepped forward.

The room that he found himself in was roughly rectangular, two metres deep and twice as wide. There were two square windows at each end but the viable daylight introduced would be minimal, largely due to the hessian drapes hanging from rails before them. There was a fixed workbench at one end, an old vice clamped to the edge, its paint peeling. Beneath was a shelving area with an assortment of plastic tubs and glass jars holding screws, nails, and other odds and ends. Lining the rear were further shelving units housing old paint tins, buckets and assorted tools, as well as the general rubbish that accumulated over long periods of time. Uses for which, Caslin could only guess at. Aiming his torch up into the pitched roof void he noticed a solitary light bulb hanging from a length of flex, along with age-old cobwebs, gently swaying in the draught.

Harman indicated to his right, over towards the far corner, beyond a petrol lawnmower and watering can that seemed to have not moved in years. Scanning the area with his torch, Caslin missed it with the first pass but caught it on the return. He edged closer, careful not to trip over the detritus that he found underfoot. Inspecting the rear wall, he found what Harman had been so excited about. Almost obscured from view was a hatch cut into the wall, little more than two feet square. It only came to waist level and was fitted with skeleton hinges, blending it in, making it almost imperceptible to the naked eye alongside the surrounding panelling. Illuminating the floor, Caslin could see that a shelving unit had been placed in front of the hatch. Repeated scratching to the floor boards and the variation in dust levels were evidence of its movement.

"Did you shift this?" Caslin asked, moving the beam onto his colleague. The angle of the light gave Harman a macabre appearance.

"No, Sir. I found it just like this. You have to see what Alice found down the rabbit hole."

Caslin was intrigued and refocused his attention on the rear wall, instinctively donning the pair of latex gloves that Harman had told him that he might need. He inspected the area and was surprised to find that the hatch was on a push latch. A gentle press brought a click to his ear and it popped forward. Another glance at Harman saw the younger man nod his encouragement and Caslin eased it open. A gentle rush of cold air, with the slight hint of damp, washed over him as he directed his torch into the darkness.

In stark contrast to the workshop the walls here were lined with block work and the floor was a concrete screed. The latter had seen better days and was visibly crumbling in places. The beam of light hit a wall, he guessed it was about seven feet away, and Caslin could make out the shadows of a corridor disappearing off to both left and right. Ducking down, he made his way through and into the corridor. Pleased to find that it was full height as he stood, he made room for Harman to follow. The passage was only wide enough for one and Harman came to stand behind him. Together they moved forward.

"What is this place?" Caslin asked, as much a question for himself as for his colleague.

"That's what I've been trying to figure out this afternoon. The walls," Harman waved his arms in a circular motion around them, "are thick enough to block mobile signal."

Their words seemed to echo as they were lost in the darkness. Reaching the end, Caslin lit up first left and then right. Harman answered the unspoken question and directed them to the left. Only a few steps along they reached a closed door. It was timber, made from ply and weighty with it. Caslin assumed it was a fire door. The surface was chipped, apparently well worn, and unfinished beyond its factory base coat. In this setting its presence seemed slightly surreal. A hasp had been fitted enabling the door to be secured, however, it was bent and the padlock that remained swung uselessly beneath. The frame bore the telltale scarring of having been crudely jimmied. Caslin twisted the handle and pushed it open.

The room beyond matched the passageway, narrow and windowless. Harman flicked a switch which Caslin had missed on entry, and two fluorescent tubes overhead spluttered into life. The brightness caused him to shield his eyes until they became adjusted to the setting. Inside the room was a desk, an office chair before it, blue-fabric covered and on castors. Upon the desk stood a modest flat-screen monitor with an assortment of cabling bunched at the base, dropping away from view at the rear.

Beneath it stood what Caslin assumed was a PC base unit. Although it had several lines of flickering blue LEDs, running horizontally in layers across the front, the likes of which he had never seen before.

"That's a server," Harman offered.

"Serving what?"

"Good question. I don't know. Not yet, at least."

"No computer?"

"I've not found one."

Caslin turned off his torch and returned it to his pocket, eyeing the rolled-shutter unit that was placed to the right of the desk as he did so. This stood three-foot high and was made of steel and, similarly to the entrance, had been secured at the base by a heavy-duty padlock. The cabinet had also been forced and recently, Caslin guessed, by the look of the damage. He examined it and glanced up at Harman who splayed his hands wide.

"Nothing to do with me. It's all as I found it."

"What's inside?"

"I haven't looked. I figured I'd come back to it."

"There's more?"

Harman nodded but he appeared to be less than enthusiastic.

"Much."

With nothing else of note in the room, the two men left. The door had a self-closing mechanism and it swung shut behind them, closing with a deep thud that carried through the darkness. Harman led them forward via torchlight, past the entrance passage and off in the other direction. Their route turned first to the left and then took a sharp right, with a couple of steps down, before bearing left once again. Caslin cursed as he almost lost his footing. Reaching out, his fingers brushed against something plastic hanging in midair, giving him no purchase. Completely disorientated now, he stumbled into the back of Harman as they came before another door, identical to the last.

"Did you see that?" Harman asked as he angled his torch in the direction they had come from.

Caslin was surprised to see that he had walked blindly past a sink unit and what looked like a shower tray. The curtain of which he figured was what had failed to brace him. Beyond the shower was a toilet with no seat. They were confined to an impossibly small area, offset from the passage and slightly into the wall, once white but now in a filthy condition. The taps to the basin were covered in limescale with green runs stretching into the waste. Water dripped steadily. The gurgling noise, as it drained away, resonated in the darkness.

Harman pushed open the door and Caslin was relieved to see him flick another switch, bathing the room beyond in light. The passageway was unsettling and claustrophobic for him and peering into the gloom did little to alleviate those feelings. Inside the next room, along the adjacent wall to the corridor, was a run of units that encompassed a sink, microwave and some shelving. The latter was piled high with pans and mismatching crockery. The sink held a number of plates and cups, stacked high in foul smelling water. At the end of the run stood a counter-top fridge, barely large enough to be practical in a caravan let alone to facilitate any domestic environment. Was this such a place? Caslin had yet to comprehend what they were looking through, let alone what it all meant.

Opening the fridge, he found a half-empty pint carton of milk that had gone off, alongside a box of eggs and an unopened pack of cheddar cheese. Something unidentifiable had turned black and decomposed within its plastic bag and he chose to leave it well alone. Against the opposite wall was a single camp bed, with a red sleeping bag lying atop it. Beneath that was a jumble of clothing, none of which looked clean, along with some newspapers that were scattered across the floor. In the far corner, there was a small table with two occasional chairs tucked underneath to the right of a second door. A glance at the table revealed a newspaper and a haphazardly arranged selection of travel guides for the North West as well as a partially completed crossword. The date in the corner of the paper was the 31st October.

Crossing over to the far door, Caslin eased it open, noting as he did so that this one had a traditional locking mechanism to it but no key. There was a light switch just inside but despite repeatedly pressing it, he remained in darkness. In yet another windowless room he had to rely on the torch once more. Scanning the ceiling he found the light fitting had had the bulb removed. Less than two metres in width and barely three in length, the room was narrow. In one corner lay an old mattress with no visible bedding, heavily stained and reeking of filth. The air was stale and the vent, nestling high in the corner, appeared ineffective. The mixture of grime and damp smelt offensive. Both men endeavoured to hold their breath in order to minimise the impact.

In another corner was a bucket and upon closer inspection, Caslin recoiled from it. Judging from the odour that it gave off, it had recently contained excrement. Off to one side stood a solitary chair, terracotta in colour and of the type common in care homes, rigid arms with a high back. The floor was again concrete and he observed the level of large stones in the mix, figuring it to be an industrial compound and therefore relatively cheap. Noting the patches of heavy disintegration and uneven areas, it had certainly been laid many years previously with a basic approach.

"Check that out," Harman said, aiming his own torch to the foot of the far wall.

Caslin turned his attention to what was illuminated, an iron ringlet attached to a metal base which in turn was bolted to the floor. A heavy link chain ran through it, rusty and approximately two metres in length with thick iron clasps attached to each end. Caslin exhaled deeply. Pursing his lips, he repeated his earlier question.

"What is this place?"

"Do you think we've found the home, if we can stretch to calling it that, of the enigmatic Mr McNeil?"

"Let's have a look in that first room. See if we can find out something useful that goes someway to explaining all this."

Harman nodded and Caslin led the way.

"Did the DCI have a problem with me not being there? I haven't phoned in."

Caslin felt bad. For the first time he was grateful for the darkness that encircled them, so Maxim wouldn't have been able to read his facial expression. No-one had even questioned where he might have been all day, let alone shown any frustration at his absence.

"No, not that I'm aware of," Caslin lied. "Everyone's pretty busy you know?"

Harman acknowledged the answer with an almost inaudible grunt. Caslin had his back to the younger man as they walked but he could tell that the latter had hoped to be missed and quietly suspected that he hadn't been. It was true though. The squad room was intense. Caslin thought Harman should get over himself.

Back where they had begun, Caslin moved the chair aside, the castors squeaking as they ran across the concrete floor. The forced cabinet was the logical, and in fact only, place to start. The shutter was so badly bent at the base that it restricted one of the runners, and it took a few moments of struggle before brute force had the desired effect and they eased it upwards. The cabinet contained a rack of shelves. Two of which had neatly stacked VHS tapes in plain black cases, bearing white labels on the spine. Handwritten dates were all that distinguished one from the next. There was a further shelf with a clutch of DVD cases and an assortment of padded folders, immediately recognisable as photo albums. These too, had homemade labels on the side. Caslin picked one at random and leafed through its contents. Many of the photos were of poor quality, taken in bad light and in an amateurish fashion but were nonetheless, still striking. Both men took a sharp intake of breath.

Harman opened his mouth but could find no words, not that Caslin noticed as he slowly turned the pages.

"It looks like that degree of yours is going to come in useful in this job, after all."

Harman happily averted his eyes from the images before them and indicated the server, Caslin nodded.

"I'll need to get a laptop to wire in."

"What is this place?" Caslin asked quietly. Harman didn't have an answer.

CHAPTER FIFTEEN

THE ROOM FELT A LITTLE COLD. The house was draughty and the curtains were lightweight. The material moved with the breeze, giving partial glimpses of moonlight beyond. The duvet however was thick, well suited for winter and covered Lizzie, tucked up to just below her chin. Her breathing was shallow as she slept. Karen always said she looked more like her father when she was asleep, Caslin couldn't see it but he had never voiced the thought. Confident that all was well, he retreated from the room. Only the squeaking of the floorboards gave away his presence as he gently pulled the door closed behind him.

It was well after ten o'clock as he slipped downstairs, his father was the only person still up. Sean was probably listening to his music in the darkness but nevertheless, had been silent when Caslin had tried the door. Rather than risk waking him, he left the door closed and made off.

"You'll have to make more time for them."

"Yes, Dad. I know."

He meant it. The guilt had already struck him and not for the first time either. It was a common thread that ran through his life. One that he felt almost powerless, or unwilling, to address. The children had been asleep when he had made it back to his father's house the night before, and he had promised to make up for it the following day. Iain Robertson had been primed to visit Radford Farmhouse with as large a team as he could spare, Maxim was happy to assist, which would have given Caslin most of Sunday before he would be needed. That was far from how it transpired.

The plan had been an early breakfast and then a trip, the destination didn't matter, the kids would choose but the point would be several hours of family time. The plan had definitely not included a visit to Fulford Road, which was what Caslin got before he had even managed a bowl of cereal.

———

"WHAT THE HELL do you think you're doing pulling forensics off the Ravenscar case?"

It was less of a question and more of an invitation for an altercation. Frank Stephens looked as if he was going to blow.

"We turned up something that couldn't wait. Iain said he could spare some time—"

"Well he bloody well can't! And most certainly not without my say so."

Caslin's back was up. With a little thought he should have sensed that this hadn't been the time but he was an experienced officer, not one to make an issue of nothing and therefore didn't appreciate being treated as such.

"We cannot sit on evidence that could indicate—"

"What?" DCI Stephens was out of his chair, fists clenched and braced against his desk. "Indicate what? It's a missing person that you don't even know is missing, in an inquiry that the IPCC has the lead on. You're *not even* supposed to be investigating the bloody case!"

"It needs to be checked."

"What about Claire Skellon? You were coming back to me on her by yesterday and I'm still waiting."

The DCI had him on that one. That was bad. His tone was barely apologetic and more than a little arrogant in his response.

"This came up and I had to prioritise—"

"Skellon *is* your priority, full stop," Stephens sat back down but his expression had remained crimson and he shot daggers at Caslin.

"Once Iain gets through on the site, then I'm sure I'll know more. Then I can see where we need to take it. If we need to take it further."

The DCI calmed down then as if a weight had been lifted. His tone changed, becoming softer, eyes straying to the paperwork on his desk.

"I pulled Robertson. He's back where he should be."

Caslin flipped, "You did what?"

It was not the most professional moment of his career. There followed a heated exchange where both men aired their views, supposedly to each other but most of CID knew what was going on. It was a slanging match that only ceased when DCS Broadfoot had entered the room. Both men had fallen silent. For his part, Caslin felt somewhat embarrassed that the argument had spilled out beyond the office.

"I would ask what is going on but I figured it out at the end of the corridor," Broadfoot stated in a manner that left neither man comfortable.

"A disagreement on resource allocation, Sir."

The Det Ch Supt eyed both men for a moment before speaking.

"This has always been a professional office, Frank. That's the main reason I gave you command of the incident team and based the unit here." His eyes scanned Caslin first and then Stephens. "Perhaps I erred in that decision? There are thirty officers on this case—"

"Which was your first mistake," Caslin interrupted, he couldn't help himself. He should have but he couldn't.

"Is that right?" Broadfoot's tone indicated it was a rhetorical question. "How so?"

Caslin cleared his throat, "They'll trip over each other, if they're not already. It's a scattergun approach, too inaccurate."

"Well, I'll take that under advisement." Caslin knew he wouldn't. "Perhaps though, that was not my first mistake. In the meantime, I trust that your.... disagreement.... can be resolved more professionally?"

Broadfoot glanced at Frank Stephens once more and left without another word. Stephens took a moment to allow the dust to settle before speaking.

"Your record indicates you're one hell of a detective but what's this I'm hearing that you've been withholding information on an assault out at Radford Farm?" Caslin closed his eyes and gave an almost imperceptible shake of the head. "Not to mention the formal letter of complaint that I received this morning, from a member of the press."

"Not that scrote Sullivan, surely?"

"Are you telling me you've roughed up more than one journalist in the past two days?" Stephens held up his hand before Caslin could protest, "You're clearly not a team player, Nathaniel. Spend as much time on the Horveds as you like. You're off the unit."

"The *Horsvedts*, Sir."

"I don't want to see you in my squad room for the next week, at least. Keep Harman with you. You're more use to each other, than me. I'll get a proper policeman to look into Skellon."

CASLIN TOOK the glass that was offered as he sat down. It was scotch. No surprise there. He sipped at its contents and appreciated the warmth spreading out in his chest. The fire crackled and Caslin glanced at his father, happy to see that he was engrossed in a book. The alcohol appeared to be more a relaxing accompaniment than the full session that he had feared.

"Did they enjoy the day?"

His father looked across, peering over the rim of his reading glasses.

"I thought so, yes. Sean got a little bored but he had his e-phone thing, so he was fine." Caslin thought about correcting him but chose not to. He opened his mouth to speak before realising he had nothing to say. His father went on, "They'll forgive you for a while but in the end, they'll hate you for it."

Caslin nodded. The job had to take a back seat at some point. His family were more important. On the verge of losing his wife, the last he wanted was to lose his children as well. He took another sip and his mind wandered. Realising that conversation was not to be forthcoming, his father returned to his novel. By the nature of the artwork on the cover, it looked to Caslin like a piece of Second World War fiction. The man had a stack of them.

Why couldn't he have left the DCI's office and driven straight back to Selby? He had the perfect excuse. Was it pride? Was it frustration? Either way he had found himself out at the farmhouse. The place was secure but no further forward in an investigation. Iain Robertson hadn't even got to the scene before being called away. Harman had left at the same time and so, Caslin had found himself there alone.

Maybe it was pure bloody-minded stubbornness that had taken him back out there. A need to prove everyone else wrong, if not merely to prove himself right, that there was something far more significant going on at Radford Farm than anyone realised. Frank Stephens was under pressure. There were dozens of officers on the Ravenscar case and a lot of ground to cover. To be fair, the DCI's reaction could have been anticipated but Caslin had tried to mitigate the impact of his own actions. There was something about this case. He couldn't leave it, he wouldn't.

"I'm going to head up, read in bed for a while."

Caslin was snapped from his thoughts as his father rose, his index finger holding his place on the page.

"Goodnight, Dad."

"Help yourself." His father indicated the bottle on the coffee table, beside his recliner. "Go easy though."

Caslin smiled. Tempting as it was, he had no inclination to drink more for he had work to do. Finishing the drink in hand as the stairs creaked under his father's weight, Caslin went out into the hall and retrieved his bag. Reseating himself before the fire, he took out his laptop and powered it up. Also from the bag he took a stack of black cases, placing them neatly on the coffee table before him. Finally, having rested a notepad and pen on the arm of the chair beside him, he returned focus to the laptop. The clock on the mantelpiece chimed eleven. It was late but sleep was far from his thoughts.

He had been reviewing the discs one by one, for over an hour, when his phone began to vibrate. Responding quickly to minimise the risk of awakening others, Caslin answered. He was greeted by silence, a pause long enough to make him check that the call was still connected. It was Harman. A hesitant voice came through.

"Are you seeing what I am?"

"Yes, I expect so."

"It's…"

"I know. It doesn't make good viewing unless you're into it."

Harman sighed, "Not this, I'm not. What have we stumbled onto?"

Caslin took a moment to consider his response. With far too many discs to go through alone, he had split them and dropped a batch off with Harman, before heading out to his father's. What they had were amateur recordings of sexual domination, featuring both men and women. That alone was surprising to him. McNeil was easily recognisable. The string of people that submitted to his will were not. At least, not yet. By no means a shrinking violet this indulgence was not one he cared for, but he had been around the track a few times and was seldom shocked by human desires.

"I think we can hazard a guess as to why that place is secreted away. He was into some messed up stuff—"

"It's more than that."

Caslin found his attention brought into sharp focus by Maxim's voice, whether through tone or reticence.

"What have you got?" There was silence at the other end of the line. "Maxim," Caslin persisted, "what have you got for me?"

"They can't ignore this. They can't ignore her."

CHAPTER SIXTEEN

THE RAIN CAME IN WAVES, lashing against the windscreen with such ferocity that ensured the wipers were ineffective. Early afternoon seemed as black as night and Caslin nearly missed the turning, braking heavily and swerving across the oncoming traffic, blaring horns decrying his manoeuvre. The suspension groaned as the springs bottomed out on the unmade road, Caslin winced. One of these days he would remember to go easy. Parked up before Radford Farmhouse were several vehicles, two unmarked white vans and another that he knew to be Maxim's.

Pulling up, he braced himself against the heavy rain and clambered out, running for the cover of the porch. No lights were visible in the house, so he made his way to the rear and again, sprinted the short distance for cover. What had originally been considered to be only a workshop now seemed wholly inadequate as a description. The labyrinthine passageways, secured doors and mass of concrete blockwork seemed more at home in an old war film than on a Yorkshire farm. Moreover, upon surveying the exterior in daylight, the construction was cleverly hidden from view. Surrounded as it was by a copse of trees, sweeping around both sides to the rear, with earthworks that covered the depth of the structure in its entirety, it would be feasible to imagine walking over it without realising what lay beneath.

The workshop was a later addition, many years old but significantly later than the reinforced structure whose entrance it shrouded. Passing swiftly through the workshop and ducking through the hatch he found Harman in the computer room, hard at work cataloguing the contents of the roll cabinet they had uncovered the previous day.

"Good timing, Sir," Harman said as he slipped his clipboard under his arm, his forensic suit coverings rustling as he walked. "SOCO's just given me a shout to take a look inside."

Both men knew the way and once Caslin had donned shoe coverings, they headed down the corridor. Iain Robertson came into view as they reached the makeshift bathroom, greeting Caslin as he did so.

"What's the matter Nathaniel, do you think I've not got enough work to do already?"

Caslin would have smiled but he knew this wasn't the time. The sanitary units behind them had been taped off. They were marked for further study as SOCO were yet to process that area. Robertson beckoned them forward but indicated they should remain in the kitchen area, whilst he disappeared from view into the room beyond. Flashes soon emanated from within as the team busied themselves photographing and recording all that they could find. The kitchen had already been processed. The units, worktop and table, were coated in a fine mist. The remnants of the fingerprint gathering process. There were areas of notable interest and each had been numbered for reference. What they found would come in the subsequent report.

Edging across the room, Caslin observed Robertson at work. The area appeared different under the light from the portable forensic lamps. Bathed in a purple hue, it was still recognisable from the shadowy memory of the previous day but more so from the images that he had seen on the laptop the night before. Those images were seared into his consciousness. A succession of people, predominantly women but not exclusively so, being subjected to what were at best deviant and at worst, profoundly sinister levels of structured abuse. Robertson was an experienced investigator and Caslin was confident in his abilities as he watched him orchestrate the team, ensuring that no trace of evidence was missed or corrupted. They moved methodically and with a purpose.

Even from their vantage point the two waiting detectives could make out some detail. SOCO had been busy with their chemicals and under the light, evidence of blood splatter and pooling was clear to see. Evidence markers indicated points on the floor, walls and ceiling. The chain that lay undisturbed on the floor had multiple markers highlighting areas for further analysis. The recorded images came to the fore in both of their memories, those chains held firm even under the greatest protest. Caslin shuddered, was it the memory or the draught, he wasn't sure.

Only once he was happy that the process was correctly organised did Robertson return to the kitchen, peeling off his gloves and removing his hood. He wiped a weary hand across his face. In his fifties but appearing far greater in years than that, Caslin could see that the workload was taking its toll. Never one to shirk his responsibilities, Iain would be the last to leave a crime scene, often competing with Caslin for that accolade.

"Well I thought I had seen it all," Robertson said ruefully.

"I don't think any of us ever gets to see it all," Caslin responded.

"Aye, you're probably right."

Harman was still staring into the room. Even in the artificial light his face appeared ashen. Caslin touched him on the shoulder.

"Why don't you duck out for a minute and get some air. It's pretty oppressive down here."

Harman didn't need a second invitation. He nodded and left them. Robertson watched the younger man leave and once out of earshot, he turned to Caslin.

"Don't you wish you could be that young again?"

Caslin smiled, "Maybe we could have had a career in a bank or something?"

Robertson laughed, "You'd have met more criminals in that job, I'm sure."

"What can you tell me about this?" Caslin indicated the room behind him.

"That will take some time," Robertson frowned.

"I'm expecting more than just.... deviant behaviour?"

"Many would do weirder, I don't doubt it for a second but I presume you're asking me if this was more than kinky sex?"

"I am, yes."

"That is hard to say at this point," Robertson's expression furrowed deeper still, "but there is a great deal of blood, even for hardcore fetishists. I should think we're looking at more than one... what shall we call it... event or incident? I must stress that is pure conjecture until we do more work and don't ask me how many, it's impossible to tell. We'll do blood types and that may give us some idea. DNA screening will take longer but with a fair wind, we could get profiles. It's a mess, though and separating one from another may take a while."

"Dare I ask how much time?"

Robertson was pensive, "We're not allowed to out-source to private labs anymore, the age of austerity and all that. So, we have to prioritise the cases. What with Ravenscar—"

"Don't worry, I get it."

"I don't like to guess, you know that, but if I had to say, then I would suggest that we are on the tip of something very dark indeed. Why were you so certain that we pull out the stops on this?"

Caslin didn't answer but thanked Iain for the information and requested regular updates as they processed the scene. He made his way outside and found a rather pale looking Harman leaning against the door frame of the workshop, staring out into the rain.

"What can you tell me about the computer set-up in this place?"

Harman glanced across.

"In what way?"

"You've got a degree in Computer Science, haven't you?" Harman nodded. "Then tell me something."

Harman thought for a moment and then retrieved his pocket book. He scanned through his notes and cleared his throat.

"Right, the discs that we've seen so far are on DVD but not all were recent. Some that I came across were time coded. That gave it away."

"As what?"

"Copies. They were originally on VHS and then transferred. Some are time stamped from years ago. Assuming that is that the maker didn't intentionally alter the date on the original device."

"Just to throw us off, you mean?" he asked, Harman nodded. Caslin felt that was doubtful. "Unlikely but you're right to mention it."

Harman continued, "There isn't the equipment here to do the data transfer. At least, I've not found it yet. It's not particularly difficult to do but nevertheless—"

"That's dedication to your hobby, though. You would worry the tape might stretch or wear out over time."

"Also, where is the camera? The recordings that I reviewed were at an angle suggesting the camera was placed at height but with no table or furniture of note in the building that matches the line, I'm assuming use of a tripod. The picture and sound quality were far too good to have been made with a phone or a basic digital camera. We're talking about some decent kit. Not stuff that you throw in a drawer somewhere. Besides that, I haven't found a computer either, just the cabling to the desk."

Caslin nodded. He remembered noting that the hardware was missing when he first arrived.

"See what you can find. Have you accessed the server yet?"

Harman shook his head, "Iain was a bit reluctant to let me.

He's onto the tech guys for support but so far, nothing doing. He promised that I can access it if they can't stump anyone up in the next twelve hours."

"Fair enough. On another note, have you had any joy with the bank about who's collecting the rent for this place, or with Horsvedt's rig and customs, for that matter?"

"Without a warrant the bank was reluctant but in the light of this lot, I should be able to get something over the phone later today. If not, I'll go in personally tomorrow. As for customs, we've got some footage of his truck driving onto a ferry at Dover but nothing more than that."

"Is it definitely Horsvedt at the wheel?"

"It's impossible to tell from the footage. And the ferry company delete their internal CCTV after three months, so there was no joy there, either. Do you think he's done one?"

Caslin shrugged, "I'm not prepared to rule anything out, just yet. Okay, good. Anything else?" Harman shook his head. He seemed about to speak but thought better of it. Caslin pushed, "What's on your mind, Maxim?"

Harman looked back in the direction of the hatch and into the passage beyond, now lit by portable lamps.

"Isn't it on yours?"

CASLIN LEFT the others and made his way over to the house. The rain had eased off, so he picked his way across the sodden ground in an effort to keep his shoes and trousers clean. He knew what Harman was feeling, for he carried the same images in the forefront of his own mind and already knew that they would never leave him. It was necessary to maintain a degree of emotional detachment from the case and it was the investigation process that enabled Caslin to do that. Years ago, he had realised that he couldn't prevent such events but was reassured that he could sure as hell try and stop it happening again. That helped maintain his sanity. With time Harman would learn that also, he would need to. Caslin felt guilty that he hadn't taken a moment to ease the pressure on his colleague but he was annoyed, and others came a distant second when he was annoyed.

That morning they had met with Frank Stephens. What could have been dismissed as an intense fetish was thrown out by what Harman had. No matter how into domination a woman could be, begging to know where your infant child was, and what had been done with him, went far beyond sexual gratification. The images of McNeil spitting in Angela Horsvedt's face, repeatedly striking, and urinating on her naked body as she wept, were not easily cast aside. By their reckoning she had appeared in at least five recordings, one of which lasted six hours and fourteen minutes. When the camera was turned off, Caslin felt he knew what had followed. The DCI had taken a few minutes to reflect on the video and the silence had hung heavily in the room before he gave the investigation the green light. Nothing more had been said. If ever a picture had spoken a thousand words, it was in that very moment.

The irritation wasn't with Stephens nor with Harman for his indiscretions, who else could have mentioned Caslin's assailant at the farmhouse? He was annoyed with his own action, or at least, his inaction. This case had struck a chord immediately but he had been slow to respond. Only time would tell what that meant. Would the cost of his procrastination be higher than he was prepared for, or did the case end with the death of Garry McNeil? Was he now merely picking over the carcass? Caslin was unsure and furthermore, he didn't know which outcome he found most palatable.

Glancing through the front window to the sitting room, he saw one of the forensics team taking photographs of the floor before the fireplace. The carpet and rug had been rolled back and even from his vantage point, Caslin could see the outline of a dark-brown stain, perhaps two feet across, on the floorboards beneath. He wouldn't need confirmation from the lab, he had seen similar marks too many times before. Whose blood it was on the other hand, would most likely take some telling.

"Too slow," Caslin chided himself as he turned away and risked a glance skyward. The rain was beginning to intensify once again. "Too slow."

CHAPTER SEVENTEEN

THE DOOR to his flat in Kleiser's Court slammed shut behind him, *something else for Mrs Ogilvie to whine about*. Caslin turned on the lights and both hallway bulbs struggled into life. The nature of low energy bulbs ensured that he remained in gloom. A small clutch of mail lay unopened on the floor and sifting through it, he picked out those that looked interesting, leaving the junk for later.

Passing through into the living room he threw his coat over the armchair, turning on the standing lamp behind it, as he went. A bank statement was not desirable reading and he discarded it. Another letter was stamped with his solicitor's address and that went the same way. The last was clearly written by a child and he opened it with a smile on his face. It was a note from Lizzie, thanking him for the weekend and instructing him to call her one evening in the coming week when he had the chance. It was signed off with a heart drawn beneath her name. The postmark was York, so she must have posted it from the train station when her grandfather had seen them off.

Caslin carefully folded the note, placing it centre stage on the mantelpiece. Crossing the room, he went to the kitchen, filled the kettle with water and set it to boil. Absently he took a mug from the drainer and retrieved a tea bag from a small tin in the cupboard above while the kettle began to quietly hum. The milk was dated for Sunday but a sniff gave it the all clear, if only barely, and Caslin reversed a chair to sit down and wait. It had been another long day. Tired hands rubbed at tired eyes but his working day was not over. There was another batch of recordings that needed reviewing and with resources stretched as they were, no-one else could be spared.

The click brought him out of his preoccupation and, stifling a yawn, he got up to pour the water. A draught washed over him and he shivered. The curtain wavered slightly in the corner of his eye. Stirring his tea bag gently he let go of the spoon and walked over to the kitchen window, open barely an inch but still enough to bring the freezing winter inside. Had he not checked whether it was closed prior to leaving for his father's the previous week? For the life of him he couldn't remember. Glancing over his shoulder, he scanned the room. Everything seemed in place. Nothing had drawn his attention when he got home and surely, he would've noticed.

The window opened onto a fire escape. From there it was only a small drop to the courtyard which in turn gave access through a locked door into the communal area of Kleiser's Court and the main thoroughfare out onto Stonegate, exiting between a café and an antiques dealer.

Caslin lifted the window on a whim, it screeched in protest, and ducked his head out. The courtyard was silent as always. Lit only by the light escaping the surrounding flats it was seldom used by the residents, except in an emergency which Caslin had never experienced since he moved in. He withdrew and eased the window down, dropping the latch and screwing the lock into place. Taking one last glance around him before shaking off his paranoia, he went back to the tea. Moments later, seated in the living room with brew in hand, he powered up the laptop. It wasn't going to be an enjoyable task but it was a necessary one.

Several hours and much caffeine later, his eyes were glazing over. His body was tired but his mind was active. Each recording followed a similar vein to the last, none of which sat well with him. On more than one occasion he had glanced at the Talisker, standing proud in a bookcase across the room, and considered cracking the seal. When the moments came, he resisted. Professional enough to bury his emotional reaction, human enough to care, he needed to stay focused. There would be something here, something worth seeing that might give him a break.

Caslin awoke with a start. Momentarily confused, he was cold and felt stiff. His computer balanced precariously on his lap. Moving it to the table he flexed his legs and answered the mobile that was tucked into his trouser pocket, noting that it was just after two o'clock in the morning.

"Caslin," he answered. His voice cracking as he spoke.

"Did I wake you?"

"No."

"Well I should have done. You'll be no good if you don't—"

"Iain, why are you calling me in the middle of the night?" Caslin recognised the voice of Iain Robertson, instantly.

"I may have some answers for you out here."

"Are you still at the farmhouse?"

"Aye," Robertson sounded despondent, "and you should make your way out, too. Although, I fear you'll end up with even more questions."

Caslin didn't know how he should feel, excited about a break or irritated at the prospect of more intrigue. Thus far, all he had managed was to feel like a blind man, punching in the dark. With any complex case he often had to wait patiently for the fog to lift even if only for the briefest of moments but often that was all it took. He let Robertson know he was on his way and hung up. The laptop was hibernating on the coffee table before him and he touched the glide pad to bring it back to life.

Inadvertently he must have paused the player when he fell asleep. The still image of McNeil and an unidentified woman was disconcerting. Hovering the cursor over the cancel tab, his finger lifted off as his attention was drawn to the corner. At first, Caslin almost dismissed it and was once again about to shut it down when he changed his mind. Instead, he took the image to full screen. Although the quality wasn't great at that resolution, he gently eased the slider control to the left and moved the image backwards. Was it a trick of the light? Restarting the recording, having first muted the sound, Caslin ignored the figures in the foreground. Once he had seen it again he repeated the review for a third time. There was no doubt. It was a subtle shift but none-theless, a movement in the bottom left of the picture, shrouded in shadow. He strained to see what could have caused it.

Sitting back in his chair, he stared at the frozen image but as time passed, he kept coming back to the same conclusion. To his mind there was a third person present.

STANDING ALONGSIDE IAIN ROBERTSON, underneath the intense glow of the portable floodlights a little after 2 a.m., Caslin found his missing person's case developing into a murder inquiry.

"How long do you think he's been there?"

Robertson knelt at the edge of the shallow grave. With a gloved hand, he raised the edge of the dust sheet to reveal the face of the man beneath, crudely buried, barely a stone's throw from the workshop.

"A while, judging by the rate of decomposition but I'd await the results of the post mortem, rather than hazard a guess."

"I'm willing to bet that the cord around his neck is related to the cause of death," Caslin pointed to the length of blue rope.

Robertson nodded, "It's similar to baler twine, only thicker. I do a fair bit of sailing, as you know, and that wouldn't look out of place on a fishing boat."

"A fisherman? Out here?"

Robertson snorted, "You're the detective, Nate."

"This is our man, though."

"The haulier?"

Caslin nodded, "I reckon so. He's roughly the right build, the location, it fits."

"Come with me and see if this does too."

Robertson led him over to another area illuminated by artificial means. A taped off patch of scorched earth, perhaps four metres square. Within the cordon were the remnants of a bonfire. A colleague, clad in a forensic paper suit, moved aside to allow them access. Robertson knelt and pointed out some charred pieces that Caslin couldn't identify.

"What am I looking at?"

"Bones," Robertson replied flatly. "At least, fragments of bone."

"Human?"

"Undoubtedly. Take a look at this," Robertson shifted position slightly, affording Caslin a better view. "Teeth. A couple of molars and an eye if I'm not mistaken."

"Adult?"

"More than likely, yes. There are more pieces than you can see here. For any detail greater than that, though, you're going to have to wait. We'll catalogue them and get them over to the lab as soon as we can."

"Anything else?"

Robertson let out a laugh, "You know me too well, Nate, too well. Before the light failed us, we identified several areas of disturbed earth, other than this, that warrant closer inspection. Two are within the copse and a third on the south side of the bunker, beneath some sprawling vegetation. Inside the bunker, we have evidence of post mortem blood staining in the shower tray and gravity splatter in the basin."

"The killer was cleaning up."

"Aye, looks that way."

CHLOE MCNEIL APPEARED VISIBLY SHAKEN as she sat in the interview room. Harman had picked her up before seven that morning and brought her in to make a statement at Caslin's request. Sipping at his Americano, one that he had bought on the way to Fulford Road, Caslin couldn't take his eyes off Chloe as he watched her via the video link. People always had a reaction to an interview room. Usually it generated anxiety but that in itself meant little, not necessarily indicating guilt. Even so, he was fascinated to observe her body language as her eyes searched the room while she waited for him.

Entering with Maxim a step behind, Caslin thanked her for coming in. The uniformed officer present departed and they each took a seat, Caslin placing a manila folder on the table in front of him.

"Can I smoke in here?" Chloe asked.

Caslin shook his head, he was grateful for that rule. Quitting was hard enough and an enclosed space with her menthol brand would guarantee nausea.

"Chloe, I've asked you to come in because we're looking to find out as much as we can about Garry," Caslin began. "I appreciate that this is a difficult time but we'd like you to help us out if you can."

She nodded enthusiastically. This meeting had been thoughtfully engineered, the time of day, location and choice of room, each carefully selected. People were less prepared at the start of the day. He wanted her to volunteer the information he needed and with this approach, he felt more likely to get it.

"What kind of a man was Garry, as a person to be around, I mean?"

Chloe smiled, relaxing a little and sinking back into her chair.

"He used to be really outgoing, always quick with a smile and a joke. The kind of guy everyone wanted to be with, you know?"

Caslin nodded, "I know the type."

Chloe continued, "He changed when he came out of the army, though. That last tour in the Gulf got to him. He was still my

Garry, only a bit more aggressive. I didn't like that side of him so much."

"Now, when did you last see your ex-husband?"

Chloe thought for a moment, "It was around August, this year."

"August?" Caslin repeated. Chloe nodded.

"We have some home movies that were found amongst Garry's possessions," Harman interjected, Chloe didn't react. "Do you know the ones that I'm talking about?"

Chloe shrugged, "No idea."

"Remind us, what did Garry do in the army?"

"He was in the Rifles."

"Was he into his technology, computers and such?"

She burst out laughing and it was genuine, "Garry? God no. He was useless with that sort of thing, didn't even have a mobile phone."

"Really?" Caslin found that interesting.

Caslin waited, letting the silence hang in the room for nearly a full minute. Casually, he opened the folder in front of him and removed some papers, placing them neatly on the table. Across from him, he saw her demeanour change. No longer did she appear nervous. Her hands were now folded across each other and resting before her. As calm as she outwardly appeared, Chloe McNeil would not meet his eye.

"Let's back up a little," Caslin was conciliatory. "You said you saw Garry in August? Previously, you said you hadn't seen him for seven or eight months. That's a little different to August, which is only around three."

Chloe glanced up at him, "You must have written it down wrong."

Caslin smiled, "You should be aware that police officers are trained to take statements and record information, accurately. This is our job. We don't make those kinds of mistakes."

She visibly tensed, "Maybe I made a mistake."

"I'll let you in on something else," he lowered his voice. "In my job, I am always looking for the *first time* someone changes what they say. It interests me and I start to question everything else that they have said and continue to say. You see, Chloe, we pay attention to what people tell us."

"There appear to be some inconsistencies in your statement and we would like to give you an opportunity to clear them up, if you can," Harman said.

Chloe looked at him and then back at Caslin, "Are you sure I can't smoke?"

Caslin ignored the question and turned to the paper before him.

"When did you get married to Garry?"

Chloe was taken aback, "You what?"

"Your wedding day, when was it? You do remember? I'm getting divorced and right now, I cannot stand my wife but I do remember the day we got married, May 21st."

Chloe remained silent, her eyes cast downward.

"That reaction would explain why we couldn't find any record of your marriage in the council archives," Harman stated.

"We got married abroad. What difference does it make?" she snapped.

"Did you get divorced abroad as well?" Caslin continued. His tone was calm and his body language relaxed. "Perhaps you could think on that, while you explain this."

Caslin laid out two sheets of paper. One was a bank statement and the other, a headed form detailing a direct debit agreement, the recipient was Sylvia Vickers. Chloe examined the paper but didn't comment. Caslin waited in order to gauge her reaction and when nothing was forthcoming, took a photograph from his paperwork and placed it on top of the other two sheets, directly in front of her. The image was black-and-white, slightly grainy but readily identifiable in the CCTV snapshot was Chloe McNeil. She was pictured in discussion with an adviser from the bank.

They waited in silence. Caslin had enough to push on but he still waited. Harman appeared to be about to speak but a sideways glance conveyed the message to remain quiet. One of Caslin's favourite techniques was to imply that he already had the knowledge, the witness may voluntarily give up more than they realised was necessary. Across the table, seated in front of him, was a liar.

"You said you had no idea where Garry had been living. No need to deny it, we wrote it down," Caslin said as he drummed his fingers on the table. "You also denied knowing the Horsvedts," Caslin ran his fingers over to the direct debit form and slowly tapped it with his forefinger. "And I think we can all agree that that also wasn't true."

Chloe shot him a dark look, her cheeks flushing.

"I didn't know where he was!"

"Come on Chloe," Caslin shook his head. "Why continue to lie to us? It only puts you in deeper."

The penny appeared to have dropped. Chloe became flustered in her response.

"Sylvia is my mother, okay. The farmhouse is hers. I just... just..."

"Collected the rent money?"

"Yes."

"After pretending to be her?"

"Yes."

"That's fraud, identity theft, tax evasion... to name but a few." Chloe nodded her understanding as she stared at the table. Caslin began to push. Indicating the recorder that silently monitored the interview, he added, "Please speak up, for the benefit of the tape."

"Yes, I know," she almost whispered the words.

"What can you tell me about the workshop?"

Chloe cast her eyes fleetingly at Caslin and then quickly to the ceiling, before returning her gaze to the table, shaking her head.

"What do you want to know? Garry built it."

"The workshop?"

"Yes, years ago. He needed somewhere to do his stuff when he was on leave and the council place didn't have the space."

"What about the rest?"

Chloe looked up as if taking a measure of what Caslin did or didn't know. After considering her response for a brief moment she bit her lower lip and exhaled slowly. Her shoulders sagged.

"My father built the shelter back in the sixties. He was obsessed with the Cold War and always talked about being prepared. As a kid I thought he was a bit crazy. We used to play in it when we were small."

"And Garry built the workshop onto the front of it?"

"Yes."

"Now tell us about the tapes."

"I know about his videos, okay," Chloe exclaimed. "And I knew he might be staying there. He did sometimes when we'd had a fight."

Caslin sat back in his chair. Now they were getting somewhere.

"He would stay in, what should we call it, the bomb shelter?"

"You could call it that, yes, or a bunker. That's what Garry said it was."

"Who did the internal works on the bunker?"

Chloe shook her head, "I don't know what you mean."

"Come on, Chloe. It wasn't all done fifty years ago. The bathroom, kitchen, running water, electrical cabling…"

"This is your chance," Harman offered her. Chloe shook her head once more.

"We already knew that you were aware of the recordings. I *know* a third person was present and that was you," Caslin was lying but that wasn't illegal. "I want you to think on this next question carefully before you answer it because it is very important for all of us in this room. Where are Daniel and Angela Horsvedt?"

"Why would I do something to them?"

"Chloe, this is as serious as it gets," Caslin paused. "We have you lying through your teeth already and with Garry gone, this will all fall on you. Juries hate a female murderer, almost as much as a judge—"

"Murder," Chloe was out of her chair catching both Harman and Caslin off guard. "You bastard!" she shouted, swinging a fist at Caslin's head. He just barely managed to avoid it, toppling backwards from his chair.

Flat on his back, he let out a groan as he looked up to see Harman grappling for control across the table. Chloe shrieked hysterically as they struggled back and forth. Caslin had touched a nerve. Perhaps his hunch was paying off. Harman's enquiries at the bank had finally borne fruit. Neither detective could believe their eyes upon opening the email attachment at Fulford Road, just as the working day officially began. Lack of sleep was forgotten. For the first time, Caslin had felt like he was going to get answers. Chloe was elevated from the status of a witness to a person of interest at the top of a scant list.

UPON RESTORATION of calm they had a recess in the interview. Chloe was reread her rights and immediately requested legal representation, much to Caslin's disgust. When solicitors were present, the interviewee invariably became less forthcoming. Within the hour they resumed and, much to his surprise, found Chloe far more agreeable than expected. Voluntarily she confirmed that the marriage to Garry had never taken place, merely changing her name in order to appear so. Not the greatest of admissions as the fact had already been established. However, she steadfastly denied being knowledgeable of, or complicit in, any criminal act that her estranged lover had been involved in.

"Come on, Chloe," Caslin said, shaking his head in exasperation. "This is your mother's property, let out to tenants by you. Your lover is living there and you expect us to believe that you are entirely ignorant of this whole situation. The beatings, the torture, the recordings, none of it rings true?"

Chloe shrugged, "Believe what you want. As long as I got the rent money, I didn't care what went on out there."

"And did you? Get the rent money, I mean."

"Regular as clockwork until a couple of months ago. I went out there to ask them about it and they were gone. People do that you know, just go. You know what these foreigners are like."

Ms Leonard, the Duty Solicitor sitting beside her client, wrote something in her notebook and then glanced towards Caslin.

"Do you actually have anything else to bring here, or are we going to re-cover the same ground again? I'm not entirely sure what my client is accused of, beyond what she has already provided. Without legal representation, I might add."

Caslin hated solicitors. He thought about calling time on the interview there and then but chose one last tack.

"Everyone has at some point watched crime drama on television, be it a Saturday afternoon *Columbo* or a bit of *Morse*. We all expect the classic line 'means, motive and opportunity'. That is very true but when it comes to murder, I focus on motive and the rest follows soon enough. Do you know how that breaks down for me in this case?"

Chloe met his eye for the first time in at least ten minutes. She glanced at her counsel, who was making further notes in her pad and then back to Caslin, giving him an almost imperceptible shake of the head.

"No."

"I call it my 'Rule of Three', three reasons that either stand-alone or contribute collectively to murder. The first surrounds *money*, the second, *sex* and lastly, *revenge*. The alarm bells ring when I am lied to and with you Chloe McNeil, *Sylvia Vickers*, they are piercingly loud indeed. This is your chance to tell the truth, your side of the story. You see, I have money covered with the Horsvedts," he tapped the bank statement for effect, "and the home movies definitely cover the sex. Now I say to myself, that's two out of three and in my mind, that's looking pretty good for me... not so much for you, though."

Caslin let the thought hang in the air and fixed her with his gaze. Even when someone sat in silence, he had an instinct that told him whether he was hitting home. She was on the hook.

"Look," she said, her tone edged with fear as she dismissed the protestations of her solicitor, who was attempting to advise her to remain silent, "it's not me behind that camera, okay. I can prove it."

Inside Caslin felt the excitement rising with the anticipation but outwardly remained stoic.

"Go on."

"I'm not filming them, I was…" she stopped, almost as if she couldn't get the words out. "I'm sorry, I shouldn't have done what I did, but I was scared and panicked."

"Done what, Chloe?"

Again, Ms Leonard tried to intervene but Chloe would have none of it.

"Shut up! I have to get this out." She stared at Caslin and this time didn't flinch. Tears fell as she spoke. "I had to get them. After your visit, I knew it was only a matter of time and I had to."

"Get what?" Caslin was confused.

"I knew that you'd find where he was living and then the tapes and stuff. I was ashamed. Garry used to make me… do things… and he… he—" At that moment she leant to her side and vomited. All present were caught by surprise. Harman even yelped as his lower leg was sprayed. Chloe remained bent double. Unqualified sobs began to emanate from her as she retched.

"Perhaps we should take a brief break?" Ms Leonard asked. Caslin was about to agree when they were interrupted.

"No! I have to say it now," Chloe shouted in between sobs, momentarily regaining some composure. All colour drained from her face. "Garry was into some twisted stuff. I hated it and when he started to record it… it just got worse. Sometimes the look on his face… I reckon he forgot who I was. It scared me."

"What did you do? You were going to tell me," Caslin asked.

"I shouldn't have… I'm sorry… I hit you but I didn't know

what else to do. I just wanted those bloody tapes, but I didn't kill no-one!"

That was an unexpected turn of events. Caslin's mind reeled as he contemplated the significance.

"What about the others? On the tapes, you knew about them, didn't you?"

Chloe nodded, "Yes. He would pick people up from time to time and even ask me to join them as well, sometimes."

"Did you?"

Again, Chloe nodded, "Once or twice."

"The third person, off camera?"

"I don't know, I swear!" Chloe implored him, looking Caslin straight in the eye. "When there were three of us, we were all on film. We were adults. We can do as we want."

Caslin sat back in his chair and sighed. The realisation hit him that the moment of euphoria wasn't coming and worse still that he was heading back to square one. He took a deep breath and glanced at Harman, whose forlorn expression meant he had reached the same conclusion.

"I'll need those tapes."

"You shall have them," Ms Leonard stated evenly.

CHAPTER EIGHTEEN

THE REFECTORY WAS OPEN BUT, apart from a few uniforms milling around, the room was quiet. The machine rattled as the cup dropped from the dispenser and the nozzle engaged. DI Atwood came alongside, placing a pound coin into the adjacent vending machine and selecting the summer-berries flavoured water. Caslin forced himself not to sneer.

"How is it going with Ravenscar?" Caslin asked casually.

"Can't say, Nathaniel. Sorry and all that," Atwood answered, without sincerity. "Broadfoot's ordered a blackout. If you're not on the case, you're not in the loop. I'm sure you understand?"

"Oh yes, completely." Caslin watched the retreating officer as he headed back to CID, cracking the seal on his bottle as he went. Atwood appeared to have enjoyed that immensely.

"That guy's an arse."

Caslin looked around to see DI Baxter approaching. He didn't respond but instead fed some change into the vending machine, selecting a bag of crisps before reaching over to retrieve his coffee, teasing out the cup whilst waiting for his snack selection to drop.

"So, are you going to fill me in?"

Baxter smiled, "Not much to say, if I'm to be honest. There's a lot of endeavour but it's not heralding results so far."

"Anything significant, at all?"

"We've set up a smaller crisis team to look at potential lines of inquiry for the perpetrator. You know the drill, escape routes along with methods of travel, possible weapon disposal locations. We're hopeful."

"No leads on the forensics, any witnesses turn up? An event like that is so rare up here, outside of the drug world, anyway. You'd expect to have plenty to run with."

Baxter frowned, "We're still looking into the family. You never quite know if refugees from war zones are all that they appear to be in their paperwork."

"Particularly when they turn up dead," Caslin added. Baxter agreed.

"Sarah Hunter is still pushing the honour killing angle but that doesn't fly with some of us. The friends are too vague and there's no evidence that they had plans to marry off the daughter. No flights booked, that we can find, and no correspondence abroad. Even the girl's diary has no mention of it, or anything else that showed she had concerns."

"What about his employment?"

"The father?" Baxter clarified. Caslin nodded. "The company were nonplussed about telling us what they were up to but they gave it up."

"And what were they up to?"

"Surveillance, but nothing for us to be concerned with. Hakim was a technician, tasked with the collection and analysis of data from the on-board flight systems of commercial aircraft. They report back to manufacturers on fuel usage, directional alterations and relaying of transponder pings. Not something that you would kill for."

"Nothing linked to military aircraft or private enterprise?"

"I see where you're going but no, purely data collection on passenger and freight traffic. The information they gather is useful for performance analysis and monitoring of international flight paths. They have no access to other systems."

"Why are the company so obsessive about keeping that quiet?"

Baxter shrugged, "It's a competitive industry, apparently. Aviation manufacturers are all looking for an edge."

"What about the brother and this inheritance dispute?"

"He swears blind there wasn't one and so far, despite our best efforts, we have to agree with him. There's nothing to the contrary."

"One wall after another, then. I'll bet that's not going down well."

"The DCS is getting antsy, which is a bit of a break from the cool persona that he likes to portray. I expect he's taking some severe flak from above."

"I can imagine," Caslin said as he stooped for his crisps, scraping his knuckles on the metal flap as he withdrew his hand. He cursed.

"It's weird," Baxter continued. "With an incident like this, there really should be a clear direction but it's not panning out as we expect. The victims' backgrounds, witnesses, forensics, motive, unusual trends in behaviour... all are drawing a blank. It's like a random act of overkill."

"Oh, I doubt that," Caslin said as he blew the steam off the top of his coffee. "There's nothing random about it at all. There will be something."

"We'll figure it out." Baxter deposited his coins and started to make his own selections. "You must be gutted to be missing out on this one." It was a statement rather than a question. "How about you and that farm thing, are you still working it? That guy from the IPCC getting around, is he?"

"Not seen him," Caslin replied, "but he knows where I am. I keep hitting my own dead ends there. It'll probably turn out that there's little else to it."

With that Caslin left and headed upstairs. He was happy to chat about Ravenscar but saw no reason to share his own case. Approaching the CID squad room, he realised that a briefing was underway. That was a shame. He wanted a clear opportunity to have a look over the information boards. Discretion would be required, particularly if Frank Stephens was chairing the briefing.

Barely a foot was through the doorway before attention turned his way.

"Just the man. Is this down to you?"

Caslin stopped at the entrance. The voice was that of the DCI and his tone, hostile.

"Is what?"

"This!" Stephens shouted as he threw a newspaper in Caslin's general direction, the pages separating en route. Several people beneath the flight path instinctively ducked. "Is this how you go about getting resources put your way?"

DS Hunter read Caslin's confused expression and offered up the detail.

"There's a front-page article in *The Post*, linking Ravenscar with your farmhouse."

"You're joking?" Caslin asked, putting his coffee down.

"It's the usual, 'Sources close to the inquiry reveal link to an isolated farmhouse', typical tabloid stuff."

Hunter scooped up the front page from the carpet and handed it to him.

"Nothing to say?" Frank Stephens asked.

All eyes fell on Caslin as he was scanning the paper. He frowned and tried to muster the energy for a rebuttal but saw little in it for him.

"Please don't tell me it was Jimmy Sullivan?"

"No surprise that you know who wrote it—"

"Now hold on a damn minute." Caslin wasn't having any of it. "If there's been anything coming out of this office, it's got sod all to do with me! You should ask who told Sullivan that I was out there in the first place? He had no reason to be snooping around."

"What's your point?" DCI Stephens asked.

"What's my bloody point? I didn't even have a case that linked me to that address. He had no business there, so who pointed him in my direction? There's someone leaking here but it sure as hell isn't me." The last comment drew howls of protest and derision from the assembled officers but Caslin was already in full flow. "This shit isn't supposed to happen post-Leveson. But I guess that's what you get for assembling an army of wannabes and plastic journeymen!" Caslin scrunched the paper between his hands and hurled it in the vicinity of the waste bin, before making to leave.

"Get out!" Stephens yelled.

Caslin didn't need to be told twice and stormed out of CID, almost colliding with DI Baxter as he stepped out into the corridor.

"Steady, old boy."

"Sorry Simon," Caslin managed to say, without breaking step.

Caslin was still seething as he reached the ground floor. Even when not on a case he was still causing ructions. His work life never used to be that way. It was always the calmness of his approach that garnered results. Remembering that he had left the cup of coffee on a desk upstairs, he swore. The corridor was empty and leaning against a wall, he tilted his head back and closed his eyes, enjoying a moment of relative peace.

Taking some deep breaths, he considered his next move. Sullivan made what he had perceived to be an idle threat. Evidently, he had misjudged that situation and now he found himself thrust centre stage, once again. Or was he? Frank Stephens was struggling, that was clear from day one, and was most likely striking out at anyone with the misfortune to walk into view. There was nothing to Sullivan's story, so perhaps it would swiftly blow over. Until then some uniforms would need to be deployed to Radford Farm to keep the press at arm's length. The unintended consequences of doing that, however, might raise the suspicion that the journalist was on to something. At some point the story there would break and the scrutiny would intensify but, for the moment at least, there was time to investigate without the accompanying circus.

The moment of reflection was pierced by approaching foot-steps on the polished floor. Caslin opened his eyes and cast a glance sideways to see the approach of Linda, easily the friend-liest as well as most capable of the civilian desk clerks.

"Nathaniel, do you have a moment?"

"For you, Linda, I have several," he smiled, and she returned it.

"I've been trying to get through to CID for the past half hour and no-one's picking up. Is there something going on?"

Caslin's smile broke into a laugh that he immediately checked.

"It's a little fractious up there at the moment. Is there anything I can help you with?"

"Possibly. There's a gentleman in the front office asking to speak with someone in CID but he won't tell me why."

"What sort of person, normal or...?"

Now it was Linda who laughed, "He seems like a pleasant man, elderly. Although, I am not entirely sure he is... how should I put it?"

"Quite all there?" Caslin finished for her.

"Yes, that was what I thought. As you know, we do get them towards the silly season. I know you're busy but do you think—"

"Of course, take me to him."

He realised then that he hadn't seen Linda for several weeks. Presuming that she had been on sick leave, he thought better of asking. Suffering from an aggressive form of bone cancer, which was taking its toll, she was routinely off work but to her credit she never once offered a complaint. Occasionally she would appear introverted and he would proffer a smile or a wink of support, safe in the knowledge that if she wanted more, he was there.

Linda led them back to the entrance foyer at her own pace and saw him through the security door, into the lobby. There was only one person present, a man seated in the corner. A dark-tan walking stick rested between his knees. The glass window to the enquiries desk was closed and the murmuring of those at work, alongside the backdrop of the gentle hum of the morning traffic outside, was all the sound that came to ear. Linda introduced them and withdrew.

"Good morning," Caslin said, taking a measure of the man slowly rising before him.

He was heavy set for someone of his apparent age and, despite being dressed in several layers of thick winter clothing, Caslin could tell that he would have been a powerhouse in his youth. Stooping forward he offered his hand. Caslin took it.

"Colin Brotherton," he introduced himself. "Detective Sergeant, from over in Leeds. Well I was until I retired, anyway."

"Pleased to meet you, Mr Brotherton. Now what brings you to Fulford Road?"

"Colin, please. I'm trying to get you lot to take me seriously, that's what."

Caslin was momentarily taken aback for he was expecting the voice of a frail individual but his was forceful, and he was aggravated. Glancing about them and then to the entrance doors, Caslin could see the bright, November sunshine beyond.

"Do you fancy a cup of coffee?"

The retired detective grinned, revealing gaps for a number of missing teeth amid those heavily stained with yellow.

Not long after, they were seated in a café on the edge of the city centre. The place was small and narrow, with only a half-dozen tables for use by the patrons. Most of their trade seemed to come by way of those heading in and out of the centre. Caslin waited patiently until their coffee arrived, along with the bacon sandwiches and a muffin. He was starving. Apparently, the retired detective had been so keen to reach York that he had travelled the day before, sleeping in a local hotel in order to be at the station first thing.

"Why didn't you just call? Believe me we have dozens of people in the office at the moment."

"I did," Brotherton explained. "Several times, and I only got through twice, but I get the impression that you boys aren't interested in the ramblings of an old git like me."

To Caslin's mind, that seemed a little harsh but in all likelihood, probably not too far from the truth. He protested anyway.

"I'm sure that's not the case."

"I can't really blame you," Brotherton continued. "I expect I would have reacted the same way myself, back in the day."

"You couldn't get anyone to listen and so you came in person?"

"Not at all," he rigorously shook his head in the negative. "I found several of your boys that would listen. They just told me I was wrong… very politely, I might say. But wrong nonetheless. Can I smoke in here?"

Caslin shook his head, "It's illegal these days."

Brotherton frowned, "Isn't everything that used to be good for you."

"What were you wrong about, Colin?" Caslin asked, taking a bite out of his sandwich, having first laced it with brown sauce.

"I'm sure I'm not, you know. It's that shooting you had out on the moors. I know one of the people involved, from a case I worked years ago. Damndest thing I ever saw when I picked up the paper, staring right back at me, a face I hadn't seen in what… nigh on thirty years."

"Whose face?" Caslin was intrigued. The light was gleaming in the eyes of the man opposite.

"Lucy Stafford."

"Lucy Stafford?" Caslin repeated. A sense of deflation settled over him. "And who is she?"

"The dead woman, on the moor. You've got those that were in the car and then Lucy, by herself."

"From the Ravenscar shootings case, you mean?" Caslin asked.

Brotherton nodded emphatically, "Exactly. But the papers and yourselves have got it all wrong."

Caslin put his hand up to stop him. He was confused, "You're talking about Claire Skellon."

"That's what I am *trying* to tell you. Her name is Lucy Stafford. No idea where you get this Skellon from. She was Lucy when I knew her. Might explain why we couldn't find her though. To think after all these years, she'd turn up like this, very sad."

Sitting back in his chair, Caslin relaxed and took a sip of his coffee. The brief rush of trade around them had died down and only the proprietor, clearing tables, was making noise. The other staff member was busying himself restocking the sandwich cabinet. Once more, Caslin found his interest piqued. The old man currently devouring a blueberry muffin seemed to be in control of his faculties and adamant about what he knew. They met eyes and Caslin exhaled deeply, picking up his coffee once more.

"I think you had better start at the beginning."

"I thought you'd never ask," Brotherton said, appearing to find a second wind. Sitting slightly higher in his chair, he began. "It was back in the early eighties, I was a DC at the time. Even though I had been in the job for a decade, I was still enthusiastic and keen to make a real difference in the world. I was young back then. Hard to believe, I know, but it's true. Anyway, we were looking into the disappearance of a young girl—"

"Lucy Stafford?" Caslin said.

"No. Don't interrupt me. Patience really is a lost art these days," Brotherton admonished him before continuing. "She was Maxine de la Grange, only eighteen and working in the Leeds sex trade. After she hadn't been seen for a couple of weeks, she was reported missing and I was tasked with looking into it. I was also a DC in '77 and so soon after Sutcliffe, we had to take violence against prostitutes a bit more seriously than maybe we used to. Not that we shouldn't have before but back in the day, people weren't so bothered, were they?"

Caslin had to agree, "I'm not so sure that opinion has changed all that much in the main. Indifference is just more concealed. Did you find Maxine?"

Brotherton stared into his cup as if seeking something at the bottom of it. Slowly he nodded but his expression had changed.

"Aye, we did. On a patch of waste ground on an industrial estate, she was in a right state."

"Dead?"

"Yes, for several days. Someone had really gone to work on her. Not just a good hiding but much more than that. She had multiple stab wounds, broken bones and other injuries that implied more torture, than a beating. Pretty girl she was. Didn't deserve that, I tell you."

"Lucy Stafford?"

"I'm getting to her, bear with me. Lucy was one of Maxine's friends. She was the one that came to us."

"Not her family?"

"Didn't have any. Maxine was brought up in care and her and Lucy met in a children's home, when the latter had a brief separation from her family. Both girls had difficult backgrounds, so it wasn't a shock that they were often in trouble. Nothing dreadful, mind you, just mixing with the wrong crowd. It was petty stuff, shoplifting, underage drinking, that kind of thing. It was no surprise to me that Maxine fell into the life that she did."

"So, Lucy wasn't in the trade then?"

Brotherton shook his head, "No, not as far as I knew, but that's not to say she wasn't without her own problems."

"Such as?"

"Her mother used to drink, heavily. Lucy sort of had to take care of herself and as soon as she hit sixteen, she was out on her own. By her volition, I should add."

"Definitely not in the trade?"

Brotherton sighed, "Never told me she was and I had no evidence to the contrary, or reason to doubt her for that matter. She was a strong-minded girl. I always felt she was in control despite the chaos that swirled around her. Anyway, they remained friends and Lucy was fired up about us finding Maxine."

"Did you collar anyone for the killing?"

"No, we couldn't tie anyone to it. There were rumours that some guy was trying to pimp her and a few others, setting himself up as some kind of gang master but we could never get a name. We interviewed as many of her friends and associates as we could but nothing came from it. Lucy was helpful up to a point but…"

"She disappeared."

"That's right, she disappeared. No word, nothing. Just vanished. We considered the possibility that perhaps she was in trouble, but we had no evidence of that and she was an adult who could do as she pleased. There were no family members that came looking for her and with apparently nothing to investigate, we drew a blank and moved on. It never sat well with me though."

"Why not?"

"Several reasons really. Lucy was so passionate about her friend. She would call me or be at the front desk asking questions every other day until we found Maxine. Then she pressed repeatedly for us to get a result before dropping off the face of the earth. When the coroner eventually released Maxine's body, not a single person showed up to claim it. *Eighteen* years old. Imagine that, and no-one cared enough to bury her. I had a whip round in the squad room and we bought Maxine her headstone. The whole of CID turned out for the funeral but that was it."

"Lucy didn't show?"

"Exactly. It just felt wrong and has bothered me ever since. We never caught the killer, nor did I clap eyes on Lucy again."

"Until now."

"Until now. Up she pops in your case. I don't know where she fits in, or even if she does. I haven't got a clue what to make of it all, to be quite honest."

"Nor do I," Caslin mused openly. "Did you get anywhere with forensics at the time, any blood, DNA?"

"We had never heard of DNA back then, this was '83. There was no evidence that Maxine had been sexually assaulted but there was an unidentified blood sample on her body. Forensics put it down as gravity bleeding, the killer getting careless with his knife."

Caslin knew what that meant. When a victim is repeatedly stabbed, the amount of blood produced often spreads to the handle which then becomes slippery and the assailant loses their grip, injuring themselves on their own blade.

"Were you able to get anything from the sample?"

Brotherton shrugged, "The lead times were horrendous for lab work back then and the focus was all about Antigen levels. We got a blood group and from there, we were able to narrow down our target range to about three million people. It was real needle and haystack stuff."

"You said that Lucy was helpful up to a point. If she was so close to Maxine, did she have any idea who had killed her?"

Brotherton looked out through the window and into the riverside park beyond, whilst considering his answer. His voice took on an emotional edge as he spoke.

"She never gave me a name and always said she didn't know, but... when we were leaning towards the theory of it being the work of a punter, she became very agitated with me. That suggested there was more going on than she was letting on. I pressed her on a few occasions and hoped that I could earn her trust so that she would open up. It never happened though."

"If she knew, why wouldn't she want to say?"

Brotherton shrugged, "You've got me there."

"Don't take this the wrong way, Colin," Caslin began. The man opposite seemed to tense as they met eyes, "But it's been thirty years. How can you be so sure that Claire Skellon is in fact, Lucy Stafford?"

Brotherton swirled the dregs of his coffee, at the base of the cup, for a few seconds before responding.

"How long have you been on the force?"

"Fifteen years, give or take."

"And in that time, I'll bet you've had a case that got to you. I don't mean one that upset you. Let's face it, in our line of work you always do and always will. What I'm talking about is one of those that really gets under your skin and the more you scratch at it, the more it itches. You can't let it go and if you were able, you'd keep going until you fixed it, no matter what the consequences. Those are the people who stay with you."

Caslin considered those words and applied them to his career. He understood.

"Have you?"

Caslin nodded, "I have."

"Were you able to fix yours?"

Caslin didn't answer.

CHAPTER NINETEEN

COLIN BROTHERTON'S words were still ringing in his ears as he pulled up outside Fulford Road. Turning the engine off, he unclipped his seat belt and reached into his inner jacket pocket, removing a tatty envelope from within. Gently opening the flap, he withdrew the handwritten letter inside, itself showing signs of wear. A young couple passed nearby. Their laughter breached the sanctuary of his car and Caslin watched them as they walked off, deep in conversation, without a care in the world.

Turning his attention to the paper in his hand, he considered whether or not to read it once more. Closing his eyes, he felt the tears welling inside. Blinking them away he took a deep breath, roughly returned the letter to the confines of its sleeve and put it back in his pocket.

"I would do it all again," he whispered to himself.

Rubbing his face vigorously with his palms, he sought to change focus. Was Colin Brotherton looking for something that wasn't there, seeing the ghost that still haunted him. Was it one last chance at redemption for a perceived, past failing? Having met the man, Caslin didn't think so but he had to consider the possibility.

Resolving to take one more look at Claire Skellon, he got out of the car. The door protested at the movement and he apologised as he pushed it to. He would have to be discreet. Having already had the suggestion rebuffed twice, Caslin realised that he wouldn't get assistance from the team. Moreover, he had no doubt what DCI Stephens or Kyle Broadfoot would make of it, not least as it was him bringing it forward. He would need to tread carefully and see if it came to anything. The real issue would be getting into the database without anyone knowing what he was up to. The names in this case would be flagged and if information control was as he expected, then questions would be asked the moment he accessed it.

Despite his awkward position he had made a commitment to look into it. The retired detective offered Caslin his old case files, with the caveat that no-one should find out. If Brotherton's information was accurate, then the angle needed investigation. They had agreed to meet that evening at a hotel in the city.

In the meantime, Caslin would see what he could dig up on Claire Skellon. In a strange way he was apprehensive about what he may turn up, for he was the one tasked with looking into her background. That in itself was a simple process, one that he failed to give proper credence, or effort to, being far too preoccupied with the events at Radford Farm. There was a distinct possibility that his lacklustre performance had ensured a vital lead was missed. Preferring to put that notion to the back of his mind, he pushed through the double doors of the entrance and stopped dead in his tracks. Of anything that he might expect to greet him upon arrival, it was certainly not her.

"Hello Nate," Karen said tentatively. She was smiling but it was at best nervous and at worst, contrived.

For a moment, Caslin was stunned into silence and stood open-mouthed in the lobby. Linda watched on with an air of entertained voyeurism and two uniformed officers passed by, each casting a glance at the pair as they went.

"Are you going to say hello?" Karen asked. She was definitely nervous. "This… this was a bad idea—"

"No, no, it's fine. I'm just… erm."

"Surprised?" she finished. "I'm probably the last person you expected to see."

"Yes, I… forgive me. I just…" he stammered, searching the area with his eyes and focusing on the solitary plant in the corner of the lobby.

"Shall we get a cup of coffee?"

Caslin instinctively shook his head, "I've just had one."

"Well, shall we go somewhere for a chat, or have you already had one of those, too?"

The last came out of frustration and he didn't bite back as he usually would. The initial surprise at seeing his wife had been replaced by a fleeting burst of exhilaration, the likes of which he hadn't felt in a long time. That unnerved him.

Regaining the composure that had escaped him, he ushered her out of reception into the daylight. It was a cold, but pleasant day and glancing over his shoulder he saw Linda give him the warmest of smiles as they left. She was one of the few at Fulford who had taken to Caslin, with no preconditioning of her attitude towards him, accepting him for who he was. Subsequently, they had got on famously. On several occasions she had asked about his family, a subject where few dared to tread, and he minded not in the least. Linda was one of the decent people, not a malicious gossip or one with ulterior motives.

Karen offered to drive and they headed into town in her hire car, making small talk on the way. Neither was entirely comfortable and they acted like a young couple feeling each other out, fearful of opening up too much. Caslin had the same question going over and over in his mind. *Why was she here?* It was a question that he was too afraid to ask. They parked the car in an area predominantly used by the coach companies for bringing tourists in to see the sights. From there, they walked a short distance through a park towards the Ouse and took the towpath running alongside.

There were daytime dog walkers and the occasional jogger, but nothing like the volume of people that descended on the area in spring or summer. A tourist cruise boat passed them by. Caslin counted three passengers, seated near the bow, listening intently to the pre-recorded diatribe. Whatever Karen had been saying, he had long ago ceased listening and cut her off in mid-flow.

"Karen, I'm not being funny but *why* are you here?"

His wife looked over at the river as if spotting something of note.

"I need to speak to you about Christmas."

"And you couldn't do that over the phone?" Caslin felt it a fair question.

"It's not as simple as that."

Caslin waited but nothing more was forthcoming. Their progress scattered a few ducks, gathered on the path. They dropped effortlessly into the water but remained nearby, keeping a watchful eye on the newcomers. In all honesty, he didn't care what she wanted. He was pleased to have her here with him, albeit with mixed emotions. There was the burning desire to throw away what had gone before and ask, no plead, for her to give them another chance. That very thought flashed through his mind and his lips moved to ask the question but no sound emanated from within. Never had he felt so powerless. At that very moment he would have given everything he had, all that he achieved in life, just to hear her say the same words. She didn't.

"Nate, I've met someone."

Those words should have hit home like a hammer but they failed to. Instead, the moment of intense emotion was replaced by a vague numbness that settled over him. What Karen had said meant nothing, changed nothing. He still wanted her back and, in his mind, that was just as likely now as it was five minutes previously.

All he could muster in reply was a tame, "Oh."

Karen was frustrated at the response, "Is that all you're going to say?"

Caslin blew out his cheeks. What was he supposed to say? The last thing he wanted was to appear hurt, which he was, or to react in an undignified manner, which he might still. There was the instinctive reaction to remain calm, aloof to the fact that she had seemingly moved on. That would give the outward impression that he was confident within himself, more than able to cope with life after her. Then there was the underlying fear that she would see right through that façade to the broken, pitiful creature that he had become. With more rational thought, the reality was that he was most likely to be found somewhere in between.

"Nathaniel?"

"Erm… congratulations," the word stung as it crossed his lips.

"Really, do you mean that?"

It dawned on him that Karen was actually seeking his approval.

"Yes, I guess so," he lied as convincingly as he could. "I've only ever wanted what was best for you." The latter was true and remained so.

"He's a doctor. He works out of the neurological unit at —"

"Now that, I don't really want to know, Karen. I'm understanding but let's not push it."

A few minutes passed in silence and they resumed their walk along the towpath. For his part, Caslin spent the time turning their situation over in his mind. How had they reached this point? He often thought that instructing divorce solicitors had been the point of no return but this appeared more finite. Karen had found a new partner, someone else with whom to share those intimate moments. This truly was a stone marker on the impending death of their marriage.

"I haven't told the kids, yet," Karen said solemnly. "I'm not sure how they'll take it."

Caslin shrugged, "Strangely, of the two, I think Lizzie will handle it better. I know she's the youngest but she's well ahead emotionally."

"And Sean?"

Caslin shook his head, "It's hard to know what he thinks about anything. Does the boy even speak anymore, or has he taken a monastic vow of silence?"

Karen laughed with genuine humour, "I get that too."

"What's so funny?" Caslin asked.

"You could almost always defuse any given situation, Nathaniel Caslin."

"Almost."

They stopped walking and turned to face each other. Karen reached out and took both of his hands in hers. The lines of her features softened by the winter sun and a gentle smile.

"You understand why I had to come?"

He nodded, "Karen, I know this isn't great timing, there never will be a good time but do you think we could—"

"Don't, Nate, please…"

"It's barely been a year. Surely we could try once—"

"No Nathaniel, just stop!" she snapped at him, releasing his hands from her grip. In that moment, Caslin went from feeling a sense of warmth and hopeless optimism to that of an embarrassed, grovelling wretch.

Karen started up the pace, once more, this time with more purpose. Her expression took on the stone-faced persona that he had come to recognise in the past eighteen months.

"Crispin has a holiday home in Normandy. He's invited us to spend Christmas and New Year with him there. I thought it would be a nice break for the kids after all they've been through."

"Sounds about right."

"Don't start with me, Nathaniel. I'll bet you hadn't even considered the holidays. You can have them for a week in January, before they start back at school, okay?"

"Whatever you say, Karen," Caslin bit back. "You've got it all figured out as always."

Caslin turned on his heel and without a second glance, stalked away. He was annoyed with himself for failing to mask his emotions and even more so, for practically begging her to come back to him. Nothing good ever seemed to come from them talking anymore. The frustration further riled him as he considered that every time he thought he had hit rock bottom, he struck another level.

THE TIME WAS WELL past 7 p.m. when his knuckles rapped on the door of Room 211. After waiting for a minute, the door creaked open and a bleary-eyed Colin Brotherton beckoned Caslin to enter. The room was like any other chain hotel that he had seen, an ensuite shower room by the entrance, a double bed, with a sofa and small desk beyond it. The smell of stale smoke hung in the air, despite the cold breeze drifting through an open window. The bed was neatly made and if not for a battered suitcase with a raincoat draped over it at the foot, he would have been forgiven for thinking the room was unoccupied. On the desk sat an archive box. Several dates could be made out scrawled on the side in faded marker pen, along with a case number.

"There it is. That's all I have."

Caslin masked his disappointment as he lifted the lid and scanned through the contents. There didn't appear to be much there, considering it was a murder inquiry. The unasked question became apparent and the retired DS saw fit to answer.

"This was all I was able to appropriate. I know it's not a lot."

"Appropriate?"

"What I euphemistically call it. *Stole* is more accurate. When the case started to go cold, people were reassigned and the team decreased in size, week on week. When it was shelved, all the paperwork was archived and there were tonnes of the stuff. This was all I managed to siphon off, on the quiet."

"You kept the investigation going then, in your own time."

"I told you I couldn't let it go. I took only what I thought was really pertinent."

Caslin was silent as he sifted the contents. There were witness statements and crime scene photographs, pathologist notes from

Maxine de la Grange's autopsy along with copious notes from a number of detectives on the case.

"Would the remaining evidence have been computerised yet?"

Brotherton shook his head, "I doubt it very much but the hard copies will still be in the archives. They're pretty good with that sort of thing."

"I wish I could say the same. In my experience if they haven't shredded it, then they've usually lost it."

Caslin saw no reason to hang about and replaced the lid. Lifting up the box, he made for the door. After insisting that he wasn't just humouring an old man and promising to keep him informed, Caslin said his farewells and walked to his car. Despite the thickness of his coat, the cold wind cut through him and he shivered. His fingers were numb by the time he rested the box on the bonnet and unlocked the door. He hoped that the alcohol on his breath hadn't been too oppressive. If so, Brotherton had given no indication of noticing.

Karen's visit had thrown him somewhat and he had failed to respond in the proper fashion. Had it not been for the agreed meeting that evening, he would surely still be in a pub, feeling particularly sorry for himself. Having considered, and then swiftly dismissed, calling Karen to apologise, he had skipped his afternoon plans and hit the beer. Now his head was thumping and his eyelids were heavy but he had managed to keep it together, for the time being at least.

Glancing at the archive box on the passenger seat, he clipped on his seatbelt and turned the key in the ignition. Knowing full well that he shouldn't be driving, he ignored the thought. Instead, he acted in the same cavalier fashion towards life that he always took when the dark mood descended. His phone began to ring, and taking it from his inner pocket, he saw that it was Harman. Caslin was irritable and wanted to be left alone. He rejected the call and threw the phone onto the seat, alongside the archive box. Pressing the accelerator, he left the car park, pulling out onto the main road. Traffic built steadily as he hit the outskirts of town, heading for home.

Once back at Kleiser's Court, with a curry and a scotch under his belt, Caslin went through the contents of the box. The autopsy report detailed much of what he already knew from his earlier conversations that day and the scenes of crime report was meticulous in its coverage. Brotherton was correct, for Maxine de la Grange had been a pretty girl, whose life had come to a shocking and premature end. Reading about her teenage years he identified several missed opportunities for an intervention where she could have been steered in a new direction. How often did he consider that when cases came across his desk? With a regularity that was far too alarming.

However, what had become of her certainly didn't ring true as a trick gone bad, which was the line of inquiry that the investigation appeared to favour. Absence of a sexual assault wasn't in itself definitive but the method of death, a combination of beating, stabbing and mutilation akin to torture, implied a more personal motive.

It was perhaps forgivable for the detectives at the time to have believed this the actions of a deranged madman, but with the benefit of modern interpretations of violent events, Caslin had to agree with Brotherton. Something didn't sit well with him either. Anyone demonstrating that level of psychopathy would not have carried out a first-time attack with such brutality, nor would they be able to make it a one off. The pressure to continue to develop even greater, bolder experiences would be all consuming and yet, according to the file that attack was a singular event. If the perpetrator had been imprisoned for another offence, or died, then that might explain the lack of further incidents but there was nothing to indicate that that was the case.

Turning his attention to the file on Lucy Stafford, he first took a look at the accompanying photograph. Taken when she was sixteen and arrested for shoplifting, Caslin tried to picture her as a grown woman, thirty years senior. Unsurprisingly, he struggled to see it and then once again found himself questioning Colin Brotherton's ability to do so from a grainy picture in a newspaper. In that moment he dislodged something in his memory. Wrestling with the detail, he fought to bring it forward but almost as quickly as it had sprung to mind it disappeared.

Reaching to the coffee table, he poured another Talisker. An unsteady hand made for too large a measure but he resigned himself to drinking it, nonetheless. Scanning through the rest of the file, he didn't see anything that caught his eye. There had been a cursory investigation into her disappearance but as he understood already, and concurred, there was no evidence to suggest foul play. Lucy Stafford was recorded as absent by will and nothing more was said.

Caslin's neck was aching and when he stood, he felt giddy and unsure of his footing. Now was most certainly the time to go to bed before he fell asleep in the chair. Tossing the file back into the box, he opted to leave the witness statements for another day and headed off to the bedroom. No clearer as to whether Skellon *was* Stafford, let alone *why* she would be, he pushed it all from the forefront of his mind.

Whilst undressing, images of Karen came to mind and he wondered whether she was thinking of him. Although drunk, he accepted that it was unlikely. Crawling under the duvet he felt his head spinning and he closed his eyes, wishing for the serenity of sleep. His smiling wife and children sitting around a roaring fire, a handsome doctor handing out presents with an illuminated tree in the background, were the last thoughts that came into focus as he drifted off.

CHAPTER TWENTY

SURPRISINGLY, the following morning began with a clear head. The sun was low in the sky and the air crisp, with only a light wind. The local radio station had a stand-in presenter who, for a change, favoured music over inane chatter and chose songs from a by-gone age, the seventies. Caslin found music from that era inoffensive and far preferable to members of the public calling in to discuss their pension schemes with a studio guest. That was the last show that came to mind.

A particular song had been lodged in his head since he had pulled up but for the life of him, he couldn't remember who the performer was. Humming the chorus as he descended to the evidence locker of Fulford Road, he recounted the thought process that had led him there. Harman had followed up the missed call from the previous night with an early one that morning.

"Iain hasn't been able to rally the tech support that he wanted, so I've got the green light to take a look. I don't think he's too pleased about it, though."

"Robertson's never pleased about anything, comes with the birthplace."

Harman laughed, "I'll let you tell him that, Sir."

"Best not. What have you turned up?"

"Nothing so far."

"Call me when you do."

Caslin was frustrated by that conversation. He couldn't help but wonder what the point of the call had been. Harman should, by this stage in his career, be capable of getting on with it. Caslin only wanted a phone call when he had something pertinent to pass on. He felt like he was wet-nursing the lad at times.

However, the conversation started him thinking. Chloe had declared McNeil to be largely illiterate when it came to technology, a response that came too fast to have been contrived. However, the evidence was indicating something different. The digital transfer of recordings, simple enough Harman had said, but Caslin's technological level was apparently far greater than McNeil's, and he wouldn't know where to begin. Furthermore, why were only some copied and not all? Caslin recalled seeing a mobile phone within the pickup and yet, Chloe claimed Garry didn't own one. The implication was that he would be unable to use it if he had. However technophobic a person was, what were the odds in this day and age of someone under fifty not owning, nor knowing how to use, a mobile phone? Caslin couldn't name anyone who fitted that bill. He found it unlikely. Moreover, how on earth did a dedicated server, situated in a Cold War bunker, fit into this scenario?

Either something worthy of note had passed them by or Chloe was leading them up the garden path once more, but if so, what did she stand to gain? For the time being she had been bailed to return in a fortnight, charged with assaulting a police officer and time would tell if further charges would be levied. In the meantime, Frank Stephens had agreed a surveillance operation, albeit a limited one, to keep an eye on her movements. Caslin suspected she was in far deeper than she was presently prepared to let on.

Signing in at the desk, the signatures of previous visitors caught his eye. Gerry Trent had accessed the evidence room earlier in the week. DI Baxter had been down on two occasions the day before, signing in first for an hour at 11 a.m. and again at 16:40, for a brief period of twenty minutes. Replacing the clipboard in its holder, he was directed to the aisle where he would find Garry McNeil's effects.

Pulling the archive box forward, he hefted it up and over to a central table. From here he lifted the lid to observe the meagre contents. All that he had examined on the first night in the vehicle was there and he found nothing new to grab his attention. Deciding that it was worth a punt to check out CCTV footage, he made a note of the date and time on the fuel receipts to follow up later. The maps and tourist guide leaflets appeared out of place but as to why, he couldn't figure. Removing the mobile phone from its evidence bag, Caslin turned it on. The screen flashed into life. Slightly taken aback, Caslin watched as the boot up process went through its cycle. An error message notifying the absence of a SIM card came up on the screen before the low battery indicator flashed, and the handset powered down. Absently drumming his fingers on the screen, he assessed what that could mean. Flipping the handset over, he prised open the cover, tapped out the battery and checked for the SIM card. It wasn't there.

Unsure of exactly what else he hoped to achieve, he reassembled the phone and replaced it, along with the other items back into the box. Then he returned it to the shelf from where it came. Turning away, he checked that he had noted down the catalogue number and headed for the exit. Whilst signing out he scanned the page more thoroughly than he did on his way in before heading back upstairs. Instead of taking the route to CID as planned, he left via the main entrance, giving Linda a wave as he passed. Once outside he reached for his phone and brought up the contacts list, dialling the number as soon as he found it. The phone rang only twice before it connected.

"Good morning, Nate," an upbeat and familiar voice came through.

"Morning Sara, is the sun shining with you this morning?"

"You are so poor at basic pleasantries. I'd go so far as to say the most transparent individual I know, apart from my mother, perhaps. Let's skip them seeing as I'm busy down here. Fortunately for you though, I still love you."

Caslin laughed, his general mood lifting higher than it had been for some time.

"Sara, forgive my persistence. Honestly, I don't mean to badger you first thing in the morning, but did you manage to get anywhere with that little favour I asked the other day?"

"*Honestly*, don't apologise. We both know you don't mean it but you have saved me a phone call. And this was not a little favour, believe me. On this one you don't just owe me, you owe me big."

Caslin was intrigued.

"Really?"

"In fact, I would go further and say forget dinner next time you're in town. I want dancing, theatre tickets and a new outfit while you're at it. And I get to choose, all of it."

"Agreed, now tell me," Caslin barely hid his impatience.

"Special Branch."

"*Special Branch?*" Caslin reiterated.

"Yep."

"You're shitting me."

"I am most certainly not and judging by whom he works for," she paused, Caslin knew what was coming, "I think it's best that we keep this short. You never know who might be listening."

The line went dead. Caslin smiled again. He hadn't even had a chance to say thank you. All joking aside, Sara would've been serious about the night out and he was in no doubt she would collect. What the hell was Special Branch doing at Fulford Road? There was always the prospect that his source was wrong but he doubted it. She was thorough and he trusted her more than almost anybody else he knew.

Refocusing his attention on the task at hand, he dialled Harman's mobile number. Surprisingly, the DC answered. Caslin was expecting to have to leave a voicemail, knowing how poor the reception was at the farm.

"How are you getting on out there?"

Harman was positive. Caslin assumed it was a result of having a task to do that he had confidence in himself to fulfil.

"Well, very well. There was a layer of encryption that I've had to work through. Seriously out of date but still a high grade and far more than your average business system would carry, let alone a domestic one."

"What does that mean to a layman such as me?"

"This isn't off-the-shelf software. It may not be the latest update but to give you a context we don't use anything this sophisticated in our office. It's military grade stuff, at least from a few years ago, anyway."

Caslin assessed that for a moment.

"Would McNeil have had access to that sort of kit, could he have brought it with him when he left the army?"

Harman sounded uncertain, "In the infantry, I don't know. Perhaps in the Signals or the old Pioneer Corp. Was he involved in that?"

"From what we've been told, categorically not but let's see what we can turn up ourselves. How about the server, what's he been using it for?"

"Storing vast amounts of data and maintaining websites, by the looks of it."

"Do you need a server to do that? My son has his own website dedicated to… something or other, but he hasn't got a server. It's all hosted in the clouds or something."

For a moment he thought he heard quiet laughter at the other end of the line but chose to ignore it.

"It's not necessary, no. Not unless you want to keep control of your own data as well as that of those who access your domain."

"To what end?"

"Maybe he's making some money from whatever he's doing online."

"Hmm… what're the orientations of the websites?"

"I'll need a bit more time before I can tell you that. I'm only just getting to them."

"Okay, when you do, give me a shout. Have you had a look at McNeil's mobile phone?"

"No, didn't know he had one."

"Well then, I've got another little job for you the next time you're back at the station. Get a hold of it from the evidence room and see what you can find for me, dialled numbers, received calls, that sort of thing."

"Locations as well. If it has an inbuilt GPS system, we'll be able to see where he's gone."

"You can do that?"

Harman laughed out loud this time, "Yes, Sir. As long as it has inbuilt GPS. With a bit of luck, we could get a trace from the signal as it relayed through transmitter towers."

"You just said a bunch of things that I have no understanding of but it sounds good, do it. Talking of signals, how come you have one today?"

"Iain's set up a booster. I think his team were getting annoyed with being off the grid."

"Fair enough. You'll find the SIM is missing from the phone. Can you still access the stuff you said?"

"Depends on the phone but I'll take a look."

"Good man. Let me know what you come across."

"Will do."

"Oh, and Maxim."

"Yes, Sir."

"Don't take the piss."

"No, Sir."

Caslin hung up. Suddenly he felt very much like an analogue watch in a digital age. He felt old. The unknown song came back to mind as he headed for his car. Remembering that Dr Taylor had left him a message to say she had prepared a preliminary report on the body unearthed at

Radford Farm, he decided her office should be the next port of call.

MEETING ALISON TAYLOR in her office, instead of across a number of corpses, was far more pleasant. Immediately struck by how attracted to her he was, Caslin had to will himself to focus on the topic at hand, the unidentified body, rather than the shoulder-length dark hair that framed her finely sculptured features. Dressed in a business suit, Caslin couldn't help but admire her style as she bid him to take a seat opposite her. She passed him a file and he began to scan the one-page summary at the front.

"Death was as you suspected, ligature strangulation. I put his age range between mid-thirties and forty and died approximately two months ago."

"Can you be more specific?"

"Not at the moment, no. The estimate fits the time-frame of deterioration but the conditions he was buried in determine rate of decomposition and what with winter coming late, it's hard to tell. I've taken some larvae off the body and sent them to the laboratory for more tests, which will help narrow it down."

Caslin felt that was reasonable.

"He was a big guy," he said aloud, whilst reading through the results. "It's not an easy thing to strangle someone to death. It takes time."

"Indeed, it does. When you push on the muscles of the neck, they push back," Dr Taylor agreed with him. "It's much easier if the victim is unconscious when you do it, which is what I believe happened in this case."

"Why do you think so?"

"There was a wound to the back of the head that would most likely have been enough to incapacitate him. There aren't the usual signs of a struggle that I would expect to find if he was putting up a fight when he died. The red spots around the eyes back up asphyxia and the lack of muscle stress is consistent with an unconscious state at death."

"Any idea of the weapon used?"

"A blunt instrument is the best I can do, as wide as your palm possibly, and flat. It could as easily be a rock as a paperweight but it struck him with enough force to cause a bleed on the brain. He would have been in trouble without seeking medical help even if he hadn't been strangled."

Caslin thought for a moment, continuing to read.

"Were there any other injuries of note?"

"None that I found, although, it is a little odd that he had signs of pressure sores on his shoulder blades and to the rear of his hips."

"What could have caused that? He doesn't strike me as a bedridden individual."

"Certainly not, he's in good shape, apart from being dead." They both smiled at the inappropriate reference. "Most likely he had a prolonged spell lying down on a hard surface, with an inability to move."

"Any signs of restraint, marks on the wrists or ankles?"

Dr Taylor shook her head, "I considered that but no, there were not. Before you ask, I carried out a full toxicological screening as well and found no drugs in his system. There is always the likelihood that they would no longer be traceable after this length of time."

"You were thinking along the lines of a *roofie* or *GHB*?"

"That would make sense if you wanted to incapacitate someone for a period of time, and they were a strong individual, or perhaps physically larger than you. Let's face it they're date rape drugs for a reason."

"In your opinion is it possible that a female of greatly inferior stature could have done this, or would we need the perpetrator to be considered stronger, as in more likely a male?"

"I would say that this could be done by more or less anyone. Provided they were in reasonable health, anyone could have killed this man once he was incapacitated. He was already very far gone by the time the air stopped entering his lungs."

"Any DNA under fingernails, unidentified blood?"

"I scraped the fingernails but they were in a state. A fair amount of damage to the flesh at the end of the fingers also as if he was scratching at something. So, in short, I expect that's unlikely but when the results come back, I'll give you a call. I was able to use water to inflate the fingers, so you have a full set of prints to work with. However, the body had been doused with bleach and I mean heavily soaked. So much so, that if there was any organic matter from your killer, it was destroyed. Although..."

"Although?" Caslin asked.

"I'm not entirely sure that the bleach was poured at the time of death. It is possible that it was done more recently."

"What makes you say that?"

"The soil and vegetation on the body are of mixed origin. As if some samples had had more recent exposure above ground than others. Have you ever heard of *The Body Farm*?"

Caslin shook his head, "No, sounds ominous."

"It's at the University of Tennessee. They have an outdoor area utilised specifically for the study of decomposition rates of the human body. Their subjects are exposed to different environmental conditions, timescales, seasonal trends, insect exposure. Almost any factor that you can imagine is analysed. From a forensic pathology point of view, it is truly fascinating."

"That sounds... a little creepy, to me."

Dr Taylor laughed. It was a gentle sound and caused Caslin to smile.

"The environmental conditions, insect infestations and the type of organic matter surrounding the body can make a significant difference in determining length of time in the ground. I've ordered some extra tests to try and ascertain if I'm right or not."

"When do you think you'll have something?"

"If I could have a couple of days, then I'll be able to give you a more definitive answer."

Caslin nodded enthusiastically, "By all means do. Perhaps we could meet and discuss the results?"

He was unsure of where that invitation had come from, but was now committed, and hoped that the wave of anxiety currently washing over him would not become apparent. Dr Taylor paused before responding, casting a momentary eye over him.

"I'm sure we will be able to arrange to discuss it. If not in person, then certainly over the phone."

Caslin was crushed.

She continued, "The effects of the bleach on the body are also unusual, which further backs up the notion that it was added significantly later, after death. That could indicate—"

"That the body was dug up, to destroy evidence?"

"Possibly," the pathologist was hesitant, "but please don't quote me on it, just yet. I haven't made too much of it in my preliminary report that you have there."

"Don't worry, I won't. That's very interesting. Good work, Doctor."

Caslin felt himself wince at his response, certain that she would see straight through the feeble praise, recognising his growing infatuation. It felt like he was back in the playground. Caslin felt his cheeks flush. For her part Dr Taylor didn't appear to notice. If she had, then she hid it well.

CHAPTER TWENTY-ONE

A MATCH for the set of fingerprints provided by Dr Taylor took only a matter of minutes to return. To Caslin's surprise it was not Daniel Horsvedt but a William Johnson whose information appeared. Previously he had been arrested for several drunk and disorderly offences, none of which were recent. He hadn't otherwise been known to the police in the past five years. His last known address was registered in Ipswich but that was several years ago.

A cursory examination had shown that Johnson had served in the British Army but only for four years, never seeing frontline service. A call to the MOD returned information that he had been removed from duty due to alcoholism, leading to neglect of duty. He had been dishonourably discharged from the Royal Electrical and Mechanical Engineers shortly after. Divorced, with no known next of kin, there was no discernable link to Radford Farm or Garry McNeil.

Having nursed a cup of coffee for over an hour, Caslin felt his frustration mounting. He had reviewed the forensic reports that were coming in from Robertson's team, without finding anything that could steer him in a useful direction. They had located a pit, barely large enough to conceal a person, beneath the filthy mattress within the bunker. A sheet of heavy-gauge ply, restrained with a padlock, prevented the inhabitant from being able to escape. This was believed to be the holding place for William Johnson, at least until his death. The underside of the wood showed clear signs of someone tearing the ends of their fingers to shreds in repeated attempts to claw their way out. The requirement for such a place was lost on Caslin. Was it as simple as a secure location to detain someone? Perhaps it was a more sinister method of control, a way of conditioning a captive to conform? The former was unsettling enough but the latter, indicated a malevolence of spirit that made him shudder at the thought of what occurred within those walls.

To further compound the issues that he faced, the press had latched onto the investigation. A lid had been kept on most of the details, Caslin was unsure how though. Considering the early admissions that had leaked out, they had largely avoided too much press intrusion up until now. However, that had changed with the early morning releases. Some had gone with links to the Ravenscar killings. That was the story that had fed the media for days with sensationalism but, without new information emerging, had subsequently begun to tire. Other publications now led with a second serial killer roaming Yorkshire.

Caslin had considered an immediate riposte to highlight that the perpetrator was in fact most likely, already dead, but thought better of it. In his own mind, it was the *most likely* part of his statement that would fuel the speculation further. After all, until the investigation was complete he couldn't categorically state that McNeil was guilty. Moreover, the press were less interested in the truth and far more so in selling copy. Any statement from him would only make the situation worse.

No matter how often he reviewed the files, Caslin could not help but think that he had missed something. There was an answer within the mountain of paper that he was sifting through. The one piece of the jigsaw that would help bring it all together, he was sure. He just couldn't find it. It was only ten-thirty in the morning but his eyes were already strained and he rubbed at them with thumb and forefinger. Tossing the last report onto the desk in front of him, he stood up and stretched. Maybe he had to come at it from a different angle, only he couldn't find the angle. The phone before him on the desk buzzed and he answered it. Linda's voice met his ear.

"Nathaniel, I have a message from Mr Trent, for you. He can't get you on your mobile."

"That's because I don't answer it but go on."

"He has asked for a copy of your latest report, to ensure that his investigation is kept up to date."

Caslin smiled, "He will have to wait, Linda. I haven't written it yet. Cutbacks mean I'm low on ink."

She laughed, "Is that what you want me to tell him?"

"No. Please tell him I will provide it as soon as I have been able to ascertain its accuracy."

"Will do, oh… and will you be contacting him as soon as you are available."

"Of course. He will be top of my list."

"Thank you, Nathaniel."

"Always a pleasure, Linda."

It was a small and childish delight that he took in giving Gerry Trent the runaround. However, there was some truth in what he said. He honestly didn't know where this case was taking him. The longer it went on, the less he felt he knew Garry McNeil and what he had been up to.

It was at that moment that something his father had said came back to him. The thread came to mind and threatened to vanish almost as quickly. Pulling on his coat he headed out of the squad room for the stairs. As he descended, he looked up his father's number and dialled it. The phone rang out and Caslin cursed. Something his father had said about his brother, Stefan, kept repeating on him. It was important, he knew it. He waited until he reached his car before trying again and this time his father picked up.

"Dad, it's me," Caslin stated as he turned the key in the ignition. The car stuttered into life at the second time of asking.

"Ah, Nathaniel, I was wondering when you would call—"

"Dad, sorry for interrupting," Caslin cut him off. "I don't have a lot of time but I need to ask you something."

"Go on."

Caslin was pleased he didn't have to verbally joust to get his father focused.

"Do you remember when you told me that Stefan was having problems?"

"Which time? He has had problems for years."

"No, I mean recently. When we picked up the kids... look, that doesn't matter but do you remember saying that he was a lot better? He had friends or something and that seemed to be helping."

"Oh yes, that group that he joined. I remember now. They seem to have things in common. I think time with them calms him down."

"Excellent. What sort of group is it, do you know?"

His father thought for a moment and sounded unsure, more than a little hesitant.

"I think it's an ex-serviceman's group. They meet every few weeks for a drink or a game of darts. I don't know where, mind you—"

"That's not important, Dad. Very helpful though. I'll speak to you soon."

"When are you going to call him, then?"

"Who?"

"Stefan."

Caslin paused before replying. He took his hands off the steering wheel and looked out of the window at nothing in particular.

"Yes, Dad. I will, I promise."

With that he hung up and sat in silence listening to the engine ticking over, phone still in hand. The windows of the car had steamed up and he could see little beyond them. Adjusting the blowers and angling the vents, he contemplated the significance of his thought process as the fans set to work. Chloe said that McNeil had found civilian life difficult following his last tour. The man appeared to be, by all accounts, a bit of a recluse. No wonder, judging by his hobbies, Caslin thought as Radford Farm came to mind. William Johnson had been ex-military. Perhaps McNeil had also reached out to former soldiers in an attempt to fit in?

Caslin went back to his phone. He wasn't comfortable doing so, finding the touch keyboard too small but he had used the internet function on occasion. Bringing up Explorer, he typed in "ex-servicemen Yorkshire". The search returned a bewildering number of entries, including several books to be bought online as well as a hotel reservation page that had nothing to do with his requirements. Modern technology was irritating. Thinking about it logically, he re-entered "Yorkshire Rifles" and hit return. Skipping the sponsored ads this time, he found links to some historical sites and a surprising number of airgun suppliers in the South Yorkshire area.

Reading through the list he eventually found what he was looking for, a webpage for ex-servicemen from the regiment. Tapping the link, he scrolled down the page, finding it fairly basic by modern standards. Little more than a blog promoting forthcoming social events there was not much detail to be gleaned, except that the next event was to be held that night, at a pub in Catterick. Caslin tapped the name of the venue and its location came up on a map in another window. The gathering was scheduled for any time after 6 p.m., they were his type of people. Looking at the clock he realised that he could make it comfortably, even stopping to grab some food on the way.

His phone began to ring and one glance told him that it was his father. Focused on getting over to Catterick, he figured he could always return the call later on. Clicking the standby button on the side of the handset he rejected the call, letting it go to voicemail. Knowing that the battery was running low, along with his father's persistence, he turned the phone off. The wind-screen was now clear enough to make driving safe and, tossing his phone onto the passenger seat, he reversed out and headed for the exit. This was a long shot and he knew it but saw no harm.

The forty-mile journey was uneventful and he found the pub with ease. The Colburn Lodge was on the main Catterick through road. Having made it there for five o'clock, he decided that it was as good a place as any to eat. Taking up a table with a clear view of the bar, he set himself up to observe who would come and go. The menu was agreeable, if a little pricey, but that was the norm when eating out in pubs these days. A microwaved main meal was just shy of ten pounds almost anywhere. Playing it safe he went with the English staple of lasagne, chips and a side of garlic bread. He waited patiently with a pint of bitter to wash the food down, whilst casually flicking through the complimentary news-paper. He deliberately avoided the front-page story in order not to annoy himself.

Only a handful of patrons had entered the bar by seven-thirty and Caslin began to wonder if he had set himself up for disap-pointment. Those present were not all together. Two were clearly businessmen, due to their attire and constant use of smartphones, another was a pensioner who sat in the corner with a half of lager and ignored the world around him. That left only a pair of men propping up the bar. Caslin guessed them to be about the right age.

Figuring that there was nothing to lose he sidled up to them and introduced himself. He saw little to gain from being coy with why he was there and asked them outright if they knew Garry McNeil. Half expecting a blank response, he was cheered to know that they not only knew him but he had also attended their meet-ings on occasion.

"Aye, he stopped by from time to time," the first man, going by the name of Rob, stated.

He was in his late forties and powerfully built, although

rapidly going to fat, with arms heavily decorated in body art. His receding hairline was cut close to the scalp.

"Can you tell me anything about him? How did he come across?"

Rob shrugged, "He was like most of us. Good for a laugh, up for the banter. You know, one of the boys."

"Most of the time," the other joined in. A man by the name of Tom, slender in build and also in his forties, Caslin guessed. He had the paunch of a beer drinker well beyond his years.

"Not always, though?" Caslin asked.

"Ah, we all have our off days, don't we? But he could be a moody sod when he felt like it. Sometimes I wondered why he showed up. Used to sit in the corner, on his own, with one drink all night and barely speak to you."

"Often?"

Tom shrugged, "No, not really. Most of the time he was a top man."

"Any of you particularly close to him? I am assuming your turnout is often higher than this?"

Caslin tried not to sound condescending. There was no need, both men smiled.

"Others will be along later. I just stick an early time on the webpage so that I have the excuse to get away from the wife at a reasonable time," Tom said.

Caslin laughed, "So was he close to anyone?"

Both men looked at each other. Caslin read their expressions as thoughtful and their responses honest. Tom shrugged and Rob shook his head.

"Not really. I mean everyone liked him, he was a good guy. Shame what happened. What's going on with that anyway?" Tom asked. There was an accusatory edge in his tone.

"Well it was a suicide, no question about that but we don't know why yet."

Both men glanced at each other. Tom appeared to sneer at Caslin's response but Rob shrugged it off.

"A real shame. Personally, I don't think your lot had anything to do with it. My old man's ex-job, so I know how it is," Rob offered.

"So is mine," Caslin added. "Well, thanks for your time. If you have any thoughts that come to mind, no matter if you think they're insignificant, please give me a call."

Caslin handed them both one of his contact cards and made to leave. He reached the end of the bar before Tom called after him.

"There was one guy."

Caslin returned, "What guy?"

Tom looked to Rob, "You remember he brought that bloke with him a couple of times, to the pool tournament and I'm sure some other time, as well. What was his name?"

Both men thought on it for a while, looking a little lost before Rob's expression brightened.

"Oh... erm... yeah, Charlie!"

"That's it, Charlie!" Tom reiterated excitedly. "He brought him along. He was a strange one though. He never spoke a word to us. It was all a little odd."

Caslin took out his notebook, "Charlie," he wrote as he spoke, "and was he with the Rifles as well?"

Tom shook his head, "Not as far as I know but definitely military. At least that's what Garry told me."

"Do you have a second name?"

"That wasn't his first," Rob chimed in.

"That's right. We just called him Charlie because he was a gook."

Caslin stopped writing, struggling to keep his tone non-confrontational.

"Because he was... what?"

"Sorry, Inspector, not meaning to sound racist. It's just Garry never introduced him, so we gave him the name. He looked VC. You know, *Viet Cong*."

"So, he was Asian?"

"Of origin, yes but definitely spoke English like a native. I heard him ordering drinks."

"What was his age? Any accent or distinguishing features?"

Tom thought about it, "He was younger than Garry. In his thirties, I would guess."

He looked to his friend for confirmation.

"Yeah, I would say so. His accent was northern, east coast. '*umberside* would be my best guess."

Caslin smiled at the mocking pronunciation.

"Definitely military, you said?"

"Well, Garry did and he always seemed on the level. Not one to bullshit, unlike most of our group."

Rob laughed at that before adding, "He didn't strike me as infantry, though. Charlie, I mean. He was short and wiry, looked like he would snap in the wind—"

"Proper geek too, I reckon," Tom added. "Peering out from behind those NHS specs like a little yellow, Joe 90."

Both men burst out laughing. Caslin was annoyed that they were providing potentially useful information as the thought came to him that he would love to be able to stick them on for something… anything.

"You think Garry was tight with this guy?" he asked, as the laughter subsided.

Tom nodded, "Charlie didn't talk to anyone else but he only came a few times."

"Always with Garry?"

Both men nodded.

"When was the last time you saw him?"

"They were both here last month. I think it was last month, anyway. Could've been a bit longer but I've not seen Garry since then, so that's why it sticks in my mind."

"While I think about it," Caslin had had another thought. "How did Garry seem to cope with his injury?"

Both men glanced at each other and then back to Caslin.

"Injury?" Rob asked.

"Yes, he had trouble with his back, didn't he?"

Tom shrugged, but his friend shook his head before answering.

"He always managed at rugby and football, right enough. Nearly won the pool comp' as well. Would've too, if he hadn't been wasted by the final."

"Perhaps I was confusing him with someone else," Caslin said, brushing off his own question. "Thanks again. If you think of anything else that might be relevant, can you give me a call?"

The men said they would and Caslin left them at the bar, confident that he had obtained all that he could from the visit. He was momentarily disturbed by the fact that he had found those men quite agreeable, right up until they revealed their bigotry. At least he had another lead to follow up on.

CHAPTER TWENTY-TWO

IT WAS past ten o'clock when the door to Kleiser's Court closed behind him. Throwing his coat across the coffee table, he flicked on the lamp behind his armchair and headed for the kitchen. Returning with a glass he poured a scotch and dropped into the seat, resting his head against the back and drawing a deep breath. What had he learned throughout the course of the day? Either McNeil had exaggerated his illness to hasten his departure from the forces, or Chloe had been lying. There was a possibility that both might be true. He had a thought and hastily got up to locate and then root through, Dr Taylor's post mortem report, only to find that she had not commented on any notable back condition. That didn't prove there wasn't one but he hated it when facts became obscured by contradiction.

McNeil appeared to find some pleasure in mixing with those of a shared background. Perhaps he was not such a loner after all. Furthermore, who was the stranger that he brought with him on occasion. What was his connection? Caslin felt that this man had a role to play. It was odd that "Charlie" didn't mix at all with the group. Why attend if you had no intention of even speaking, let alone forming bonds of friendship? It was yet another piece that just didn't fit, at least not to Caslin.

Reaching for a top-up, he caught sight of his phone on the table. He had switched it off when his father had called and hadn't bothered to turn it back on. A frustrating five-minute search ensued for the phone charger, eventually locating it in the socket next to his bedside table. Returning to the living room, he plugged it in and then turned on the phone.

Gerry Trent came to mind and Caslin thought that he had better produce something for him to read in the coming day. As much as he enjoyed testing the man's patience, he was well aware that there were limits and knowing when to push, and when to concede, was essential. His phone vibrated momentarily before a swift succession of beeps came to his ear. Nursing his drink casually as he leant forward, he scanned through his notifications. There were five missed calls, two from Harman's mobile and a further three from Fulford Road. The last was received at just before 9 o'clock that night. There was a voicemail notification also and Caslin tapped the link.

The phone took an age to connect before playback began and he was grossly underwhelmed when it eventually did so. There was no voice, only a little indistinguishable background noise lasting for less than twenty seconds, before the call was ended. The number was not stored either and Caslin put his phone down on to the table in relative disgust. His thoughts moved onto Karen and the kids. As much as he was aggravated by their situation, he knew that he would let them go out to France for Christmas, without making a great deal of fuss. What could he offer them anyway, another visit with their grandfather? He could count on one hand the number of holiday periods where he had been present the entire time without interruption. Why would this year be any different? The phone call he would have to make to Karen would no doubt stick in his craw but with the alcohol currently washing through his system, he felt that he would manage.

Reaching for his phone again, he called Terry Holt. It was his shift to be keeping a watchful eye on Chloe McNeil that night. A bored and despondent voice answered.

"Hello."

"Anything happening tonight, Terry?"

"No, Sir. She went out around five, to a neighbour's place. He's a known dealer, soft recreational stuff, nothing to get excited about. She was back home within an hour and hasn't left since. No activity, no visitors. If I try, I think I can see the green haze coming out of the air bricks."

"Okay, stay at it and don't fall asleep."

"No, Sir."

Caslin was hanging up and overheard Holt muttering to himself in the belief that the conversation was over.

"No activity. No visitors… no point."

Caslin ignored him. Pressing the phone to his lips, he contemplated their approach. Was he on the right track? In the absence of any clear indication to the contrary, he would persevere. Suddenly he felt tired to his very core. Glancing at the time, he saw it was barely eleven but his eyes were closing of their own volition. Standing, he realised he was unsteady on his feet and decided to go to bed. Finishing his drink, he switched out the light and didn't bother to wash. Throwing himself onto the bed without undressing, he was asleep within minutes.

Rising, feeling refreshed, he made it into Fulford Road before 8 a.m., having first called in at the café below his apartment to pick up a breakfast roll and a cup of coffee. On the way through he noticed that Linda wasn't in reception and hoped that she was just running late. She was never late. Taking the stairs up to CID two at a time, he found the squad room was deserted. Why that was, he could only guess at. For once ignoring the progress boards for the Ravenscar case, he pulled up a chair and powered up his laptop. As expected, he found several emails marked for attention. One was from Harman, sent the previous afternoon, and scanning through it he picked up the general information.

The websites managed through McNeil's server had been mixed content, from pornography to get-rich-quick schemes. Caslin didn't understand the reference to something called "Tor" but Harman highlighted it as particularly notable.

Sifting through the spam in his inbox, he opened an email from Dr Taylor. She had been able to ascertain that William Johnson had indeed been buried twice, apparently uncovered and reburied within the previous ten days. Caslin found that time-frame curious and figured it was significant. He was also pleased to see that Dr Taylor had signed off her email by pointing out that he hadn't left her his personal number. He reflected on what she had written, not regarding the case, but as to whether she was inferring a social engagement. After several minutes of rereading and analysing the one sentence, it dawned on him that he had no way of knowing her intentions and decided that he would call her later that day.

Pulling out his phone he dialled Harman's number but the call wouldn't connect and was directed straight to voicemail. Looking around CID at the lack of presence, he decided now was a good time to pen an update for Gerry Trent and his investigation. He had no idea what the IPCC would make of everything that he had turned up to date. If he was honest, he couldn't comprehend it yet himself. It took well over an hour for him to compile a relatively complete time-frame of where his investigation had taken him thus far. Certain aspects he chose to not to share, therefore limiting his writing to the core detail alone. Once he had reviewed the piece several times and he was satisfied with the content, he attached it to an email and sent it directly to Trent.

The unhealthy breakfast left him still feeling hungry and he pulled on his coat to head down to the refectory to get something else to eat. There was a general background noise as he entered, not in itself unusual but there was a level of disquiet that was palpable. Caslin joined the queue. Picking up an apple and some fruit juice which he placed on his tray, he glanced around the room. There was something going on. He waited until the line shuffled up and he reached the till. No-one stood behind him and once clear he asked the operator, a retired lady whose name slipped his mind, what was going on. She shook her head, her face conveying a look of genuine sadness.

"That young lad in CID, it's very sad."

"Which lad?"

She seemed amazed at Caslin's ignorance, "That smartly dressed chap, the Chief Constable's son."

"Harman? What's he done now?"

"You haven't heard?"

Caslin stopped. Giving her his full attention, he conveyed an expression that demonstrated he truly had no idea what she was about to say.

"He was found early this morning, dead."

Passage of time ceased. The noise in the background no longer registered. It was as if the world had stopped spinning for the briefest of moments before Caslin was able to register the information. The lady before him was still talking. He could see the lips moving but no sound appeared to be coming to his ears.

"… cleaner found him, I heard—"

"Where?"

"In the bedroom, is what people are saying—"

"No, where? His apartment?"

She nodded, "Hanged they say. He was such a polite young man. Tragic really."

Caslin left his tray where it lay before the till and stumbled out of the canteen. He felt nauseous and with each step his feet felt heavier. Two officers greeted him as he passed by but he didn't respond. Once out in the corridor he stopped, propping his back against the wall and looking to the ceiling. He took a deep breath. Surely there was a mistake? Harman had seemed perfectly fine when he had spoken to him... when was it... yesterday, perhaps the day before? Quickly he made his way to the gents and after first checking that he was alone, ran a basin full of cold water. Cupping with both hands, he threw some over his face. Drawing his palms across his cheeks, he eyed himself in the mirror between breaths.

What was Harman looking at? The question sprang to the forefront of his mind. Had he stumbled across something that might have got him killed? Massaging his fingers into his cheeks and eyes, he let the water trickle from his chin, dripping back into the basin. A uniform entered behind him and Caslin pulled a couple of paper towels from the dispenser on the wall to dry his face, depositing them in the waste bin on his way out. Back in the corridor, he headed for the DCI's office with a determined pace.

DCI Stephens beckoned Caslin in, despite the latter's failure to knock.

"Is it true?" Caslin asked. Reading the haunted expression from across the room, he already knew the answer.

Frank Stephens nodded. His voice almost broke as he spoke.

"It's true. The housekeeper found him this morning, it was too late. There was nothing to be done for him."

Caslin stood just inside the office, thoughts coming to him in a random fashion.

"It's not right," he mumbled.

"We've seen it a hundred times, Nathaniel. But you're correct, it's not right."

"No, no. That's not what I meant. He's not the type."

"Well, I was there first thing this morning, with Atwood and Hunter. It's pretty clear. We found a bottle of anti-depressants in his kitchen, along with a repeat prescription. From the date on the label it seems he's been on them for some time."

"I had no idea."

"Nor did anyone else, by the look of it."

"It still doesn't make any sense."

"In these cases, does it ever?"

"Did you look for—"

"Of course, we bloody looked," Stephens' anger flared but he swiftly brought it back under control. "I know it's hard—"

"Did he leave anything?"

"No, nothing."

"That's unusual—"

"You're reaching," Stephens interrupted him. "It's not unusual and you know it. Michael pointed it out and he was right, that more often than not, people don't leave anything. Unless of course, you know something specific that the rest of us don't?"

Caslin thought about it but shook his head. Harman suggested that the content of his email was important but there was nothing to set alarm bells ringing.

"He tried to get a hold of me last night but I... my phone was off."

"Don't beat yourself up, Nathaniel. The lad was trying to escape his demons. He managed it."

Caslin sighed, "He was working on the computer set-up, out at Radford Farm."

"You think there's a connection?"

Caslin shook his head, "I can't see how it would be. He implied that he was on to something."

"Such as what?"

"I don't know."

"Check it out, make certain, if you feel it necessary."

"You're sure there was nothing to find, nothing out of place?"

"The apartment was what you would expect from Maxim. It was as immaculately turned out as him."

"Suicide," Caslin said softly.

"It doesn't sit well with me, either. He's one..." the DCI paused as his words caught in his throat, "one of our own."

THE ARTIFICIAL GLOW from the mixture of street and Christmas lights emanating from outside the apartment, lent the sitting room an ethereal appearance. He blinked several times. The sash window was cracked open and there were some revellers passing below. Their voices grew faint as they moved on. He hadn't imagined it. There was another knock at the door, it was his door. Looking around, Caslin tried to ascertain what time it was but he had no idea. The day had passed in a blur.

This wasn't the first time he had come across a colleague in similar events. Once he was called out to find a constable hanged in a garage, only two weeks following retirement, and three days after his wife had left him for another man. This was different, Harman was just starting out. The job shouldn't have worn him down so soon. He was inexperienced without a doubt but intelligent, and far more able than he was often given credit for, even by Caslin. Such a waste. However, no matter how often he replayed the conversation with Frank Stephens in his mind, the feeling of unease surrounding the circumstances tugged away at him. Could he have done more? Undoubtedly. Would he have been able to guide the younger man? Most probably. The thought that lingered more often than not, was that perhaps Maxim had chosen him to be his saviour. The number of calls made that day to Caslin's mobile could have been entirely professional, but were they? Unanswerable questions that constantly repeated in his mind.

The knock at the door came again, only this time more forcefully. Dragging himself upright, Caslin made his way out. Unlocking the deadbolt and opening the door without looking through the spy hole, he wished he had.

"Good evening, Inspector. Your landlady let me through the outer door."

"Good evening, Mr Trent."

The two men stared at each other in the dim light of the communal hallway for a few moments. The visitor offered up a brown paper bag. Caslin took it and inspected the contents. A bottle of Jura.

"Very nice. You had best come in."

Caslin led them back inside, putting on lights as they passed through into the sitting room. Trent took his coat off and for the moment at least, slung it over his forearm, choosing to remain standing.

"No need to break the seal on that just because I brought it for you."

Caslin laughed, "I've not had a drop all day, if that was what you were getting at."

Trent smiled easily in return, offering his hands out apologetically.

"Nothing was further from my thoughts. I remember that you are picky about who you drink with that's all."

Caslin headed out into the kitchen to pick up some glasses. Trent lay his coat across the back of a chair at the dining table, confident that he would be staying for a little while longer. Casually he took in the archive box that sat atop the table, running an index finger along the top of the files contained within. Tilting his head to one side, he raised an eyebrow as Caslin returned with two glasses in one hand and an ice cube tray in another.

"I prefer water with mine but I don't know how you take it."

"Ice will be fine," Trent replied. Indicating the files, he asked, "Who is Lucy Stafford?"

Caslin passed him a glass, now containing three ice cubes and offered up the scotch. Trent nodded and found his glass filled with a healthy measure.

"Just a cold case that I've had on the go."

Caslin put the bottle on the table and replaced the lid back onto the archive box.

"It was only a casual enquiry. I'm not here to give you any cause for concern."

Caslin smiled, "Up until recently, cold cases have been all that I've been tasked with. I don't mind telling you that it's been pretty much ball-ache for the past year."

Trent swirled the ice around in his glass.

"Bad Karma?"

Caslin assessed the man before him. There didn't appear to be any malice in his demeanour and he chose not to look for any. Raising his glass, they met eyes.

"To absent friends," Caslin said solemnly.

"Absent friends," Trent repeated.

Caslin took a seat and indicated for Trent to do the same but the latter declined, crossing to the far side of the room. He glanced down into the street below, taking in the view of the scaffolding against the building opposite. Without turning he began to speak. Caslin was stunned at what followed.

"I believe that I owe you an apology... of sorts," Trent said evenly. He glanced over his shoulder and could read the expression on Caslin's face, "No need to be concerned, Inspector. You're not dreaming. I feel that despite my best intentions I may have allowed our past connection to, how should I put it, influence my approach to this current investigation."

"Prejudice you, you mean?"

Trent turned and inclined his head ever so slightly, which was the closest Caslin would get to an acknowledgement. Both men took another sip before Trent continued.

"I have read your report and although your investigation is yet to be concluded, mine on the other hand, is pretty clear and concise. The full publication will have to wait for the conclusion of all official protocols and so on, but I feel it only fair and prudent to indicate—"

"Spit it out, Gerry."

"You are in the clear... well in the clear."

"I didn't put a foot wrong."

Trent shook his head, "I will admit that was not the conclusion that I was expecting to reach, but no. Nor did any of your colleagues, I might add. Perhaps a better search procedure but let us be candid, who looks for ampoules of poison with a Road Traffic Accident? Strange business."

"Not a lot stranger, to be sure."

"I was sorry to hear about your colleague."

Caslin didn't answer. He merely took on a distant look as he stared at nothing in particular.

"Any idea what would drive him to such a rash action?"

"Not really," Caslin sighed. "Work stress, self-esteem issues, overbearing parental expectations... pick your cliché. Maybe all of them, maybe none."

"It is hard to ascribe rational thought to such an irrational act."

Caslin had to agree. It was an assessment that summed it up in a nutshell. However, he was still struggling to resolve Harman's apparent suicide in his mind. Was that because of the burden to his conscience or was there really something else that he expected to find? If, as everyone kept telling him, it was self-inflicted, then the chances were that he would never know the reasoning behind it. That saddened him further still. Realising his glass was empty he rose and poured himself a refill, offering the same to his guest, who accepted. Ignoring the water this time, Caslin sipped at the neat scotch. The thought struck him how odd it was to be sharing this moment with a man whom he had hated with such a passion over the past two years.

"Just thinking about our situation, were you?" Caslin shrugged off the question. Trent held up a hand, "No need to answer. I could read the look you just gave me. Believe me I didn't think that I would be sharing a drink with you under the circumstances, either. It's funny how things go sometimes, isn't it?"

Caslin smiled as he re-seated himself.

"Seeing as we are breaking the moulds here, you should probably know that you were right."

Trent was intrigued, pulling out a dining chair. He sat down opposite Caslin and leaned forward, elbows to his knees.

"How so, with what?"

"I broke the rules and you punished me for it. Not saying that I agree with you. I had my reasons."

"You found the girl."

"Yes, I brought her home," Caslin glanced into his glass before drinking from it. "I promised her mother I would do just that."

"And you did."

"I did and her family were grateful."

"So, it would appear but in doing so, you prejudiced a future trial and the killer will never face justice for that crime."

"He's inside, he'll never get out. I can live with that and more importantly, so can her family."

"But not the family of the previous—"

"They had their day in court. He was found guilty and that's why he's never getting out."

"They wanted more."

"They usually do," Caslin said forlornly.

"The family felt that he should have gone down for the second girl as well."

Caslin shrugged, "We can't all have what we want, can we? They have no cause for complaint in my book."

Trent appeared rueful, "I did my job."

Caslin glanced up, his expression lightening, "And I did mine. It's just a bloody pity that you're so damn good at yours, though."

Both men laughed as they raised their glasses once more.

CHAPTER TWENTY-THREE

HARMAN HAD both called and sent Caslin an email, the latter was under review again today. At no point was anything other than case-related material contained within it. There was no indication of a mercy call as far as he could tell. At least that was his conclusion until 10 a.m. that morning. Answering the phone, he was surprised to find the caller was Anthony Harman, Maxim's father. Caught slightly off guard, Caslin didn't know what to say apart from the standard condolences that one offered. The words appeared wholly inadequate to him as they came out. The reason for the contact quickly became apparent, making the conversation even more uncomfortable.

"… my son admired you greatly," Chief Constable Harman said. "You were making a great impression on him."

Caslin felt like a cheat.

"… I don't know what to say…"

"There's no need to say anything. Only that you would do as I wish."

"I'm not sure that I can. I mean no disrespect, merely that there must be someone more qualified, more suitable—"

"I understand your concerns, Inspector. However, I must say that I had not seen my son so enthused with his work as he was in the past few weeks. This case, although disturbing to him, was inspirational. Much of which, I put down to you."

"I am still not sure, Sir."

"No need to make up your mind today. I appreciate that I've put you on the spot. Will you consider it over the next few days?"

"I'll do that, Sir."

"Perhaps I can come back to you once we have a date set?" Caslin agreed. Taking a role in Maxim's funeral service struck a sense of dread into him. The passing of a few days would not make him change his mind, of that he was certain. The call left him questioning what he thought he knew about the young detective. Having worked with him briefly, Caslin did not feel a particular bond with the lad, nor did he feel that their relationship was anything other than basic at best. Evidently Harman held a different view, one conveyed to his father. This was unsettling. Had Maxim called for help that night?

A question that he had compartmentalised returned to haunt him once again. Was he really the only person that Maxim could call upon in a personal crisis? It would seem that the old adage was true and you never really knew people. Although, Caslin had never claimed otherwise. Putting all that aside he considered Harman's rationale one more time. If he was so enthused why would he feel the need to die? An action fuelled by substance, perhaps? The lad had never struck him as an abuser of drink or drugs, and of all people, Caslin should be able to recognise one.

Michael Atwood appeared alongside and Caslin refocused his attention on the screen before him. Letting out a deep sigh, he glanced up.

"Struggling with something?" Atwood asked.

"Just going over the last email that Maxim sent me, you know, on the day…"

Atwood nodded, "Anything interesting?"

Caslin shrugged, "Get-rich-quick scams by the look of it, presumably a source of income. It's this *Tor* thing that Harman was banging on about, that has me wondering."

"*Tor*, what's that about then?"

"Well, I've no idea what it is for a start. Harman seemed to think it was significant though. I suppose he had planned to elaborate but…"

"Other things got on top of him."

"Something like that, yes. I'll have to check it out myself. I wish he was…" Caslin left the thought unfinished.

Atwood patted him gently on the shoulder and moved off, "I know."

Caslin put the thoughts to the back of his mind and brought up a search engine, typing "Tor" into the box. The enquiry returned thousands of hits and he navigated the list, ignoring the sponsored returns, until he found a Wikipedia entry. He double clicked the link, figuring their explanation would be comprehensible. The listing proved to be interesting. Tor was a software program that masked the identity of the user, thereby rendering them untraceable by anyone seeking their origin. Popular with political activists in oppressive states, the program was greatly utilised in places like China and Iran where internet content is strictly monitored. The IP address of the host computer would be replaced with a fake, providing genuine anonymity.

According to Harman, the number of such entries in McNeil's server indicated widespread access by a network of people using the program. The possibility of such a network made Caslin shudder. He hoped that wasn't the case, preferring a reality where McNeil's fetishes were his alone, the far lesser of two evils.

The conversation with Harman's father came back to mind and Caslin found himself considering who would stand up at his own funeral, when the time came? Probably his children. Logging out of the computer he shut it down, watching until the process completed and he was left staring at a black screen. Deciding that fresh air would be advantageous, he got up and headed for the exit. Perhaps this was a good time to follow up on Claire Skellon.

TRAFFIC WAS sparse around the city centre, an experience to be enjoyed seeing as it was so infrequent. Leaving the car in a small car park just beyond the city walls, Caslin made his way to Claire Skellon's place of work, a women's refuge within sight of the perimeter. A Victorian house, three storeys in height, had been adapted to provide a home for the charity. Approaching the main door, he rang the bell, noting the combination lock to the exterior as well as several dead bolts. The ground floor windows also had added security that was visible from where he stood.

There was movement within and after a moment the door opened. A lady in her fifties with straw-like, greying hair and half glasses, stood before him. He offered up his warrant card and was bidden entry. The door was closed and locked behind them. A figure appeared from a doorway further down the narrow hallway, a young woman with shoulder-length brown hair. As swiftly as she appeared she was gone again. Her age was impossible to tell in the gloom of the interior space. Sixties floral patterns adorned the walls beneath the dado rail, clashing with yet another floral design on the carpet. Neither lent an air of light or space to the hallway.

"You will have to forgive the reaction," the lady who'd identified herself as Ruby said, leading him further into the building, towards an office. It looked like the former sitting room to the house. "We don't get, nor encourage, many male visitors. Our residents have trust issues."

"Completely understandable."

"Don't take it personally, Inspector."

Caslin shook his head, "I don't wish to make anyone nervous. I'll get out of your way as soon as possible."

"No need, I am happy to help in any way I can."

"How well did you know Claire?"

"Oh, for at least ten years. I joined the project soon after she set this place up."

"Where did you meet her?"

"Initially in church."

"And this," Caslin indicated the refuge. "This was Claire's idea?"

"Indeed, it was. There were several years of raising money before the doors opened. Since then we've been able to move to bigger premises and we were looking to open a second refuge. Still, I dare say I don't know if that will happen now."

"This may sound an odd question but have you come across anyone who may have had a grudge against Claire in particular, or the refuge itself?"

"You don't think her death had anything to do with us? It is such a dreadful business, that poor family as well."

"It's just a line of inquiry we have to follow up, if only to rule it out."

Ruby thought for a moment, a look of stern concentration on her face, "There are the occasional unwelcome visitors here."

"Abusive partners?"

Ruby nodded, "We try to keep ourselves under the radar, so to speak. We aren't secret, just low profile. It's safer that way for the women."

"But some do show up?"

"Occasionally but not often, and we can keep them out until the police arrive. No-one has ever got past the front door. We tend to relocate every once in a while, anyway, so that our whereabouts don't become common knowledge. This building has been our home for a little over a year. No location is ever too permanent."

"No specific threats directed towards Claire herself?" Caslin asked as he scanned the framed pictures on the wall. Claire Skellon was prominent in several. Hiking trips by the look of them and once again he felt that he knew her.

"None directly, no. She would be able to handle it anyway, were it to happen. She's a strong… was… a strong woman. She didn't tolerate any nonsense."

"How well did you know her outside of this environment?"

"Not very well, really. Claire was so driven. She didn't have time for much else, what with this place and her church work."

"So, before she came to York, you don't know what she did, where she lived?"

Ruby's expression went vacant, "Come to think of it, no. I thought she was from York. Claire never talked about anywhere else."

"What about family, friends?"

Again, Ruby shook her head, "I guess it's true what they say, you never really know people, do you?"

Caslin had to agree, the déjà vu struck him as he said his farewells. The downstairs seemed deserted as he made his way out. No doubt his presence had impacted on the residents. The need for such a refuge was a damning indictment of society as far as he was concerned. Domestic violence had been an issue for as long as there had been relationships but women shouldn't have to disappear to be safe, certainly not in the modern age.

On the face of it the trip had been unsuccessful and yet, Caslin still felt it was worthwhile as he drove back to Fulford Road. The rain began to fall and the temperature outside was already barely above freezing. Despite being just past midday, it had the feel of night time already. Ruby was as helpful as she could be and her distinct lack of knowledge about Claire spoke volumes.

Claire Skellon was very private. If a fellow congregational member and co-worker of ten years knew absolutely nothing about your private life or personal history, then you were endeavouring to keep your past a secret. Perhaps there was just cause for her to do so, and in Caslin's mind, it went beyond mere privacy. Claire was hiding, running, or both but most definitely starting afresh. Whichever was the truth, there would be a motivating factor that made her choose that path.

No relatives had been uncovered when he had first looked and she had failed to show up in any police background check, nor any other inquiry that he had subsequently made, either. With hindsight there may have been good reason for such a lack of detail. For the first time, Caslin felt that Colin Brotherton could well have been right. The nagging sense that he was missing something came back to him, a feeling that he was unable to shake off, no matter how much he tried. Whatever he was missing, he was certain the incident team were too.

His return to Fulford turned out to be little more than a brief visit. Having spent much of Tuesday attempting to surreptitiously gain access to the files held by the Ravenscar incident team, he had been forced to abandon the task. His attempts had not gone unnoticed however and upon returning from the refuge, he was summoned to the DCI's office.

"You had your chance on Ravenscar but you couldn't be arsed. So why are you sticking your nose in?" Frank Stephens said with thinly veiled aggression in his tone.

"Professional curiosity, Guv," Caslin countered.

"Bollocks. *Professional* is not you at the moment, Nathaniel. I've briefed the team and you'll get nothing out of them. So, in future, don't bother asking. Get out!"

Banishment from CID hardly felt like a punishment to Caslin. Sitting at home, immersed in Brotherton's files as well as his own notes, Caslin was forced to try and reconcile what he knew about Claire Skellon with the facts listed before him. Needless to say, he was none the wiser in the pursuit of the elusive woman. The snooping had been a response to the brick walls that he repeatedly came up against at every turn. Prior to ten years ago she barely registered in the United Kingdom with no tax record, either council-held or at the Inland Revenue. Medical history was also non-existent and no records of marriage or divorce could be found. More tellingly, there was a distinct lack of financial data. The only significant lead that came to light was another person of the same name who shared the same birthday. However, she had died in childhood, as a result of a car accident, alongside her parents in 1976. There were no other living relatives listed.

The more that Caslin thought about it, the more he had to consider that these were one and the same person, at least in terms of identity. It was an alarming reality that with only a birth certificate it was still possible to obtain documentation to become that person. Indeed, the police had been using exactly that method to safely place deep-cover officers for many years. Any cursory inspection would only return genuine information.

There was little need to disguise his happiness at being out of the station. Perhaps it was a case of paranoia but he felt some were looking at him differently in the past week, more so than usual. All he could put that down to was Maxim Harman. If anyone felt that he should have seen the signs or done more then they kept their counsel. In this scenario people always looked for someone to blame and, having worked so closely with Harman recently, he was an easy target. He didn't doubt that the rumour mill was well underway. Ill will had followed him like a shadow for over a year, so a little more wouldn't make much of a difference.

Turning his focus towards the archive box, he compared the files relating to Lucy Stafford with his own cursory check and, just like Brotherton had found decades previously, there were no hits against that name in births, marriages or deaths. Furthermore, there had been no criminal arrests or convictions. Lucy had vanished. This didn't in itself link directly to Claire Skellon, who appeared over a decade later, but Caslin couldn't help drawing a parallel between the two women. After all, their age range matched, they shared a skill in living below the radar and in Claire Skellon's case at least, helping others to do likewise.

This was the coincidence that he now pondered. The documents received from the retired detective were meticulously documented in handwritten, as well as typed, formats. The team had been thorough. There would certainly have been no accusation of lax practice in a cold case review. What that meant now, though, was that it took an age to get through. The cross-referencing system was all done by hand and linking documents was excruciatingly slow. How complex crimes were solved prior to computerisation, Caslin could only wonder.

Progressing through the witness statements was particularly depressing. Over two hundred people had been interviewed by the team although Caslin had access to barely two dozen transcripts. Of these, many had been interviewed on at least two occasions. Often the statements contradicted each other, even when given by the same person within a month of each other. Many who occupied Maxine and Lucy's circle were drug users and this posed inherent problems for the investigators. People moving in the drug world lived outside of mainstream society and largely mixed with each other. This often led to passages of time with no recognisable markers. People honestly didn't know where they were at given moments. Statements would become vague and it became nigh on impossible to form an accurate picture.

Another unfortunate reality that detectives would encounter in this scenario was that substance abuse fuelled fall outs over money, drugs, debt and more often than not, people wouldn't even remember the cause. Put all that together, along with a healthy distrust of the police, and it was clear why the leads dried up. No wonder they struggled he thought as, not finding anything of note, he tossed the last of the files back into the box.

The vociferous nature of Lucy Stafford's statements had been evident, despite recording methods toning it down but Brotherton was right, she gave few details that generated leads. Almost in despair, Caslin picked up the inventory and scanned the list of witnesses, his index finger almost reaching the end before something caught his attention. Holding the list to one side, he thumbed through the folders looking for one in particular but to no avail, that statement was missing. Letting out a frustrated sigh, he sank back into his chair. He didn't believe in coincidences and never had. Replacing the list in the archive box, Caslin picked up his phone and dialled DC Underwood's number.

"Hello."

"Hayley, how are things? Any movement?"

"No, Sir. It's quiet but I'm pretty certain that we won't turn anything up here."

"Why not?"

"We stick out like a sore thumb. Everyone knows everyone around here and they will have scoped us out days ago."

"No doubt. Alright, let me know if anything interesting happens."

"Will do, Sir."

Caslin hung up. Why he thought that Chloe McNeil would do anything that would help their investigation momentarily escaped him. *No, that wasn't true*, criminals did the most stupid of things which led police to evidence all the time, even when knowingly under surveillance. If Chloe had something to hide, then a presence around her might just push her into taking a risk. She had already demonstrated an inability to cope with pressure if her interview was anything to go by. Maybe he was barking up the wrong tree and she was another victim in Garry McNeil's twisted existence, but there was more to her than they had seen, of that he was sure.

The intercom snapped him from his reverie, a shrill sound that cut through almost all other noise. The bustling sounds from Stonegate, beneath his apartment, were in the background as he rose and went to the door. Lifting the receiver, a familiar and not welcome voice, came to his ear.

"Good afternoon Inspector, could I have a word?"

The voice was distorted through the system but clear enough for Caslin to recognise Jimmy Sullivan's tone.

"To what do I owe this honour?"

"I would rather discuss it inside, if you wouldn't mind."

"That could lead me to another letter of complaint. At least out there we have the benefit of two hardwood doors separating us."

Sullivan laughed, "Oh come now, Mr Caslin. We are grown men. What's a bit of ink between... I hesitate to say friends. How about colleagues... with a degree of separation obviously?"

Caslin buzzed him in, hearing the lock click on the outside door and the journalist passing through before he replaced the receiver. The man was odious but Caslin was intrigued as to what would bring him to his door. For some reason he felt sure it would be unpleasant. He opened the door to the apartment and waited patiently as Sullivan made his way up the stairwell.

"Lovely place you have here," the journalist said as he crossed the threshold, wiping his shoes as he passed.

"Keeps the rain off," Caslin replied, leading them into the living room before asking the inevitable question. "What can I do for you?"

"Well for once, Inspector. Perhaps it is what I can do for you."

"Go on."

"Your little gremlin that has caused you so much trouble, I may be able to cast a little light on his shadow for you."

"You've lost me."

"Garry McNeil."

"What about him?"

"His past is even more interesting than I expect you realise. What would you say if I told you that his military service was not quite what we've been led to believe? Unless you are already up to speed?"

Caslin was interested but he maintained his composure, appearing to be quite the opposite.

"What do you have for me Jimmy?"

"Officially McNeil was invalided out of the army on a medical discharge, full honours."

"That is what we understand, yes."

"What if I told you he was perfectly healthy, physically anyway."

Caslin was very interested.

"Go on."

"His last tour saw him stationed just outside of Basra, Iraq. At a detention centre for former military, insurgent types."

"And?"

"My sources tell me that there was an incident at the prison, a number of inmates... how shall we say... came to an unfitting end."

"As a result of actions by British personnel?"

"Systematic abuse, along the lines of the US at Abu Ghraib, is what has been alleged."

"Alleged by whom?"

Sullivan smiled, "Now, now, Inspector. I must protect my sources. This is extremely sensitive information—"

"That you will publish at the first available opportunity. What has this to do with McNeil?"

"He was one of those involved… according to my source, anyway."

Caslin thought for a moment. Sullivan was fishing, of that he had little doubt. There was enough in what he was saying however, to make Caslin have to consider this was a possibility, at the very least.

"A reliable source?"

"One of the best."

"Was your source present?"

On that Caslin realised he had him. Sullivan didn't want to play his hand but he couldn't be emphatic. The journalist chose not to lie.

"That is what I am led to believe. Any of this ringing true with you?"

Caslin shrugged, "Sounds a lot like hearsay to me but if you want to submit your details to the relevant body, I'm sure they'll look into your concerns."

"Already been done, whitewashed and filed away. No doubt, in the bowels of the MOD for the next seventy-five years."

"What are you expecting me to do with it?"

"Nothing Inspector, I am merely performing my civic duty."

Caslin laughed with genuine humour. Sullivan headed for the front door.

"I'll look forward to your next headline."

Sullivan smiled, giving a wave as he descended the stairs.

"Should you wish to go on record, do please give me a call."

Caslin let the door slam shut. Returning to the lounge he looked out onto Stonegate, watching the journalist exit the building, heading east. Sullivan looked over his shoulder, up at Caslin in the window and grinned before resuming his course, weaving his way amongst the pre-Christmas shoppers. The potential lead on Claire Skellon would have to wait a little longer. Coincidence or long shot, either way, it didn't matter. Immediately, Caslin was concerned that he was seeing movement in the shadows where there wasn't any. Sullivan had provided another more pressing avenue. Meeting the source would have been ideal but experience told him that those details would not be forthcoming. Despite knowing that anti-terror legislation gave police the power to seize such information from the press, he was reluctant to push that button, at least for now.

What the journalist proffered left him with an uneasy feeling. Watching the departing figure in the descending darkness, he couldn't help but wonder how deep this particular rabbit hole went.

CHAPTER TWENTY-FOUR

THE OFFICE WAS DRAB, even by the standards of Fulford Road. Three desks were in the room with only one currently occupied by a young corporal tapping away at his keyboard with frequent bursts before pausing to review his work. On the right of his desk were trays full of paper. Roughly a dozen manila folders were stacked to the left, three inches high, each tied with string. The white-painted walls were heavily marked, highlighting a need for a refresh. Several notice boards were mounted with even spacing between them, bearing a vast array of information from charts to lists. Behind each desk were large format calendars for the incumbents to keep track. Two of which had clear crossings out to mark the passing of the days but the third did not, remaining on the month of September.

The phone rang again, the fourth time since he had arrived, and was swiftly answered by the only person present. The call was put through. The typing began in earnest once more. The clock on the wall read 9:46 a.m. and Caslin checked his watch to find that they were more or less in sync. He waited a day to be granted this appointment, giving him ample time to consider his approach. That culminated in a decision to be direct without getting carried away.

Maxim's funeral was set for Monday 27th November and was yet another reason for him to avoid the office. Anthony Harman tried to contact him twice the previous day but Caslin had ducked the calls, easy with a mobile but less so at Fulford Road. Having given the invitation to speak at the funeral serious consideration he had not wavered in his desire to avoid doing so. It didn't feel right and he trusted his gut instincts. His attitude was certainly not garnered from a position of not caring. He just knew he would feel somewhat of a fraud. Strangely, he already did. The two were hardly close and Caslin had shared his colleagues' view that Harman was a nice lad but sorely lacking in professional ability. Even so, he glimpsed a different side to the young DC while they worked together recently and that ensured a modicum of guilt over his stance. The fact that he hadn't definitively said no to Maxim's father meant the door remained open.

The word from the top was that all officers not required for urgent duty should attend the service in their dress uniform. Caslin was unsure if his would fit. That was a flippant thought and he chastised himself for it.

His decision to actively avoid the station in entirety saw him set off at the wrong time and catch the commuter traffic heading for Catterick. The approach roads seemed to be in perpetual contra flow whenever he needed to be in that part of the country. Arriving suitably early, despite the congestion, he was ushered through the main gate and directed to the fourth building on the right. Parking was set aside just in front. His request for an appointment welcomed with a customary military response, emotionless efficiency. Sadly, the meeting was not taking place with the punctuality that one would expect. Another glance at the clock. Eighteen minutes had now passed since he was due to meet with Colonel Edwards. Sitting back in his chair he yawned, looking to the ceiling as he did so, resisting the urge to count the tiles. The room was warm. The radiators were kicking out much needed heat this close to December. The draught drifting through from the single-glazed, Crittal-framed, windows was awful.

Another uniformed body knocked and came through the entrance, carrying some forms. She casually glanced at Caslin, seated to the left of the door, before handing the papers to the clerk. The two soldiers exchanged the briefest of pleasantries before the newcomer departed, Caslin smiling at her as she passed him, more out of courtesy than any desire to communicate. The desk clerk flicked his eyes in Caslin's direction and swiftly away again, as the look was met. Twenty minutes. He was beginning to feel the delay was deliberate. The army was an institution that liked to keep its business internal. The police were begrudgingly welcomed only when protocol dictated it. At least that was his personal experience.

More time passed before the phone eventually rang and Caslin was shown through into the colonel's office. Surprising as it was to him, the room beyond was similar to the last. Notably there was only the one desk but also a lack of the pomp and grandeur that he expected. Various metal filing cabinets lined two walls, which themselves carried pictures documenting the officer's various spells abroad. The barren desert backdrops could well have been from any number of postings. The colonel kept a tidier desk than his subordinates though. Minimal paperwork was set alongside photos of his family.

Colonel Edwards came from behind his desk to greet him. He apologised for the delay as he offered his hand in welcome. Caslin was shown a seat which he took, as the clerk departed, closing the door behind him. Having dispensed with the pleasantries they got to the subject in hand.

"You were inquiring about a former serviceman, Rifleman McNeil."

"Yes, I need to clear up some contradictions that have arisen during an investigation."

Colonel Edwards opened a drawer to retrieve a folder from within it, presumably McNeil's service record.

"I had his file brought up following your telephone call on

Wednesday. Having familiarised myself with it, I am happy to clear up any discrepancy that I can."

"Could you clarify the cause of his release from the regiment?"

"That's easy, medical grounds. He had an ongoing condition with his back that ultimately left him unfit for duty."

"That was what I was led to believe, Sir. However, is there a possibility that he was faking it?"

The officer looked up and met Caslin's gaze. He blew out his cheeks and glanced back at the file, appearing to scan a page before leafing through the next couple and shaking his head.

"He was assessed by the medical team at his last posting and again, by a specialist, here in the UK. Both came to the same conclusion, so I would have to say no."

"And that was the only reason for his discharge? There wasn't anything untoward?"

If the colonel was surprised by that question, he remained impassive.

"Forgive me. I don't know what you are getting at."

Caslin sat back in his chair. Taking his small notebook from his pocket, he also made a show of leafing through the pages. Stopping at a certain point, in truth, one completely unrelated to his line of questioning.

"Only I have made a note here that a witness suggested McNeil was involved in an incident in Iraq, facilitating his discharge."

"What incident?"

"I would rather not go into the specifics. It is only a brief mention. I'm endeavouring to see if there is anything in it at all."

"There is no mention of anything in his file."

"Was he a decent soldier?"

"I would say he was solid, not the best but experienced. I never had cause to have him in front of me. His record was better than average."

"And yet, he didn't progress. For a man with such a length of time served that is unusual, is it not?"

"Not really," Edwards shrugged. "Some soldiers are where they should be, at their level. Not everyone has leadership ability. Once you reach a certain age, how much more can you learn?"

"I see. We've also come across evidence of a historic brain injury, during his post mortem."

"Right."

"Do you know when, or indeed, how that may have been sustained?"

Colonel Edwards returned to his paperwork. Moments passed as he reread the information. Shaking his head, he replied, "There is nothing that warrants a specific mention of a brain injury. He did suffer a fall from height during a training exercise but subsequently, made a full recovery in a short space of time. That doesn't imply a serious condition."

"When was that, Sir?"

"July '97."

"And the nature of his injury?"

"I'm sorry. The details are not documented here. I could arrange for the full medical file to be released to you. I must say though. Should he have suffered an extensive brain injury during his service, I would find it difficult to comprehend how he could return in an active, frontline capacity, so soon. Perhaps it was before he enlisted."

"Perhaps," Caslin agreed. He was frustrated at that response, having hoped for something more. "It has been suggested that such an injury could have affected his personality. Wouldn't that have shown up during the selection and training processes?"

"That would be impossible to say without knowledge of the injury sustained. I couldn't possibly speculate."

"I understand Rifleman McNeil was assigned to a detention centre in Basra."

"I am not sure how you came by that but," the officer consulted the file once again, "yes, he was part of a detachment. Is that significant?"

Now it was Caslin that shrugged, "There was nothing unusual

that occurred there?"

"Not to my knowledge."

"Would it be possible for me to speak with some of his former colleagues, or perhaps his platoon commander?"

"Certainly. Provided you can wait three months."

Caslin frowned, "They are deployed?"

"Overseas. On active assignment."

"Do they have phones?"

He didn't mean to sound sarcastic but it came naturally to him, and that was exactly how his question came across.

"I can relay your request. Once they are out of the field, I'm sure the men will be happy to give you a call during their limited, free time. Perhaps you can leave us with your contact numbers. I cannot guarantee the time of the call though. I hope you're a light sleeper."

"Where are they deployed?"

"I am afraid that theatres of combat are classified. I am sure you understand."

Caslin didn't. He considered asking to speak with the medical staff but quickly dismissed the idea. The chances that he would get a different response were slim.

"Would I be able to see a list of people who served with Rifleman McNeil? Not his entire career, I know that would be ridiculous, but his immediate surrounding group. For example, those on his last tour?"

The colonel returned to his file and rapidly flicked through a number of pages before drawing one out and passing it across the desk. Caslin was genuinely surprised. He imagined that such information would take some time to gather if it was at all possible.

"I pre-empted your request. Inspector, is this really the pressing matter that you came all the way over here to discuss? I was under the impression that you had more far-reaching inquiries, than this."

Caslin thought for a moment about what Sullivan had told

him as he scanned through the list of names before him, none of which struck a chord. Was there anything to the allegation? The colonel was giving very little away but in fairness, if there was no substance to it, what else would he be saying? Always having prided himself on an ability to read people, he had to admit that this was a scenario that left him wondering. What could he expect, a scandal to be admitted the moment he asked the question? Dare he ask the question? Yes, he dared.

"It is alleged that detainees were systematically abused and tortured by British personnel, at that detention centre. Furthermore, that Rifleman McNeil is implicated in those actions and also, that the incidents have been buried to avoid embarrassment."

If there was any element of surprise at the allegation, then it remained well hidden, too well hidden. An experienced officer, shaped in the military tradition of holding firm, Caslin knew that he would get little reaction. Colonel Edwards fixed him with a stare that neither confirmed nor denied anything.

"I hope that your witness has evidence to corroborate such a wayward allegation. Were it to be true, then it would indeed be shocking. There was no such event to my knowledge and goodness knows there is enough scrutiny on our actions that something like that would not remain secret for long."

"Perhaps it hasn't."

"No-one, I repeat no-one, under my command has knowledge of what you are saying. Whoever your witness is, they are at best mistaken and at worst, lying in the gravest of fashions. Have I made myself clear?"

The last was said in a controlled tone that seemed to only afflict officers of rank in the British armed forces.

"I understand."

"Are we finished?"

Caslin realised that the question was more rhetorical than it sounded and he nodded. Rising from his chair, he took the offered hand and made to leave the office.

"May I keep this?" Caslin asked, indicating the typed list he held in his left hand.

"You may."

MAKING his way out to the car, Caslin considered the meeting. The day was overcast with the constant threat of rain. The wind rattled through the camp throwing up the multitude of brown leaves that lay around. He braced against the cold until safely in his Volvo. The reality was that he hadn't expected a confirmation of the allegation. A denial, on the other hand, was a foregone conclusion. The real point of the exercise was to assess the man opposite and try to gauge the reaction. Had he gleaned anything from the brief encounter? Probably not. Without speaking to Sullivan's source directly, there wasn't going to be much mileage in this angle of the investigation.

Starting the car, he wiped down the interior windscreen with his sleeve, smearing rather than cleaning the mist away. Turning on the blowers he sat back, drawing his coat about him as the cold air blew through. Thoughts turned briefly to Chloe McNeil and Caslin considered calling DC Underwood, to check if Chloe had done anything that aroused suspicion. Dialling Hayley's phone he found she answered within a couple of rings.

"Hayley?"

"Before you ask, yes, I am watching Chloe and no, there is nothing of note going on. She left home about twenty minutes ago and went to the supermarket. Nice lady. She waved to me from the end of her path. I thought about giving her a lift, seeing as I'm going her way."

The response to his unasked question did little to veil her frustration at the surveillance detail. Caslin wasn't annoyed. So far Underwood and Holt had produced nothing of note that aided them in moving the investigation forward. Spending a twelve-hour stint watching the policing equivalent of paint drying was a task that few relished. The operation was yielding so little that the resources were under threat if nothing turned up soon.

Caslin laughed, "Let me know if anything happens. You can never be sure when the big break will come."

"If you weren't my DI, then I would have a rant about your sarcasm."

"… have a rant about my sarcasm, *Sir*," Caslin admonished her, in mock seriousness.

"Oh yeah, sometimes I forget about that bit, *Sir*," Hayley replied, her grin almost evident down the phone line.

Caslin smiled as he ended the call. Whether true or not, it did seem that he was the only one that found keeping a watchful eye on Chloe to be anything other than pointless. Her connection to the case at Radford Farm was clear but there was little to tie her to the crimes. With that in mind, he looked up Iain Robertson's number and dialled it. The gruff Scot picked up almost as soon as the call connected and Caslin asked for an update.

"The scene has been processed in its entirety. I'll have a summary written up for you by close of play Monday. But as for the finer detail, you can whistle. It'll take months."

"Can you give me any of the headlines?"

"You're going to be busy, or at least I will continue to be. We have potentially twenty sets of prints to process through the system. Once duplicates are filtered out, it may be fewer. Many are historic and have degraded but the conditions in there have helped retain them. Likewise, we have DNA profiles. Some of which will require a great deal of study, down to cross contamination. However, with a fair wind and a bit of luck we may get hits on the database."

"Any further joy with the server?"

"No, afraid not," Robertson sounded dejected. "That was young Maxim's work. I haven't been able to get a techie to take that on yet. I'm sorry, it's just—"

"No need, Iain, I understand. That's hit us in many ways."

"I'll be there on Monday, for the funeral, but I'll still get my findings to you beforehand. We could head over together if you like?"

"Thanks, but I'll make my own way, no offence."

"None taken."

"Any word on the bone fragments that you turned up in the woods?"

"Not only in the woods, also in the furnace of the heating system."

"Jesus."

"Yeah, too right. By my reckoning we have at least four bodies buried in the woods, to be certain will take more time as they appear to have been scattered."

"Scattered?"

"Dismembered, burnt and or scattered. It's a misconception that human bones burn down to ashes, even in a crematorium. They dry out but need to be pulverised in order to achieve that result. My guess is that has been done rather crudely, in this case, and then strewn about to get shot of the evidence. Once we can assemble all the remnants, we will have a clearer idea."

"The child?"

Robertson paused.

"We will have a clearer idea once we assemble the…"

"I understand," Caslin said with a heavy heart.

He had suspected for some time, that when Angela Horsvedt had asked what had become of her child, the reality was that he was already dead. Robertson was unofficially confirming that hypothesis. How the monstrous scenario of Radford Farm matched the general opinion that seemed widely held on Garry McNeil, did not sit well. How this man who was so easy going, fun to be around and an above average soldier with a largely unblemished military record, could inflict such evil on those around him was almost unfathomable. *Almost.* The only negative descriptions came from an unknown source, courtesy of an untrustworthy hack, and the deceased's ex. The latter was not unusual in itself and coming from this particular ex, gave him further cause for concern.

The skill of mirroring others was well documented in those with the propensity to kill. How many times had he heard someone state that their friend, or neighbour, was the last person that could ever be involved in such a horrendous act. That inherent ability to blend in, to operate in plain sight was something that few could learn, it was a natural talent. What Caslin often referred to as the "Divided House" of a person's psyche, the public face versus the private reality. The more he thought about it, the more Garry McNeil fitted the criteria.

The seemingly unproductive meeting in Catterick took a new twist when his phone rang. The car was warming up and Caslin, having fastened his seatbelt, was reversing from his parking bay when he stopped to answer the call. An irate Frank Stephens was at the other end.

"What the bloody hell are you doing in Catterick?"

Looking back towards the building that he had vacated only a quarter of an hour previously, Caslin exhaled heavily. Word certainly travelled fast.

CHAPTER TWENTY-FIVE

DRESSED IN DARK BLUE, Caslin was able to blend into the shadows as he silently nursed the glass before him. The drink had been sitting on the table since he took his seat half an hour previously, but no scotch had passed his lips as yet.

The smell of damp was once again present, not surprising considering he was seated well below the level of the Ouse, barely twenty feet away through the wall behind him. Once the heaters and dehumidifiers were fully engaged, the smell would soon dissipate. A couple descended the steps to the lower cellar of Lendal's and occupied a booth at the other end, well away from the lone figure hunched in the far corner. The recessed lighting illuminated the vaulted ceiling but did little to bathe the patrons in revealing detail.

It came as a great surprise to Caslin that he had no guilt for his vanishing act. Having risen in plenty of time, with every intention of making the service, he walked to his car only to divert his path back into the old town and head for the Cellars. Once beneath ground, the anxiety subsided to be replaced with an all too familiar apathy. He drained his glass in a single motion. Closing his eyes as the aftertaste bit, he replaced the empty glass on the table. Laughter permeated from the far end and he glanced across.

The simple pleasure of lunch with a friend or loved one, he missed that. Not nearly enough to encourage him to make more friends but he felt sure that their day was infinitely better than his.

A waitress walked past, a full-figured woman in her thirties. Caslin couldn't remember her name. Noticing the empty glass, she scooped it up and placed it on her tray.

"Same again, Nate?"

"It's a little early, probably shouldn't."

"Let me know if you change your mind."

The waitress smiled as she made off, Caslin returning it with one of his own even though his was forced. At the far end the young man rose from the booth, with a menu in hand, and headed upstairs to the bar. His partner remained seated and quickly became engrossed in her phone. Apart from an odd sound emanating from the next level up of the Cellars, silence prevailed. Caslin retrieved the vial from his inner pocket and with one last furtive glance around he unscrewed the top. Tapping a little of the contents onto the reverse of his hand, he swiftly sniffed the powder. Wiping the remainder off his hand with his forefinger, he rubbed it along the length of his gums, secreting the vial back inside his coat as he did so. Today was not going to be a day of abstinence.

Withdrawing his own phone, he could see that he had no signal, which pleased him. One of the attractions of this pub was that very fact. Although others seemed to manage without issue, his network wasn't strong enough to penetrate the brickwork. The couple at the booth were reunited and a quick conversation took place as the man sat down. A glance in Caslin's direction from both of them made him realise it was time to leave. Putting his phone away he stood up and quickly pulled on his overcoat, concealing the uniform as he passed through the cellar. All of a sudden, he was sweating and his gums felt as if they were tingling. Ensuring that he didn't make eye contact as he went, he climbed the stairs, crossed the upper bar to the exit and up out onto the street. He blinked rapidly as his eyes adjusted to the daylight, albeit an overcast morning. The smell from the kitchens of the Italian restaurant next door drifted through the air, and he realised he was hungry. Two gulls landed on the railings of the balcony above, squawking at him in a demand for food. Drawing his coat tightly about him, he turned left up the cobbled street and headed into the city centre as the rain began to fall.

Picking up a takeaway coffee and a ham sandwich from an independent café, he made his way back towards the river. The rain had turned out to be a light drizzle that soon passed off, leaving a brighter, yet cloudy sky. The towpath was relatively empty and he slowly walked the route, keeping within the tree line that edged the park alongside the river, as he ate.

Frank Stephens had given him another three days to generate something useful from the surveillance on Chloe McNeil's address before he had vowed to pull the plug on the operation. With Iain Robertson's team completing their on-site investigation and little to associate her with active participation in the events, the DCI was keen to tie the case off.

A successful conclusion would make good copy for the press and therefore relieve the burden of pressure on both CID and the management. Radford Farm and Ravenscar were proving damaging to the notion that law and order were being maintained. The cases had become a political issue, Ravenscar in particular, which was never a good development in an investigation. The team spent precious time attending briefings and answering telephone enquiries from councillors, as well as the office of the constituency MP, who all thought they should be kept aware of progress. In reality, they were tying up resources better utilised elsewhere. A quick win with the closure of the file on Garry McNeil would be advantageous, neat and tidy. He could even put a pretty bow on it for them if that was their desire.

Caslin took out his phone and looked up Colin Brotherton, hitting the call tab as soon as he found the number. The phone rang for some time and he was about to hang up before the retired detective answered. They exchanged greetings before Caslin got to his motivation for the call.

"Colin, can you tell me anything about a girl by the name of Vickers?"

There was a pause at the other end of the line and Caslin had to consider that the link was so insignificant that it may have escaped the detective altogether.

"Vickers, Vickers... doesn't ring a bell. Can you help me out a bit?"

"Sure. She was interviewed in your investigation, not by yourself but a DC Flanaghan—"

"Chloe Vickers," Brotherton interrupted excitedly. "She knew Maxine."

"Excellent, do you remember any details taken in her statement?"

"Oooh, vaguely but I don't recall it being significant in any way. Why, what did she say?"

"Well, that's why I'm asking. Her statement isn't in with all the evidence that you passed on to me."

"It can't have been useful if that's the case. Otherwise I would have taken... I mean, kept it all together."

"Can you tell me anything about her?"

There was silence as Brotherton thought for a moment, not wishing to get himself mixed up with any of the dozens of others interviewed along the way. The rasping nature of his limited lung capacity was all that came to ear.

"If memory serves, she knew Maxine. She was another girl from the care home."

"Chloe was in care also? I didn't know that."

"Yes, I think I'm remembering that right. Her mother had some mental condition, or another and struggled to cope."

"That certainly fits."

"And her father had some abuse allegations thrown at him as well. He was a teacher, I think, and so Chloe spent some time in care."

"Was he ever charged?"

"No, not that I recall. The case never made it anywhere near trial. Thinking about it, he passed away at some point. Sorry, I can't remember when exactly but that might have been why it never progressed. Not my case. I think he was much older than his wife."

"Anything else? Was she there at the same time as Lucy Stafford?"

"No, I don't believe so. At least Lucy never mentioned her as far as I know. Why are you so interested in her, have you turned something up?"

"No, not at all. Just came across it and thought I would ask. I'll let you know if and when I do, though."

The two men said their goodbyes and Caslin found himself sitting alone in the park once again. The wind whistled through the barren trees above his head as he considered his next move. A rustling sound caused him to look beneath the bench. The remnants of a discarded newspaper had been blown underneath and were currently flapping vigorously against a cast-iron leg. Caslin picked it up with the intention of putting it in the bin before it blew off across the open grass. As he made to deposit it, he caught a glimpse of the front. Opening out the page, whilst shielding it from the wind, he saw that it carried a black-and-white photo. A team of female pool players were huddled together, proudly displaying a trophy before them, their hands resting against the edges of the table. Caslin stared at the picture, he knew no-one within it or had any real idea of what the story was about but that wasn't the point.

He put the page into the bin and stood there for a moment, trying to tease the thought to the front of his mind. The feeling that had been nagging at him for weeks finally delivered something tangible. Turning around, he picked up his coffee and headed back into the city. He had to pay a visit to Fulford Road and another chat with Chloe could wait until later.

The station was nigh on deserted, considering the time of day, and Caslin was able to slip in and down to the evidence room without having to make conversation with anybody. Signing himself in, he headed for the Radford Farm evidence boxes, hoping that Robertson and his team had already indexed the materials and placed them in storage. He was surprised to find as much as he did. Effectively two properties had been photographed, catalogued, and packed up for use in the ongoing investigation.

With little to go on as to where he would find what he was looking for, he set about opening and scanning the index for the contents of each box. The third that he opened listed the items found in the living room of the farmhouse. Flicking past the ballistics report on the bullet lodged in the wall, he was looking for something far more mundane. Leafing through the photographs taken at the scene, he saw what he was looking for and cross-referenced the photo with the folders arranged before him. Moments later he had it in his hand, a folded copy of *The Post* that had lain on the floor beside the armchair.

Caslin exhaled slowly as he read the cover story, a good news angle about a local woman who had turned down an OBE in the Queen's Birthday Honours. The grainy photo showed a face that seemed ill at ease with the attention. He was right. Sure enough, here was Claire Skellon looking out at him. Angry with himself for not having put it together sooner, he swiftly replaced the items in the archive box and returned it to the shelf. Signing out, he took the stairs two at a time and made for his car.

The evening traffic was heavy with everyone heading out of work on the first day of the new week. A power cut affecting street and traffic lights did little to help. Whilst en route he called Terry Holt but there was no answer. Caslin hoped that the DCI hadn't already pulled him off the surveillance. Assuming Chloe would be at home that was where he headed.

The street was in darkness when he finally arrived. Cloud cover ensured that headlights and a few candlelit windows cast the only light. Pulling up outside Chloe's house he turned off the engine, catching the briefest glimpse of a CID number plate parked up the road before finding himself in gloom. Getting out, he first cast his eyes towards Chloe's front room which was also shrouded in darkness, before crossing the road. There was no movement from within the CID vehicle and Caslin found himself slowing as he approached it. The hairs were standing up on the back of his neck as he clocked the mist on both the driver's window and the windscreen. The rest of the car was clear and as he stepped onto the verge alongside he could make out the dark splatter, through which a figure was slumped across the passenger seat. It was far too slight to be the stocky form of Terry Holt.

Caslin opened the driver's door. The body lay away from him, face down but clearly female. Stretching out a hand he found matted blood-soaked hair. Searching for a pulse proved fruitless as his fingers slipped into a wet opening and he recoiled at the sensation. Grasping a shoulder, he attempted to lever her up. The vacant, yet unmistakable face of DC Hayley Underwood stared up at him. Her body was warm but little blood emanated from the wound to her neck, which passed almost from one side to the other. The moment of shock was replaced by seething white-hot anger. Caslin retrieved his phone with his free hand, managing to unlock it and call an ambulance. Having seen many such incidents in his career he knew that it was a futile gesture. Hayley was never going to make it. Even with only the dim glow emitted by his mobile phone, he could see the wound was deep enough to almost sever her spinal cord.

Laying down the still form of his colleague and stepping out from the vehicle, he was suddenly aware of how vulnerable his position was. Alone in the dark, unsure of whether Underwood's attacker was still present, watching him from the shadows. Knowing that waiting for support and preserving the crime scene was what protocol dictated, he knew he should remain where he was. However, anger flared within him. Potentially the only witness to the events at Radford Farm, Chloe was important to the case and the realisation that perhaps someone else thought similarly spurred him into action.

He set off at a run back down the street and up to her house. Deciding that discretion was a better tactic, he listened outside for sounds from within but all that greeted him was silence. He moved slowly but with purpose around to the shared access alley. Tentatively he passed through the pitch black emerging to the rear moments later. Once again, he stopped and listened. Nothing came to his ear. Edging forward, he risked a glance into the first window he came to but the inside was in darkness. Ducking underneath the opening he approached the door to the kitchen and waited. Crouching, he reached up to the handle and gently twisted it, finding it unlocked. Taking a deep breath, he realised his hands were sweating despite the cold and he actively forced himself to calm down. His adrenalin surged.

The possibility that there was a person waiting to ambush him with a weapon aimed directly at the door, poised to unleash a barrage as soon as he entered, worried him. Taking another deep breath and psyching himself up, he eased the door open a fraction and waited. Nothing happened, so he pushed it open just enough to peer through. Even in the gloom he could see there was no movement, his eyes having adjusted to the lack of light.

Slipping through into the kitchen there appeared to be nothing untoward. Everything looked as one might expect. His attention was drawn to a knife block on the worktop. Two blades were missing. Tiptoeing through the kitchen, he paused as he reached the threshold of the living room. He remembered that the room beyond was substantially wider than the kitchen. Therefore, an assailant had three locations in which to lie in wait, either side of the through entrance or in the hallway beyond. Caslin risked poking his head around the corner and once again saw nothing unusual. One more look and he was satisfied that it was safe to proceed. Checking the hall was clear he progressed through the house with greater urgency.

The upstairs appeared undisturbed and Caslin had to accept

that nothing seemed to have happened here. All of which added to his sense of unease. His initial fears for Chloe's safety were being eroded by the notion that she was culpable in the attack on Underwood. Had he underestimated, not only, her complicity in McNeil's crimes but also her propensity for violence?

Sirens alerted him to the forthcoming presence of his colleagues and he returned outside to direct them as the first two patrol cars approached. The second of which was an armed response vehicle. Looking back at the house, one question came to mind over and over, *where was Chloe McNeil?*

CHAPTER TWENTY-SIX

THE LATER HOURS of Monday 27th November passed in a blur. A full-scale man-hunt was underway in York with every available officer deployed in an attempt to snare a killer. The paramedics at the scene believed DC Underwood had a chance. Pupil dilation following exposure to bright light was indicative of brain activity, albeit not a great deal of activity but nonetheless, it was still a sign of life. Despite their best efforts however, she was pronounced dead on arrival at University Hospital, information that came as no surprise to Caslin.

The utilities restored power by eleven o'clock and the area was able to be properly explored rather than the more haphazard search carried out by torchlight. There was no evidence of a struggle, either in Chloe's residence or in the car where Hayley Underwood had been discovered. Early conjecture indicated her attacker was concealed within the vehicle, taking her unawares from behind. In any event, she had been unable to defend herself from the attack.

As the night wore on the tracker dogs returned nothing. Neither did the hastily erected road blocks on the arterial routes in and out of the city. Officers were going door to door and despite expressions of much horror at the events taking place, the results of the inquiries were yielding little. No-one had seemingly seen or heard anything of note. The anger at losing another officer so soon after Harman was rapidly surpassed by the frustration of stumbling around in the darkness, despite the restoration of the street lighting.

The most anger on display came from Terry Holt. An outburst in CID saw him hurl a chair across the room in a fit of pique. Caslin directed him to the washroom and followed him in. The momentary peace gave Holt an opportunity to calm down.

"That shouldn't have happened," Holt said with anguish in his voice.

"But it has."

"She shouldn't have bloody been there, it was my shift."

Their brief conversation was interrupted by the arrival of Simon Baxter entering. He stopped at the entrance as the door closed behind him, the self-closing mechanism squeaking before the door slammed against the jamb.

"Sorry, gents. Am I intruding?"

Both men shook their heads and the inspector passed between them, going to stand before the urinal.

"There's no blame to apportion to you on this, Terry. Don't beat yourself up, although I know you're going to," Caslin said almost apologetically.

Holt sighed, "If I had been there—"

"Then maybe I would be having this conversation with someone else."

Baxter finished up and came to wash his hands.

"You were supposed to be there?" he asked.

Both Holt and Caslin looked across but it was the former who answered.

"I… I had a thing. Hayley said she didn't mind staying on and covering for me, so I could… she wasn't supposed to be there."

Baxter dispensed with the dryer and took a handful of paper towels, rubbing his hands before depositing them in the bin.

"Nathaniel's right. You can't legislate for these things. It could well have been you. Focus your anger on finding the bastard who did it, feel bad later."

They were once again alone as Baxter left and neither man spoke for a few minutes. Caslin could see that his colleague's head was still spinning. Survivor's guilt was a strong emotion, one that would take time to overcome, if ever.

"What time did you head off this afternoon?"

Holt thought on it for a moment.

"Around half-past three. Hayley got there about twenty minutes before and we had a catch up."

"Anything unusual happen during the day?"

"No, it was quiet. Some of the locals were checking me out but then they've been doing that all week."

"What about as you left, anyone hanging around?"

"No, definitely not. There wasn't a soul about."

Caslin felt his own frustration building. This was not how he had expected the day to go when he had pulled on his uniform that morning. No-one asked him directly why he didn't attend Harman's funeral. However, he had overheard two officers slating him for the no-show as he passed them in the corridor that night. They wouldn't be the only ones. Others would no doubt say it to his face, sooner or later.

"What was the thing?"

Holt shot Caslin a dark look and his anger threatened to boil over once again.

"It's okay, you don't have to tell me. I can see that it's on your mind, that's all."

"It was... I was just..."

Tears came unbidden to his eyes and he blinked them away furiously. The sight of such a burly figure reduced to that state made Caslin feel self-conscious and he decided to give Holt some space.

"Take some time and come back to the squad room when you're ready. We need everybody on this one."

With that, Caslin returned to CID. He couldn't help but

wonder what had required Holt to need extra time when for most of the day he hadn't been on shift, anyway. It was a strange consideration bearing in mind all else that should warrant his attention, under the circumstances. Maxim Harman came to mind and Caslin was acutely aware of how unlucky they were to have lost two colleagues in quick succession, *far too unlucky*, in his opinion. There was no cause to link the two deaths but Caslin was struggling to reconcile that fact with the reality. The situation felt so very wrong to him, more so, than merely a sense of injustice. He forcibly reminded himself that Harman's suicide had no indication of external influences and yet, he remained unconvinced.

The members of the investigation team, who were not still at the crime scene, had assembled for a briefing, much of which was to be delivered by Caslin for he was the first in attendance. The immediate focus was to find Chloe McNeil. Formally she was to be treated as a witness but in the light of the attack on DC Underwood she was to be considered armed and dangerous until proven otherwise. Her absence from the scene was suspicious but as Caslin was at pains to point out, there could still be another player in the game. The man known only to him as Charlie came to mind but Caslin remained tight-lipped.

"Maybe she cracked under the surveillance and made the drastic move you were hoping for. Although it was one we didn't see coming," DCI Stephens offered.

"Perhaps, but how did she get the drop on Hayley? I'm as open-minded on Chloe as you are but it doesn't make a lot of sense. She would know that we would suspect her. If she's as innocent as she makes out, she wouldn't have done it and if as calculating as I suspect, she wouldn't be stupid enough. With that said though…"

"Let's get her in before we rule her out?" Stephens finished for him. Caslin agreed.

"So, we could be looking for someone else then?" Baxter offered. "Who?"

Caslin thought for a moment as he scanned the faces before

him, noting the absence of those that he had gotten used to. He was unsure of whether he should reveal the lines of enquiry that he was following, none of which were even close to being considered concrete.

"With a bit of luck SOCO might turn up something from the car, or the house. Has the search of the area turned over a weapon?"

Frank Stephens shook his head, "They've found a blood trail, that's a generous description, mind you. A few drops, predominantly around and to the rear of the car, but it only went thirty yards before it stopped."

"Hayley's?"

"We don't know but that's the presumption that we're working with. The trail ended on the road."

"The attacker got into a parked car?"

"Again, that's only a working theory. We've nothing to substantiate it."

"Chloe's the key," Caslin stated, almost as a matter of fact. "We need to shake up her peer group, dealers, fellow junkies, whoever she has been in contact with. Terry should have a few good leads on that with what he and Hayley have documented in the past week. Meantime, start checking homeless shelters, missions, anywhere that she might try and get her head down. Likewise, get traffic to give us a hand around truck stops, all-night diners and red light pick-up points. If she's running, she'll do it under the radar."

"What makes you so sure of that?" Baxter asked.

"Something tells me she's got form for it."

"Would you care to enlighten us?"

"No."

THE TEAM SET about their new tasks whilst Caslin scooped up his coat and headed for the exit. He pretended not to hear Frank

Stephens call after him but the DCI followed and caught up with him as he hit the stairs, falling into step alongside.

"We missed you today."

"I doubt that, Frank, I doubt that very much."

"I know you care, even if you pretend not to. Would it have hurt you to put in an appearance? To at least act like part of the team."

Caslin stopped on the half landing. Leaning his back against the handrail he fixed his superior with a gaze.

"I intended to. I just… couldn't."

"It wasn't your fault, you know. Hell, we all should have seen the signs. Most of all me seeing as I'm his boss."

"He was struggling with the job."

Stephens nodded, "I should have done more."

"Self-flagellation can wait, though, can't it? We have more going on right now."

"Exactly, which is why we need to be a team, in spite of any personal misgivings we have about one another."

"Fair enough."

"So, we can't be holding out, can we?"

"What makes you say that?"

"Because I am too long in the tooth, Nathaniel. What are you keeping back?"

Caslin first glanced down the stairwell and then up, from where they had come. He broke the following eye contact with Stephens within moments, nervously brushing his face with the flat of his hand and sucking in a sharp intake of breath as he did so. He may not rate his boss particularly highly as a detective but he had never doubted his integrity.

"There might be more going on here than we realise."

Stephens lowered his voice to match Caslin's.

"Such as what?"

"I need to check something out first, until then it's nothing solid. Can you trust me for a few hours?"

"What are you up to?"

"It's best and I think you'd prefer it, if you didn't know for the time being. I need to shake a tree and see what drops."

Stephens fixed Caslin with a stare as if contemplating the potential outcomes of his next decision. It was certainly against his better judgement to trust Caslin without further details but on the other hand, plausible deniability was appealing. If his DI were to hang himself, then so be it.

"Lunchtime tomorrow, twelve hours max."

Caslin nodded and set off down the stairs. He knew what he had to do. There was only one link left that he had access to but it was a long shot. Once outside and in his car, Caslin rummaged around in the glove box, eventually finding what he was looking for. The following telephone call he made was answered within three rings, despite the early hour.

THE TRUCKS SHRIEKED as they passed over the rails, the freight train stretching through York Station. Caslin nursed a cup of coffee as he braced against the early morning cold, heavy-eyed but still alert. The fog had rolled in through the vale during the night, giving the air a moist chill, and without a breeze it lingered all around. Standing on the open bridge that spanned the platforms, he casually looked first one way and then the other. There were precious few people around. A handful of station staff toiled alongside those opening up the variety of concessions on the platforms beneath him. Sipping more of his Americano, he stifled a yawn. A glance to the clock told him it was 6:30. He was left wondering if the appointment would be kept.

Footsteps approaching to his left caused him to turn. The oncoming man was in his late thirties, dark hair shot through with grey, of slight build, and walking purposefully towards him. He was easily over six feet in height, clean-shaven and smartly attired. Caslin drew himself upright from his slouched position against the railing. Taking a deep breath, he opened his mouth to speak just as the man passed by, without a glance. Turning, Caslin watched as he descended to platform five before disappearing from view.

Under his breath, he cursed. The long shot appeared to be infinitely longer than he had thought. Ready to abandon the plan, he made to set off in the direction of the car park. At which point his phone began to ring. Taking it out he saw that the number was withheld, he answered.

"I apologise, Inspector Caslin. That wasn't me."

Caslin stopped in his tracks and as casually as possible began to look around, eyeing the kiosks and coffee bars on each platform below.

"You won't see me but I don't blame you for looking."

"I thought we were set to meet this morning?"

"No, no, I agreed to speak to you this morning. I certainly did not agree to meet you."

"We could have had a conversation over the phone from anywhere. Why bring me down here?"

Caslin continued to look around, trying to find anyone who was talking on a phone or standing with an earpiece. There were several possibilities although they were just as likely to be catching a commuter train as talking to him.

"I wanted to see you, take in your measure."

"To what end?"

"You interest me," the voice said. "Very few people interest me but you are persevering in a case that has no victory for you. Why would you do that?"

"Who says there is no victory?"

There was gentle laughter at the other end.

"Come on, Inspector. You are stirring a hornets' nest with a very big stick and you know it. What you've learned about Garry McNeil so far is only the tip of the iceberg. No-one wants this in the public domain."

"And you know more about it?"

"I should do."

"You were there?"

Silence.

"Were you there when Garry McNeil allegedly carried out these abuses?"

"No, I wasn't there."

"How then, can I take your word for it?"

More silence. Caslin decided to take a different approach. If this person was on the level, then he had to have access to the information that he was quoting. Either he must have been present or was a whistleblower, perhaps an MOD employee, civilian or military.

Caslin pushed, "Clearly you have things to say, you wouldn't have contacted Mr Sullivan if that weren't the case."

"Ah yes, James Sullivan. He has his uses but taken as a whole, I find him to be a trying little man."

"On that we can agree. You have me at a disadvantage. You know my name. Will you tell me yours?"

"I prefer anonymity for now. Please don't insult me with promises of discretion. James said something similar and I know that technically, he hasn't broken that promise. However, you and I are still talking, so he has at best… stretched the boundaries of our agreement."

"It is only a matter of time until I find out, if I choose to."

"There may come a day when I offer it."

"So, you work for the MOD then?"

The voice laughed once more with genuine humour. Caslin was certainly not unnerved by it. This person was confident and at ease with maintaining control of the conversation.

"Ever the detective. What is it that you're looking for from me today?"

"The truth. Was Garry McNeil involved in what you have alleged? Do you have some evidence to back it up?"

"What evidence would you find sufficient?"

"What have you got?"

"Hearsay."

"From whom?"

There was the briefest of pauses before he continued.

"From Garry."

The last threw Caslin somewhat, he hadn't expected that. Dozens of questions ran through his mind in quick succession.

"You knew Garry?"

"Well enough, as much as you can ever get to know someone like that, anyway."

"Someone like what?"

"You know what he was capable of, you've seen the pictures."

This time it was Caslin's turn to stop and think before speaking. Of all that he had anticipated coming out of this morning, he was very surprised to be where he was now.

"Inspector, is it too early in the morning for this conversation? You appear to be going a funny colour."

Caslin spoke slowly.

"What pictures?"

"Oh, come now. Let's not be coy on the detail, Garry did enjoy his mementoes."

"You and I both know that this information hasn't been released—"

"To the general public, no."

"You are not the general public?"

"No, general implies standard, utilitarian. I prefer to think that I am more than that."

"Don't we all?"

"Although life has a way of battering that out of us. At least it has with you."

"What do you mean by that?"

"Following my link up with James, he furnished me with some information. I was intrigued and so I have checked you out, Inspector Caslin. I felt it prudent."

"And what did you find?"

"Oh, the easy stuff wasn't hard to turn over. You were once quite the poster boy but the bright lights have faded slightly, haven't they? To be honest, I sided with you. Your judgement was sound and yet you were destroyed for it. That was grossly unfair but life runs that way sometimes, doesn't it? Good guys finish last and all that."

"What makes you think I'm a good guy?"

"Good guy, lousy husband and as for a father… well, the jury is still out on that one. How are Karen and the kids, Sean and young Lizzie? She's precocious by all accounts but that's endearing, I find."

Caslin felt his blood run cold. There was something in the manner of the voice that didn't sit well with him.

"Clearly, I'm not going to get anything from you, am I?"

"Where would be the fun in that?"

Caslin tried to focus on the tone of voice, use of vocabulary, accent, any detail that he could take note of that might generate a lead.

"In which case, what are you looking for from me? I am certain you didn't get up at this time to play verbal cat and mouse at a railway station."

"I told you, you interest me."

"In what way do I interest you?"

"Perseverance, tenacity, you won't let it go. I admire that. You know professionals believe that the British Police are the most competent in the world."

"Professional what… criminals?"

"Indeed. If you are planning a crime, you should do it elsewhere, far less likely to be caught."

"You have spent time abroad then?"

"I have, no harm in you knowing that. However, I would argue that your competence is what makes you a challenge."

"Who is challenging me, you? Chloe McNeil?"

There was silence once again.

"And that is why I like you, Inspector. You can throw a curve ball with the best of them. I always found Chloe less than interesting, I must say."

"How well do you know her?"

"Not particularly well, she's Garry's wife after all."

"If you know Garry so well, you must have spent time with her."

"Occasionally, yes. Why are you so keen to know?"

Caslin ignored the question.

"DC Underwood, was she interesting?"

"Who?"

"I thought you might know her."

"Can't say that I do. Are you reaching, Inspector?"

"You tell me."

He waited but there was no response. Checking his phone, he found that the call was still connected. Looking around, he tried again to find someone that stood out in the station, hoping to catch sight of something that could grab his attention. Straining his eyes, he scanned the fog that hung across the ends of the platforms at the outer limits of his vision. An announcement came over the public-address system and Caslin could hear a delayed version through his phone, he was close. The dense fog indicated the caller's vision should be just as impaired as his own. He was certainly within the station itself. Caslin began to walk the length of the bridge, but the platforms were beginning to fill with commuters and people were now crossing the bridge in both directions around him.

"Hello. Are you still there?" he asked but again, there was no response.

Checking the phone once more, he still had an active line. A man walked past chatting on his mobile. Caslin snatched it from him as he passed.

"Hey!" the man protested.

"Police business, shut the fuck up!"

The man stopped in his tracks, unsure of what his response should be and within moments accepted the statement. He looked decidedly irritated at the inconvenience. With distinct trouble, Caslin managed to look up Iain Robertson's telephone number on his own handset without disconnecting the call before dialling it from the one recently acquired.

"Iain, it's Nate. I need you to trace a call for me." It took an hour, but a little after 7:45 a.m. a uniformed officer plucked the handset from a waste bin towards the end of Platform One, where it had been discarded. Within an hour of that they knew it was a prepay burn phone that had only ever made one call, the one to Caslin that morning.

Furthermore, the handset was devoid of fingerprints. The subsequent review of CCTV showed that there was a blind spot in the coverage of that area. No-one had been picked up depositing the phone in the bin. The entrances and exits from the station were covered but that meant sifting through images of hundreds of people, without knowing if any were the caller. The target could just as easily have crossed the tracks and cleared the perimeter fence without anyone being any the wiser. That is, if he hadn't boarded a train and left that way.

If it had been possible to be any more frustrated with the events of the previous fifteen hours, then Caslin certainly was now. In disgust, he left Fulford Road before 9 a.m. and headed over to Sullivan's apartment, located south of the city centre.

CHAPTER TWENTY-SEVEN

THERE WAS no answer as he stood before the faceless intercom panel at Sullivan's home address. Nor did the hack answer his mobile, despite repeated attempts made throughout the course of the morning. Forced to abandon his second visit without success, Caslin walked back to his car. A sense of dejection took hold as he went. He momentarily considered the journalist's well-being. Was Jimmy avoiding him, so as not to discuss the handing over of any more details regarding his source? After all, there had been a huge amount of coercion in arranging the meet at York Station. Caslin felt that further assistance would be less than forthcoming without a warrant. He was about to open the car door when he saw a woman leaving via the communal entrance to the apartments. Trotting over, he took out his warrant card.

"Excuse me, police," he said, brandishing his identification.

"What can I do for you?"

"Do you know a resident here by the name of Sullivan?"

"Jimmy? Sure. Why, what's he done?"

Caslin shook his head and smiled, "It's nothing like that. I was wondering if you've seen him recently? Yesterday or today, in particular."

"Can't say that I have. Usually I would, he has the apartment above mine. We often cross on the stairs. Come to think of it, I haven't heard him for a couple of days either. He likes his music. I don't care for his tastes."

"Okay, thanks," Caslin took out one of his cards. "Do you think you could give me a call if and when he does? Don't worry. You'll not be dropping him in it or anything."

The resident said that she would and Caslin excused himself. The concern for Sullivan was somewhat heightened by that exchange. What also struck him as slightly alarming was the level of knowledge that the source held on Caslin's own personal situation. Granted, any internet search would've returned the majority with minimal effort, but it remained an unsettling part of the conversation. Caslin had expended a great deal of effort over the years to keep his work out of his home life, principally away from his children and didn't appreciate this unknown showing an interest in it. Taking out his phone, he decided to call Karen, although he was unsure of exactly what he would say. However, his mind drew a blank as he tried to unlock the screen, his security pattern eluding him. A flash of irritation shot through him before he realised that he had been on the go for nearly thirty-six hours straight. He hadn't eaten for at least the last twelve of those.

Putting his phone away, he walked the remainder of the distance to his car and climbed in. Instead of putting the key in the ignition he sat back in the seat. Laying his head back against the rest and shutting his eyes, he sought a moment of peace. Traffic buzzed past with regularity. The size of the lorries and buses making the old car shake slightly with the combination of air flow and vibration. Sleep wasn't desired but Caslin endeavoured to clear his mind, just to give his brain a break if nothing else, to perhaps sharpen the senses.

His thoughts drifted back to the call with Sullivan's source, playing out the transcript as he recalled it. Not necessarily in the order that the conversation had taken place but more randomly in the way it came to him. The person appeared to have spent time with Garry McNeil but in what capacity, he was unsure. The way that he structured his comments and the level of reticence in his responses, implied that he may be identifiable should he give too much away. Was he another veteran who had served with McNeil in Iraq or elsewhere? Had they met through some other route, a shared interest in fetish, perhaps?

Taking the caller at his word would indicate they were strong acquaintances, if not friends, and he did appear to be more knowledgeable about McNeil's interests than had been disclosed to the public. Was this Charlie? That notion scanned pretty well, the more he thought about it. However, Caslin had to reluctantly concede that he didn't know enough overall to draw any useful conclusions.

Of one thing he was certain. Sullivan was a canny enough journalist to have figured this out too and was more than capable of unearthing a bigger story. If the source was involved, or knew substantially more, then Sullivan would find it. Would that put him at risk? It might, if the source had something incriminating to hide. Could he be the elusive third person that Caslin was searching for? He shuddered at that prospect and once again considered the significance of the journalist's absence. He reached for his phone. Karen answered almost immediately. They exchanged pleasantries before his tone changed to one that made her take particular interest. She remembered it well.

"Tell me, when are you and the kids heading to France?"

"Not for another couple of weeks. The sixteenth, I think. Why?"

Caslin paused for a moment, reluctant to go into detail.

"This guy that you're staying with, do you trust him?"

"Nate, what kind of question is that?"

"Do you?"

"Of course."

"Could you head out earlier?"

"Why?"

"Could you?"

"Nate, what's going on?"

"Probably nothing. I'm just a little uneasy about something I'm working on and... look it's nothing to be overly concerned about, but I thought that it might be a good idea if you and the kids took off a bit earlier, that's all."

"That's all? Are you in some kind of troub—"

"No, no it's nothing like that. I'm fine, honestly. I'm not trying to frighten you unnecessarily—"

"So, you think it is necessary then?"

"Bloody hell, Karen. Can you do it?"

"I'll have to get the kids out of school early, not to mention have a chat with—"

"Good, do it, please."

"Okay," Karen sounded nervous, which was understandable. "When do you want us to leave?"

"Yesterday."

"Right, now you are scaring me. What's going on? I thought you weren't on that big case anymore."

Caslin silently fumed. His father must have been at it again.

"It'll turn out to be nothing, just something someone said... I want you all safe somewhere for the next few weeks, that's all."

"Okay. I'll take care of it and give you a call when we're ready to leave."

"Thank you."

"You will fill me in on all this later?"

"I will."

"And not leave me in the dark while we're away? I'll keep my mobile with me."

"I promise. I know you'll worry."

"I was thinking about you also... I still worry about you..."

"I'll sort things out this end. It'll all work out, soon enough. I expect I'm going over the top a bit."

"*Going over the top* is not something you do, Nathaniel. But I know you'll take care of it, whatever *it* is... I heard about that detective that was killed, on the news, this morning. Did you know her very well?"

"Reasonably well, yes."

"If there is anything—"

"Thanks. Look I have to go, someone needs me. Call me when you're set."

Caslin went to hang up but Karen stopped him.

"Oh, and Nate…"

"Yes."

"Take care of yourself."

"I will. Speak soon."

With that they both hung up. Caslin was suddenly left feeling cold, sitting alone in his car. The windows of the vehicle had steamed up and the light was fading even though it was only a little after lunchtime. Momentarily he considered whether he had done the right thing. Generally, a cautious person, with the occasional lapse into headlong abandonment, upon reflection he knew he would feel more comfortable with his family safely tucked away in Normandy, for a while. Putting the key in the ignition he started the car. It spluttered into life begrudgingly. Following a quick wipe of the windscreen with his sleeve he set off back to Fulford Road.

THE CID squad room could at best be described as an organised chaos and at worst, in borderline anarchy when Caslin reached it. In the previous week the sizable area, along with its resources, had been turned over to the Major Crime Unit investigating the Ravenscar shootings. All of a sudden, following the death of DC Underwood, there were two high-profile incidents being aggressively pursued. The upshot of that was the fracturing of a team who had been on top of their personal tasks only the day before. They were now finding their assignments hastily reallocated on a priority basis. DCS Broadfoot was taking root in Frank Stephens' office, as close to getting his shoes dirty as he was ever likely to get. Expressions on the faces of those around him ranged from serious to strained. No-one had been home and no-one expected to be doing so any time in the near future.

Caslin collared DI Baxter as he passed him in the congested entrance, guiding him out into the corridor.

"Any updates that I should be aware of before I head into the lion's den?" he indicated the DCI's office.

"SOCO are picking up the pace on Hayley's car. They've lifted a number of prints but whether they're our guy's, we don't know. Likewise, we're fast tracking DNA from under her fingernails. Maybe she got a hold of her assailant at some point. We're also processing some of Chloe's personal effects from her place to get a DNA profile."

"To try and match it with anything that we can get from Hayley, or the car?" Caslin asked. Baxter nodded. "Good. What about witnesses?"

Baxter shook his head.

"Nothing yet. So far the attacker is a ghost."

"That's becoming a common theme at the moment."

"You don't think it was Chloe, do you? Are you leaning towards your mystery man being the attacker, the one you spoke to?"

Caslin sighed and considered the point. It had occurred to him, he couldn't deny it but there was nothing to substantiate a link between the two. Nevertheless, Caslin's lack of belief in coincidence was pushing him in that direction. However, Chloe was the one with motive and opportunity and he couldn't ignore that.

"We need a break. Right now, I'd settle for anything, even a sketchy report on a suspicious vehicle."

"I know what you mean, how often can you keep banging against a brick wall?"

Caslin nodded and Baxter excused himself, heading back into CID. Baxter had a point. They were being thwarted at every turn that wasn't in itself unusual in any investigation until all the evidence had been gathered. Caslin had had the feeling for some time that they, he, had missed something. Walking into CID he went to his work station, avoiding eye contact with anyone who might engage him in conversation. Sifting through his files he took out the transcripts of the interviews he had made with Chloe McNeil. He took them with him and left CID to find somewhere quieter. In the absence of speaking to her directly, their previous conversations would have to do.

Ten minutes later, seated in the canteen with a cup of vending machine coffee before him, he began to reread her statements. The occasional person passed through but to all intents and purposes, he was alone. His concentration drifted away from the subject as he read Harman's comments. The young DC's death brought into sharp focus, once again. Pushing the thoughts from his mind, Caslin continued to scan the documents and it was on the second pass that he found what he was looking for. He read the lines for a third time just to see if he formulated the same conclusion. He did and, not for the first time, he was left cursing himself. How could he have missed such a classic deflection?

Perhaps it was because he had not considered the question to be the most searching at the time but Chloe's response had been text book. When asked *"where are the Horsvedts?"*, Chloe had responded with *"why would I do something to them?"*. Such an innocuous comment was telling. If a suspect replied to a question *with* a question, then it was odds on they had a desire not to answer the former. Again, Caslin castigated himself for missing it at the time. The suspicion lifted from his mind and left him with a certainty. Chloe was far deeper into this than she had admitted. Whether or not she had killed DC Underwood, they needed to bring her in, urgently. Swiftly packing up the transcripts he hurried upstairs to speak to Frank Stephens. The heavily reinforced belief that Chloe McNeil held the key piece to this particular puzzle, well at the forefront of his mind.

CHAPTER TWENTY-EIGHT

RISING before dawn he had showered, eaten, and made his way across the city well before the press of the morning commute. The trip on this occasion proved successful and he was beckoned into Sullivan's apartment by the bleary-eyed journalist, who seemingly hadn't benefitted from a similarly upbeat morning.

The apartment smelt funny to Caslin. It was an odour born of the mixture of human sweat alongside a lack of fresh air and fast-food containers. A shamefully familiar smell. The only other addition was that of the overflowing ashtrays dotted around. As if on cue, Sullivan sparked a cigarette while Caslin drew back the curtains in the living room. The apartment block was a modern one, built in the previous decade. Bland and uninspiring to look at from the outside, with precious little to redeem it from within. The daylight stung his eyes as he looked out over the car park below. The logic of the French doors and the Juliet balcony escaped him entirely. The haze of stale smoke was illuminated by the stream of winter sunshine and Caslin wafted his hand in a futile gesture to try and clear it.

"What brings you here, Inspector?" Sullivan asked from a seated position on the sofa. The folds of his dressing gown did little to flatter his appearance.

"Your source."

"What about him? I set you up as... requested."

"I want him."

"Don't we all, Inspector. Don't we all."

Sullivan laughed as he took a steep draw on his cigarette, exhaling the smoke directly at Caslin.

"You misunderstand me. I'm not here to force more out of you. I came only out of courtesy."

"I don't understand."

"That isn't surprising to me, Jimmy. You did me a favour, under protest I'll grant you but it led me to him. We're onto him and we're confident he'll be in custody within the next couple of hours. You had better find yourself another meal ticket, this one is spent."

Sullivan sat back into the sofa. His expression was unwavering but he didn't draw further on his smoke, the ash curling away at the end of the cigarette but yet to drop.

"Why would you be telling me?"

"It turns out he's not quite what you... and I, to be fair, thought that he was. He was convincing but—"

"He was full of it."

"Definitely full of something, yes."

"So why are you telling me?"

"Some strange, misguided notion, that I owe you one. To give you a chance to minimise your professional embarrassment. Depending on how far you took the story, of course."

Sullivan, at first appeared to be crestfallen before he managed to process the information. After that his expression conveyed an element of fear as the realisation dawned on him that he could come unstuck as a result of this.

"Why should I—"

"No reason why you should but then there's no reason for me to be here. I don't need to squeeze you. I would if the need was there, but it isn't. Call it even?"

The journalist stubbed out his cigarette in an overfull ashtray, disturbing the pile and sending some grey matter cascading to the coffee table below. Sullivan rubbed his face with the palms of his hands before their eyes met and he nodded. Caslin made to leave without another word, seeing his own way out. Pulling the front door closed behind him and heading downwards, his footfalls echoed around the concrete stairwell. The charade had played out as expected and Caslin hoped that the remainder would work just as well. There was a momentary flash of guilt at using Sullivan in this way. After all, Caslin still felt that the source was potentially dangerous and by stoking the hack's paranoia, there was a chance that this plan could backfire. He resolved the internal dispute by concluding that Sullivan was sharp enough to take care of himself. He wasn't entirely convinced of that, but it was too late now. With a bit of fortune, the journalist would be beating someone else with a stick soon enough.

Caslin had needed the respite and the few hours' sleep afforded him before the visit to Sullivan's had worked wonders. Three days on from DC Underwood's murder, Caslin could feel that they were close as he walked back into CID. The sounds of an energetic team came to his ear, he was buoyed.

"Where's the DCI?" he asked no-one in particular.

"Briefing Broadfoot and the other brass upstairs," DS Hunter said. "Word's come through that a parliamentary question is going to be asked in the commons today and they're concerned."

"Shitting bricks is more like it," Caslin replied. Undoubtedly some would feel their careers would be threatened by such a high-profile development, fortunately he no longer had that problem. "Okay, where are we with Chloe's known associates?"

"The bad news is no-one has seen her," Hunter said.

"And the good?"

"Is very good. She has few contacts outside of the York area, by all accounts. We've run down all those local to us and they haven't seen nor heard from her. She has some distant family down south and local police are chasing those up. Although, I doubt she'll reach out to them."

"Terry," he called out to Holt. "Financials?"

The DC dutifully walked over with notebook in hand.

"Chloe has limited funds in her bank account, deposits and withdrawals are much in line with patterns over the past few weeks. No withdrawals since she went missing. If she is running, she's not going to get far."

"Good work, Terry. Phone?"

"No activity," Baxter answered, having joined the conversation.

Caslin's confidence was growing. "It's only a matter of time."

"You think she's running then?" Hunter asked. "You don't think she's been abducted."

"Do you?" Caslin countered.

"No, I don't. There was nothing to indicate a struggle at her place."

"The more I think on it, I agree with you. She's running. Lack of activity on her account and phone tell me she's trying to be clever about it."

"Did she kill Hayley?" Holt asked, uncertainty edging into his tone.

Caslin bit his bottom lip before replying, "On that I still don't know. Let's find her first."

With little in the way of wealth and even fewer resources to aid her disappearance, Caslin felt sure that after a couple of days the net was tightening. The frustrating element to it all was that she had been under surveillance for so long that it seemed counter-intuitive to now be chasing her shadow.

The phone on Hunter's desk began to ring and she reached down to answer it. Caslin walked towards the information board to cast his eye over the enlarged map of York, coloured pins marking known haunts of Chloe and her associates. Attached slips of paper denoted which had been checked and crossed off. He almost failed to hear Hunter's excited shout. Turning, he went to her desk as she offered him her phone.

"We have a positive sighting."

Caslin indicated for Hunter to put the phone on speaker, telling the squad room to quieten down. Activity ceased as everyone stopped to listen when the call was put through.

"This is DI Caslin, with whom am I speaking?"

"Jack Martins," came the reply.

"And what do you have for me, Mr Martins?"

"I'm a haulier, long distance. I think I came across this woman you're looking for."

"You think? Can you be sure?"

"Yeah, sorry. I'm sure. You've got posters up all over the services here. I stopped for an early lunch and I saw—"

"Great, Jack," Caslin interrupted him. "Where did you see her?"

"Woodall Services on the M1, southbound. Just east of Sheffield. She was hitching."

"Good man, when was this?"

"Couple of hours ago, maybe. I didn't see the picture until just now."

Caslin cursed. He was pleased that the information flyers had generated a lead but gutted with the time delay. Putting his hand over the microphone he looked to Hunter.

"Flood that area with everything you can get your hands on. She's had enough time to get off in any number of directions but we might get lucky. I want all traffic units on major arterial routes within a hundred-mile radius of that location on alert." He then returned to his conversation with the haulier. "Did you speak with her, Jack?"

"Aye, I did. Like I said, she was hitching. I offered her a ride but she knocked me back."

"Why?"

"I was passing by the southbound services but crossing over to head north. She said that was the wrong direction for her."

"Well, she was right about that. You're sure it was her."

"Absolutely. I thought it a bit weird at the time."

"In what way?"

"Several, really. She didn't have anything on her. I mean, I pick up hitchers all the time and they travel light but she had nothing, bugger all. That doesn't happen. She was also a lot older than most people you meet. And looked in a bit of a mess, like she hadn't slept for a bit."

"Did you see her catch a lift with anyone else?"

"Err… no, can't say as I did, sorry."

"That's okay, thanks. Listen, I'm going to pass you over to a colleague to take some details from you but I appreciate your help."

A tense atmosphere replaced the initial elation in CID as they waited, the bubble of expectation deflating as the minutes ticked by. Chloe was tantalisingly close and yet, remained out of reach. Caslin sat in his chair observing the team swirling around him as they optimistically hoped for the results that their efforts deserved. He didn't share their positivity. For his part, he spent the time reviewing reports from the previous twenty-four hours, looking for the slightest detail that may have been missed but failing to come up with anything. If he was honest, he was merely killing time.

He contemplated his meeting with Jimmy Sullivan that morning. His brief excursion to the journalist's home had a purpose. The wheels had been set in motion and the results would come. He wasn't certain but he was confident and until then, it was a waiting game. The surprise came soon after when his phone rang. He had been expecting a call, perhaps not so soon but anticipating one, nonetheless. However, the caller was far from whom he had expected.

"Inspector Caslin?" the voice asked quietly.

"Yes."

"It's Chloe… Chloe McNeil. I need your help."

THE WINTER SUN sat low in the sky. The ornamental trees cast long shadows and the water feature gurgled away as if it ran through the most natural place in the world. To his mind, the wooden seats may well lend a stylish edge to the Winter Gardens in Sheffield but they did little for his back. Caslin arched it from his seated position in a vain attempt to release the pressure. A small group of boys and girls sat off to his left, deep in conversation, with only the occasional explosion of laughter to indicate the lightness of their mood. Caslin guessed they were students on their wind down to Christmas.

Glancing up and through the branches, adorned with decorations, he watched as the clock ticked round to 3 p.m. before picking up his coffee cup. The temperature outside was dropping away rapidly. Snow had been forecast again but he hoped they were wrong. The whiteout was always stunning in Yorkshire, beauty not altogether lost on him even during the recent tribulations. However, if you had to get anywhere or achieve anything beyond the four walls of your home, it was a severe pain in the backside.

Another glance towards the clock. It now read five past. If she didn't show in the next ten minutes he would call it a day. Having already sat there for an hour, he was in no mood to stay much longer. The call received from Chloe ensured a frenzy of activity, not least a hair-raising drive south at speeds he could hardly imagine travelling at. Even in a convoy of traffic cars with all the bells and whistles, it was still frightening. That journey had given them a window of little more than thirty minutes to set up their operation.

Beyond Caslin's view there were two officers holed up with the security guards in their control room, poring over the CCTV system, waiting to clock her arrival. Further to that there were plain clothes officers all around the Winter Gardens, blending in with the public. They had even managed to supplant DS Hunter into the coffee shop as a waitress for the afternoon. She was the only member of York CID that they felt confident Chloe would never have met. Apart from DI Baxter, the remaining officers on the operation were all sequestered from Sheffield. It made sense as they knew the area far better than the team from York. A hasty briefing was convened at the Nunnery Square Station where photos of their target were passed out. Every officer was fore-warned to expect the unexpected and no-one was in any doubt that this arrest could be far from straightforward.

Despite Chloe having initiated the meeting they were all well aware that at one end of the scale, Caslin could be dragged into some kind of an ambush and at the other, Chloe might lose heart and change her mind. With either eventuality, or anywhere in between, they would need to move fast to secure her in custody. Casually, Caslin glanced around. Baxter was seated within twenty feet reading a newspaper, or at least that's what he appeared to be doing. DS Hunter was clearing tables a short distance away. The remaining officers' whereabouts he could only guess at, as their faces had all merged into one since the rushed briefing.

Operations such as this were unusual to Caslin. More often than not they would have had a far greater lead time to get them-selves organised. With that said they had been praying for a break and this certainly qualified as such.

Placing his cup on the bench next to him, Caslin realised that his hands were sweating and he wiped his palms on the flat of his thighs. At that moment a flicker of movement from Baxter caught his attention, only the slightest darting of the eyes but it was enough. Looking over to the eastern entrance, a figure had passed through the glazed door and was glancing around her as she walked. She wore a heavy coat that shrouded her figure along with a woollen hat, pulled down to just above her eyebrows, frizzy hair protruding in all directions from beneath. Unmistak-ably, it was Chloe McNeil. She made eye contact almost immedi-ately and headed straight for Caslin. Instinctively, he stood up to greet her. Nervous as he was, he didn't show it and managed a soft smile. Although his was deeply contrived, she returned it warmly with one of her own.

With an open hand he bade her to sit down, which she grate-fully did. Caslin also returned to his seat and offered her the second cup of coffee that he had purchased along with his own, fifteen minutes earlier. Taking her measure, he thought she looked dreadful. To be fair, she wasn't in great shape when he had seen her previously but her appearance had certainly altered. She was haggard, her eyes bloodshot and sunken, with far darker rings beneath them than he recalled. There was little colour in her heavily lined face and he wondered when she had last managed any meaningful sleep.

"It's only a latte, but it has milk and more importantly, should still be warm."

"Thank you, I know I'm later than I said but I wanted to be sure."

"Sure, about what?"

Chloe looked around.

"Sure that no-one was watching."

Caslin had to try very hard not to laugh at that as he too glanced around.

"True, that would be awful."

"Not by your lot!" Chloe snapped. "There is probably a dozen of you around here somewhere. Don't worry. I'm not planning on doing one."

"Then by whom?"

Chloe's eyes scanned the Winter Garden once more, as if expecting to see a face in the crowd. Satisfied that that wasn't the case, she tentatively sipped at her coffee.

"The same person that I think you're looking for and if you're not, then you damn well should be."

"And who might that be?"

Chloe fixed him with a stare.

"Lee."

Caslin saw fit to keep the conversation going rather than take her into custody, there and then. If she was opening up, now was as good a time as any. A voice crackled in his earpiece but he chose to ignore it. Casually reaching up, he removed it from his ear and put it in his pocket.

"Your friends?" Chloe asked. Caslin nodded with a hint of a smile. "Keen, aren't they?"

"They want you in handcuffs."

"Me?"

Caslin nodded once more, accompanied by the slightest of shrugs.

"By all accounts, you fled a crime scene. Doesn't look good."

"My place?"

"Yes," Caslin sat back a little. "Can you tell me what happened?"

Chloe took a deep breath followed by a mouthful of coffee, closing her eyes as she swallowed before fixing Caslin with a stare.

"Lee came to mine. He scared the crap out of me."

"And Lee is?"

"A friend of Garry's. I was in the kitchen looking for a torch under the sink. You know there was a power cut?"

Caslin nodded, "I know."

"Then, there he was at the window," she continued. "Just standing there. Proper weird."

"You let him in?"

"Didn't see as I had much choice."

"What did he want?"

"Me to go with him."

"Where?"

Chloe shook her head.

"No idea but I told him that your lot were outside, anyway and I couldn't go anywhere. He didn't like that. Said he had already seen the car which was why he came around the back."

"What happened then?"

"He told me he'd take care of it. He went to the front window and had a look before going back outside."

"And?"

"And what? As soon as I thought he was clear of the back yard, I grabbed a coat and took off."

Caslin had been listening intently, assessing her words as she spoke them. They didn't appear to be well rehearsed but he had been wrong before. Keen to keep her talking, he chose to leave Hayley's murder aside for the moment. He took another sip of his coffee.

"Why did you run?"

Chloe laughed. It was a nervous laugh without genuine humour.

"You would too, if you knew him."

"Tell me about him."

"Garry brought him home one night, said he was a mate from the army but I didn't see it."

"Why not?" Caslin asked, remembering the visit to the pub in Catterick and the conversation about Garry and his withdrawn friend.

"Never mentioned him before and I got to know most of them over the years. Don't doubt that he was military. He had the walk, you know?"

"Not really, but I'll take your word on it."

"Anyway, he was proper weird, Lee. Quiet, didn't say a lot but creepy."

"Creepy?"

"Yeah, always watching me as I did things. Even just folding the washing or something and there he was. He'd smile when I looked at him but it was… just…"

"Weird?" Caslin offered. She nodded enthusiastically.

"I reckon he's on the run."

"Why do you think that?"

"He never had anything, no ID, no pay cheque. Always did stuff cash-in-hand, he was shifty."

"Why are you so scared of him?"

Chloe looked at the floor. She rubbed at her eyes with her left hand and sighed deeply.

"Him and Garry, they had the same interests. He's the one you were talking about."

"The video recordings?"

"Yeah, he's the one you want. He did them… well, some of them."

"Chloe," Caslin sighed. "Why didn't you say so earlier?"

She shook her head and once again failed to meet Caslin's gaze. She could only repeat what she had already said.

"They liked the same stuff."

"Why do you think he wanted you to go with him?"

Chloe considered her response for a moment before answering.

"I've been thinking about nothing else. Lee and Garry, they sort of thought I was theirs… like they were entitled to… you know?"

"Both of them?"

"Yeah, I guess Lee still sees it like that but it never was… it never was… he's weird."

"What's his full name?"

"It's something Chinese. *Lee Nargong* or *Nehon*, something like that. Sorry, I don't know for sure. He was only introduced to me fully once. The first time that Garry brought him home."

The conversation was cut short as Simon Baxter came to stand before them. He pulled himself upright in what seemed to Caslin to be a somewhat stuffy manner.

"About time we took this back to the station, wouldn't you say?"

Baxter was clearly annoyed. It didn't take a detective to figure that out. Caslin glanced up at him and then across at Chloe.

"The night you took off a police officer was murdered, DC Hayley Underwood. She was sitting in a car outside your house."

"I didn't know… I…" she stammered.

"We'll find him, Chloe," Caslin said softly. She smiled weakly at that. "And you're going to help us."

The smile faded rapidly.

CHAPTER TWENTY-NINE

ONCE SAFELY RETURNED TO YORK, the senior team assembled in Frank Stephens' office to plan their next move. The success of bringing in Chloe quickly forgotten as fractures within the Major Crimes Unit threatened to widen.

"Why have we got her sitting comfortably in an interview room? It beggars belief. She should be sweating in a holding cell," Baxter stated forcefully. Ranking the same as Caslin, he was stepping above his pay grade but he wasn't alone.

"That would be a mistake," Caslin argued.

"You're kidding me, surely?" Baxter was dumbfounded. "You kill a copper and get what, a cup of tea and a toasted sandwich?"

"We don't know that she's killed anyone—"

"Piss off, Caslin!"

"Calm down, Simon," Stephens said, verbally stepping between the two of them. "She can be charged this afternoon. Let's see if we can get a confession out of her first. Nathaniel's right, we don't have enough yet but we'll get it."

"Sorry, Guv but you're both wrong on this."

The DCI was somewhat taken aback as he looked to Caslin.

"I'm listening."

"Chloe is still our best shot at tracking down this Lee. He's proving elusive at best but I'll put everything I have on it that this is the same guy the ex-servicemen, that McNeil associated with, referred to as 'Charlie'. He's the new focus of this investigation and Chloe is a link to him. The *only* one that we currently have."

"We've got half a team sitting through there throwing high-fives at each other because we've got Hayley's killer downstairs and you want me to sit on it? Are you serious?"

"You said it yourself, Frank," Caslin was into his stride. "We don't have enough on her for the CPS to prove reasonable doubt. Maybe the forensics will turn something up, we'll have to wait and see on that. *Maybe* we can get a confession out of her *if*, and it's a big *if*, she actually did it."

"You've got to be winding me up," Baxter said solemnly. His anger having subsided if only a little.

"Wanting someone to be the killer doesn't always make it so," Caslin challenged. Baxter looked away in disgust.

"What then, are you suggesting we do with her?" the DCI asked.

"Let's give the white coats a chance. In the meantime, we can try and elicit something positive from her in the coming days and figure out what to throw at her in the future. If we charge her now, she'll demand a solicitor and the barriers go up. I need... *we need* her on board."

Frank Stephens appeared to visibly slump in his chair. Caslin understood the frustrations of the team. They wanted someone in custody for the murder of a colleague and there was enough circumstantial evidence to convince many of them that they already had her. The DCI looked to the one who held the casting vote. He had maintained composure throughout the exchanges and said nothing, Kyle Broadfoot. All eyes looked to him.

"I know many on the unit see this Lee character as just that, a name in a play. A cover to mask the McNeils' actions. We all want a result and sooner, rather than later," he paused and Caslin wondered whether he was still to make up his mind. "I'm prepared to go the extra mile on this one. I'm backing Nathaniel. We have nothing to lose and so much more to gain."

Caslin appreciated the vote of confidence, "Thank you, Sir."

Broadfoot looked him square in the eye, "As long as you play it right."

Caslin knew exactly what that meant. The meeting broke up without further discussion. The decision had been taken. Broadfoot's support had come as quite a shock to Caslin. Entering CID, he considered that the DCS also wanted a greater result than just Chloe, albeit for altogether different reasons.

THE CLOCK on the wall of the squad room had just passed eight o'clock when a file dropped onto the desk before Caslin. He glanced at the beige folder and then up at a smiling Simon Baxter, who appeared almost gleeful as he looked down.

"What's this?" Caslin asked, whilst unwinding the looped string holding the folder together.

"I called in a favour from an old friend in the Military Police."

Caslin opened the folder and inside were several sheets of printed copy. The first was a personnel form from the MOD. The grainy black-and-white image in the top right-hand corner depicted an Asian man of oriental appearance, round-faced and youthful. A quick scan through saw his birth date was the 3rd August 1984.

"That's our boy."

"That's our boy," Baxter reiterated. "Arrived from Hong Kong, along with his parents in '88, well ahead of the handover. His father worked in the RHK Police. The family all took British citizenship a year later."

Caslin continued to read through the file, looking for connections to anyone in the case. He didn't see any.

"A familial residential address in Hull is listed here," Caslin read aloud.

"He's a Private in the Royal Logistic Corps, at least he was," Baxter stated. "He had five years in until going absent without leave, in the February of last year."

"Lee Na Honn," Caslin read out the name. "Chloe wasn't far off. How does he tie in with McNeil?"

"No clue as yet. As far as I can see there's no obvious link."

"Not in Iraq or Afghanistan."

Baxter shook his head.

"No, this guy wasn't frontline."

"He received training in telecommunications, though," Caslin indicated a line on the second page. "Looks like Harman was right."

"Harman? About what?"

"His training in telecoms and weaponry. It's the old Pioneer Corps stuff."

"What's that?"

"Oh, they would drop in with the forward infantry. You know, first boots on the ground. They'd set up the comms for those that were following on," Caslin replied absently, whilst reading through the document.

"Maybe they met around then?"

Caslin shrugged. It was possible but comparing his recollection of McNeil's service history with a cursory inspection of the detail before him, he couldn't see a crossover. He considered pulling out the page that Colonel Edwards had provided him with, back in Catterick, but then thought better of it. They could analyse it at a later date. Lee Na Honn had an exemplary record for the first three years of his service but had subsequently been in trouble on numerous occasions. In the latter two years, he had been placed on warning on two occasions. There were no details as to why this might be the case.

"Let's get his face out there."

"No, wait a second."

"What for?" Baxter challenged. "We're onto him."

"But he doesn't know that. He still thinks he's a ghost. I have a better idea. Let's go and have a chat with Frank and my new mate, Kyle."

"YOU MUST BE out of your mind!" Chloe said defiantly, folding her arms across her chest and sitting back forcefully in her chair.

"You wanted to be safe. This will achieve that."

"If it doesn't get me killed first, you mean?"

"We'll be right there the whole time. There is a risk, I'm not going to lie to you, but this is your best shot. And ours for that matter."

"Why don't you just do your job and leave me out of it?"

Caslin sighed. The planned course of action had been a tough sell to Broadfoot, even with his revitalised faith in Caslin's abilities. Getting Chloe to buy-in was proving far more difficult.

"If you want this to be over, then here it is. It's your choice," Caslin placed a mobile phone on the table. It was hers.

"He'll never go for it."

"We'll see. Lee doesn't know that we have you here. Your image has been up in lights for the last two days and we haven't let it out that we're no longer looking for you."

"Oh yeah, and you guys are so good at keeping things quiet."

"Let's not forget that helping us will help you. It's your choice," Caslin stated once again. He gently pushed the phone across the table towards her.

There was a pause in the conversation where everyone present waited patiently, keeping a watchful eye on Chloe as she considered her situation. Her eyes never left the phone on the table, almost as if it was a prize possession that she dared not touch. After what seemed like an age she gently bobbed her head forward, which Caslin took as an acknowledgement. He instantly swept up the phone. Turning it on, he passed it over to her. After a moment of scrolling through her contact list, she selected a number and glanced up at Caslin.

"What do you want me to say?"

THANKFULLY THE FORECAST snow had thus far held off. The clouds had still rolled in, obscuring the moonlight and leaving the night slightly warmer than it would otherwise have been. That was the only positive to be taken from the situation. Caslin's plan appeared to be working but as he sat in the car, alongside Frank Stephens, he contemplated the potential for disaster.

"I don't mind telling you that I'm a little nervous with this one, Guv. We've not had enough time to set this up."

Stephens passed him a wry, sideways smile, "Now you tell me. Na Honn has taken the bait. Let's reel him in."

Chloe's frightened call had been almost believable to those at Fulford Road and now, three hours later, they waited just off the A1 at his chosen spot. Chloe sat in the all-night diner. It was an American 1950's style restaurant, all stainless-steel reflecting pink and blue neon. The location lent itself conspicuously to an almost altogether surreal situation.

They waited roughly three hundred yards from the diner, on a service road used only by local traffic. In this neck of the Lincolnshire farmlands, there was precious little of it. Elsewhere in the darkness were three other CID teams. Terry Holt and DS Hunter held positions off to the south and west, respectively. Another car, containing DI Atwood and two further officers, was parked to the south east on a farm track, behind a small copse of trees. The location was fraught with operational constraints. Vantage points were limited due to the exposure of the open farm-land encompassing them. The car park was accessed only from the southbound side of the A1 and apart from the local minor roads, the sealing off of the area without making it apparent, was nigh on impossible.

Chloe sat at the counter, absently sipping on a glass of cola that she had bought. Through his binoculars, Caslin could see that she was nervous. Ordinarily, this operation would never have gone ahead so late in the day, with such little prior planning but this was Na Honn's demand. To delay the meeting may well have tipped their hand. They felt that there was no choice but to agree.

Caslin was grateful that Chloe wasn't alone inside the building. Baxter had taken up a position to the left of the entrance. That seat gave him an uninterrupted view of anyone coming into the car park as well as the diner itself. Further to that, there were four armed officers in the kitchens to the rear, ready to move in if the signal was given. Another two sets of armed response officers were waiting a short distance away in unmarked vehicles, ready to deploy at a moment's notice. The last piece of the tactical jigsaw was the police helicopter, which was flying a holding pattern over Lincoln City, some ten miles away. Everyone present knew that the helicopter would only be deployed in the event of things not going to plan.

Checking the time, he saw that it was approaching ten-past eleven. Caslin quietly reviewed the positioning of the various teams and reassured himself that they had covered as many variables as possible. The only option that was available to them now was to wait. The tension had been growing since the very moment Chloe had agreed to the meeting.

"All teams, check-in," DCI Stephens requested.

There then followed a response in numerical order of all those present. All reported no change in their status.

"Do you think he'll show?"

Caslin pursed his lips before answering.

"He'll show. He won't be able to stay away."

"What if he's rumbled us?"

"He'll show."

Another twenty minutes passed by without incident. Stephens took radio checks at ten-minute intervals. As the time passed, the feeling that they would get a result began to fade amongst the waiting officers.

"How long do we give it?" Frank Stephens asked as he checked his watch once more.

Caslin glanced at the clock on the dashboard and was about to reply when his phone rang. Removing it from his pocket bathed the interior of the car in blue light. The number was withheld and he took a deep breath before answering. A familiar voice was at the end of the line.

"Did you honestly believe that I was going to walk straight into your little gathering?"

"What are you talking about?" Caslin played dumb.

"Credit me with a little intelligence, please. You're insulting me."

Caslin glanced over at Stephens who understood who the caller was and got out of the vehicle as quickly as he could. Once outside the DCI began relaying details to the teams positioned around the diner. For now, they were to hold position.

"I figured that you would be calling me at some point."

"What, after that little stunt you pulled with Sullivan? For someone of his experience, he is certainly naïve when it comes to playing the game. You on the other hand, Inspector, are another matter entirely. Although, that was a clumsy effort to flush me out."

"What are you playing at, Lee?"

"Ahh, so the little bird has been tweeting? It was only a matter of time, I suppose."

"What's the end game here?"

"I'm not giving you all the answers, Nathaniel. You're paid to figure these things out-"

"I'm paid to get you off the streets and that's exactly what I intend to do."

"To stop me in my tracks. Is that it?"

"Something like that, yes."

"We'll see. Wait a moment, would you?"

"Why? You have something more pressing to—"

The sound of a gunshot tore through the silence. For a second,

Caslin thought he was the target before he heard a delayed sound relayed through his earpiece, preceded by that of breaking glass. There then followed a momentary pause before shouting emanated once more, through his earpiece.

"Delta One is down. I repeat, Delta One is down," a lone voice crackled, quoting the code name for Chloe McNeil.

Caslin raised his binoculars but all he could see was the pandemonium within the diner. People appeared to be running in every direction. Another voice cut through on the network, it was Frank Stephens.

"All stations secure Delta One, secure... Delta... One. Does anyone have eyes on the shooter?"

"From the east," was the reply but Caslin noted the response was via his phone.

"The shot came from the east, repeat, from the east. I have no eyes on," Baxter's strained reply was transmitted.

Stephens issued orders as Caslin tried to make sense of his own confused state.

"All stations converge to the east. Exercise extreme caution. I need that chopper in here now."

Caslin heard laughter coming down the phone line. Anger flared within him and he scrambled from the car, bringing his own radio to bear.

"Switch to the alternate channel. I repeat, switch to the alternate channel. Suspect has our comms."

Frank Stephens looked across. His ashen-faced expression was one of fear as the realisation of what was happening dawned on him.

"Shit!"

"What are you playing at, Lee?" Caslin shouted. "Tell me!"

There was a period of silence. Caslin swore he could feel his heart pounding within his chest. His breath was coming in short, ragged gasps. He stared into the darkness trying to make out what was hidden beyond his sight. The reply, when it came, was crystal clear.

"Cleaning house."

Further silence followed before a monotone beeping signified that the call had been disconnected. Caslin hurled his phone across the bonnet of the car where it bounced off and disappeared from view.

"Bastard!"

"Status on that chopper?" Frank Stephens asked.

Caslin didn't pick up the response as he was in a daze and stumbled away from the car. Closing his eyes, he sought to control his breathing, whilst taking in what was going on. The outlying units were approaching the scene. Quick statements were flying in as each reported their position and began the search. A voice requested the condition of Delta One but by this point, Caslin was on his knees, head cradled in his hands as a wave of nausea passed over him.

The roar of the engine starting up snapped him back into focus and he swiftly clambered into the passenger seat. DCI Stephens glanced over as he floored the accelerator and they took off down the access road. They were on the scene within moments. The sound of the police helicopter came to their ears as they got out of the vehicle. A searchlight from above began scanning the area to the east. Caslin knew they would be using a thermal camera to try to pinpoint Na Honn's position. The barking of an Alsatian announced the arrival of a dog handler and Caslin silently hoped that between the resources on the ground and in the air, they would have success. However, his instincts told him otherwise.

CHAPTER THIRTY

THE EFFORTS of the previous evening left a hollow feeling within the unit. The atmosphere in the squad room was notably flat during the debriefing. Search teams were still out scouring the vicinity of the diner but no trace had been found of Lee Na Honn or his firing position. The suspect had vanished into the night. The apparent lack of speed to the search was reasonable under the circumstances. Pursuing an armed suspect under the veil of darkness was always precarious but the presence of the helicopter had given them some sense of security. No hits on the thermal camera implied he had fled the scene. Even so, the going was slow with caution key to their approach. With the benefit of hindsight that should have been the view they took to the whole operation. Hindsight truly was a wonderful thing.

"When did you last get some sleep?"

Caslin looked up at Kyle Broadfoot, not having heard his approach. A glance at the clock and a quick calculation later, he replied.

"It's been a while."

"You should go home, take a shower and get some rest. I've sent most of the others home too. We can pick things up first thing."

First thing, Caslin thought about it. That was only in a little over three hours' time, what with it already ten to four in the morning. He didn't reply and merely shook his head. Broadfoot shrugged and walked away. Caslin couldn't help but wonder how the DCS was going to explain this debacle. His paranoia began to creep back in. Despite gaining approval for the operation, it was ultimately his plan that had failed and Caslin felt responsible. Accountability and responsibility were, however, two very different things. Sensing, rather than observing, people milling about he needed some space and left CID. The rest of the station was pretty much deserted but instead of going downstairs, he chose to head up. Pushing open the door at the top of the stairwell he walked out onto the roof.

Picking his way around the vent covers he made his way across the flat roof. To the north lay York, its orange glow illuminating the sky above. Even without the cloud cover there would be precious few stars visible. The wind was getting up and the resulting chill caused him to shiver. Thrusting his hands deep into the pockets of his overcoat, he pressed his arms to his side and stamped his feet to try and generate some much needed warmth. The bout of nausea that had struck him hours earlier had been replaced by a banging headache. That was a condition more familiar to him but one that basic painkillers failed to counter. Caslin had to consider the cause. Was it diet, general fitness, lifestyle or a reaction to stress? He found none of those answers palatable. Each would require some monumental effort on his part to tackle them. In truth, there was little motivation for that.

Approaching the edge of the building he sat down on the surrounding ledge, side-on to the drop below. Ignoring the cold touch of the concrete beneath him, he drew one leg up and hugged his knee. A patrol car left from the rear of the station and engaged its blue lights, accelerating away in the direction of the city centre. Taking out his phone, latterly retrieved from where it lay a short distance from a boundary drainage ditch, he surveyed the damage. There were a couple of scuffs to the rear of the unit and a small scratch to the screen, much to his surprise it had held up well. The build quality was impressive, rightly so for the money. He typed out a text to Karen, nothing particularly insightful, asking after her and the children. He sent it knowing not to expect a reply until the morning.

Turning his thoughts back to the events of that evening he contemplated how they had got it so wrong, or more to the point, his complicity in the enterprise. They had discussed the potential pitfalls of the operation, the public place, as well as the nature of their suspect. Having considered virtually every conceivable factor they believed they could realistically contain him. No-one considered the scenario that played out.

If he wanted Chloe dead then why hadn't he killed her at her home, three days ago? Was it as simple as believing that she had betrayed him to the police or had he planned to kill her all along, perhaps in a different way? Why was Chloe the only victim, why not take down some police officers as well, just for good measure? All rational logic indicated to him that Lee was the most likely suspect in Hayley Underwood's murder, so the precedent was there.

So many questions and nowhere near enough answers. Lee Na Honn was intelligent, of that there was no denial. Reviewing his file, Caslin had read that he was an Oxbridge graduate, achieving an upper second, reading law. Not usually the qualification that leads one to a career in the RLC. Not without a commission at any rate. There still appeared to be no direct link to Garry McNeil either, which Caslin found an ongoing source of frustration.

What Iain Robertson and his team had turned up on the first victim, uncovered at Radford Farm, indicated that McNeil somehow moved amongst those who either had little or nowhere else to go. The dead man, William Johnson, had been a homeless veteran with no family to miss him. The Horsvedts also appeared to have disappeared unnoticed from the radar. Likewise, Lee Na Honn was living off the grid. Was that how McNeil found his victims? That would certainly explain why he had gone undetected for so long but where the two men came together, and how their dynamic worked, escaped Caslin entirely.

Not for the first time he considered his position. Having always believed that he was cut from the right cloth for this line of work, he now faced the reality that maybe he was falling short. If that was the case then lives may have been lost as a result. Tears welled in his eyes but he forced them back, along with the despair that threatened to overwhelm him.

Reaching into his coat pocket he took out the vial that contained his release. The confidence that he had once held in such abundance, now reduced to little more than a craving for the contents within. Holding the tubular plastic in the palm of his hand, his attention passed to another liveried car making off from the station rear. The vehicle only engaging its lights as it reached the main road. Returning the vial unopened to an inner pocket, he rubbed at his face. His cheeks were cold and his nose stung with the pressure.

The conversation kept repeating in his mind. Two words that were so simple and yet telling, or at least should be. Despite the little that they knew about him, it seemed that Lee Na Honn had a process, what appeared random was not so. He was organised and methodical, albeit in a brutal fashion. What had he meant by "cleaning house"? Initially, Caslin saw it as simply tying up a loose end, that being Chloe. However, the phrase kept returning over and over. Standing up, he headed back inside.

Briefly ducking back into CID, he scanned through Na Honn's file once more and made a note of what he was looking for. He then swiftly headed downstairs and out into the car park. Getting into his car he took his phone from his pocket and tossed it onto the passenger seat. Thankful for the cloud cover so no ice had been able to form on the windscreen, he started the engine and drove off.

The car appeared to stutter as he turned south onto Fulford Road, heading away from the city centre. He continued on until entering Barlby where he took a left, towards junction 37 of the eastbound M62. The motorway was empty with the exception of a few lorries, who were presumably aiming to depart for the continent from the docks of Hull. The slow-moving traffic, occupying the nearside lane, failed to slow his journey as he breezed past them.

Long ago he came to the conclusion that once you had exhausted all possibilities and felt there was nowhere else to go, the best course of action was to start again at the beginning. In this case, he would go home, not his own but to the former of his chief suspect.

Unfamiliar with the city, not to mention having become overly reliant on sat nav in the past few years, it was approaching 7 a.m. by the time Caslin finally pulled up outside the address. The residence was an imposing old Victorian terrace, located just beyond the pedestrianised high street, at the edge of a traffic-controlled area. The limited parking on the street was occupied. Multiple signs denoted designated timeslots for permit holders only. Waste collection must be due that day as blue wheelie bins lined the pavements.

Caslin was surprised how light he found the traffic to be at that time of day and decided to leave his car double parked. He assessed that the width of the road was sufficient to allow free movement of vehicles. Locking the car, he approached the house. The white-painted exterior stood out against the red brick façade of its neighbours. The house was in need of some maintenance. The paintwork around the windows was peeling and plants grew from the guttering that edged the roof. Net curtains hung in the bay windows, obscuring what was within. Even if the darkness beyond had been illuminated, the detail would remain masked.

No lights appeared to be on inside. After walking up the hedge-lined path he took a quick peek through the letter box. All that achieved was to give the impression that the inside was as dated as the out. The hallway was carpeted with a pattern that Caslin found vile and the walls were adorned with pictures hanging from the original rail. Standing up he rang the bell. Three short bursts and he stepped back to enable him to see if a light came on in any of the upstairs windows. Nothing happened.

Squatting down, he peered through the letter box for a longer spell, only to catch a glimpse of movement beyond. Looking more intently, he tried to make out what he had seen. In the gloom of the hallway and kitchen beyond, he saw and heard nothing. He waited patiently to no avail. Writing it off as a trick of the mind, he stood up once more and walked back along the path. Reaching the car, he turned to face the house for a final time. He had his keys in his hand and was about to unlock the door when he glanced off to his right, away from the high street.

Putting the keys back in his pocket, he stepped onto the pavement and set off down the street just as a bus negotiated his obstructively parked car. The driver first gave Caslin a frown, followed by a gesticulation when he was ignored. It only took a minute and Caslin found himself passing through a side passage running adjacent to the terrace. Making his way around to the rear, he struggled to identify the Na Honn house. It wasn't painted in the same fashion as at the front. Each building appeared much like any other. Rubbish bags were piled high in places within the confines of the narrow alleyway. He had to pick his way past them. Remnants of discarded takeaways and broken bottles littered the area, having been cast aside at frequent intervals. A dog barked as he passed by one yard. The animal hurled itself against the boundary fence as he approached.

Selecting what he guessed to be the right house, he tried the rear gate. It was locked and a quick shake confirmed he wasn't getting through. The fence alongside was six feet high but he judged the structure should support his weight. With a quick glance to either side of him he hoisted himself up and over into the yard beyond. Landing with a thump, he braced himself against a brick out-building to get his balance. The floor beneath his feet was paved with concrete and there were some raised planters off to one side. The contents of which had long since died. The house was still in darkness. Several of the neighbouring buildings now had lights on upstairs.

Carefully, he made his way to the rear entrance. Stepping over upturned plant pots and catching his foot on a patio set, obscured in the darkness, he nearly tripped over. The resulting screech, as the leg of the chair scraped across the concrete, sounded loud at that time of day. *What did he think he was achieving here?*

Moving on to the back door which was located in an extended dog-leg to the building, incorporating the old coal shed, he made to peer through into the kitchen. He stopped dead in his tracks. The rear door was ajar. The jamb showed signs of fresh damage as if the door had recently been forced. Caslin's heart rate increased and he rapidly considered his options. Almost instinctively he nudged the door further. It squeaked on its hinges but opened effortlessly. Caslin waited outside. No sounds emanated from within and he chanced a look through the doorway. With nothing to deter him, he cautiously looked to both left and right as he entered. Reaching into his pocket for his mobile, he found it missing. A frantic search of his coat revealed he didn't have it. Silently, he cursed himself as he remembered it was still in the car. *Proceed or retreat?*

Taking another couple of steps, he cast his eyes about the kitchen. Scanning the worktops, he didn't see anything that he had hoped to. There were a few dirty saucepans, a microwave with some occasional trays stacked on top and what looked like unsorted mail, piled alongside. The draining board had a few cups and plates sitting on it, with a half filled washing-up bowl in the sink, containing dirty water. Coming to a drawer unit next to the cooker, he opened the top one. It was full of assorted cutlery. The second had tea towels and long boxes, most likely cling film and tin foil. The third had something more useful to him, a wooden rolling pin, roughly an inch-and-a-half thick. Caslin hefted it. The solidity gave him a reassuring sense that boosted his confidence. Resuming his search, he looked for a telephone but there was no extension in the kitchen.

There was only one exit from the room. One that went into the main body of the building and he edged his way towards it. The adrenalin surged and he sought to remain calm. Breathing deeply through his mouth, he tried to get oxygen into his system faster. Reaching the threshold to the rear reception room he stopped. Taking another deep breath, he leaned around the corner, ready to react to anything untoward. There was nothing. Once again, he moved forward. The ticking of a clock above the fireplace was the only sound that carried to him.

On the far side of the room were two doors. One opened into the hallway and the other was in the opposing corner. That door was closed. Caslin thought the second was either a cupboard or gave access to the cellar, the latter was more likely. The room had an antique dining table and chairs positioned at its centre with a matching sideboard, adorned with ornaments, running adjacent to the kitchen wall. The furnishings conspired to make the room appear far smaller than it was. The varnished floorboards creaked under foot as he progressed but there was nothing he could do about that.

The hall was as Caslin had seen through the letter box. Spartanly furnished, with an occasional table set just within the front door, he saw a telephone upon it. He considered phoning for support but all of a sudden, he had a crisis of confidence. Could he afford to make two bad calls in one twenty-four-hour period? Choosing to wait, he turned his attention to the sitting room. Smaller than the room he had just vacated, it also appeared to be inappropriately furnished for the space available. An oversized leather sofa and two non-matching chairs dominated the space before the period fireplace. A small television stood in one corner, upon a unit with shelving above, which was rammed full of books. Outside the dawn was breaking. The darkness gradually passing into daylight but Caslin did not as yet, receive any benefit.

Increased traffic noise came to his ear, followed by something else. He stopped and listened intently, trying to ascertain what it was he had heard. Remaining motionless for at least two minutes, he faced the doorway. Nothing could now be heard above and beyond the noise outside. He moved back out to the hall and made his way around to the stairs. Taking the first three steps quickly, he stopped once more and strained to see into the darkness above him. The balustrade was open and he resumed his course at a slower pace. Ascending sideways and remaining vigilant to any movement on the landing above, he progressed.

The landing had four doors off it. The first was open and evidently led to the bathroom. Edging forward, he looked through the crack between door and frame to see nothing unusual. Of the remaining three doors, two were closed and the third, the front room with the bay window, was pulled to. The landing had a creased runner and he caught his foot, stumbling forward. At that moment he heard what he thought was a muffled sound. Gently testing the first door he came to, he found it firmly shut. Moving on, he went to the open door, feeling sure that the sound had originated from there. Gently, he touched the door and it swung open into the room. In the grey of the dawn light beyond, he could see the outline of a person sitting in the centre of the room. Even without the lights on, Caslin could tell the man was bound, arms behind him and ankles to the chair legs.

The figure appeared to turn slightly as if in recognition of his arrival but the head listed from left to right. Now Caslin wished he had made that call. The adrenalin surge reached new heights. Instinctively looking over his shoulder, before stepping into the room he moved forward, expecting an attack that never came. Hugging the interior wall, he observed the restrained man. He was elderly and of Asian origin, with receding hair. This was thinning and predominantly grey. He was clearly in a bad way, with only an irregular murmur to confirm that he was alive but barely conscious. Blood was seeping from a wound to his forehead. A closer inspection saw much of his features were barely distinguishable due to the mass of swelling and damage. All were consistent with a severe beating.

Confident that they were alone in the room, Caslin went towards him and knelt down, placing his improvised weapon by his feet. The captive flinched when he felt Caslin's presence but relaxed a little as the policeman whispered to him in a reassuring tone. The response came not in English but, Caslin guessed, Chinese. Be it Mandarin, Cantonese or another dialect, he had no idea but interpreted it as a request for help. Turning his attention to the cable ties that bound him to the chair, Caslin realised he had no way to sever them. He would have to return to the kitchen and find a knife or scissors.

"I'll be back in a moment," he said calmly, not knowing if he would be understood or not.

Rising to his feet, he heard a click, not particularly loud but one that he recognised. It was unwelcome.

"You are persistent, you really are."

"I try," Caslin replied. Slowly, he turned to face the newcomer.

"Not as bright as I first thought, though."

The figure stood in the doorway. Caslin couldn't make out detail but from the silhouette alone, he knew who he was talking to. A brief glimpse of reflected exterior light caught on the rim of Lee's glasses, as well as the metal of the rifle that he now pointed at Caslin.

"A veiled compliment if ever I heard one."

Lee laughed, "Coming here all by yourself. You must be desperate for redemption."

"Far from it," Caslin countered. "If I'm honest, I didn't expect you to be stupid enough to be here."

"You were wrong."

"Indeed," Caslin said quietly, never a truer word had been spoken. He pointed to the old man. "Your father?"

Lee nodded, taking a couple of steps into the room. His eyes never left Caslin, indicating with the barrel of the rifle for him to step aside. Caslin did so, moving two paces sideways towards the window. A glance through the net curtains saw the street below beginning to fill with the morning traffic.

"Yes, at least in name."

"I can tell that you don't see eye to eye."

Caslin backed away another step, Lee's face now visible in the rapidly approaching light. He looked younger than expected and Caslin was taken aback. Were it not for the piercing stare and the weapon he brought to bear, this boy could have been a geek, slightly built and rather effeminate looking.

"Much like you and yours, wouldn't you say?"

Caslin shrugged, "I've never beaten mine to a pulp, though."

"You should consider doing so. It's quite cathartic."

"Maybe I'll pass, if it's all the same."

"What's that old saying, 'you should walk a mile in a man's shoes'?"

"Again, I think I'll pass on that. Was it also cathartic taking down Chloe tonight?"

Lee sneered, "Bitch deserved to die."

Now it was Caslin's turn to laugh, "Pity you can't shoot for shit then, really."

"She went down, I saw her—"

"Yes, she did. You nearly got her. Two-metre high plate-glass, industrial glazing. Thick stuff. It can change the trajectory of a high velocity round," Caslin indicated the rifle with a nod of the head, "even from something as powerful as that. Of course, you'd be aware of that, what with you being a telecoms guy."

"Bullshit."

"Well, she'll be in recovery for a while," Caslin shook his head. "But she *will* recover. It was a nice try, you bypassed us with ease. One step ahead every time. I'm impressed, in a twisted sort of way."

"I won't make the same mistake twice."

"You may not get the chance."

Lee took a couple of small steps forward. His gaze lingered on Caslin as he appeared to consider his next move.

"What made you come here?"

Caslin blew out his cheeks.

"What you told me on the phone. That you were 'cleaning house', it got me thinking. You weren't just talking about Chloe, were you?"

Lee slowly shook his head.

"I knew I should've just hung up."

"Probably," Caslin agreed. "Is that what all this has been about, finishing off the loose ends?"

"Since Garry, yes."

"Who's left then?"

Lee thought for a moment but his eyes never strayed from Caslin.

"I thought I was virtually done. The trail, Chloe, my old man, that charity bitch—"

"Claire Skellon?"

"Yeah, that's what she called herself."

"What was your problem with Claire?"

"Didn't have one," he shrugged. "She'd pissed Garry off somewhere along the line, never seen him so angry. He had been reading the paper when he just flipped right out. Anyway, seeing as he wasn't able, I thought I'd take care of it for him."

"The family?" Caslin asked but Lee looked at him without understanding. "The ones in the car park."

"Oh, them. What can I say, wrong place, wrong time," Lee was nonchalant. "Shame, shame."

At that point Lee's father began to mumble something. It was barely audible to Caslin and he wouldn't have understood even if he could've made it out.

"What's he saying?" Caslin asked, attempting to buy time as he sought a solution to this impossible problem.

"Nothing," Lee snapped. "Old fool."

The mumbling increased, momentarily taking the gunman's attention from Caslin. He considered making a move but dismissed it as Lee's focus swiftly returned to him.

"Must be saying something?" Caslin asked again. The old man was repeating himself in a monotone voice.

"Shut up, you old bastard!" Lee shouted at his father, turning the gun on him.

"I made... a... man out of... you," his father stated in halting, broken English, "... at last."

"Shut up!" Lee screamed, swinging the butt of the gun. It made an odd sound, a hollow thud, as it connected with the old man's head.

The mumbling ceased. Caslin made to throw himself forward but pulled up as the barrel turned back to him. The end was now barely an inch from his face.

"Steady," Caslin said in as reassuring a tone as he could manage, his hands raised in supplication.

"You disappoint me, Inspector. I had *such* great plans for you and I," Lee admonished him. Caslin's stomach began to twist in knots. "But you had to ruin it."

"It doesn't have to end in a bad way," Caslin said. The barrel of the rifle was far too close for his liking.

"Oh, it has to end. It has to end," Lee stated with conviction.

Any emotion appeared to have left him, to be replaced by a cold stare that conveyed nothing but emptiness. Caslin felt an end was certainly in sight. Surprisingly nothing came to mind. No thoughts of loved ones, either past or present. No images of his life leapt to the fore. He just stood there, staring straight ahead, waiting for someone else to make the decision. Reflecting on such a hypothetical event, he would have sworn blind that he would fight to the last. Now, here he was and there was nothing, no spark, no reaction, merely resignation.

Movement in the corner of his eye caught his attention and Caslin's gaze crossed to the street below. A patrol car was taking an interest in his illegal parking, pulling up behind the old Volvo. An officer stepped from the vehicle, his high-vis jacket appearing as a beacon from heaven. A colleague remained in the car, flicking on the blue lights to visualise their presence to passing vehicles. The lights flashed through the net curtains. Lee glanced over and Caslin swung his hand up and away from him, knocking the barrel from his face. The momentary relief from dislodging the weapon was replaced by a blow to his cheek from Lee's elbow. The gunman's forward momentum conveyed his full weight behind the connection. Caslin's head flew backwards, his senses stunned. Determined to maintain his position in the struggle he reached for the gun, his hand closing on the barrel as Lee fought to bring it to bear.

Caslin struck out with his fist. Making contact with his opponent's face, he extricated a groan of pain from the younger man. The two tussled for the upper hand. Caslin was surprised at how strong he found Lee to be. Somehow, they managed to knock the old man and the chair clean over, sending all three sprawling to the floor. A sharp intake of breath, containing a great deal of dust, made Caslin gasp as he struggled to find his feet. Sensing, rather than seeing an attack coming, he hurled himself forward. His head struck Lee's abdomen and with all the force he could muster he shoved his opponent backwards. They picked up speed as they went. Off balance, Lee failed to gain any purchase on the varnished floorboards.

Beyond the bedroom they stumbled together before clattering into the balustrade on the landing. The spindles creaked for a split second before splintering and giving way under the weight. Caslin fell to the floor, air escaping his lungs at pace. Meanwhile, Lee toppled through the broken wood to the stairs below, still clutching his rifle. Caslin hauled himself up and crawled over to the edge just in time to see the gun raised in his direction. All he could do was drop to the floor. For a fraction of a second he didn't think the gun had gone off but then a bullet fizzed past his forehead, driving into the door frame above and behind him.

He lay there attempting to merge with the surface and thereby make himself invisible. He knew he should move but he was frozen by fear. Listening intently, he could tell Lee wasn't coming back up the stairs and he lifted himself up onto his haunches. Then there came several rapid bursts of gunfire. The echoes of which reverberated around the buildings outside. The draught of cold air told him the front door was open. Glancing back into the bedroom at the old man lying on his side, still bound to his chair, Caslin made towards him before changing his mind and running for the stairs. Cautiously, he glanced down the stairwell to ensure he was clear before descending.

At the front door he poked his head out. Several pedestrians were sheltering behind parked cars. All were anxiously looking to Caslin's left. He looked at the police car. Its windscreen sported several bullet holes and Caslin saw an officer lying on his back in the middle of the street. His colleague was crouched behind the offside door to the patrol car, radio to his lips, calling in the shooting. Another body lay on the pavement a few metres further up the road. A rapidly spreading pool of blood beneath her showed that she too, had been wounded.

Caslin ducked low and headed down the path using the hedgerow to shield him from view, stopping as he reached the end. Risking a glance up the street he saw a struggle going on as one man was unceremoniously dragged from his car, a blue hatchback. The other was undoubtedly Lee Na Honn. Caslin called out to the officer taking cover, identifying himself as CID, and indicating there was another casualty inside the house. The constable appeared to accept the information with a brief nod. Caslin was unsure whether he had conveyed the message clearly enough. Another quick look and he saw that Lee was making off in the hijacked car. The owner stood in the street with a somewhat perplexed expression on his face. Caslin considered that he didn't know just how lucky he had been. Three feet away lay the rifle. Caslin presumed the magazine was spent and was silently pleased that he wouldn't face that again.

Sprinting to his car he unlocked the door and got in. Not bothering with his seatbelt, he turned the key in the ignition, only for the engine to stutter as it turned over, before dying. Trying twice more, he found the car obstinate and it was on the fourth attempt that the engine engaged, roaring into life with his foot depressing the accelerator like a man possessed. The tyres screeched in protest as the car sped away from the scene. As an afterthought, Caslin reached across to the passenger seat to retrieve his phone. The action jerked the steering wheel and caused him to narrowly miss a parked car that he hadn't seen. The shock saw him drop the phone which bounced into the nearside footwell, far beyond his reach. He cursed openly as he sought to make up the ground on the hatchback, roughly a quarter of a mile ahead.

CHAPTER THIRTY-ONE

THE TRAFFIC BUILT as they sped through the outskirts of Hull. Caslin was well aware that he was partaking in an ill-advised pursuit. The speeds that they were achieving, often approaching sixty miles per hour in built-up areas, could become lethal at any moment. The Volvo strained to keep pace with the newer car. The engine bounced off the rev limiter repeatedly as he progressed up through the gears. Much to his frustration, the gap between them was still increasing. Blasting his horn at almost every intersection, he attempted to alert other road users and pedestrians to his approach.

In contrast, Lee Na Honn accelerated through every hazard and held no truck with using the oncoming lanes, as well as the pavements, to facilitate his escape. Driving with an apparent belief that he was somehow charmed, he was reckless beyond measure. Nevertheless, his flight continued unabated.

As the signs flashed by, Caslin figured they were heading south towards the Humber estuary. Finding it difficult to believe that Lee's headlong flight was crafted by design, Caslin felt it was more likely that he was improvising. This made him even more dangerous. Desperation often led to extreme reaction and Lee Na Honn qualified on both counts. What he might be capable of once backed into a corner featured heavily in Caslin's thoughts as he gave chase.

Up ahead the hatchback swerved out into oncoming traffic to pass a slower vehicle. The startled occupants seeking to maximise the width of the road as Lee powered between the two, delivering a glancing blow to the side of the car he was overtaking. The driver of that vehicle struggled to maintain control and the impact sent him towards the verge. The car snaked from left to right before finally reducing speed and coming to a standstill. Caslin eased off but didn't stop as he passed. The shocked man stared blankly ahead, trying to comprehend what had happened.

Lee Na Honn was nearly out of sight as Caslin crested the next hill, bringing the Humber into view. The road before him swept down and away before widening into a dual carriageway. Pressing the accelerator to the floor he encouraged his car to find something extra as he tried in vain to gain ground. Looking up, he saw a helicopter in the sky and believed he could make out the yellow and blue livery, thus identifying it as that of Humberside Police. Reassured that he was no longer alone he returned his focus to the road, negotiating his way past the vehicles that he came to.

Passing signs that indicated they were heading for the Humber Bridge gave him renewed confidence. Should Lee maintain that course there would be an opportunity to contain him there. Glancing over to where his phone lay he felt helpless to make the suggestion. He would have to rely on his colleagues to reach the same conclusion.

Their arrival at a roundabout where several high-volume roads converged, brought the two cars to the closest they had been in the previous fifteen minutes. Lee entered at great speed, far too quickly to maintain his course, putting the car into a barely controllable four-wheel slide. He only managed to correct the manoeuvre at the last moment. Commuters around them came to a stop and Caslin had to thread his way through the stationary vehicles to an accompanying chorus of blaring horns. Pleased to see his quarry maintain course towards the bridge, Caslin looked skyward to ascertain where the support was but could no longer see the helicopter.

Pushing the doubt from his mind he accelerated hard, willing the car to hold out as he did so. The distinct smell of burning was permeating through to the interior. Several warning lights came on in front of him. The oil pressure indicator was one and some of the others he could only guess at. Ignoring them, he pushed on. Traffic began to build once again as they passed the last exit before the bridge. Both cars flew over a mini roundabout, hurtling onwards. The giant suspension cables, rising far above them into the harsh brightness of the low winter sun becoming ever more present.

Lee weaved his way between the vehicles, jockeying for position to access the toll booths or to take the central express lanes. Misjudging the available space, Caslin watched as Lee's hatchback clipped a van as he cut in front, putting him into a sideways slide. The van driver broke off, swerving to the right and colliding with another car. The resulting impact flipped him back into the side of Lee's car. Forced up onto two wheels, the car threatened to be upended, at any moment. All four wheels came crashing back to earth, Lee battling to keep the car under control as it snaked from left to right. The open express lanes were no longer a viable option and he careered headlong towards the toll booths, approaching at an impossible angle. The barrier descended but Lee accelerated and drove through the bar at speed, splintering it into pieces. The vehicle's trajectory caused the rear to mount the kerb as it passed, blowing out a tyre on impact. The momentum pitched the car sideways, elevating the rear end before coming back down fiercely, Lee, still wrestling with the steering wheel.

Caslin anticipated that the chase was now at an end but to his dismay the car continued on. Sparks showered from the rim as it bounced along the carriageway, albeit at a greatly reduced speed. Caslin picked his way through the now stationary vehicles, whose passengers were already getting out to inspect the damage, and pulled up at the booth with a screech of his tyres. The attendant was on her feet within, a phone pressed to her ear, as she watched the fleeing car. He had to shout to get her attention.

"Close the bridge!"

She turned slowly towards him. In total shock, she appeared not to understand what he had said. Caslin brandished his warrant card, holding it at full stretch towards her as she strained to read it.

"I… don't—"

"Close the bloody bridge, now," Caslin reiterated.

"I don't have the authority. I'll have to speak to the Bridge Master."

"Do it," Caslin shouted once more, putting the Volvo in gear and resuming his course.

Several vehicles had driven onto the bridge via the remaining booths. Two of which had slowed after witnessing the incident, unsure of whether they should remain where they were or continue on. Others proceeded across the bridge. Their occupants gawped at the bizarre man, driving the crippled hatchback up the slope. As Caslin got closer, he watched as the stricken vehicle came to a stop in the nearside lane, less than a quarter of the way over. Lee Na Honn jumped out onto the carriageway and attempted to flag down the first car that drove past. The driver showed great sense not to stop, despite the protestations and frantic gesturing of the lone figure, trying to block his way.

Lee turned as Caslin approached. Withdrawing something from underneath his jumper and pointing it towards him, Caslin was horrified to recognise it as a pistol. Instinctively, he lifted off the accelerator and thought about stopping before quickly realising that he was well within firing range. Considering that a moving target was harder to hit, he pressed the pedal hard. The roar of the engine rose as he accelerated straight towards Lee.

Whether the gunman recognised Caslin as the driver or not, he couldn't tell, but a brief flash of white light was followed by a sharp crack as something struck the windscreen of his car. Bracing his hands on the steering wheel he expected to run Lee down but at the last, he hit the brakes and pulled the wheel to the right. The car swerved violently. His tyres howled in protest as he battled to regain control but it was no use. Caslin was unable to focus his vision as a blur of colourful images flashed before his eyes. The feeling of being out of control and almost weightless dominated his senses as he was flung around inside the cabin. The car spun several times before colliding with the central reservation. His head struck something, be it the window, dashboard, or passenger seat, he didn't know. When the car finally came to a stop, relief washed over him before dissipating to be replaced by a numbness that filtered throughout his body.

Now facing back towards the toll booths, Caslin could see the information boards flashing to signify that the bridge was closed to traffic in both directions. People milled around watching the drama unfold. Everything had gone quiet and Caslin first surveyed the hole in his windscreen. It was little more than the width of a fingernail with three hairline cracks creeping off in different directions. Then he reached up to make sense of the damp patch that was spreading down the side of his face. Blinking his way through a dizzy spell he looked at his hand, there was blood on it.

After a moment of confusion, he remembered where he was but there was no sense of urgency or panic. Shaking off the lethargy, he opened the door which protested with a screech followed by the sound of grating metal. Easing his way out he heard crunching glass underfoot. He cast an eye over the car. Steam, or smoke, was escaping from under the bonnet and the smell of something burning filled his nostrils. A cursory glance reassured him that the car itself wasn't on fire, at least for now, and he looked over towards the blue hatchback some thirty yards away. There was no-one in view.

Coming around to the rear of his car, Caslin looked for Lee on the ground but there was still no sign of him. *Had he hit him after all?* For some reason he dropped to his knees and looked underneath, half expecting to see the crumpled form of the gunman but he didn't. The whirring of rotor blades accompanied by the distinctive roar of the twin-engine helicopter above, made him look up. The police helicopter was taking up position, hovering approximately two hundred feet above the bridge. Another look towards the south side saw the approach of flashing blue lights. Caslin scanned the carriageway, catching sight of Lee Na Honn making off along the pedestrian walkway. His progress appeared laboured and Caslin concluded that he was somehow impaired. Lee also seemed to acknowledge the significance of the police presence and checked his disjointed flight. Turning back towards Caslin, he rested his hands on his thighs to catch his breath.

At that point, Caslin felt he could allow the cavalry to make the arrest. Leaning against his car he used the sleeve of his jacket to wipe the blood from the side of his face. Examining the dark smear upon the fabric, he figured that the wound was superficial. Looking skywards once again he took a deep breath and appreciated the slight warmth of the sun on his skin. Returning his attention to Lee, he saw him approach the outer edge of the bridge, examining the barrier of the walkway. *Where did he think he was able to go?* His next actions answered that unspoken question as Lee took a run up, hurling himself against the barrier in an attempt to scale the fencing.

At the third attempt, Lee managed to gain a hold at the top and was well into the process of climbing over as Caslin raced towards him. His pace aided him in a terrific leap as he attempted to make up the ground on Lee's progress. Both men managed to haul their way up with some difficulty before levering themselves over to the other side, dropping to the maintenance access bar below. A gust of wind caught Caslin unawares and he lost his footing whilst trying to compensate and maintain his balance.

Grasping the structure, he breathed a sigh of relief. Lee appeared before him, striking out with a booted foot and catching Caslin in the stomach. The wind was knocked out of him with some force. A punch to the face followed and he fell backwards, his one-handed grip on the bridge was all that stood between him and a hundred-foot plunge to the freezing water below.

Swinging himself back towards the bridge, he sought to take hold of his opponent rather than strike out with his free hand. Lee responded by trying to brush him off and back away. Caslin took the opportunity and went with him, contrary to what his assailant expected. In doing so, he managed to improve his hold. Taking advantage of the surprise move, Caslin tugged at Lee's collar, pulling him out and away from the structure. Before Lee could react, he lost his footing. A flailing arm shot out and grasped Caslin's forearm just as his feet went from under him. That action arrested his fall but left him dangling precariously over the edge.

Whether Lee had planned to jump or not, he now clung to Caslin in acknowledgement that his life depended on it. A yelp of pain escaped from Lee due to the stress his muscles were under. Caslin had his right arm wrapped around a stanchion and through gritted teeth, he held on as they were buffeted by the wind. There they remained, apparently locked in a timeless embrace. The roar of the wind almost drowned out the gasps that each man gave out with the exertion of their efforts. They met eyes but neither spoke, such was the concentration required to maintain their position.

The conditions were beginning to take their toll. The wind chill, along with bare skin on freezing metal ensured that Caslin began to go numb, not only his hands but his entire body. He dared not look up for fear of losing focus and desperately hoped that assistance would arrive soon. As if to reinforce that point, Lee's grip began to wane and his hand slipped further down the length of Caslin's arm. In turn, Caslin felt his arm was about to be torn from its socket.

"I had such plans," Lee shouted, trying to be heard above the noise of the wind.

Caslin didn't reply, grimacing at the pain that he now felt throughout every muscle. To his dismay he saw Lee release the tenuous grip that he had on his forearm. That left him as the only difference between life and death in the Humber far below.

"Take a hold of me," Caslin yelled, but Lee only looked at him with a placid expression that conveyed little. "Take a hold, damn it."

"This is the difference between you and me, Inspector," Lee shouted, his voice barely audible. "When all is said and done, you can't do it. You're not like us but you need us. Without us, you are nothing."

"Grab a hold of me or you're going to die," Caslin yelled back, feeling the tightness of his grip loosening.

"You could have killed me on the bridge. Ended it there and then but you couldn't." Lee gave him a wry smile. "Even after everything I've done, you still… need… me."

Those words sent a cascade of fleeting images through Caslin's mind. The family photo of the Horsvedts, the expression on Claire Skellon's face, Hayley Underwood and finally his own children.

"No, I don't," Caslin whispered softly.

The wind rattled throughout the surrounding steel. That, coupled with the extra weight and the imbalance of his poise, had threatened to blow him off the bridge at any moment. Placing two hands on the structure, he was able to brace himself as he watched the diminishing figure of Lee Na Honn until he disappeared from view, striking the freezing water below.

CHAPTER THIRTY-TWO

LITTLE HAD CHANGED in the waiting area of the x-ray department. The total reached eighteen once again. However, the solitary brown chair appeared to have been breeding at the expense of the green ones. The reason that Caslin could retain such information was lost on him but, he considered, it was still some form of an art. Summoned into a consultation room to review his injuries he was grateful to have to wait no longer. The last time he sat there he was not alone and the memory was unwelcome.

"You'll be thankful to learn that you have a mild concussion, nothing more," the doctor stated with a genuine smile.

"Take it easy in the office for a few days?" Caslin asked.

"Best to take a few days off. Put your feet up but try not to go to sleep as soon as you get home. It would be better to stay awake for a while. If there's a change in your condition, blurring of the vision, nausea, any symptoms such as that, then you should come back immediately."

Caslin nodded and offered his thanks before leaving. The doctor's words almost made him burst out laughing but he had kept himself in check. A few days off were likely but not anytime soon. The chase for Lee Na Honn was over. At least it would be once his body was recovered from the Humber or the North Sea, bearing in mind the nature of the tides.

The Coastguard had called out the Spurnpoint Lifeboat crew immediately after Lee had fallen from the bridge. The vessel was on the scene with frightening speed but as of yet, the body was still missing. Apparently, the Humber Bridge had recently been ranked ninth in a league of favoured suicide locations around the world, with only five people ever having survived the drop to the water below. The search assumed Lee was still alive but Caslin doubted it very much. Lasting twenty minutes in the freezing water of the estuary would have been impressive and it had been hours.

Walking past the newsagent's kiosk he glanced at the cigarettes behind the counter, bringing a smile to his face.

"Not this time," he said to himself. Continuing on out into the sunshine, he had to shield his eyes from the glare.

The day was cold with a bitter wind but despite that, he felt good. The best he had in days. The toot of a car horn made him look to his left as DC Holt pulled up. Winding his window down and waving to get Caslin's attention, he beckoned him over.

"The Guv suggested that you might need a lift."

Caslin nodded and got into the passenger side, putting on the seatbelt. The action made him wince. It was a harsh reminder of the bruising to his ribs. Holt noticed and grimaced in sympathy.

"Painful?"

"Not too bad," Caslin replied, remembering the crash, the hole in his windscreen as well as the potential of plummeting to his death from the bridge that morning. "All things considered, I think I got away with it."

"Good to hear," Holt said. He pulled out of the collection zone and made his way from the car park, completely oblivious to the extra meaning behind Caslin's response.

"Any word on the father?"

"Aye, he'll be grand but it will take a while. A few broken bones, plus fractures to his cheek and jaw. It was the fingers that the little bastard broke, strangely enough. They reckon he was dishing out a bit of torture on his father. Twisted or what?"

Caslin didn't answer but he figured Holt was right. It had been quite telling, after the event, that Lee's father had said that he "made a man out of you" to his son. Presumably he viewed the latter as a weak child, either mentally or physically, perhaps both. Had Lee been a let-down growing up? If so they had something in common there. It was also possible that his father was taking an opportunity to score some kind of victory over his son, in what he perceived were his last moments. Caslin didn't know and ultimately didn't care.

Whatever had driven Lee to do what he did was of little interest to him. Nothing could justify or rationalise them in his mind's eye. Although he felt certain that psychologists would attempt to do so in the coming weeks, months and years.

"The DCI says that there will have to be an investigation. Most likely it'll be referred to the IPCC, what with it being an officer-involved death," Holt said, glancing across more frequently than Caslin liked. He would've much preferred him to keep his eyes on the road. One accident in a day was enough.

Caslin shrugged, bringing another stab of pain via his shoulder.

"So be it."

"You'll be fine. You tried to save him, after all," Holt said with an intimation of reassurance.

Caslin stared straight ahead at the early afternoon traffic they were encountering along the A63. He paid little attention to Holt's apparent attempt at support. Arriving at the station an hour later, they took the circuitous route into the car park and entered via the rear yard. In doing so, they bypassed the melee of journalists camped at the front entrance.

The news broke first thing about the failed operation at the diner the previous night and followed onto the fast-evolving story that climaxed upon the Humber Bridge. The media had been clamouring for interviews since dawn, having only been drip-fed information from the police. Social media had played a part in the ensuing frenzy. People were putting two and two together following the events of the morning. Correctly for once as it turned out.

Entering CID to rapturous applause, Caslin felt rather self-conscious and more than a little embarrassed but he handled it with good grace. The noise level was far greater than he would have appreciated under normal circumstances. Simon Baxter was one of the first to approach him.

"Well done, Nathaniel. Good job," he said as he offered him his hand, clapping Caslin's shoulder at the same time. That brought about another stab of acute pain through his upper body.

"Thanks Simon, I'll bet you're pleased. You'll be able to head off soon, then."

Baxter looked back at him quizzically.

"I don't follow."

"Any talk of Basra also died this morning, didn't it? One day you might tell me what you're really doing here."

"Just what are you saying?" Baxter countered.

"Only you and Gerry Trent accessed the McNeil evidence in storage, after it was submitted."

"Yes, so what?"

"Lift anything useful from the mobile phone?"

"No idea what you're talking about."

"Even so, the whitewash is complete, isn't it?"

Baxter grinned in a telling manner, lowering his voice so that no-one else could hear his reply.

"It is my favourite colour, after all. Very clean and precise."

"You're going to let them get away with it?"

Baxter shook his head vigorously, "That's not my call, Caslin. That situation has so much negativity attached to it already. It's in no-one's interest to add more."

"We were supposed to be there to help those people."

"Just remember. Over there, we were the good guys."

"So, we're told, yes—"

Caslin was about to respond further but the all too brief conversation was interrupted. The throng of well-wishers, wanting to proffer their own congratulations, swept Caslin away.

"Good work, Nathaniel." A voice came from behind. Caslin turned to receive a firm handshake from DI Atwood. Mercifully, it was far gentler than Baxter's. Caslin was unsure as to his level of sincerity. The expression appeared genuine and the tone hit the right notes. However, he was still uncertain whether his fellow DI was slightly put out by the case breaking without him at the centre of it.

"Thanks," Caslin said. "I'll be honest and say I would rather you had been there, than me."

DI Atwood smiled at that.

"Of that, I am sure but you get the plaudits this time. Rightly deserved too."

"You'll get your day, Michael, don't worry," Caslin said.

Whether DI Atwood took offence at Caslin's implication that he was keen to be in the limelight or not, he didn't wait around to see. At the first opportunity where it wouldn't appear rude, he made himself scarce, heading to the washroom for some peace. Running a basin of cold water, he doused his face first and then his neck. The water refreshed his rapidly stiffening muscles. He saw Frank Stephens' reflection in the mirror as the DCI entered behind him, acknowledging his arrival without turning around.

"How are you doing, Nathaniel?"

Caslin shrugged, "I've had worse days."

Stephens smiled as he spoke, "I'm pleased that you managed to pull it all together."

"Not very clean though, was it?"

"No, it wasn't. You know there'll be an—"

"Investigation, the IPCC. Yeah, Terry Holt told me."

"Just routine, under the circumstances we have to refer it to them. It's no reflection on you."

Caslin nodded. For once he thought that that was reasonable.

"I've nothing to hide."

"The chopper has it all on camera, so it will be tied off quickly enough."

Caslin returned his gaze to his own reflection and watched the water dripping from his face into the basin below. He took a deep breath.

"Good."

"And you know we'll have to have a conversation about you going off by yourself this morning. Not to mention that you should've obtained a warrant before going in. Whatever made you think he would go back to Hull, anyway?"

Caslin smiled, "I didn't. As much as some people think I'm some kind of Sherlock Holmes, I just couldn't see myself going home to bed and thought I'd check out his father. I got lucky. And don't worry about the improper procedure. The door had been jimmied, so I knew a crime was in progress."

"Turned out nicely, then." Frank Stephens appeared pleased with the outcome. "Holmes might be pushing it a bit. Columbo is more like it. Speaking of which, I'll send someone back to yours for some clean clothes. Broadfoot will be wanting a word before wheeling you out in front of the press—"

"Bugger that, Frank. Leave me well out of it."

"They'll want to hear from you. You're the talk of the internet, news bulletins and the like. It's all in meltdown after this morning's drama. No excuses."

"Oh, bloody hell," Caslin put his head down and submerged it in the water. There was no way he was going to a press conference. Moments later he came up for air, "Any word on Chloe?"

"She's out of surgery and the prognosis is good."

"What are we going to charge her with?"

"Now that is a question." Stephens appeared thoughtful. "My guess is we'll wrap it up as neatly as possible and throw it to the CPS. Let them figure it out. One thing for sure though, she'll not be walking away."

"Damn right," Caslin agreed as he rubbed his face with both

hands. Tilting his head in the mirror to examine his latest head wound, he had a thought, "One thing that came to me..."

"What's that?"

"When McNeil was picked up on the A59, he was heading towards York."

"Yes, so?"

"Radford Farm is in the other direction," Caslin said without breaking the stare at his own reflection. "Where was he going?"

"You think he was going to Chloe's?"

"Just speculating but it would make sense. She has been lying to us from the word go, mitigating her actions at every opportunity."

"We'll have a job to prove that."

Two MILDLY EXCRUCIATING hours later and Caslin was clear of the briefing room. The flash of media bulbs had done little for his headache. Keeping to as few details as possible and relying on the "unable to comment due to ongoing investigations" line, Caslin found the press conference to be less painful than anticipated. Fortunately, Kyle Broadfoot was more than keen to pick up the slack, not only comfortable in front of the cameras but also pleased to be the face of such a high-profile success. Caslin found the description of "success" to be bittersweet. The passer-by shot that morning in Hull had died of the injuries she'd sustained and one of Humberside's officers remained in a critical condition following the incident. DC Underwood's family would also be facing their first Christmas without their daughter.

Not wishing to face CID once again and having been advised to remain at the station until he could be debriefed by the IPCC, Caslin headed upstairs. Bumping into Linda on his way brought a genuine moment of comfort in what had been a trying week. She gave him a hug and kissed his cheek. He felt like the favoured son of a beloved mother. She looked well in herself, having been off work for a spell due to a particularly nasty reaction to her most recent bout of chemotherapy. Caslin hadn't realised how many days had passed since he had last seen her.

"I was so sorry to hear about that young lad you were working with."

Caslin smiled appreciatively, for she was talking about Maxim Harman.

"It was a shock."

"He had seemed so energetic that night. Such a shame."

Caslin had told her how well she was looking and promised to see her later in the day, for a proper catch up. Resuming his course, he headed for the newfound sanctuary of the roof. The sun had set and the clear sky saw the air temperature rapidly dropping away. His coat still bore some blood but it had long since dried and he saw no reason not to wear it. After all, it was his blood. Pacing backwards and forwards to jolt his circulation into warming him, he contemplated the events of the day. Knowing that there should be, at the very least, a modicum of joy at finally stopping Na Honn's rampage, he was annoyed with himself for the apathy that he was experiencing. Previously, he had felt elation upon the breaking of a big case but today there was nothing. Writing it off as fatigue he flexed his shoulders. Immediately he regretted that decision.

Putting a call in to Karen, he was disappointed to only reach her voicemail. Leaving a message, he told her that all was well and that the case was over. At the point of hanging up he paused for a moment, allowing a thought to develop in his mind. Having taken a deep breath, he apologised in a heartfelt manner. Not only for instigating the headlong dash to France but for all that had occurred in the previous two years. Tears welled in his eyes as he hung up.

Glancing up at the night sky, he wondered what the next chapter life had in store for him. For the first time, he genuinely gave consideration to his options. Turning such thoughts away he tried to focus on something more positive and knew that he was about to make someone's day. Looking up Colin Brotherton's number, he dialled it. Unexpectedly, the call was answered immediately.

"Hi Colin, it's Nate Caslin."

"Strewth, are you okay? I've been watching you on the news all day!"

Caslin laughed, "Who would have thought that you knew a celebrity?"

"Pleased to see you're alright. What do you have for me?"

"Straight to the point."

"Why else would you be calling?"

Caslin had to concede that Brotherton was on the ball.

"I think that we have a good shot at putting your case to bed. You were right about Skellon, she is Lucy Stafford."

"I bloody knew it!"

"We still don't know why she disappeared like she did. It's all a bit circumstantial. This guy that I'm all over the media with today, he took her out. The family in the Mercedes were just in the wrong place at the wrong time."

"Did he say why?"

"All this isn't out there yet, so discretion required, alright?"

"Of course."

"An associate had a long-standing grudge against her from years back. He took it upon himself to settle it on his behalf, seeing as he was unable."

"Why couldn't he do it himself?"

"He was already dead."

"So why the need?"

"There was no need. At least not for a normal human being, anyway. This associate was knocking around with Chloe Vickers for several decades. Knowing what I do about the two of them, I think Lucy would've had good reason to be concerned. Now, if you ask me, what are the odds of Maxine de la Grange and Lucy Stafford coming in contact with different serial killers? This guy was on the scene when Maxine was murdered and had connections to her, through his partner. Then he turns up years later, harbouring some kind of rage towards Lucy. I'd suggest that you'd have a better chance with the lottery jackpot."

"True. Were it a horse, I wouldn't back it."

"That would explain why she felt the need to pull a fast one and vanish," Caslin offered. "Like I said, it's largely supposition but I think it'll be enough to get a review of the case, if not get it reopened. Once things settle this end, I'll put the wheels in motion. With you so involved back in the day, you should expect a call." There was silence at the other end of the line and Caslin had to check that the call was still connected. It was. He had been expecting an outburst of excitement at bringing closure to the case that had dominated the retired officer's latter years. Instead, there was silence. "Colin, are you still there?"

"I'm here," Brotherton said but his voice was barely a whisper.

Caslin realised then, that he was emotionally overwhelmed. Having worked towards a result for all these years, the reality of a resolution was almost too much to take in.

"Time to let it go, Colin."

Fighting back the tears, Brotherton replied, "Thank you, Inspector Caslin. Thank you."

"I'll be in touch," Caslin said. With that, he ended the call.

Alone with his thoughts once more, Caslin suddenly felt happier within himself. Reaching into his pocket he took out the battered envelope that accompanied him everywhere that he went. Opening it, he slid the paper out and scanned the contents. There was no need for the words were committed to memory long ago. A letter received shortly after the spectacular collapse of a trial at the Old Bailey. The writer had reason to hate him but quite the opposite was true. He made good on his promise, a promise to a grieving mother. He closed his eyes, concentrating on the cold breeze passing over him. Returning his focus to the letter in his hands, his eyes lingered on the content.

"Follow your own advice, Nathaniel. Time to let it go." He folded the paper in on itself twice and then gently tore it into pieces. As the wind picked up, he waited for a strong enough gust before launching them into the air. Watching with a smile on his face as they were carried away, he felt the release of the pressure from the last two years. "Time to let it go."

Moments later his phone rang.

"Could I speak with Mr Caslin, please," a soft, female voice asked.

"You're speaking to him."

"Mr Caslin, my name is Louise and I would like to talk to—"

"I'm not in the mood for buying—

"I beg your pardon?"

"You've got the wrong man at the wrong time. I don't have PPI or need anyth—"

"No, no, you misunderstand. I don't want to sell you anything," she countered.

Caslin let out a sigh, "I'm sorry, forgive me. What can I do for you?"

"I am calling from a company called 'Safely Home' and we have you down as a recipient for one of our clients."

"I'm afraid I don't understand."

"You are to be provided with the information lodged with us. You know that we have you on record?"

Caslin was confused and becoming irritated.

"You have me at a complete loss. Are you sure you've got the right person?"

"Nathaniel Caslin, of York?"

"What is it that you do?"

"We like to think of ourselves as the benevolent Big Brother. Amongst other things, we operate a service where people can provide details on their whereabouts of an evening. So, in the event of something going wrong, friends or relatives have a starting point."

"Starting point?"

"Yes. Often our clients are nervous singletons going out on a first date. They'll give us their location via an upload with our app and then update it as the evening progresses."

"Why would they need that service?"

"Well, for instance, if you were invited back to a guy's place unexpectedly, you could upload the address quickly. It only takes a few seconds with the app. That way, you'd have peace of mind without the major buzz kill of making a phone call."

"Not wanting to kill the mood, you mean?"

"Exactly. No more 'excuse me while I call my friends because you might turn out to be a rapist', kind of scenario."

"Wow. The things you can get from technology these days never ceases to amaze me. And what has this got to do with me?"

"Firstly, I must apologise that we have not been in touch before now but usually the nominated recipient contacts us. It is just by chance that we saw the news today and his name was mention—"

"Perhaps you could enlighten me faster because I'm hanging up in about ten seconds?"

"The notification wasn't generated as it should have been when your friend... erm... passed away."

"Whose passing?"

"Mr Harman's."

Caslin was dumbstruck for a fraction of a second. His mind raced in circles before becoming alert, pain and fatigue forgotten in all but an instant.

"Harman? He was a client of yours?"

"Yes. We have a message that he lodged with us on... let me just look it up... here. On the Sixteenth of November."

"That was the day he..." Caslin left the thought unfinished. "What did he leave with you?"

"He uploaded a picture along with a short... it's probably easier if you view it for yourself. Would you like me to send it to you?"

"Yes, could you email it to me?"

"Certainly, we have your email... oh," Louise faltered.

"What is it?"

"Oh, it's nothing. Your email listing here, it's a police address."

"Correct. Is that a problem?"

"No, no, of course not. Sorry, it just caught me by surprise. Usually it's a relative or friend—"

"Never mind," Caslin pushed her on. "Have you sent it?"

"There. Done. If there is anything el—"

"Thanks," Caslin said, hanging up the phone.

Replacing the handset in his pocket he headed inside and down the stairs at a rate of knots. Wishing the whole time that he had learnt how to synchronise his email and phone set-up. Resisting the urge to break into a run he made his way along the corridor of the third floor, accepting the acknowledgements of a handful of colleagues as he went. Just outside CID, he pulled up as he came face to face with DCS Broadfoot.

"Inspector, I've been looking for you since the close of the press conference."

"Sorry, Sir. I needed a bit of quiet time after the... well, the events of the day."

Caslin was keen to get past and access his laptop in the squad room.

"Understandable," Broadfoot said, waving his limited entourage onwards whilst he remained. Once they were out of earshot he continued, "I have to head off to brief the Chief Constable but I wanted to have a word with you before I left. I know we got off to a rough start."

"Not at all, Sir."

Broadfoot smiled, "It's okay, Nathaniel. I jumped to the wrong conclusion about you, influenced by prior events no doubt. I dare say I listened to a little too much hearsay. I feel that I might owe you something by way of an apology."

"Not at all, Sir," Caslin repeated, anxious to have the conversation over with.

"Good man," Broadfoot offered his hand. Caslin accepted it with a smile. "I think that there may be an opportunity opening up for you in the near future. Perhaps we could discuss it in the coming days?"

Caslin was caught slightly off guard. That was possibly the last thing he expected to hear coming his way.

"Getting rid of me, Sir?" he answered with a hint of humour.

"Far from it," Broadfoot replied with a large grin. "We'll talk then?"

"Of course, Sir," Caslin replied.

Both men said their goodbyes and Caslin slipped into CID. The squad room was almost deserted as the vast majority had been allowed to head home, or to hit the pubs, for some much needed relaxation. Caslin unearthed the laptop from his desk drawer and powered it up. The whole time he was mulling over what Harman could have left for him. He was still none the wiser as he connected to his email account. The inbox stated that there were two hundred and eighty-one unread emails, all highlighted in red, requiring his attention. The latest was all that he was interested in and he opened it, immediately double clicking the attachment. The following seconds passed slowly while the file downloaded.

The wait proved to be a disappointing anti-climax. The file opened to reveal a close-up photograph of a road sign, "Clement Avenue". Caslin had to close down the picture and reopen it again to make sure that there was nothing else to it. There wasn't. Puzzled, he minimised the photo and looked again at the email. Underneath the attachment icon was a sequence of numbers that read "192168245245 47". Reading and rereading the email, he found nothing else to elaborate on what either the numbers or the photograph meant. Frustrated to say the least, he sent both to the nearest printer before bringing up a map showing Clement Avenue on the screen. Noting that it was south-west of York, in a residential area not far from the station, he wondered what it could mean.

Thinking that he wanted the email readily accessible, he spent a quarter of an hour setting up his phone to have access to his email account. He had to resend the email to himself in order to ensure he could access it from his phone. Then he powered down his computer. Retrieving the printout from the machine, he folded the copy and tucked it into his pocket. Then he left the squad room, making his way downstairs.

The representative from the IPCC hadn't arrived yet and Caslin thought he could slip out for an hour or so without rocking the boat. Finding Linda in reception, he asked if he could borrow her car to run an errand. She agreed. Journalists were still encamped at the main entrance so Caslin made for the station rear. Almost as an afterthought he returned to reception and, ensuring no-one else was within earshot, he beckoned Linda over.

"You said that you saw Maxim on the night he died?"

Linda nodded in response.

"Yes, I was working late, trying to get some things done before heading home. I was going into hospital the next day for, well, you know? Why do you ask?"

"How was he? Did you speak with him?"

She shook her head, "No, he appeared to be in a hurry."

"That's a shame. I was wondering what he was up to. He left me a message but it doesn't make a lot of sense, really."

"You should have a chat with the others, they might know."

Caslin's interest was piqued.

"Others?"

"Yes, he was with a couple of the officers from CID when I saw him. They all left together."

"Where were they going, did they say?"

"I didn't speak to them. I'm assuming they were leaving together, anyway. Maxim was chatting with that new one, from London."

"DI Baxter?"

"Yes, that's him. Young Terry Holt was only a step behind."

"Terry was with them as well?"

"Like I said, I assumed so but maybe not." Linda clearly sensed something was amiss. Her gaze narrowed slightly as Caslin digested the information. "Why, what's going on?"

"Probably nothing," Caslin said reassuringly. Linda's expression gave him the feeling that she was distinctly unimpressed with his response. "Honestly, it's just something has come up but I'll have a chat with them and let you know. If anyone's looking for me, just say, I'll be back in half an hour or so."

Stepping out of reception, Caslin passed through the ground floor of the building and left the station by the rear entrance. Following a brief hunt amongst the parked vehicles, he located Linda's Fiat in the far corner of the car park. Feeling slightly out of place cocooned in the little car, surrounded by the cream leather seats and chrome trim of the interior, he left Fulford Road, determined to take a drive down Clement Avenue. Following the route from memory, having swiftly given up on the in-car navigation system, Caslin made several wrong turns before taking a left into the road that he sought.

Bringing the car to a stop underneath the overhang of a large silver birch, he looked around.

CHAPTER THIRTY-THREE

CLEMENT AVENUE BORE nothing of any note. It was simply another residential street in Fulford, lined with a mixture of non-descript detached and semi-detached housing stock, constructed in the sixties. Getting out of the car he stretched out his arms, stifling a yawn. Despite being only around five o'clock it felt much later. The road was quiet, many residents having not returned from work yet. Whilst others were already hunkered down due to the inclement weather.

Caslin took a walk down the street, taking in the various properties as he went but once again, found nothing untoward. Having reached the other end, he came to stand before the road's name plate. Withdrawing the printout from his pocket he compared the two in the orange glow of the streetlight above. They were identical. This was where the photo had been taken. Caslin glanced around once more, trying in vain to see what Harman may have been looking at from this vantage point. Nothing remarkable stood out. Why take a picture here?

Crossing over to the other side of the road he began walking back towards the parked Fiat. All the while he looked to the left and right, searching for inspiration. Regrettably, he reached the car without coming to a conclusion. Getting back in, he sat there in the dark, remaining thoughtful. Unfolding the printout again, he stared at it intently, seeking inspiration.

Taking out a pen, he began to play around with the numbers. Firstly, he tried to reorder them as if they might be a combination to something. Rapidly he discounted that notion, there were far too many. Considering they might be a primitive code, he began to list them. The first number he allocated as a page number, the second a line, and then lastly, a word in that line. That was a classic method of generating a code. The words when put together spelt out the message. The problem with the theory was that he would need the source book that Harman used in order to make any sense of it. Furthermore, the picture and number sequence had been uploaded together. If that had been done on the move then Harman would have had little time to carry out such a procedure. He discarded the idea as nonsense.

The windows of the car began to steam up around him but Caslin was almost oblivious to the outside. Harman must have anticipated that the puzzle could be solved, and by Caslin, otherwise why would he leave it for him? The notion that it was unsolvable by design came and went in a fleeting moment. Harman was far too straight to have carried out such a pointless exercise.

Headlights illuminated the interior as another car made the turn into Clement Avenue. Caslin glanced up as it passed by. The vehicle had his attention and he watched as it made its way a hundred yards, or so, before turning right into the driveway of a house. The driver got out of the car, pulling his coat about him as he walked up the path. The indicators flashed twice as the alarm was set before the figure unlocked the front door and passed into the darkness beyond.

Caslin stared at the house for the next couple of minutes. Areas of the interior lit up as the occupant went from room to room. Tossing his pen onto the passenger seat, Caslin folded up the paper in his hands and tucked it into an internal pocket. Taking out his phone he saw that it was a quarter to six. In all likelihood, he would be missed back at Fulford Road soon. Typing out a brief message, he sent it before replacing the phone in the pocket from where it came and got out of the car.

Light drizzle was starting to fall as he crossed the street and headed for the house. Walking up the driveway, alongside a neatly manicured lawn, he approached the front door. Glancing to the right, noting the piece of numbered slate fixed to the wall beneath the exterior porch light, he took a deep breath before pressing the bell. Then he thrust his hands into his pockets, shielding them from the cold.

"Good evening," Caslin said as the door opened. A surprised expression crossed the face of the man standing before him.

"What are you doing here?" DI Atwood asked.

"Thought we could have a chat."

"About what?"

"That's what I was thinking," Caslin replied, silently pulling the pieces together in his head.

"You'd better come in, then," Atwood replied, beckoning Caslin inside.

Caslin hesitated, glancing back towards the street, "I'm supposed to be—"

"C'mon, you're letting all the heat out," Atwood persisted. He looked past Caslin to the street beyond, casually scanning both left and right. Standing to the side, he allowed Caslin room to enter. The hallway was wide by modern standards with stairs off to the left, tastefully decorated in neutral colours.

"Nice house," Caslin said. "Live here by yourself?"

"Thanks. Yes, I do, but it's only rented. I didn't see much point in buying as I planned this to be a stop-gap solution."

"Big house for just you, though. What is it, three bedrooms?"

"No, four," Atwood corrected, "but I like the space down-stairs. I don't want to live in some pokey one or two-bedroom flat like a middle-aged student."

"I always had it in my head that you were married."

Atwood led him through to the back of the house and into the kitchen.

"I am. Well I was until recently."

"I can relate."

"Do you want a coffee, tea, or something a little stronger? You'll no doubt need it after today."

"You have no idea," Caslin said. "Coffee will be fine though, I'm driving."

Caslin watched as Atwood filled the kettle and took down two mugs from a cupboard above.

"I wondered how you got out here. Your car was totalled, wasn't it?"

"You could say that. It doesn't matter. It was a piece of shit, anyway," Caslin said as he looked about the kitchen with a curious interest. There was little of note to grab his attention. The counters were all clear, without any dirt or loose implements to clutter them up. The stainless-steel sink appeared to reflect the light from the overhead spots like a mirror. The room was immaculate. "Do you actually live here?"

The question caused his host to smile as he glanced over his shoulder whilst retrieving a bottle of milk from the fridge.

"I like things clean and tidy."

Caslin nodded, "It's like a show house."

Atwood laughed. The kettle clicked and he added the boiling water to the cups.

"Do you take milk?"

"A little. And some sugar, if you have it," Caslin said reluctantly. Had he realised it would be instant coffee he would have chosen tea but it was of little consequence. "I gather your promotion has come through."

"More of a transfer than a promotion, but yes."

"You're heading off then?"

"Yep, next month, all being well."

"Diplomatic protection, wasn't it?"

"Yes, should be a good one for the CV. I can't wait."

"I'll bet," Caslin said, sipping at the steaming brew that had just been passed to him. Despite the sugar, it remained bitter and lacking in flavour.

"So, what brings you here?"

Caslin took another sip of his coffee and placed the cup down on the breakfast bar. Undoing his coat, he reached in and withdrew the paper, clearing his throat as he unfolded it.

"A message from beyond the grave."

DI Atwood raised an eyebrow as he also took a mouthful of coffee. Stepping over, he watched as Caslin placed the paper on the counter and flattened it out.

"What on earth do you have there?"

"That was exactly what I was contemplating, until you happened to drive past."

"I don't understand."

"Really?" Caslin said, narrowing his gaze. "I think I'm beginning to."

Michael Atwood stepped away, resting his back against the counter behind him. With both hands, he cupped the warm mug in front of him. With a nod of the head he intimated for Caslin to continue.

"Do you remember the email that Harman sent to me, the day before?"

"The day before he committed suicide? Yes, but only vaguely."

"Aye, that one. He was telling me all about that 'Tor' program. Apparently, it shields your identity online, untraceable. At least, that's what I found out. I read that the CIA developed it to aid political dissidents and the like although I'm not sure about that bit."

"Okay, go on."

"Well, I didn't think too much of it at the time but that's the kind of software that any officer spending time with CEOP would surely be aware of," Caslin said, fixing Atwood with a gaze. The latter appeared unmoved.

"I don't recall the conversation. Only that I was checking that you were okay. I probably wasn't paying much attention."

"I asked you specifically."

"I don't recall," Atwood repeated. Moving over to the sink he filled a glass of water from the tap. He took a moment to drink half of it before turning back to Caslin. "What's your point, if you have one? Are you pulling me up on my competence or my listening skills?"

"Like I said, I didn't think much about it. Until I got this," Caslin indicated the photograph. "And of course, the number sequence. That had me running around in circles right up until I knocked on your door."

"And?"

"This house. Number forty-seven, correct?"

"Correct," Atwood nodded. "So, what?"

Caslin pointed to the sequence. The last two digits were separate from the others, a four and a seven.

"I'm not a strong believer in coincidence."

"Nor am I, I think it comes with the warrant card," Atwood grinned. Passing Caslin, he went over to a sideboard and retrieved a glass from one of the shelves. He then took a bottle of red wine from the rack and returned with both to where he had been standing. Opening a drawer, he glanced across at Caslin. "You'll forgive me, I'm not driving and it's been a long couple of days."

"So that has me thinking," Caslin continued. "A photograph of your street, your house number and these others, what could they be?"

"Please, do tell," Atwood replied, bringing out a corkscrew and setting about opening the wine.

"Harman wasn't the greatest of detectives, it must be said. Not exactly a chip off the old block but he had a thing with technology. In that, he excelled."

"Damn it," Atwood snapped as he withdrew the corkscrew

with only half of the cork attached. "I hate this thing. It's cheap as shi… excuse me, while I get another."

Caslin watched as his colleague disappeared into the dining room, returning only moments later with a different corkscrew and began teasing the broken end of the cork from the neck of the bottle.

"Those numbers, they're a reference to this house, aren't they?"

Michael Atwood stopped what he was doing. He slowly put the bottle down and turned around to face Caslin.

"How do you figure?"

"What are they, an IP address for your computer, or ident number for your mobile?"

"Been reading up?"

"I'm thirty-nine, not a dinosaur."

Atwood took a deep breath, "What are you saying, or should I say, *accusing* me of?"

"Who says I'm accusing you of anything?"

"Let's not be coy, Nathaniel. If you have something to say, say it."

"What happened? Did Maxim come across a link to your address amongst all those fake ones? Did he challenge you—"

"He wouldn't have the balls."

"He was just a kid, Michael. Why did you have to kill him?"

Atwood took on a look of consternation as the two men stared at each other across the kitchen. Shaking his head, he exhaled heavily.

"Kill him? Come on, Nathaniel. You've seriously lost it, this time."

"Don't take me for a fool, Michael," Caslin admonished him. "It won't take much you know, revisiting what Maxim explored. Iain will find it sooner or later. Plus, what he sent me the night he died."

"That's all circumstantial, Nathaniel. You know that—"

"So far, yes, but I wonder what we'll find if we look at the suicide with fresh eyes. Can you be absolutely certain you left nothing behind?"

Atwood began to laugh, "You crack me up, Nathaniel. You always have done. And I'll give it to you, you're a pretty good detective but, unlike me, you never look far enough ahead."

"I'm going to have to take you in, Michael. This ends here and now," Caslin stated, stepping forward.

"And don't I know it," Atwood replied. At that moment he brought out a revolver that he had concealed in the rear waistband of his trousers, bringing it to bear in the blink of an eye. Caslin froze.

"I wasn't sure," he said softly. "I really wasn't."

"And now you are, good for you."

"You'll never—"

"Get away with it? I already have. To think," Atwood said, indicating the gun in his hand, "my grandfather's old service revolver would come in so useful. I keep it well oiled but I've never had cause to use the thing."

"Until now, you must be chuffed to buggery," Caslin said. The realisation hit him that he had just dropped the ball in the biggest way possible. "So, you might as well tell me what happened. Was there an unexpected knock on the door, just like tonight?"

"He was standing in the street when I came home. That ever-present, gormless expression on his face, same as usual."

"You invited him in?"

"I had a feeling that he had come across something, when I pulled up and wound the window down. He was behaving oddly, even by his standards. It's a strange thing that afflicts so many people. That they stand when they should run, remain polite when being rude would be far more appropriate. Or even," he used the end of the barrel to indicate Caslin, "accept an invitation when their good sense tells them they should decline it."

"Sometimes it's a measure of your own self-belief."

"That was always Harman's problem. He never knew when to trust his instincts. More often than not, he just got carried along with the current. It was so typical of the lad though, to stumble across something and not have the confidence to speak up. He would rather go it alone than risk looking like a fool and getting it wrong as he had done so many times before.

"Well, arguably that was a reaction caused by the rest of us, as much as by any personal failings."

"That's where you and I are very similar, Nathaniel. We're not too worried about what everyone else thinks about us."

"Perhaps," Caslin mused openly. "I would never have thought of you as capable—"

"We're all capable. When push comes to shove. You should know that in our line of work."

"Debatable," Caslin shrugged. "Even so, you… an arsehole, definitely, but a killer… I wouldn't have pegged it."

"It's not wise to insult a man holding a gun on you."

Caslin placed his cup down on the counter.

"I'm banking on you coming to your senses."

"Really? Explain it to me."

Caslin cleared his throat.

"You figured that you had a good chance of getting away with taking out Maxim. Quite rightly, as it turned out. You must know that you won't get away with this."

Atwood fixed him with a stare. It was cold and made Caslin doubt his own logic. Why had he engaged with him? He had had the upper hand and should've taken his chance. Now he was boxed into a corner. He felt foolish, like he had tripped over his own arrogance. Despite the outward appearance of calm, Caslin felt his heart going ten to the dozen.

"I'll find a way. It's not the first time that you've gone off on your own. I'll bet that no-one knows where you are."

Inwardly Caslin cursed. Atwood knew him too well. The two men remained motionless, facing off. Each was waiting for the other to make a move. For his part, Caslin had only one more card to play.

"Come in with me, Michael. This doesn't have to get any

worse but it has to end, now." Caslin immediately regretted the turn of phrase. The last thing he wanted was Atwood considering finality. "We're not going to accomplish anything standing here. You see, you are wrong about one thing."

"What's that?"

"I've passed the information Maxim left me onto Gerry Trent. I emailed him before I knocked on your door."

"You bastard," Atwood snapped.

Turning to face him with a somewhat resigned demeanour, Caslin shrugged.

"If you want to shoot me, then go ahead. It won't get you anywhere. Maybe a bit of a head start but... if it makes you feel better, go ahead."

"I would've lost everything... and for what?" Atwood shouted, tears welling in his eyes. Caslin was unsure if they were born of frustration or anger. "For checking out a website after a few beers... everything?"

"Come off it, Michael. Don't trivialise it. There was more going on than that, wasn't there?" Caslin said accusingly. "Were you paying for downloads, streaming it live and getting off on it like those other sick bastards?"

Atwood shook his head but Caslin could see that his words were hitting home.

"I never went looking for it... I swear."

"Technology is neither good nor bad but it is great for removing barriers. You're able to get in on things that you wouldn't seek in the real world."

"I don't know when it started to happen. I used to look at stuff but it was never over the line—"

"The line gets blurred on the internet. You know that as well as I do. If you didn't realise it before when Harman showed up you knew you'd crossed it. Your private reality was about to become public."

"You know nothing about me!" Atwood bit back.

"What the hell happened to you, man?"

"Fuck you, Caslin! I wasn't about to risk losing it all. I've come too far."

"And therein lies the irony," Caslin said. "Despite all that you've done, you still will."

Atwood's shoulders appeared to visibly sag. To Caslin it seemed as if the awareness of his situation had struck him. The breakthrough had been made.

"I never thought it would come to this," Atwood said. He was looking to the floor, his free hand aggressively massaging his forehead.

Caslin tentatively took a step forward, gently reaching out with one hand.

"Come on, Michael. Give me the gun, it's over now."

Without warning, Atwood lunged, shoving Caslin forcefully away before retreating himself. Caught off guard, Caslin stumbled backwards, putting some distance between them. He offered up his hands in supplication as the gun was brought to bear. The fear he exhibited must have been recognisable because Atwood stopped to glare at him. He sneered as he almost spat his words out.

"You think you're so bloody clever, Nathaniel. You're not."

Caslin had to agree and not just because he had a gun pointed at him. His own stupidity had put him in this position.

"Just take a moment, Michael. Think this through."

"I have," Atwood replied.

There was no emotion in his tone. Cocking the pistol, Atwood extended his arm and Caslin tensed.

"Wait!"

He made to turn and break for the hallway. The impact came like a hammer blow to his chest, spinning him like a top and sending him sprawling to the ground. He hadn't heard the shot. Struggling to breathe, panic flashed through him and he tried to stand but his legs gave way. Slumping back, he fell against the wall, eyes wide as the onset of shock took hold. Atwood remained standing in the centre of the kitchen. He wasn't looking at Caslin.

He didn't appear to be focusing on anything. The gun was at his side.

Atwood lifted his head and, after a moment, his eyes fell on the colleague now sitting on the floor before him. He stared at Caslin briefly before glancing at the weapon in his hand.

"How did it come to this?" he asked. Raising his arm in one fluid motion, he put the barrel in his mouth and pulled the trigger. Caslin closed his eyes and swallowed hard, hearing Atwood's body drop to the floor.

There he sat as an eerie silence descended on the room. His heart raced and the smell of cordite drifted over to him.

Time stood still. After a short while, although probably in reality, a few seconds, Caslin opened his eyes and his senses recoiled from the scene. Blood and brain fragments had been sprayed across the kitchen units, walls and ceiling. In places it was beginning to run. Suddenly he became anxious to know how bad his own wound was. Surely it should hurt more than it did? Reaching up, he found his hand was shaking uncontrollably. He willed it to stop but he couldn't manage to, such was the adrenalin coursing through him. Forcing himself to take deep breaths helped and within a minute he felt better.

He winced as he put his hand inside his coat. Withdrawing it, he saw there was blood on his fingers but not as much as he would've expected. Upon a second inspection, his fingers brushed across something cold and sharp. Removing his phone from the pocket he found the screen had shattered. Flipping it over he saw that the aluminium casing was heavily damaged and twisted in a way he didn't think possible. From nowhere he began to laugh, finding that painful, he soon stopped. Somehow, he doubted that the insurance company would see this as accidental damage. As the moments passed his left side began to burn, similar to a deep muscle injury, only far worse. With difficulty, Caslin raised himself up on his haunches and used the wall to brace himself as he stood. His legs were wobbly but he managed to stagger a few paces towards the hall, stopping briefly to cast an eye over the still form of Michael Atwood.

"You got off lightly," he said aloud.

Moving into the hall, he paused at the mirror adjacent to the front door. Teasing aside his coat he took account of the dark patch soaking into his shirt. Probing the area gently brought a significant amount of pain. Instinctively, he felt that it wasn't as serious as he had feared. The bullet had been deflected in a sideways trajectory and he hoped, hadn't penetrated too deeply but had still managed to tear through muscle and quite possibly, bone. The force of the initial impact had done some damage but an initial search for an exit wound found nothing. His chest ached with every breath and any movement brought forth a wave of pain.

Picking up the landline he dialled Fulford Road. As the call connected, he realised that he had no idea what he was going to say.

CHAPTER THIRTY-FOUR

CASLIN LED the group from the confines of the small chapel, out into the afternoon sunshine. The breeze was gentle and, despite the cold of midwinter, the day was pleasant. Caslin could feel his toes were going numb. The service had been short, due in the most part to the lack of knowledge about the family. Much to the regret of Fulford Road CID and everyone else involved in the investigation, no-one had come forward to claim the Horsvedts as their own. Extensive contact with officials in the Czech Republic had failed to trace any living relatives. The family were destined to become a footnote in the local paper or worse still, a statistic in regional crime figures.

Reaching the grave, the pallbearers, made up of officers from the station, laid the casket in place. Caslin stood to the side as the priest came to stand before them to consecrate it and deliver the final blessing. The little that they had found out about the family was that they were Catholic and as such, they warranted a service in keeping with their faith. Protocol regarding burial under state control was forgotten on this occasion. The lack of any significant human remains had not deterred the team from arranging the casket. The symbolism of the act of laying them to rest was what mattered.

"I'm pleased, if that's the correct word, that you pushed us to do this, Nathaniel," DCI Stephens said, as the priest led the mourners away.

Caslin cast a glance sideways to the grave diggers waiting patiently, off to their left, for the signal to begin their next task.

"It's a good turnout," Caslin replied.

Stephens looked towards the vast crowd of locals who had answered the call made earlier in the week.

"Hunter did a good job there. The social media, local radio, and that interview she gave to your friend, Sullivan. I think there must be several hundred here, at least."

"They deserve it."

Caslin looked down at the grave marker, gold lettering inlaid on a slab of polished, black granite. The words were simple and honourable. He judged it to be a fitting epitaph for such a young family, known only to the people of York in death but sadly, not in life.

"Nice touch, by you," Stephens said. "Arranging the marker."

"I wanted a headstone but apparently, you can't set it for a few months. I needed to do it in one go."

"I understand."

It was right that the Horsvedts had something to mark their passing that was a little grander than would otherwise have been. With the investigation complete and only Chloe's forthcoming trial to provide closure, the coroner had released what little remained of the family, for burial. Other victims were still waiting to be identified. Whether or not that would prove to be possible was yet to be determined. Caslin indicated to the burial team that they could commence and the two men stepped forward, shovels in hand. With one last, solemn look at the casket, Caslin silently paid his respects. He then joined Frank Stephens on the path back to the car park.

"How are you feeling?" the DCI asked.

Caslin frowned, "I've been better, but..."

"But?"

"I'll be alright. The ribs are healing nicely and any pain that comes along with movement is bearable, these days. Painkillers help."

"It took a lot out of you, I think."

Stephens let the following moment of silence carry as they walked. A few of the CID team were lingering in the chapel grounds. Caslin spotted Iain Robertson amongst them. Of all involved, it was most probably Iain and his team who bore the psychological brunt of the investigation. After all, they had to pick over every detail of Radford Farm and unearth the grisly secrets contained within.

"I think it's impacted on all of us," Caslin said. He intimated towards the assembled group, standing a short distance away. "This is one that will be difficult to move on from."

Stephens cast an eye over them while he thought on that. Touching Caslin's forearm gently, he indicated they should stop walking.

"When do you want to come back?" he asked. "I'm presuming you want to. It's been a month and, like you say… it's going to be hard to leave this behind us."

"We won't."

"No?"

"McNeil, Na Honn, the farmhouse, they were extreme but you can argue they come with the job," Caslin said. Shaking his head, he continued, "Maxim, Hayley… Atwood. Get past it, maybe. But this will never leave us."

"We stopped them, all of them. You must remember that."

"I do. Every day," Caslin said evenly.

"Are you still thinking about quitting? In my mind, you'd be making—"

"I'm not quitting, Frank. I'm not," Caslin said, looking his boss square in the eye. "I just need a little time."

Stephens accepted that with a nod. He appeared relieved. Caslin thought that was quite a turnaround, bearing in mind their complicated relationship during the past year.

"Take as much time as you need. I'll clear it with Broadfoot. He's as anxious to have you back as I am."

Caslin thanked him. Excusing himself, he made his way back into the chapel to have a word with the priest. Emerging outside shortly afterwards, Caslin found the CID team waiting for him. He approached warily. He felt on edge having not seen many of them since the night of Atwood's death.

"We're all going for a drink," Sarah Hunter said. "You coming?"

Caslin smiled.

FREE BOOK GIVEAWAY

BLACKLIGHT - PREVIEW
DARK YORKSHIRE - BOOK 2

THE OVERNIGHT STORM had left the car park treacherous in places. The pooled water at certain points highlighted where not to stop, or walk, once beyond the confines of the interior. The distinctive crunch of hiking boots on gravel carried as he climbed out and made his way to the rear, dropping the tailgate. Pulling the red and black rucksack out and slipping it over his shoulders, he locked the vehicle and cast his eyes skyward. The day was still overcast but held some promise as shafts of light split the grey, changing the landscape beneath from grim to stunning. Far off to the west was an ominous sight. Swathes of rain lashed the distant hillside and he was thankful that the wind direction was favourable.

The pack on his back felt strange, being nigh on empty, an unnecessary addition to the all-weather gear that he wore. Surprisingly to him, there was another car parked up already. This early in the morning, he found that unusual. Granted, he had only been here twice before, once scouting and once to leave his kit but nonetheless, he had never come across another soul. That was the reason he had chosen the location. There were so many better, no, not better - more travelled places that drew in the tourists and locals alike. Leaving the car park from the east side, he set off on the well-worn trail.

Starting out in a valley, the path trekked east before changing direction and tacking north, his destination point would never see him leave the confines of the hills to either side. On a dreary day, such as this, there was always the likelihood that a walker would barely see the sun, let alone the views that Yorkshire was famous for. The going was tough as the trail narrowed and the gravel passed into mud. The water drained into the valley, leaving the soil wet and sticky underfoot, slowing his progress. Despite this, his destination was well within a fifteen-minute walk. He knew that to be almost exact. The need to make notes was never required that was his gift. The ability to commit details to memory, even trivial ones, that would slip the mind of lesser people in moments. He knew where to make the turn from the trail; after the boulder, one hundred yards beyond the sprawling gorse ahead.

The sound of voices came to ear and he stopped. The first was young, a girl, and after that an adult male, her father? Their chatter carried to him on the light breeze. Another, a young boy was complaining about his feet getting stuck in the mud. A shriek followed as someone presumably lost their footing. Resuming his course, he clocked them rounding the forthcoming turn in the track, the boy now being led by his mother. The man was at the head of the party, a furrowed brow, born of frustration, upon his face. They were equipped for a hike, judging by their gear but none of them looked comfortable.

"Good morning," the father said, glancing up from the OS map, enclosed within a transparent case, hanging by a cord from his neck.

"Having trouble?" he asked, reading the look of concentration on the man before him. The group had all stopped behind the two men, the children's expressions one of hope and expectation.

"Is it that obvious? We wanted to visit the bird sanctuary at dawn but we've taken a wrong turn on the way back to the car."

That wasn't surprising. He knew the sanctuary, a well-tended area returned to its natural habitat by a wilderness group over the past eight years. It was easy to get disorientated there, not for him but certainly for the general public. The group were good on nature, bad on signage. They planned to not only reintroduce native tree species but also the indigenous animals, wolves and lynx, to national parks in the future. That is, if they managed to overcome the objections of local landowners.

It would be easy. *Too easy*. He dismissed the thought. Stepping forward, he located their point on the map before tracing a line with his index finger, walking them through the route back to the car park. Even with the children in tow, it would take them under twenty minutes. With many spoken thanks and smiles of gratitude, the family moved on. Once again, he was alone. Picking up the pace the sense of excitement rose within him as it had done at this time in each of the previous three years. He left the trail where he remembered to, skirting the heather and jogging up a shallow incline before coming to a stop alongside a solitary silver birch. For some reason this species loved the landscape here and was one of the few managing to thrive.

Looking around, he was struck by the isolation of where he stood. There was nothing to indicate an urban presence, no roads, artificial light or noise, beyond the breeze passing through the nearby foliage. He was most definitely alone.

Removing the backpack, he put it on the ground before him and dropped to his knees. From inside he took out the only item contained within. The collapsible shovel was assembled in moments and with one last look around, he set about digging. Barely five inches beneath the surface, he found the rim and within a minute of that he had unearthed the top. Clearing more space around it, he put the shovel down and used his fingers to pry off the lid to the orange plastic tub, breaking the airtight seal.

Immediately, a smile crossed his face as he examined the contents. There was no evidence of moisture penetration, as he anticipated, and all was as he had left it. Firstly, he took out the length of coiled climbers' rope, cable ties and duct tape, placing them all in the open rucksack. Next, he picked up the mobile phone, removing the cover and slotting in the battery from his own handset, deliberately chosen to be interchangeable. Switching it on, he watched as the screen illuminated and went through its start-up process. Putting the phone in his jacket pocket he returned his focus to the container. A re-sealable bag came out, the three hundred pounds in used tens and twenties were swiftly transferred to his pockets.

A bottle of drain cleaner and a pack of refuse sacks were added to the rucksack. Retrieving a small red and white cardboard box, he opened it to reveal it was full to capacity. Lastly, he took out the semi-automatic pistol and checked it over. The slide was well greased and moved with ease back and forth as did the hammer action. Several years of military service had taught him how to prepare a firearm for these conditions. Releasing the magazine, he loaded it with rounds from the cardboard box and, having replaced it, chambered one. Ensuring first that the safety was on, he put the weapon in the pack alongside everything else.

Quickly reattaching the lid, he buried the container once more, covering the disturbed earth with detritus that he found lying around. Finally, he collapsed the shovel and returned that to the rucksack. Lifting it onto his shoulders he bore the newly acquired weight with ease. With a last glance at the ground, content that almost any sign of his presence was fleeting, he set off back towards the car park. The family came to mind once more and he wondered whether they had reached their car and set off already. A wave of exhilaration passed over him and he fought to subdue it. *This wasn't the time*. Although, he had been raised to never look a gift horse in the mouth and for a brief moment he considered breaking into a run before quelling the urge. That was getting harder and harder as time passed. The recognition of that fact made him stop to draw breath.

There was a process and it was successful. One that had been developed through experience and had never failed him. Why should he change it now? Was this becoming mundane? Perhaps it was time to broaden his horizons a little bit, mix up the status quo. *Maybe so, but not today.* That would require some thought. Unless an opportunity presented itself again, of course. That would signal something else was at work, a power far greater than him.

Retracing his steps back to the trail, as the sunshine broke through the clouds in ever greater bursts, he made it to the car park soon after. The family had made worse time than predicted and were still loading the car as he approached. The mother smiled warmly in his direction before leaning in and clipping their daughter's seatbelt in place. The father offered a small wave of acknowledgement. No doubt his pride slightly dented at having to ask a stranger for help in finding their way. Their son was hopping around in the rear, apparently searching for something lost amongst their gear.

Whistling a nameless tune his thoughts drifted to the contents of his rucksack, all easily accessible if required. He must have slipped into a daydream of possibilities because he found the father staring at him as he finished stowing their kit, closing the boot to their people carrier. He looked on as the family closed their doors, the father casually walking around to the driver's side and taking out his keys. The man stopped and glanced over towards him. At that moment he realised he had stopped walking and was standing in the middle of the car park, watching intently. Still, he didn't move.

The excitement was building once again. This coming weekend was shaping up to be a great one.

Blacklight - Dark Yorkshire Book 2

Audiobooks

The entire Dark Yorkshire series is available in audio format, read by the award-winning Greg Patmore.

Dark Yorkshire

Divided House

Blacklight

The Dogs in the street

Blood Money

Fear the Past

The Sixth Precept

Audiobook Box Sets

Dark Yorkshire Books 1-3

Dark Yorkshire Books 4-6

Hidden Norfolk

One Lost Soul